Love, Life and
NAUGHTY BITS

TANIA COOPER & RICKY COOPER

OTHER TITLES
co-written by these authors:

Heaven's Scent Book 1

OTHER TITLES
by Tania Cooper:

Too Broken to Love – The Broken series, Book 1

Too Easy to Love – The Broken series, Book 2

Happy Little Horrors - Anthology

OTHER TITLES
by Ricky Cooper:

Designated Infected – Designated series, Book 1

Designated Quarantined – Designated series, Book 2

DEDICATION

To the reason this story exists, Frankie.

A woman who is just as beautiful on the inside as she is on the outside.

Who would've thought a conversation in London about the weird and obscure books of the world would lead to this?

Thanks for the encouragement to be a little off centre.

xxx

ONE
She

Mmm, what a peaceful morning. I need this quiet moment after such a restless night, well ... many restless nights lately. I feel a shift in her, something is changing and we know how we feel about change; we don't like it! So to say I'm a little nervous is an understatement. That's it, a nice long stretch to wake the body up, hun; let's conquer the world today, shall we? Let's put the past few weeks behind us and start fresh. Wait, what ... no, not again! I am still raw from the three times last night!

"Buzzzzzzzz ..."

You have got to be kidding me! It's Friday. Can't you just wait until we hit the bar later tonight with Zali and Mel? You know they help you make better choices with which junk you invite back here. We could get a good one tonight, no need to ruin me for that possibility! This is not the answer to all our problems ... ah ... hang on ... ah ... oh ... what the hell. She won't listen anyway. I might as well help to hurry this up, ride the wave and get this over and done with so we can get on with our day.

Okay ... there we go ... that's the right place, just relax and I'll get us there. That's right; find your sexy happy place ... oh yeah, think of *him,* think Mr. Uptight in a suit who dares to walk past us all snobby and smelling so freaking good *every* morning. Mmm ... oh yeah, if we get him alone we will start with his tie, dragging it from his neck nice and slowly and … ah … that's it, that's it, here it comes, let the tidal wave begin. Ahh … oh, oh, ohh …. That's what she needed.

We never do get past that damn tie!

Now to meet some suits in real life. I know exactly what she will wear to the office today; her uplifting outfit with that tight navy skirt, a little short for her liking but one that has a lot of eyes turning her way apparently. And she will match it with the white sleeveless silk shirt that shows off all her cleavage, the one Zali *made* her buy to try and catch the eye of Mr. Uptight.

Ahh … Mr. Uptight. He gives us *real* good feelings, but he also makes us feel like crap on an almost daily basis by acting as if we don't exist! We have tried to ignore how handsome he is, how good he smells, how the hormones his body releases affects us the minute we are within a mile radius of him, and how incredibly charming he can be to everything with a vagina but us. On those days, when she witnesses him being so nice to everyone, then turns and gives her the cold shoulder, we don't like the hormones *that* produces in us. We call them the Vodka days, 'cause *that's* what we need the minute we get home, back to the non-judgmental, non-moody male, non-biased for some unknown Godforsaken reason, cocoon of our apartment.

As much as I would love to get to know Mr. Uptight's junk intimately, he's just not worth chasing if it results in a roller coaster ride of emotions, so I will keep my pheromones in check and not spit them his way. What's his freaking problem, anyway? I know my girl is all kinds of hot. Everyone tells her so, male and female, which she just brushes off shyly, but doesn't he see what others see? We were nice and friendly to him when we first discovered his handsome aura in our work building, but let that die off after his continual coldness towards us. I know he's not gay because his junk sends out bloody testosterone to almost everything that reeks oestrogen. So what does he think is so wrong with us?

Fuck him. We don't care; we can give a cold shoulder just as good as he can. And he's not our 'Mr. Long Term Guy' anyway. We want someone warm, someone who loves all of our faults, and someone who will support and encourage all of our dreams no matter how crazy they are. We want someone who will laugh with us and gently wipe away any tears. We want kindness and understanding and love. We want deep, soul reaching, heartbeat skipping and constant wet panties kind of love. We know it's out there … we are just looking in all the wrong places.

Okay, time to get our head out of the man zone and into work mode, because we pay our *own* bills. No man, toy boy, or sugar daddy needs to take care of us. So to do that, we *really* need to haul our arse to work right now instead of looking in the bloody mirror. Let's go earn some more dollars to spend on pretty shoes, oh yeah, like those red ones we couldn't stop looking at last week. Oh, they gave us *nice* feelings.

••••

The smell of power can be intoxicating and exhilarating, but it can also swallow you up and spit you out if you let your feet lift off the ground. That's why we like our job. It's the right balance of power, where we achieve great pride when a project we have been working on is accepted or praised, yet, not being the *head* honcho, means we don't get our arse caned when it goes wrong or even fired by someone with *more* power than us. We are happy to stay on the sidelines.

'Creative Square' is our second home, not exactly the cosy beachside cottage we dream about, with an open fireplace, a fur rug in front of it and some wine and some hanky panky on the fur rug in front of that fireplace after consuming said wine, but it's our place of work and we sometimes feel as if we live here more than our one bedroom, barely room to swing a cat, apartment at the Docklands. Apparently it has some of the best views of this beautiful city of Melbourne and is situated on South Bank along the Yarra River, so for a business location, it couldn't get any better than this.

Our building is tall, like *really* tall. If we have a busy week and don't get to our Pilates classes as much as we would like, we take the stairs, much to my dismay. I mean seriously, chafing can be a bitch on a hot day and that is *not* the kind of friction I like. Not that our thighs chafe much outside of summer, but just the uncomfortable thought of it makes me want to vomit discharge everywhere.

Our building holds many businesses, everything from IT companies to top accounting firms, along with all sorts of digital and media services. And we're not the only advertising company here. Our building also houses '100 Design,' an innovative and award winning ad company which offers salaries somewhere in the southern hemisphere. But we don't often compete for jobs because their CEO and our CEO are the best of mates and often throw jobs each other's way. We are more of a boutique style company, so we may offer our larger jobs to them and they offer smaller ones to us. We have heard whispers that the same man owns both companies to try and cover all corners of the market, but we are yet to confirm that at the great and sacred meeting place: The Water Cooler.

There have always been whispers of a merge but we pray it doesn't happen, because Mr. Uptight is one of their top account executives so we would bump into him much more than we do, like today, in the lobby of our building. She hasn't spotted him yet, but I can smell him, and no matter how hard I try, I can't stop the reaction I have to that one particular male spice. Oh, there she goes, she has spotted him and comes to a stop, like always, as much as she doesn't want to. It's just an automated reaction we would need a scientist to explain. Stupid chemicals and stupid male spices that make our stupid brain momentarily freeze.

That's it, keep walking and don't look his way. Yep, look left, oh but not towards Mr. Garlic Breath first thing in the morning, we don't want to encourage him any more than he encourages himself. Good, let's pretend we didn't see him. Yep, looking down is safer and OW! Knocked to the floor on our arse was not the plan and freaking, freaking, freaking that hurts no matter *how* much cushioning you have back in your trunk. I can feel the impact all the way through my bones and straight to my centre and that place doesn't like that sort of impact, damn it.

"I'm sorry, I didn't see you," a deep, husky man voice tells us. And holy shit, there go all of our brain cells on vacation for God knows how long, because that voice belongs to the one, the only, Mr. Uptight. He reaches a hand down to help us up from the floor gracefully. And when his hand makes contact with ours, ohhhhhhhhhhhhhh ... what was I thinking again? Ha, what just happened? Oh yeah, knocked on ground, being helped up from said ground, by *him!* His grip is solid but not overbearing and he places his other hand on our shoulder to steady us as we stand. And, and ...

Oh dear God, we are standing right in front of him, with our mouth opened, with no words coming out, looking like a fool, a mute fool! Oh come on, girl, don't give him even more reason not to talk to us. Give him the evil eye and storm off. Pleaseeeeeeee. Let's not stare into his beautiful warm whisky brown eyes, or let our eyes run over his chiselled jaw and plump, deep pink, oh so kissable lips, or stare at his dark brown hair that's just a bit too long, almost hanging over one eye, just about needing a haircut, or take an obvious deep breath in to smell that sexy as fuck aftershave he always wears. Oops, too late.

He knows, he knows we just sniffed him! Yep, couldn't get any more embarrassing than this. Fix this, talk, woman, you can do it! Even if you're not wearing your Nikes.

"It's okay, I had my head down for a moment and didn't see you there. I'm sorry also."

What the? Are you kidding me, girl? We were supposed to stomp away, giving *him* the cold shoulder for once and you go and tell him sorry? It wasn't his arse that hit the dirty, full of feet germs, but somehow still shiny and clean looking, tiles of this lobby. We will be the ones with the black and blue battle scars on our butt, so why are we apologising?

"Are you going to be okay if I let go?"

Who does he think he is, Hercules, the only man who can help a woman to stand? No buddy, we are woman, we can stand on our own, hear us roar and all that shit. That's right, shrug out of his hold. Show him we have two capable feet, well, while we're in a standing position anyway, not the same story when we dance after too many cocktails. Oh yeah, we're going to need some of those tonight to stop the pain in our arse, literally.

"I'll be quite fine, thank you."

"Yeah, we're walking away! You go girl, you show him who can be cold. You can now call us Ice Queen, we will not fall under your spell of muscled arms and sexy as fuck aftershave again!"

"Yeah right. Keep telling yourself that, baby."

What? Who said that? Stop, turn around, go back. Pretend to have dropped something from your purse, I need to know who said that. I hear a contentious snicker and can guess exactly where that comment came from. Him. Mr. Uptight, well, to be more exact, Mr. Uptight's junk, who's also good at ignoring us. I will not comment, I will not comment, I will not comment. Oh who am I kidding? I am sooooo freaking commenting.

"Oh I will, because a nice smell doesn't mean a nice guy. My girl's too good for him and he knows it."

"So much for what you know. A smell says a lot about a guy."

"Oh you're right, your smell is saying a *lot* about you right now. Have a nice day, stinky." I can't help but giggle to myself as we make our way towards the far end of the lobby and hit the elevator button to go up as Mr. Uptight continues towards the front doors.

"Wait! What? I just got out of the shower only an hour ago. I don't stink!"

And out the door he goes. See ya, stinky junk. Well, not really. That was kind of a lie, well, not kind of, it *was* an actual lie. I couldn't exactly tell him that I found his smell as intoxicating as his owner's aftershave. We have enough trouble trying to ignore that man without extra scents dragging us under his spell. Nope, his junk does not smell good at all. *Think garbage bin, think fish market, think rotten eggs.* Yep, that's done the trick. No memories of nice smelling men and their junk left in my brain.

"Hold the door please." I'm not the only one distracted. Thank God an old gentleman whose tan suit smells like formaldehyde holds the door open for my girl as she rushes in. We're almost running late, so if we had missed this, the stairs would have been our only sucky option.

As we go to open the door to Creative Square, a man's hand grabs the handle before we can, and oh yum, he smells good and his looks must match his yumminess because my girl is blushing. Mmm, we needed these nice feelings after the epic arse crash only minutes ago.

"Please, let me." Oh an accent! A charming French accent. A charming *Oh la la* accent. That'll brighten up our crappy morning. Yes, good feelings are a blooming. And we're forgetting that arse crash caused by, who? See, forgotten already. We take a step through the doors while Mr. Oh la la follows close behind, so we add a little extra swing to our hips, just for his benefit of course and … well … just because it feels damn good to do sometimes.

We keep walking past the main reception desk. As we go to open the door to our office, we turn our head around and sure enough, Mr. Oh la la is still staring at our arse. A little extra wiggle just made the day a whole lot better. Men, so *easy* to please.

We get straight into work, opening up the accounts we need to work on this morning. Just as she reaches for the phone to check in with a client, it rings, scaring the crap out of us both. Yes, we scare easily. It's the boss, asking her to join him in the conference room. She sighs, not wanting to leave the groove she just got herself into. But we never keep the boss waiting.

Not because he is a mean tyrant or anything like that. Mr. Andre Black is actually a really cool boss. He has a great dry sense of humour and is very understanding when any personal issues arise with his employees, and he is the best mentor anyone could possibly have in this field of work. Everything she knows has come from him. But he is no softy when it comes to the nitty gritty of this job.

He expects everyone to be just as professional and hard working as he is on every project this company handles. And he has been nagging my girl for the past year to move up in her field of work, but she keeps repeating herself, she's happy here and honestly wouldn't like the stress of being number one. But it is a good boost to our ego that he holds that much confidence in her abilities.

We gather our tablet and head down to his office. We knock once and wait for him to say his usual 'come on in' then open the door to see ... Mr. Oh la la giving us a sexy smile. *Pay no attention, pay no attention, this is our place of work.* Yeah, that didn't work, especially when we notice him so obviously scan up and down our curves. But seriously, we do not, I repeat, we do not mix work and pleasure, so now that we know Mr. Oh la la is here for work, his yumminess factor just dropped a few good notches. Damn!

Introductions are made and Mr. Oh la la, a.k.a. Mr. Rene Arment, shakes my girl's hand a little too long to be considered polite. A bit too charming, Frenchy. We take our places at the large table and the boss begins. Apparently Mr. Oh la la is from a large advertising firm in Paris and has a client who wants to bring their product to Australia, starting with Melbourne.

By the end of the meeting no firm deal has been made, but our French friend seems very impressed, hopefully more with our company than with my *girl's* company. We say our goodbyes and wish Mr. Oh la la well before we return to our office to catch up on our few lost hours. We make calls to a few clients, tie up some loose ends, and receive texts from Mel and Zali throughout the day, firming up our plans for the night. I love Fridays. The end of the working week is so near which brings hope. Hope for some *nice* attention from the opposite sex.

Oh my girl is no floozy or easy for that matter, but when we do receive some attention, preferably from a man who actually *knows* what to do with a vagina, it's a good boost to our confidence and those good feelings can last a while, well, at least until the ones we want to call us never do. Which seems to be the last three we were brave enough to invite back to our place. My girl is picky, so her besties tell her. She doesn't take home nearly as many men as those two do; actually, she never used to take home anyone she wasn't actually dating for a few good weeks or even months.

That was until Mr. Confidence Smasher ruined my girl. Boy, did he do a number on her. He was charming, too charming for my and her besties' liking, but my girl was swept away for months. He praised her constantly and told her how beautiful she was and how wonderful she was at her job. For a girl that struggled for years with low self-esteem mainly due to her shyness, he built her up in a way nothing had been able to do before. She felt more powerful and she even felt sexy for the first time in her life when she was with him.

Until, six months into the relationship, she decided to surprise him after telling him she couldn't come over for dinner because she had to work late. She had been to a lingerie store during her lunch break that day and bought, not just pretty lingerie, but really pretty and kinky lingerie *and* a black trench coat. After working until seven, she went into the ladies room and changed into her new purchases, excited to see the look on his face when she rocked up to his home where he claimed to be working from.

When she knocked on his door and there was no answer, she decided to use the key he'd given her for emergencies and let herself in, thinking he must be too engrossed in work to have heard her knock. The noises she heard after a few steps in should have had her running out of there, but for some reason she still kept walking towards his bedroom. If I had a voice, I would have screamed at her not to open the door, but as the tears started to stream down her face, she opened that damn door.

And her heart fell to the ground and shattered into a million pieces.

He and his *companion* both looked up in surprise to see my girl standing there, and to add insult to injury, the extra-large-busted young thing straddling his lap said, *"Oops, maybe I should have stuck to Tuesdays."* Tuesday was the night he said he played poker with his brother every week. But wait, it gets worse. As my girl, on shaky legs, turned around and made her way to the door, Mr. Confidence Smasher, who we'd been beginning to think could be our Mr. Long Term Guy, ran after her, grabbing her arm to turn her around, and said, *"I'm so sorry, but seriously, your niceness was just getting to be a bit much, princess. We can still make this work though."*

Thank God she slapped him hard across the face before leaving and never hearing exactly *how* he thought they could work it out. Knowing that scum, he probably wanted to put her on a roster system with Miss Not Looking Quite Legal. But even though she walked away, the damage was already done. Which led to many nights with our head buried in a bottle of wine or too many cocktails with Zali and Mel, which also led to the plan we currently live by. That they all would seek out guys for pleasure only. Give the male species a good dose of their own medicine, hook them in and let them go when we have had our sexual fill of them.

Well, my girl and I have tried to live by that plan, but our pesky emotions seem to get in the way no matter how much we try to push them down. Pesky feelings and pesky body chemicals, always causing pesky trouble.

So even though we don't do the one-night-stand thing too often, we do go out and enjoy ourselves with our girls, and if a specimen of the male species so happens to turn our head, then we just play along and see how the night turns out. And to be honest, no matter how much of a nympho I would be if she let me, sometimes a long dry spell is better than the feeling of rejection when our plan backfires and the guy is quicker at hitting and quitting than we are. To not be the first one to get up and leave hurts sometimes.

This is our end of Friday ritual. Shut our computer down; check. Take our little garbage bin to the door of our office for the cleaning staff; check. Duck into the ladies for a quick pee and re-apply of our lipstick, ahh that feels better; check. Give ourselves a quick pep talk: *You're an accomplished woman who is smart and caring and has a lot of love to give the right man who deserves it, and is also great at giving mind blowing, body shattering, raw throat screaming orgasms, who will come along when the time is right*; check. Okay, we are ready for take-off.

As we hop off the lift and walk towards the exit, we smell his aftershave before she even sights him. And it's not just Mr. Uptight's sexy as fuck aftershave, it's also him. He has a unique smell that I swear we would smell from another state if he was to move. And as luck would have it, he's talking to our boss so there's no avoiding the close proximity to his male hotness. Stupid testosterone, causing stupid oestrogen to think this stupid male is hotness.

We speed our steps in hopes of our boss just saying a quick goodbye and not asking us to stop so he can introduce us to Mr. Stupid who knocks woman on their arses. As we get close we take one quick glance their way, and as quickly as Mr. Uptight catches our eye, he turns his head to avoid us, which results in anger rising in us again, which also results in our snappy *"Goodbye"* to our boss. Damn, that was a bit rude. I hope Mr. Black takes it as if she's just busy or running late for something other than we're shitty at him, when it's Mr. Uptight's coldness that has our feelings hurt again. Fuck him. It's Friday night and we will not let him bring us down again.

Well, that doesn't really work, because the moment we arrive at the pub, sit down in the booth next to Zali, and wince in pain, memories of how that pain in the arse got there and who was responsible for it come rushing back to the forefront of our mind.

"*Oooooo, someone has been having some naughty fun,*" Zali tells my girl, while Mel starts cheering loudly. I can feel my girl's deep blush all the way to my core. God, I love our besties. My girl goes into the details of why and how she has a pain in the arse. And wait for it, here it comes, the holy and sacred best friend advice we all can't live without.

"*The hold Mr. Uptight has over you is ridiculous. You need to screw him out of your brain, then he won't affect you so much or at all.*"

Yep, money can't buy that shit. Mel has always been my favourite. Such a clever woman.

"*I don't agree with your plan, but even if I did, he won't even acknowledge that I exist. So how would I possibly get him in a situation where I can screw him out of my brain?*"

Good point. Every time our eyes meet he turns away, so it would be impossible to start a conversation that could possibly lead to anything more than just passing in the lobby of our building.

"*Men are simple creatures and that's because it's a fact that half their brain resides below their belts. So, you know what office he works in, pay him a surprise visit. Just walk in unannounced, say 'Oops, wrong office' when he looks up in surprise to see you there, then quietly lock the door, walk over to him silently and slowly, with extra sway in those sexy hips of yours, turn his chair around, fall to your knees and give him the best damn blow job of your life. But just before he comes, pop that mouth of yours off, lift your skirt, push your panties to the side and ride him all the way to O town. Then hop off just as silently, fix your skirt, and walk out of there. Then, next time you see him in the lobby and he is desperate to get your attention, begging you to pay him another visit in his office, say 'No thank you, I really do not want a repeat of "that" performance' and walk away with your head held high.*"

Wooohooo! I like that plan, but going by the emotions swirling through my girl, she is *way* overthinking Mel's plan.

"*But what if he's amazing, what if that one moment is epic and life changing, then what? How would that possible help me to get him out of my system?"*

Damn. I feel this plan falling apart before we even have a chance to try it out.

"Um, yeah. I think I need a few more drinks before I dole out any more freaking awesome advice. I'll get back to you after drink number five."

I really liked that one. Maybe the next will be even more rewarding. The night continues as usual. Booze, laughter, and guy fishing. It seems tonight all the good ones are already caught, but I'm happy just to get to talk to *my* girls. Zali's and Mel's vaginas live a much more adventurous life than I have, so I can live through them vicariously.

"Did you seriously say that you had some nookie for lunch today?" I just have to ask Mel's vag so I can live precariously through her.

"Yep! And it was a mighty tasty lunch indeed. This time he surprised us. He came in, shut the door, kissed the hell out of us before lifting my girl up onto the desk, spreading her thighs and feasting on us with that talented tongue of his. It was the best damn lunch break we have ever had."

Okay, rules are being broken here and it's usually Mel who enforces them. "What happened to the rule, never at work, well, unless it was in the stairwells?"

"They've both been so busy lately that the only time they can hook up is during work hours, and there are more options in their offices than the bloody cold stairwells so the risk is worth it. This fuck buddy business is hard work sometimes. As much as I'm *not* complaining, because seriously, that mouth of his is worth it, but I sometimes think I'd like a regular guy, who is devoted solely to servicing me on a nightly basis, in our own bed. And one that preferably doesn't confuse our name with his other fuck buddy, because that little slip has me drying up faster than smelling some other skank's perfume on him."

"At least you're getting some attention. Our last two were the 'wham bam thank you mam so sorry forgot to please you too' kind of men. How did we not pick up on that before we got to the bedroom? We're seriously losing our radar if that has happened twice in a row. There will *not* be a third time. If I sense that's about to happen, I will clamp up so hard nothing will get through my tight muscles."

That's true. Guys have been jealous of how strong Zali's internal muscles are; they wish they had the strength in their arms. If she shuts up camp, nothing will get through that barrier. At least repeat fuck buddies are better than one nighters, but I would still prefer something a little more substantial than both those options.

"Are we ever going to find our Mr. Long Term Guy? I mean, I thought the plan of seeking pleasure only was fun for a while, but it's not really suiting my girl. She needs a bit more nurturing than a one night stand can offer."

"It won't happen overnight, but it will happen, if that's what she really wants. Her Mr. Long Term Guy is just having trouble finding her. For my girl, she's not ready for long term yet, so I will just hang on tight and enjoy the ride."
Zali might like the constant ride, where I would like to at least add a constant cuddle to the mix, preferably with the same guy and for more than a few nights here and there.

Tonight's a bust, well almost. Just as the girls all get up, ready to leave, two handsome men walk in the door, one we actually recognise.

"Oh no, don't look. That's Mr. Oh la la I was telling you about, and by the way he was looking at me today. I really do not need him trying to pick me up right now. I am so not messing up the deal my boss is trying to get him to sign. Let's go through the crowd and hope he doesn't spot me."

"Just because you can't go there doesn't mean I can't. I feel like some 'Crème Brule' for desert. Night, ladies."

Yep, she went there. And as my girl and Mel sneak out through the crowd they look back and can see Mr. Oh la la ready to feed Zali whatever she wants.

TWO
He

Ugh, what a bloody night, I've gotta get that taste out my mouth, we have really got to get you some better toys, mate. What the fuck were you thinking? She may have had a plump arse and huge cans, but fuck, have you never heard of coyote ugly? Come on, wake up, I need a stretch. My balls are turning blue from how much I need to drop one. Wake the hell up, you gotta wash this crap off me, I'm starting to stink! The bathroom is right there, how hard is it to get up and go wash me off before falling asleep?

She wasn't that good. You do know she never made us pop last night. You fucking owe me, sleeping beauty, I mean come on, she looked like a ten when you picked her up, I'll give you that, but bugger me bro, she ended up looking like a minus ten when I woke up. Seriously, what were you drinking last night to make you go home with that? Oh right, I forgot, tequila and vodka, who the hell mixes tequila and vodka? All you're doing is ruining the tequila and doubling on an easy way to get smashed. I mean, come on mate, they're both forty per cent proof!

Finally, the drama queen is up. Come on, let's have a stretch, lover boy, that piece of fluff from last night is long gone and no way in hell was I going to drop a wad into that. So come on, get a grip and let's have a stretch.

Oh yeah, that's good, get a good grip, ow fuck, not that tight, Jesus. Okay good, slowly now, that's right, find the rhythm. Oh yeah, good one, right there, nice and easy. We need this, last night was *not* a good night. Seriously mate, all she did was bounce up and down and make a dent in the bloody mattress, you need, no, you *deserve* better than that.

Hey, what did I say, slow down, for fuck sakes, this ain't a race. Besides, you're gonna give me a sore head if you keep yanking on me like that. Work ain't for another three hours, we've got time. Somebody's feeling the letdown, ain't they. Well, dumb arse, that's what you get for beer goggling your pick up. I always tell you to go on the hunt sober *then* get smashed *with* the piece of candy you snag, but nooooo, do you ever bloody listen to me, do you hey? All you seem to be doing lately is getting plastered and going from one train wreck to the next.

I swear, ever since Miss Queen Bitch ripped our heart out through your arsehole, it's one dumb floozy to the next. None of which ever give me or you a proper release. Take last night for example. I swear she was going to break me off at the bloody root rather than make us pop our cork. Great, now I'm pissed off, back to the stretch. Oh yeah, that's my boy, slower, good, you're getting there, a little slower. Damn, that's it, keep it there, oh good one.

Okay, a little faster mate, that's it, keep the pressure, rub my head, oh yeah, just like that. Okay, nearly there, just a little more. Oh, oh, oh, there we go, fuck me was that good, nice big load, oh yeah now we feel better, all nice and empty.

Would have preferred a nice, tight, wet pussy, but hey, we make do. Right, up ya get sleepy, *to the shower*!

●●●●

Okay, that feels a hell of a lot better, no nasty tramp gunge on me and no more blue balls. Right, what am I going to wear today? How about that silk Armani pair Miss Queen Bitch left behind? Those always make me feel good and ready for anything, that, with the DG suit and those Italian loafers your mum bought you. Oi dipshit, you paying attention here? Hurry up or we're going to get caught in the rush again, which makes us late, which means we miss the nice bits of T and A walking into the office first thing, which makes me grumpy and you don't like me when I'm grumpy, so bloody move it!

Oh yeah, those feel nice, I like these, only thing she left behind that I do like. Yet you, you dopey bastard, you still insist on keeping that bloody banana hammock of a set of briefs, all because they were one of the last things *she* bought you. Man the fuck up and toss 'em out, they feel like crap, look like a set of tighty whities, and squash me up so much I end up sniffing your butt crack for half the day. So are we getting rid of them? Yes or no? Oh for crying out loud, you're seriously putting them back ... *again*! I'd tell you to sack up and act like you've got a pair, but right now I'm seriously wondering why I still hang around.

Okay, enough of this crap, suit up and ship out, we've got some T and A waiting in the office and I have some pussies to chat up. Not that you really pay attention to any of them, too busy playing Mr. Executive and while ignoring all the good ones. You know, that tight little thing that acts like a door mouse but I *know* will be a demon if you ever got her in the sack. But do you notice her, do you, fucker? All you see are those plastic bimbos that wander around with their jugs hanging out. Hell, even the mail room clerk has seen more of those than their own mothers.

Okay, okay, I took that a little too far; don't go all pissy on me. I know why you ignore her, I think you're being a pansy, but I know why. It's Miss Warm Sunshine, the one that smells like Miss Queen Bitch but looks like a blonde Scarlett Johansson. I mean come on; you must be blind if you haven't noticed the goo goo eyes she fires your way every time she sees you. And yet, there you are being the biggest arsehole you can be to her, ignoring her like you would the creepy kid in science class, you know, the one that always turned the frog into a puppet.

Right, you ready now? Done moping around again? Good, off we go, don't forget your keys this time. I'm not sitting on the marble steps again getting numb nuts because your dumb arse locked us out.

••••

Here we go, take a deep breath, dude, its wild country now. God do they smell great today, all pheromones, shampoo, and Chanel No. 5, you've gotta love this. Oh hell yeah, you smell that, come on, you have to smell that.

"Hey sexy, why don't you swing this way and we can play soldier."

Oh shit, wrong one, damn it, this is that prissy muff from the office down the hall. Abort, abort, no, don't get closer to her, ahh fuck.

"Seriously, what else you gonna ask, if I want to get a taste of a salty salami?"

He just had to walk closer to this uptight kitten.

"Yeah, yeah, whatever love, just keep moving, I wasn't talking to you. I wouldn't offer friendly fire your way let alone anything else."

Come on, move on, we need something else. Okay we're moving into the good stuff now.

"Hey girly, why don't you send your spicy self this way, we love a little oriental flavour. No, okay then, that's alright, we'll catch you later."

Okay what's next, what's next? I know we've got to get upstairs and the elevator is right over there, but really dude, do we have to leave all these gorgeous girls. I mean that Chinese girl was damned *hot* and has got to be worth a hit. I don't think we've had a Chinese girl yet ... have we ... no I'd remember that ... I think.

Ooofff! What the bloody hell, hey you dozy muff saddle, watch where you're ... oh damn it's Miss Warm Sunshine. You know you want to hit that, can't you smell her, she is gagging for it. Seriously, man up, she's just playing hard to get, does it matter she reminds you of Miss Queen Bitch? You cannot leave her on her butt on the floor; help the lady up, damn it.

This is master brain calling big brain, *help the lady up!*

"Sorry I didn't see you there."

What are you being sorry for, she's the bloody idiot that walked into you, did you not notice her head in the clouds when she rammed us in the bloody back?

"It's okay, I had my head down for a moment and didn't see you there. I'm sorry also."

See, she even admits it. Okay, she's getting inside the zone now, wake the fuck up. Oh come on, you had to notice that, she just *sniffed us!* Who does that? No normal person does that.

"Are you going to be okay if I let go?"

Seriously, you're trotting out the charm and the ice, what the hell is wrong with you, dude, you're acting like a freaking frat boy. This is Miss Warm Sunshine, damn it, not a typing pool tart. Wise up.

She just sniffed us, bro, and you're asking if she's okay enough to let go? Even her own muff is screaming at her to get you to let go and walk away. *What is going on, are you even listening here?*

"I'll be quite fine, thank you."

Finally someone with some common sense in this stand-off.

"Yeah, we are walking away! You go girl, you show him who can be cold. You can now call us Ice Queen, we will not fall under your spell of muscled arms and sexy as fuck aftershave again!"

"Yeah keep telling yourself that, baby."

"Oh I will, because a nice smell doesn't mean a nice guy. My girl's too good for him and he knows it."

"So much for what you know. A smell says a lot about a guy."

"Oh you're right, your smell is saying a *lot* about you right now. Have a nice day, stinky."

"Wait! What? I just got out of the shower only an hour ago. I don't stink!"

Saucy lips that one, telling me I stink, she's the one who was bloody dribbling all over the place, telling me I stink and she damned well knows my boy ain't so easy to walk over. Did she not see her girl sniff us? I mean come on, she snorted on his collar more than a coke addict at Christmas. He's going to thaw her faster than a hair dryer on an ice cube, and by the time we're done she's going to be little more than another notch on his belt, even if *she* is Miss Warm Sunshine.

Right, now what? Oh right, work, yay. That means I get to sit tucked next to your thigh all day sweating like a hog in a sauna. The least you could do is undo your belt and pants when you sit down. I mean it's not as if anyone else is in your office, unless you count me, but I doubt you do.

I guess I'll just sit here, sweating away. Hidden inside some silk boxers until you either need a piss, a wank, or we head out with the lads tonight. I swear mate, sometimes being attached to you is a pain in the freaking arse.

Oh great, now someone is knocking, let's see what door number one gives us today. It's probably Viv with your coffee.

"Sir, I have your coffee, are you ready for it or are you still going through paperwork?"

Told you, every day like clockwork, don't you get tired of the routine?

"Thank you Vivian, just leave it on the coaster here, then can you please hold my calls until I'm done here? I'll buzz through once I'm ready to receive any."

Well that shuts me up. Guess you're all set on your routine. Okay, might as well make myself comfortable, this is going to be a long day.

••••

Okay, we need a drink, are we heading straight to the bar or home first? If we're going straight there can you at least go to the loo first, I really need some air. Being stuck against your thigh all day ain't as fun as it sounds. Although I don't doubt several of the bimbos around here would love a chance to be stuck on you *and* me all day.

So you made up your mind yet, dude? We heading straight out to get shit faced, it is Friday after all, or we heading home for the three S's before hitting the bars with the boys?

I need to know. So come on, tell me what we're doing. Oh, okay, answer the phone, just ignore me. And people say *I'm* a dick.

"Benji, hey mate how's it going? Oh, yeah, not too bad. Paperwork and the usual bull, you know how it goes. You heading out tonight? Cool, me, no I'm heading home first, need a shower and that. This place may have A/C but it gets hot as hell when the sun hits the window. Yeah mate, later days."

Well that settles that, though an answer would have been nice. So are we going or aren't we? Oh good, you're actually getting up, come on then, let's get home, it's hot as hell in here. Okay you got everything, we ain't gotta come back for anything, no calls to make at the last minute, no paperwork to sort out?

Good. Let's go.

Oh for fuck sakes! Who's this now? Oh great, Viv again, probably just sneaking in to fawn all over you as per usual. Bloody woman just can't take a hint, and the odour that comes off her, sheesh, smells like a cat crawled up there and died. Ugh.

"Okay Mr. Anderson, is there anything you need before I head home?"

Well that was an open ended invite. Hell, her body language says miles more than her words and count yourself lucky you're not me at the moment mate, she is *oozing* fuck me juice. Seriously, if you had a funnel you could bottle the crap, she's giving off so much.

"No Vivian, thank you, I'm just leaving myself so just lock up once I'm gone."

Thank God we're out of there; she really gives me the creeps at times. It's not what she says, or the way her muff squeaks whenever it gets a whiff of us, it's just the way I can feel her staring at us. A kind of 'I want to chain you up in my basement' kind of stare, there's not a patch of it that shows anything other than Annie Wilkes level of creepiness. Remind me again why they keep her around? Oh that's right, you can't file worth a shit. You really need to learn how to file.

Okay, *to the pub*!

••••

Someone is already pumping the tunes out here, are we really hitting a club first? Well sure, if you really want to listen to some dodgy techno rip off and drink watered down lager, then by all means head on in, but I'm not raising my head for anything in here, sod that for a game of soldiers. Bloody hell it reeks in here, it's all hormones and sex sweat. How old are some of these people? Oh hell no, she can't be more than eighteen, put your eyes back in your head, mate, I'm going nowhere near that. She may look hot, but seriously, do you want that on your hit list? She probably still listens to Bieber for crying out loud.

Oi, watch where you're going, bloody Uni kids are pissed as farts and twice as stupid. Come on dude, let's get out of here. The boys ain't here and *we* need to get to some place where there's an ounce of intelligence attached to something older than twenty-one. That bar there seems like a good place, so let's find the boys and get some grog in. Benji and Booker should be around here somewhere, come on, go find them, I need to find out if they did better than your dumb ass last time we were on the prowl.

"Oi, Lane ass."

Yes! Booker's here, finally get a chance to find out if he copped one with that chick from his office.

"Bookend, took you long enough, I was starting to think I'd be partying with the kids again. What the fuck took you so long?"

"Like you'd mind that, some of those sheilas are pretty loose when you get a few in 'em."

Yeah, don't encourage that again, dipshit, you know what happened last time, bloody moron ended up with a black eye and almost got arrested because of you.

"Shut the fuck up, you still owe me from last time. Where's Benji?"

"Oh you mean Mr. I need to finish the filing before I can leave? He's on his way in. I was going to catch a ride in with him, but the dipshit was taking too long. Besides, I knew you'd be lonely without me."

"Oh will you shut up, bloke talks more shit than a bloody u-bend," I said.

"You're telling me, try being stuck in his jocks all day, crustier than a week old slice of pizza, he hasn't changed them in three days."

Man, I feel sorry for Booker's junk.

"Damn mate, I thought Lane's were bad after an all-nighter, but Christ, that's gotta suck. So you're telling me he's still rolling around in the set he went home in with that chick from last time?"

"Yup."

"Fuck, that's gotta suck."

"Eh, you get used to it, although I do have a bit of a sore head from all the chafing, but nothing I ain't used to. The hook up was worth it though; I dropped more bombs on that one than the opening minutes of Wind Talkers."

"Nice, that sheila that we went home with, well, let's just not go there."

"I get ya. Booker wasn't too impressed with your man's catch that time and she wasn't exactly the uh ... cream of the crop."

"You're telling me. I swear I couldn't wait to be out of there, it was like being trapped inside a sweaty sock and you and I both remember these idiots at Uni."

Thinking of Uni, I wonder what these two are still yammering on about. They should be head deep in lager and shots by now. Oh yeah, that's right, their stupid bro code, all for one and one for all, blah, blah, blah, never leave a bro behind blah, blah. Typical chest pounding crap. God it's nauseating at times, and with all the drama *that* has caused these two, I'm surprised they still keep up with it. Some things just never die, I suppose, no matter how many times certain members shoot the code in the back of the head.

"Well it doesn't look like Benji is going to show up, he's probably balls deep in that piece of ass he's been after for the past month, it's some new girl a few cubes down from him. Pretty hot, but has this really odd quirk in her voice, if you combined Elvira and Velma from Scooby Doo, you'd be in the right ball park." Booker's always referencing freaking cartoons.

Well that was … disturbing. I guess people all have their preferences. I really wouldn't want to be attached to Benji right now. It's bad enough being Lane's thunder cannon with all the crap decisions he's made since Miss Queen Bitch tore him apart. But forget that for now, *we* need to get drunk and I need to meet some yummy muff.

"So, how do you reckon these two chuckle heads are going to play it tonight? I'm betting on Booker being a fight promoter and Lane being an up and coming boxer." Lane would so pick up more if he really was a fighter. Maybe we should hit the gym more often.

"Ha, Lane a boxer, that'll be the day. With how Booker has been lately I think they may go for the white knight routine, with Lane playing the arsehole and Booker swooping in to save the day. Then switch half way through."

"We'll see."

"Okay, bro, what one we hitting first? There's P.J. O'Brien's or we jump the river and hit Young and Jacksons, although The Duke's always a good choice. Depends on if we're hunting for some pussy or just out to get hammered and wake up cross eyed."

Well, it looks like Booker is an easy gamer. Why can't Lane be like that, just pick some random places to either get pissed or hunt out a tasty piece of muff for me to get lost in? It's not as if he has a missus at home to be worrying about, all he has to do is make sure he isn't all devil eyed when he shows up for work. Then again, when he drinks too much, it's always like I'm firing battery acid the next day, all hot and greasy. Ugh, never can figure out why it does that to me, although Mr. Coffee Guzzler does stick to the spirits unlike his two brainless amigos.

"Mate, I don't give a shit where we go as long as I get either of two options, laid or wasted, either is preferable to how this week has been."

"Pissed and a good shag it is then, let's do this," Booker said.

Okay, let's see what goes down, shall we? Hopefully it'll be some cheeky bit with a mouth like a hoover, those always feel good.

••••

"Hey, you up?" I know I'm not alone, but I'm confused as to why Booker is apparently in the same bed as us.

"Yeah, what's up?"

"You remember what happened last night?" Please say yes, please say yes.

"No not really, although I am half gloved and smell like an old tuna can, so it was something fun."

"Ha, me too, so we know there was at least some muff involved." Thank fuck!

"Who you calling a muff? I'm a fucking lady, dickhead, and you two owe me big time. It's been a long time since my girl has handled two guys in a row."

Oh God, we shared one. Fuck, Lane, bro, what the fuck happened? We have never gone that hard on the booze before that we ended up sharing one. Although it is a notch on his belt, and more the merrier in my opinion, I know how bad he is going to feel when he finally wakes up; poor fucker's going to hate himself.

"I have never been this sore or stuffed in my life. You two aren't exactly the little woodies my girl is used to."

"Ha, just goes to show this is what you get when you come south of the Yarra." Booker and his junk can be such snobs sometimes.

"Yeah, yeah, keep blowing your own horn, big boy, although I'll give credit where it's due, you two can satisfy a girl. I can't say the same for your fella; he conked out after two rounds up the spout."

"Ha! Benji is going to hate himself for that one, you really need to get him to do some stress training mate, you're letting the side down. Talking of which, it looks like my boy's waking up. I'll chat to you two in a bit, we've got a morning constitutional to take care of." I'm about to fucking burst!

"What's he on about?"

"He needs a piss."

"Oh."

Staring at a toilet bowl ain't exactly a good way to start a day. I'm just hoping my boy can aim this time. Last time we did this he missed the mark by miles and really cheesed off his mate. Well, I say did this, taking a piss with a hangover is never an easy thing to do, and coupled with the thoughts no doubt rolling around in his head, if he has even realised yet exactly what he has done, well, it's enough to throw off anyone's aim.

Oh, here we go, let's see what my boy has to say for himself.

"What the hell happened? Oh Christ no, please tell me we didn't go there, ugh, how much did I drink to think that was a good idea? And with Booker, oh fucking hell!"

Afraid so bro, you went for the three way and I, personally, have *zero,* count them, *zero* regrets, although I doubt I can say the same for you. Yeah, you sound pissed at yourself more than the situation, although this chick ain't half bad. Tight arse and cans, a bit shorter than our usual take away date, but not too bad all in all. Then again, I bet Booker picked her out didn't he, he always has preferred the shorter woman. What was it he called them? Oh yeah, that's right, travel sized.

"Booker, you fuck nugget, wake up. What the hell did we get into last night?"

"Huh, wah? Oh shit yeah, figured you'd forget, you were drinking like a freaking fish last night. That's Erin by the way, she was all over you, that was until I slipped out the tickler."

"Ha, ha, ha, tickler, he calls you the Tickler."

"Yeah laugh it up, Love Gun." Yep, Booker's original, alright.

"Oh fuck."

"Yeah, I know yours as well, so keep it to yourself or I'll tell Benji's boy when we see him next."

"Yeah, Love Gun." Cheeky girl.

"You can shut up too, Twinkle Cavern, your girl wasn't exactly quiet when screaming out about having two snakes creep around her fairy cave. What exactly goes on in that head of hers?"

A fantasy about having a threesome apparently. Nothing wrong with a kinky chick.

"You know what bro, I don't wanna know, I needed to vent and I did, just text me the story later. I'm gonna bounce, catch ya."

Oh great, I can see it now, a weekend spent watching old Van Damme and Schwarzenegger films, while wallowing in self-pity. We really need to hook you up with a new woman and I swear Miss Warm Sunshine would be all over you if you gave her the time of day. But no, you're being a freaking pansy about it all. Ah shit, let's just get this over with, maybe I can get a stress wank out of you later, to at least get some endorphins through that depressed mind of yours. You're freaking tiring when you're like this.

THREE
She

What a boring weekend. After having to ditch early Friday night, not wanting to bump into Mr. Oh la la, who, by the way, apparently turned out to be not as well hung as Zali was hoping the French man would be, but still so freaking awesome at oral it kind of made up for it, all we did was a little work from home and cleaned. It was kind of lonely. Apart from guy fishing, which has been mostly on Friday nights, we have been getting more and more … well … lonely.

Maybe we need to get a pet. Yeah, maybe a cat. Oh, but we would have to hide it when the girls came over, because there is *no* freaking way we would risk being labelled into the lonely old cat lady zone at the tender young age of twenty-nine. If we got a pussy companion, we would never live it down. Ha, pussy companion! Isn't that what married men call a mistress? Yeah, I crack me up some times.

It's fun going out with the girls, but when we come home here, to our apartment, and it's just us, we get sad feelings sometimes, more than ever lately. It would be nice to come home to a man, a boyfriend or partner, someone who would do the cooking occasionally, or surprise us after a long day at work and have the bath already run. Someone who would bring our feet onto his lap and massage the stress of the day away. And someone who knows exactly when we need to be whisked away, from the smog and noise of the city, to our dream beach cottage where we can just be us.

Mmm. One day. Maybe. Oh please maybe.

Thank God we decide to walk to work today. It's a beautiful morning and the rays of the warm sunshine and the crisp morning air is helping to clear my girl's head. It's better than trying to clear it with sweet vodka drinks. Just as our work building comes into sight, so does the sight of the man standing at the waterfront opposite our building. Is it a coincidence that he has been there every morning *right* at this time for the past three weeks?

As we get closer he notices us and that sly, slightly creepy smile appears across his face, again, like it does every time he sees us. We smiled back the first week to be polite, then we smiled back the second week in case it was someone we might have met who is associated with one of our clients and we didn't want to seem rude. By the third week we pretended to ignore him as alarm bells started going off inside our head. But we still can't be overly rude just in case he is here because he *is* a potential client.

As we walk past him and head into our building, we hear him say *"Good morning"* but thank God we're already walking through the doors and can ignore him politely. My girl gets an uneasy feeling rush through her and so do I. We need to be careful, I'm just not sure why.

When we reach our floor, Alecia tells us that Mr. Black wants to see us in his office. It's a little earlier than most mornings. Usually he lets us all get in and enjoy our coffees from the awesome hi tech coffee machine my girl talked him into purchasing while we check all of our correspondence before he starts checking in with us all. My girl asks Alecia if he's had his coffee yet, thinking that if he hadn't she would make it for him before she goes in. Yep, my girl is always thinking of others. The receptionist tells her he was in early this morning and already had his coffee, so we walk straight down to the boss's office.

His door is open so we just walk in as per his constant request when his door is open. My girl anxiously stops after a few steps. *"Okay. Why do you have a smile that looks like a cat that just ate the mouse? Please explain why that makes me nervous, Andre."*

Right from the start, as soon as he could see her potential, he insisted she call him by his first name. Most of his employees get the privilege eventually.

"I have some exciting news to share with you."

Ooo, let's hear it. My girl sits in the chair opposite him but only relaxes slightly as she eyes her boss warily.

"As you know, I have been working on a deal with Woody from 100 Design. You may think it's a deal that would involve me working on the project for them, but ..."

Oh no. My girl instantly tenses up, knowing exactly what Andre is going to say.

"What have you done, Andre? I've told you before, I'm happy swimming amongst the little fish. I've no desire to swim in the ocean with the big fish."

She also knows that what the boss has proposed will have her working in the same building as him, Mr. Uptight. Damn that has made my girl lock up with stress something shocking. As much as I'd *love* to work within close proximity to him and his junk, I know how uncomfortable that would make my girl. And I don't want that. She loves her work, so to have her dreading coming here every weekday would be rather miserable.

"Okay, hear me out. You're bloody brilliant at your job, I've been telling you this for years. I know you're not running after the big time, but girly, it could do with a woman like you in it. This project is not only perfect for you and your talents, but it'd also be prestigious for our company to be associated with it. You won't be one of their employees, you'll be one of ours contracted out to them so our company's name will be associated with the campaign. It's a win, win for us all."
My girl knows he's right.

"Low blow Andre, using the fact that our company's name will be riding on this deal. See, too much stress already. And how will this play out? Do I get to work from here, or do I have to move two floors up for the duration of the campaign? By the way, what campaign is it?"

At least she is entertaining the idea. I mean really, we can put up with bumping into that cold dick more often for a few weeks. Well, I would prefer his dick to be warm or more so, hot, but hey, some of us can't afford to be fussy about these things. At least I could get drunk off his scent more often than I have had the luxury to do before. And damn, his smell is a good kind of liquor to get plastered on. As long as his junk doesn't start mouthing off any more, because I will not hold my tongue if he does, well, more to the point, my lips. Ooo what I wouldn't do for a tongue. Now *that* would be fun.

"All that'll be explained when you meet the head ad exec. Woody will introduce you two later today. Then I guess you can both work out the logistics of it together. Even though you'll officially be the junior on this campaign, you'll work as an equal with whomever he's going to have head up the campaign. So remember, don't back down on your ideas. I count on you not to. It's one of the reasons Woody is so keen to have you on board with this project. He's been trying to secretly poach you from me forever. Show him what you got, Lex."

She knows she can't say no now. I'm excited for something different, so I try to bubble those feelings up to my girl, but so far, she's paying no attention. While they go through the finer details, my girl stops thinking about Mr. Uptight and is finally beginning to get a little excited about this new adventure. It'll be good for her to step out of her comfort zone for a while. Hell knows she needs something to shake her out of the funk we were falling into.

We walk down to our office, not knowing what to expect or where we'll be working, so we pack our briefcase with everything we may need to save coming back. Always better to be prepared than look like a fumbling fool in front of a new boss.

Her nerves skyrocket when the elevator doors open up to reveal the entrance to 100 Design. It's a much larger company which takes up two whole floors compared to our meagre half a floor. There are people buzzing around everywhere. So many staff. I wonder if they all know each other's names like we do. My girl begins to have hope that with it being this busy, she may never bump into Mr. Uptight. But the reality is that we know through seeing Andre talk with Mr. Uptight in the lobby along with his mate and boss of this company, Mr. Woody Hardwick, that it's likely that Mr. Uptight is one of this firm's top ad execs, so there's a real possibility that *he* could be heading up this campaign. Oh God, let's hope he's not.

My girl introduces herself to the pretty little blonde receptionist who informs us she has been waiting for our arrival and we can proceed straight down to Mr. Hardwick's office where his personal assistant will announce our arrival. Seriously, why couldn't she just do that? What a waste of staff. If I had a mouth I would so whip this company into shape. But I guess they're not doing too badly, by the looks of this fancy place, so I'll just bite my lips.

Our arrival is announced and we are introduced to Mr. Hardwick, CEO of 100 Design and best mate to our boss Andre. He looks a lot more formal and commanding than our boss, but once he starts talking and getting to know my girl, we can see his friendly nature start to show. He's excited to have her in his grasp, his words, not ours, and informs her of the basics of the campaign while telling her that he has his number one heading up this project.

Then, before we know it, we're walking past an office, then a massive boardroom twice the size of ours, past two more offices, before he's knocking on a door. I can feel her pulse start to quicken and I know why. I can smell *him* nearby. Yep, that damn sexy as fuck aftershave is nearby alright. I can hear my girl chanting inside her head, *Don't let it be him, don't let it be him, don't let it be him.* Then the door opens and ...

Fuck! It's Mr. Uptight himself, looking just as shocked and displeased as we are.

"Lane, I would like to introduce you to your newest co-worker, Alexis Ryan. Alexis, meet our brightest star, Lane Anderson. Oh, do you prefer to be called Alexis or Lex? I have heard Andre refer to you as both."

We've lost our tongue. Emergency, emergency, we have seriously lost our freaking tongue! Maybe we swallowed it the minute we laid eyes on Mr. Uptight freaking Anderson and our brain was too busy short circuiting to realise our tongue is down our throat! Girly, snap out of it!

"Either name is fine, but I usually use Lex at work. Nice to meet you, Mr. Anderson."

Thank God our brain cells snapped out of their utter shock and saved my girl from looking like a fool. As much as this is her worst nightmare, working so closely to this attractive yet cold man, determination washes all through her as she straightens her spine and places on her best poker face. This is our chance, our chance to show him how cold and fierce we can also be. We will prove to him we're his equal in the business world and someone he couldn't possibly ignore. All he's got is a handshake and a nod? Seriously?

I'm surprised his junk is quiet in this awkward situation. Maybe he's been gagged. Ha, ha, that would be an amusing sight. Nope, no response? Okay then, I'll ignore you like all the other pedigree pussy that walks right past you. Still nothing? Damn, this is going to be boring.

I can hear a plan formulate in my girl's head and I'm so damn proud of her right at this moment. She is in business mode and is about to show him who's boss! Yep, we're roaring, so watch out Lane. Ooo, I really like the sound of his name flowing from my lips.

"I'll leave you two to sort out the finer details. Lex, please let me know if you need anything or if this guy becomes too difficult to handle. Lane, remember your manners in front of the lady, a lady who is damn good at her job. Play nicely, children."

We really like Mr. Hardwick already. Now down to our roaring!

"Andre and Mr. Hardwick have filled me in on the gist of the campaign,

but what I need from you is a full analysis, if you have one already, on the direction the client wants us to take. Then I would like to go over the ideas that are already forming in my head. I think if we can get the client to think outside the box on this project, they'll see it'll be more beneficial for their business."

Yeah! Take that you mother! Roar, roar, roar! We're not some piece of pretty arm candy, and if you'd taken the time to be nice to us when passing in the lobby, you'd already know that. Be prepared to be our bitch on this project, Mr. Uptight. Seriously, junk? Still not biting? If that's how you want to play it, so be it.

"Of course I already have a full analysis and I know exactly what the client wants. They're very traditional, so once you get to know their needs, you will see that 'thinking outside the box' won't work for them. Take a seat and we'll go over exactly what the client is asking for."

"How would the client possibly know they don't want to 'think outside the box' if we don't show them the possibilities? Isn't that our job, to show them what would benefit their campaign the most? If their 'traditional' ways were working so well for them, they wouldn't have sorted out the services of the best advertising company in the country. I think they need a change if they want to claim the number one spot in the market."

His only response is a grunt. We got this, girl. He'll see you for who you truly are, then he won't be able to resist your natural charms. Then ... then ... I'm not sure I'd even want to be with a man who's treated us so coldly. Well at least when he gets to know my girl and see how friendly and caring she is, he'll realise what he let slip by.

After a few tense hours of going over the entire campaign and arguing, quite heatedly at times, over the best direction with which to start, it's lunch time and my girl seriously needs a break from all his intensity. She goes to get up and leave but Mr. Uptight stops her with a hand around her elbow. No, no, no, I will not pay any attention to the zap of electricity that just shot through our arm and travelled all the way down to my core. Nope, no attention being paid here to the electricity bouncing off my internal walls. Trying not to clench, trying not to clench. Back off wetness!

"We've a busy day ahead so I ordered lunch. It'll be delivered here shortly. And I think it'd also be best if you moved into the spare office just down from mine so you don't waste anytime going back and forth to your floor."

Who the fuck does he think he is, bossing us around? Yes, we're technically working on *his* company's project, but we will not take orders from Mr. Uptight, no we won't, not even if those orders were in the bedroom, no, no we would not. Mind out of the gutter and back into the office.

"I've my own lunch already back in 'my' office, and I'm a quick walker and I also pee fast, if you must know. So I'll not 'waste' anytime in getting back in here. And as for the 'offer' of an office up here, no thank you, my office will be just fine and I'll only be a phone call or an email away if you need to see me in person. I can even run up the stairs if something is that urgent."

And with the sarcasm dripping on the floor, my girl walks out of his office. Girl power! Fist bump me, girlfriend! Well, not literally cause that would be too freaky thanks. As much as she held herself together in front of Mr. Uptight, my girl's *not* liking the tension. Tension doesn't sit well with us and it's mainly because my girl takes everything to heart. Thick skin is something she does *not* have. And this project could take six to eight weeks to complete! Damn, this is going to be stressful. It's worrying, as sometimes she doesn't choose the best ways to release the stress; do you have any idea what it tastes like when vodka comes out? Well, it isn't yummy; let's just leave it at that!

The day actually flies by and before we know it, there's only an hour left before we can hightail it out of this igloo. As much as he's still continuing with his cold shoulder routine, which he doesn't seem to show when any of the other staff comes in and out of his office, my girl and I are quite impressed with his work ethic and how talented he is at his job. It's plain to see why he is Mr. Hardwick's number one. God, for all we know, he could be the number one in the country, but we are sooooo not Googling that in the quiet of our apartment tonight, after a few glasses of wine and maybe some vodka shots thrown in if our thoughts turn to his sexy as fuck aftershave and the yummy scent of his junk. No. No. Not happening!

When Mr. Uptight takes a rare toilet break (well trained junk), we take that chance to text our girls.

CODE RED. Bar 31 tonight!

After such an awkward and tension filled, but also somehow very productive day, we need to see our girls. How the hell are we going to continue to work with Mr. Uptight for the entirety of this project? We need a plan, and by the way my girl is angry and hurt at the same time, we need as much help with our plan as possible.

I would say I don't know why he has such a hold over us, but I do know. It's his beautiful whisky eyes. They've so much kindness in them when he smiles; they just don't shine it our way. And despite him openly being a flirt, we've never seen in it anything remotely close to sleazy. He's also such a gentleman, always opening doors for the fairer sex, except us. He's as hot as hell and smells better than chocolate and that's a hard act to beat. He seems like the total package, someone we could actually want in our lives, someone who we see as our perfect Mr. Long Term Guy, but he just doesn't see my girl. Not for the wonderful person she is, no, he just doesn't see her at all. Sometimes it seems deliberate, but we've no idea why.

When he gets back they begin to wrap up their day and make plans for what each of them needs to research this week. My girl's excited about this project despite its rocky start and is determined to do herself and her real boss proud with what she knows she can achieve for the client and within herself. She just needs to continue to hold her ground with Mr. Uptight. Which is going to be hard to do considering, as she was packing her briefcase up for the day, he just grabbed his and mumbled a sullen *"See you tomorrow"* and walked out the door, not even waiting to hold the door open for her to leave his office first, which would've been the polite thing to do. Damn, this is going to be hard.

Let's not think about that now. Let's concentrate on what's important at this very moment. *Get to Bar 31, get to Bar 31, sauv blanc, sauv blanc.* We're so focused on that mantra that we barely notice the creeper, who's been loitering out the front of our building each morning, following us down Southbank along the riverfront. I don't like the feelings he's giving my girl. Maybe it's not a coincidence, maybe he's actually following us. Damn! That's all we need. Just before we get to the bar we turn slightly but can't find him, thank God.

As we walk into Bar 31 just after six, we see our girls already sitting at a booth towards the back with concerned looks on their beautiful faces. We can always count on our girls when we need them the most.

"Okay, spill. Why the code red? Are you okay?" Zali's voice is panicked.

"I'm okay, but I don't know if I will be after six to eight weeks."

"What the fuck is going on?" Poor Mel, she is just as worried.

"I was asked to go into Andre's office as soon as I got to work today. The project he has been trying to set up with 100 Design, which I thought was for himself, was actually being set up for me to help headline."

"Oh my God! That's awesome, Lexi. But why's there no awesome look on your face? You know you're going to show them how freaking brilliant you are." Zali has always thought we could conquer the world.

"Because, when I was introduced to the ad exec who is the senior on the campaign, it turned out to be ..."

"No." Zali knows exactly who my girl is talking about.

"No freaking way." Yes freaking way, Mel.

"Oh yes and yes freaking way, Mr. Uptight himself a.k.a Mr. Lane Anderson. He's every bit as cold and uptight in person as he is from a distance. Today was horrible. He's a freaking arsehole, demanding and

condescending, but still damn good at his job and he smells even better in an enclosed space. And this project is big, I mean really big and long and important for both our companies. How the hell can I survive this? You all know the effect this man has on me. This is a disaster!"

"No sweetie, this is perfect. This is an opportunity; to not only prove yourself beyond your comfort zone, which we all know when it comes to work you're snug as a bug in your comfort zone, and to prove to this man that you can be his equal in the advertising world. It's also an opportunity to show him who you really are. And that you're the sweetest person we all know and not someone who deserves a blast of ice every time you end up on his radar. You don't need to prove that to try and hook him in, you need to prove that to make yourself feel better about the way he's treated you. Fuck what he chooses to do with that information when he sees the real you. He's already lost you before he even had a chance to have you."

Zali hides her brains so well sometimes.

"Umm, how'd you get so wise?"

"Well I had three glasses during our lunch meeting today. So I'm on fire. Ask me anything." Yep, wine is an intelligence builder alright.

Besties are the best for a reason. As the giggles subside, my girl goes into the details of the whole day, then they all decide on a plan my girl should follow. Operation "Kill him with Kindness" takes shape. Which is basically my girl being herself but upping the niceness factor a few sickening notches. I'm not sure she'll resort to cooking his whole office blueberry and yogurt muffins like she does her own on occasion, but she'll definitely not let his freeze smother her fire.

As they order a selection of Tapas for dinner with some wine, they notice a group of five businessmen eyeing them quite obviously. Bar 31 is not usually where the girls pick up, since the class is generally a little to snobby for the girls' tastes, but hey, if the interest is there, why ignore it? So they throw sly smiles back.

Two of the men have beards, which results in some ... interesting conversation.

"Seriously, I couldn't stand the pash rash you'd have on a daily basis, let alone the possibility of swallowing a piece of yesterday's lunch every time you went in for a kiss. I see the hotness factor of a beard, the rugged caveman look is damn hot, but the constant prickly feeling would be too much for me."

I think my girl needs to take her own advice on how to "look outside the box" because that prickly feeling would be sexy as fuck.

"Oh Lexi, Lexi, Lexi. Think of that pash rash somewhere else. But think of it as more of a hot friction than a sore rash." Mel sounds like she has experience with such a situation.

"Pash rash, down there? No thanks!"

"Friction not rash! Believe me, it's hot. Don't knock it till you try it."

Oh yeahhhhhh. *I wanna try, I wanna try, pleaseeeeeeee.* Fuck the pash rash, make a sacrifice for me, girlfriend. Mmm prickly friction, yum. It'd be so much better than the friction from our vibrator; that seriously needs an upgrade by the way. Ooo, suggest a trip to the XXX superstore again, that was hilarious, even though we nearly wet our pants with laughter. Zali's demonstration of what to do with that three headed contraption will forever be etched into my brain and some new toys *would* spice things up a little. No? Okay then, but please consider some beard friction, for me.

"If you took home one of the Mr. Cavemen, you'd be sure to wake up happier in the morning and that'd be a good start for day two of working closely with Mr. Uptight. You'd walk in glowing like you just received the best morning sex of your life and have him wondering all day why you're in such a good mood. It's a win, win."

Yes! My girl is actually considering it. Oh my God, make me a bearded lady, please.

"Is it getting hot in here or is it just me?"

"Beards will do that to you. You're going to love it. Just don't push up too hard, those prickles can get a bit … tricky sometimes. I can't wait to hear of the results." Mel's vag loves all the dirty little details.

"Aren't you going to tell her what happened when ...?"

"Shh. She needs to experience it for herself. And it's different for everyone. I can't wait to hear what you think. This is the most excited I have been since you told us about Mel and the guy who couldn't get off without his cock ring."

"Okay, what're you not telling me, girlies? Is a beard a go or a no?" Please say go, please say go.

"Oh it is definitely a go! Very much a go, hoe."

"Cheeky cat."

By now the group of men have made their way over to our girls' table and are politely buying them drinks. This is a refined place, not a place where the dudes are shouting all the girls shots, but hey, there's a time and a place for shot shouting and this bar is too refined for that and so are their clientele. But hey, free alcohol is still free alcohol. And after a few more drinks one of the hot bearded cavemen, who surprisingly has tatts like a rock star under his business shirt, turns out to be pretty cool and ... well ... pretty to look at too.

After a trip to the ladies, which yes, as all men joke about, can't be taken alone, safety in numbers when you gossip like bitches behind closed doors, my girl decides to throw Mr. Uptight from her brain, take the plunge and invite Mr. Tattooed Bearded Dragon back to our place for some prickly friction. I'm so freaking excited I'm flooding her panties in appreciation.

Once our apartment door is closed, he wastes no time and, to begin with, the prickly kisses are a nice sensation. But it doesn't take long for my girl's lips to cry out in raw unhappiness as the infamous pash rash takes hold. My girl subtly dodges his lips by moving over to nibble on his ear, which going by his growl, he likes. This gives him a chance to move his bearded lips down my girl's neck. Ahh, now that's a nice sensation, sending sparks to our core.

He's good with his lips as he slowly travels down, nipping with his teeth as he sensually travels over her collarbone and down between her breasts. When his mouth travels over her nipples and his whiskers graze the sensitive buds, we almost convulse into oblivion. Mmm, why haven't we tried a beard before? Oh this will not be the last time, I'm sure of it.

He loves her nails lightly scratching down his back as he reaches the apex of her thighs and takes his time to admire my sexual beauty.

"Oh yeah, I'm wet and ready for you, handsome."

"You smell so freaking hot, kitty cat."

"Umm, maybe less talking and more doing, because 'kitty cat' don't do it for me, spiky."

"Whatever you say, sugar. Just lie back and enjoy the ride my guy is going to take you on. To the moon we go, babe."

"Yeah, still less talking please. You're interrupting my mojo."

Oh, oh, oh, the first feeling of his beard is delicious as he lightly brushes it over our clit. I am sooooo not going to last long. Yey, multiple orgasms tonight! But as he starts to apply more pressure as he digs his tongue into my core, the prickle actually starts to hurt a bit.

"Ow, ow, okay, lighten up a bit dude. Ow, ow, this is not pleasant anymore."

It's starting to feel like a thousand tiny needles attacking me all at once.

"Just relax sweetheart, we got you. It will get better soon I promise."

"Ow, ow. Needles, needles, jabbing, stabbing. Ow, ow, OW! No more! Get that hairy weapon of mass destruction and pain away from me!"

Oh come *on,* girlfriend, I can tell you are *not* liking it either. Get him off of me, find a way to move him somewhere else. Hey, offer him a blow job, offer him anything just pleaseeeeeeee get him off of me before I bleed to death from all the pricks.

Oh no! Fuck me! What is that smell? Is that … is that sticky stuff in his beard? What the fuck? A piece of buffalo wing … from *yesterday!!!*

FOUR

He

Well that was tense, what the hell got into you? Miss Warm Sunshine was within your reach the whole damned day and you sit there acting like a complete tosser. Seriously, I know how you feel about her, I can read you like a bloody book, and yet there you were, blowing more cold air than Antarctica in winter. I mean, seriously dude, what the fuck is up with you? Yes, Miss Queen Bitch messed us up good, but that is no damned reason to go and destroy one possible ray of kindness that isn't attributed to blatant and overwhelming flirting with airheaded bimbos.

I just don't get it mate, what could she, Miss Warm Sunshine, ever have done to deserve it? The pheromones coming off that woman are phenomenal; she is a cracking sheila and here you are acting as if she pissed in your cornflakes. Ahh fuck, you know mate, you're being a right dickhead at the moment, and that's coming from me, *your dick.*

Sod this, if you're going to be like that for the next few months or so, you can forget about any help from me. I'm going to stay silent on everything, show Hot Lips that even I am pissed with how you're acting towards her girl. Oh, you're looking for a pop, are you, forget it mate, until you buck your ideas up and start treating that woman with some respect, I'm staying limper than a wet sock in winter. See how you like that reaction.

Right, so you're pulling down your zip, I told you no matey, I'm not raising a whisker until you treat that girl with some respect. Yeah, your hand feels great, nice and warm around my shaft, but you can forget about it if you think *anything* more than a tingle in your hand is coming your way. I'm just going to lie here, nice and floppy, like a wet sausage until you, matey boy, decide to act like the man your mother raised you to be.

"What the hell is wrong with me? I need this, but fuck, I can't get it up. Why can I offer her nothing more than a sneer and a cold remark?"

I told you mate, you're a freaking dickhead. At the moment Miss Queen Bitch is still up in your head, messing with your wiring. Oh come on, don't go and pick up that poxy photo for crying out loud. Have you gotten rid of nothing of that bitch's? The jocks, the photos and the bloody teddy that sits on a shelf in your bedroom; what the fuck is the point in saying you want to move on when you can't move twenty feet here without being reminded of that whore.

She tore your heart out, hell, she made you so depressed and melancholy that you ended up popping pills for a year just to feel bloody normal. So why in God's name would you want to keep any of the shit that reminds you of her?

You know what, sod it, not my problem; until you get your shit together you're on your own big boy. Let's see just how well you do flying solo. Great, phone's going, probably Benji judging by the ringtone, most likely phoning to say sorry for bailing and asking if you're free for a quick spin to The Dukes for a few ambers.

"Yeah, hey Benj. No, no mate. Sorry, not tonight, I just got a massive project rolling and I need a clear head, maybe at the weekend, but for at least the next two months mid-week sessions are cancelled, bro."

Ha, so there is a brain in that head of yours, any other time you'd have said yes and gone and got plastered again. But, ah, like I said, not my problem, but good on you for keeping your head on straight, maybe there is some hope for you yet.

••••

Up ya get, time for work, nope, no play time. You don't deserve it, yet. So up you get, I told you yesterday I wasn't rising for anything, least of all a bit of self-love. Phone's ringing dickhead, you going to get that?

"Hello, yeah hey Vivian, how's it going? Okay yeah, give me twenty minutes and I'll be there. Tell me, is she already there?"

Ha! She is, ain't she, serves you bloody right. Oh you're pissed now are you, pissed at being proved wrong at her not being good at her job, she's bloody brilliant and you can't stand it. Or could it be that you thought you'd be working with a bloke and end up working with the one sheila in the world that actually makes your heart beat faster? So which is it boy, both are as bad as the other.

••••

Oh there she is, the fuck me personal assistant. God she stinks. You need to do one of two things, either get a new PA or learn to freaking file your own shit. But hey, at least you have a good long day of being a dick to make up for it. So what is it going to be today?

"Okay Alexis, if you want to keep your office, that's fine, just don't blame me if you get sore legs from running up and downstairs all day."

So that's how you're playing it today, well shit, you are being a bigger dickhead than I thought. Oh well, at least I get to play the hardworking gentleman and not act like a complete tosser with Hot Lips.

••••

"Hi Vivian, is Lane in his office yet?"

"Yes Miss Ryan he is, although he seems in a bit of mood today."

"I'm a big girl, Vivian, I can take care of myself, and call me Lex."

"Oh of that I have no doubt, Lex, it's how much a dick Mr. Anderson can be when he puts his mind to it that I'm worried about."

"Oh have no fear love, my girl can take care of herself, just wait till you hear us roar, your precious Mr. Uptight won't know what hit him. Now come on girl, let's go kick some ass. Mr. Uptight and his gorgeous smelling junk are going to kneel before the Queens of this jungle when we're done. Ooo gotta be quiet, Uptight is on the phone. Baby steps, girl."

Glad I heard that little rant from Hot Lips. This is going to turn out to be an interesting day. I kinda like their spark.

"Woody, this is just going to cause problems. You told me I would be working with Lex Ryan, I wasn't expecting some bloody blonde centrefold, no, and I am not saying she can't do the job. No, I'm not saying it's because she's a woman. Well shit, Woody, what do you want me to say, I'm just not happy to be sandbagged like this. Well, guess what, I bloody ain't. You tell me one thing and I get another, how else do you expect me to react. Yeah, yeah, whatever Woody, thanks for nothing."

"If I didn't know better, Mr. Anderson, I would get the feeling that you weren't enamoured with the idea of working with me."

"You heard that huh?"

"Damn right my girl heard that, Lane Anderson! You pompous arse, you jumped up sack of elephant crap."

This Miss Hot Lips is feisty. Fun times ahead.

"Yes, unfortunately I did. If you want a new partner on this, take it up with my boss, otherwise we're stuck with one another. Now, if you need me, I'll be in my office, you have my direct line."

Damn it, Lane, you're killing me here, why are you being such a prick all the time? She literally just heard every awkward, contentious word you said. Fuck, Hot Lips is going to be pissed.

"What? No fuck you, no dragging an apology from him? Come on girl, let it rip, I know that hurt a bit so where's the fiery girl that I know you can be? No, don't walk away, come on, I haven't even had a chance to tease the shit out of Mr. Stinky; you have to at least give me that. Come on girl, after my putting up with Captain Porcupine last night, you at least owe me that much."

I hate being right, but Hot Lips is still using Mr. Stinky, which I kind of find funny now and it gives me a little bit of hope, despite what my boy's doing. Strange but true. And I wouldn't mind being teased by that kitty cat right now.

"Whatever Lex, just keep the phone close by."

Well, that was awkward. I can't believe you, she was in such a good mood when she got in here. Hell, she probably got laid last night and laid good by the looks of it. But no, there you go, just ripping it all apart as she walks in willing to work with you and make a decent go of this project. Why are you being such a dickhead anyway? She wants you as much as you do her. I know she smells a little like Miss Queen Bitch, but that doesn't mean she *is* her. Hell, she's squirting so many girl pheromones in our direction that we could go swimming, and yet you're doing everything you can to push her away. When did my boy become such a pussy? And that's not the good kind, the kind I love to slip deep inside and plough hard.

But like I said, until you get your head out of your arsehole, I'm staying silent. Zero help from me. You are on your own, Lane. How's it feel to be all alone, again?

"Well she's probably there by now. Let's have some fun, see if she is all bright and cheery by the end of the day."

Hang on, what are you doing?

"Yeah Lex, can you come up here for a moment, got a design plan I need you to go over quickly. No, I can't email it down to you, they sent over a solid packet design."

Oh you arsehole, that is one hell of a dick move, bro, that's just plain nasty. Damn she's fast, flushed and a little out of breath, but fast as hell.

What did she do, sprint up those stairs? That's just nuts, and I should know, I have two of them.

"Your girl looks more than just flushed. Thinking about it, looking like that, she does have a certain air of vibrant sexuality about her, well, more so than usual."

"Damn right my girl does, she's the hottest chick around here, just take a look at Sally Foot Fungus out there."

Well, I'm just going to stay quiet, she's going to see just how much of a gentleman I can be, even if Lane is being a complete dickhead at the moment.

"Really, you're not talking to me and King Prick there is giving my girl the run around!"

No, no, don't say anything, just stay quiet, just stay quiet, show her that you are completely neutral in this war.

"Lane, what was it I had to rush up here for?"

"Oh, nothing now, turns out the digital packet was just delayed; you'll find it in your in-box."

You what, you're playing this game? Come on girl, give it to him, rip his damned head off and stick it up his butt pucker.

"Fine."

What? No! Get back in there and let him have it. Damn it girl, get the hell in there. Bro, that was not nice, what are you playing at? No, do not phone her again, you are just being childish now, this is not the way to be man, your mum did not raise an arsehole.

"Oh Lex, I'm sorry, I need you to come back up, the company just sent through some proposal revisions and it'd be easier if you were here rather than doing this over the phone."

"Oh, ow, ow, this is getting stupid, that's the second time in twelve minutes he's dragged us up here, you do realise how much I sting from Captain Porcupine's tongue bashing. He was good with that tongue, but damn I'm freaking sore and you keep taking the bloody stairs when there is a perfectly good lift."

Captain Porcupine? I'm so tempted to ask, but I'm being a gentleman."

"Thanks Lex, it seems as if the client is looking for a more … modern twist."

Ha, did you or did you not shoot her down over that yesterday, bro. How's it feel to know you're wrong for once? Yeah look at her smirk, she knows you're chafing over being wrong and having to admit it.

"So, they actively asked for a more up to date look to their campaign? Interesting that." She sure knows how to give it to Lane. This is fun.

"Yeah, that's my girl, oh ow, ow, ow, bloody hell that stings."

Don't laugh, don't laugh, keep quiet, she needs to know we're a gentleman and not like our boy. How long are they going to keep babbling on about this? I know for a fact that it was only two revisions to their original idea, so unless my boy added some crap, he is making up crap to keep her here.

"Okay Lex, that about covers it. I'll call you if there is anything else."

What? No thank you? No sorry for dragging you up here again? Can't you see how pissed off …. Oh, okay, you really are being an arsehole right now, aren't you? Doing all this just *to* piss her off, what are you going to do, sip your coffee for a few minutes then call her up here again and hand her a printed out version of the entire segment you just went over?

"Oh Lex, yeah, can you pop back up, got a few bits you forgot earlier."

For crying out loud, you're really pushing your luck here. You don't ease off on this crap, she is going to smack you with a freaking laptop! You do know she carries a notebook in her purse right?

"What is it now, Lane?"

"Oh fuck, ow, ow, fucking ow. Seriously, haven't you got something to put on me, come on, do you know how much it stings down here?"

Now I'm just *too* curious to stay silent any longer.

"Okay, I can't keep quiet anymore. I was trying to stay quiet and be the gentleman since my boy is being a complete dickhead at the moment, but what the hell is up with you? You've been wincing and groaning every time he calls your girl up here."

"Why do you care, it's not as if you give a shit."

"Well sorry for showing concern here, I was just trying to be nice and show some concern for another. Next time I'll just stay quiet and not say a damned word."

"Yeah, you do that. Besides, what's the worst a dick like you has to worry about, razor burn?"

"What the hell has that got to do with it?" What the fuck is she talking about?

"That has everything to do with it. I had some bear faced moron slathering all over me last night. It was like being tongued by a greasy roll of barbed wire and my girl let her dumbass friends talk her into it. It was awful, he was good with his tongue but that bloody beard was like freaking sandpaper when it got inside."

"Uh, hmm, umm. Yeah, I got nothing."

Seriously, how am I supposed to respond to that? Only way sandpaper would get near me ... well ... I don't think my boy will ever be *that* drunk. Drunk enough for a three way maybe, but to try and ... no, I'm just going to leave that thought alone. Let's all just be thankful lunch is here, I don't think I can take the cold in here much more.

"I thought we would have lunch in the office again, unless you have another idea, Lex."

Oh yeah, you're really enjoying watching her stew, aren't you mate. I really don't get this, what has gotten into you?

"I'm fine with that, Lane."

Damn it, even I can feel how pissed off she is. Christ, this is going to be a *long* few of months if you keep this crap up. Hot Lips is going to get really pissy with me and it'll be all your bloody fault. I hope you appreciate the situation you're putting me in here. Sometimes, I really do wish you could hear me.

••••

"Well, not that I'm being picky, but I think Thai food is getting a bit much, especially every day. Is your boy addicted to it or something?"

"I don't know, but what I do know is it smells like rotten asparagus on the way out." Yep, it really does.

"You're not kidding. I'm getting to the point where I'm scared when she goes to the loo, and it's, well … not exactly an enjoyable experience, especially at the moment."

"You think a pash rash on your lips is bad, try having a chick get her braces caught on your head. That *hurts!*"

I wince at the memory, making my boy jump as I twitch. I can't help but chuckle as Hot Lips giggles at her girl. The quirk of her girl's brow making my boy blush slightly. There's no way in hades she could have known what made him jump, but, well, she could probably make a decent stab after my boy turned into a human shaped tomato because of it.

"What was your boy doing with someone who needed braces in the first place, do you know the kind of image that conjures up?"

"Whoa now, he was like eighteen at the time."

"Oh."

"Yeah."

"Sorry."

"No drama."

"So, regardless of what happens with our respective people, what do you say to us being friends?" I enjoy this chick's company and it's better than talking to myself.

"Is this some ploy for you to get inside me? I've had swingers like you try that move before."

"Ha, seriously, the likelihood of that happening at the moment is nil. Do you really think your girl is going to open up to Lane when he is acting like a bigger ball bag than the clackers hanging off King Kong?"

"True, but then again, my girl is firing off goofy juice faster than the fire brigade during a Code Red bush fire."

"So, friends then?"

"Yeah, don't see why not. Just avoid the fourth week of the month."

FIVE
She

My girl's head is pounding and so am I. She just sat down after being called to Mr. Uptight's office for like the hundredth time today, and knowing we're going to be too busy to make our Pilates classes this week, she has been taking the stairs, with no respect to my life threatening condition! Pash rash down here can kill! Well, if you let it get infected that is, and my girl is too clean and tidy to let that happen. But for the love of God, I hope she lets me heal before our next wax appointment. I do not want to have pieces of flesh ripped off me because of that stupid porcupine.

Alexis starts to pack up for the day, making sure to take all the research she printed out so she can work from home tonight and get a head start on Mr. Uptight. And what was it with him complaining to his boss about Lex turning out to be Alexis and not the man he thought he was working with? My girl played it off well, but she was hurt, deeply hurt. She knows her industry is male dominated, but she has never experienced that kind of prejudice against her before. She should have been angry and stomping around the place, but the hurt smothered all that.

But instead of retreating in pain, it has hardened her and made her more determined to prove to him she is his equal, hence the overly heavy briefcase our body will have to haul all the way home. Damn, I hope we get a tram instead of walking tonight.

The elevator ride down is not pleasant; too many lunchtime sushi eaters in a confined space *is not* an enjoyable experience and someone has to tell Mr. Fake Italian Suit that he should add some deodorant to his morning ritual because we shouldn't all have to suffer because he prefers au naturel. Can you imagine the type of women he takes back to his place if he loves au naturel? They would have forests growing out of all their covered spots. Eww itchy. No thanks.

Once off the lift, we head for the front doors and as soon as we place a hand on the handle to push the doors open, we see the creeper, our very own Mr. Stalker. Just as he spots us we turn back to re-enter our building as if we've forgotten something. The unease flowing through my girl is unnerving. This may be something we have to seriously address. There is only so much you can blame on coincidence. Maybe we should start a log of how often we see him. Damn, I hope it's just someone who has recently started working in the same building and just happens to start and finish when we do.

Not feeling comfortable walking out there on her own tonight, she scans the lobby area for someone she knows and can hopefully walk through the doors with. And as luck would have it, she spots her boss Andre, who is speaking to none other than Mr. Uptight himself. Lane. What type of name is Lane anyway? Wasn't Lane the name of a famous cowboy who lasted eight seconds on a bull? Ha, ha. I will call his junk Mr. Eight Seconds from now on. I'm sure that will rouse him up a bit. Oh, that sounded naughty.

Okay, back to my girl's safety. She's standing still, debating whether to go over to them or just chance walking out on her own. When she looks out of the glass fronted wall and still sees Mr. Stalker out there towards the waterfront, she knows it wouldn't be wise to ignore her intuition. She takes a deep breath and walks over to the two men. Anyway, she shouldn't feel as if she can't even approach her own boss.

"Alexis, how has this clever young man been treating you?"

Well isn't that a question with lots of answers. Where shall we start? He's cold and rude and a downright pain in our freaking arse, who also seems to have a fetish for sweat, going by the amount of times he has had my girly running up and down two floors of our building and enjoying it when she turns up all rosy cheeked and flustered. And then, it seems he has an issue working with a female, that, or it's just one female he has an issue with. Ow, that kind of hurts just to think it. What is so wrong with us? I may have to have a quiet word with my new friend, Mr. Eight Seconds and see if he can give us an insight into why his Mr. Uptight despises my girl so much, even before they started working together.

"He's treating me quite well, Andre. We have some exciting ideas between us and we're excited to see what the client will think of the end result."

"That's if we don't throw something at his pretty head for being an arsehole first and storm off the project all together."

"Aww don't be like that. Just give it time, he'll thaw out eventually I promise. Truth is, apart from the way he reacts to your girl, he's genuinely a really nice and caring guy. He'll show it soon."

"So tell me, why the fuck's he so cold towards Alexis? Before they even started working together he was so rude to her. The first time she saw him in the lobby was the first time she had smiled in a long time. Seeing his cute grin and the dimple that formed on the left of his cheek and the kindness that shone through his smiling eyes was like a sunrise for my girl. And for a split second, when their eyes met over the crowd, he seemed just as enamoured with her as she was with him. She was drawn to him like nothing she had experienced before; her feet started walking towards him without her even thinking about it. But as she got closer, that sweet grin on his face started to disappear and was replaced with a blank stare before he turned away altogether, and that's how it's been ever since. I want to know why?"

"Well ... that's complicated and I'm not sure I should be talking about it. It's Lane's story after all."

"Oh, so you have only recently been attached to him? I mean, if it's not your story also then, that raises a *lot* of questions about your man."

"Funny fucker; there's been no attaching anything. I'm as real as he is, but his emotional rollercoaster of a love life is not something either of us likes to dwell on. Well, I don't dwell at all; he, on the other hand, let's just say he hasn't thrown out all the garbage yet."

"Ahh I get it, still holding onto those painful mementos. I was surprised when my girl threw out everything that reminded her of her ex. But considering the way that ended, I think a cold firm break was exactly the way to move on from that disaster."

"That bad huh. What happened?"

"Well, let's just say she will never surprise anyone again with a late night visit. The last thing you want to find is someone in a bed that doesn't belong there."

"The bed or the woman? But seriously, ouch, that's just cruel."

"Yep I don't think anyone can recover from the view. But seriously, why does he hate us so much?"

"It's not that he hates her, it's that she kind of smells like his ex and to be honest, at certain angles or with certain lighting, she looks a little like her too. But I'm sure that part is just in his head due to the recognition of the scent."

"What? So you're telling me it could be the perfume my girl wears that just so happens to be the same as his ex?"

"No, it's not her perfume, it's just ... her. She smells sweet and innocent; like a beautiful sunrise on a warm summer's day."

"Aww, aren't you the poet. That's really sweet, in a sickly kind of way, but still sweet."

"Yeah, yeah, cheeky girl. But seriously, he associates anyone that is that sweet as being false, someone who may be faking it with a hidden agenda behind their niceness."

"Well, you can tell him right now, that's not my girl. She is genuine. And that goes for all her parts."

"It's exciting for both Wilson and I to see our two best working on a project together. You are a match made in advertising heaven. I cannot wait to see the end result. But watch out Lane, this sweet girl can be a tiger when she needs to be."

"So can I, Andre, so this should be interesting."

Oh, you do not want to turn her into a tiger, mate. She will eat you alive. It's a relief when Andre starts to head to the door with my girl walking safely beside him and Lane following close behind, so close that his sexy as fuck aftershave washes over us making my girl shiver and swallow hard. No, we do not need those reactions now, we're working in such close contact with him. I will stomp those feelings down.

As the doors open she can still see Mr. Stalker out of the corner of her eye, and his eyes are definitely trained only on her. She sucks in a breath as the realisation that this could become a serious issue finally takes hold and a slight panic takes over her senses.

"Hey, what's wrong with your girl? I'm getting some uneasy vibes floating from her scent. Is everything okay?"

"Umm, we're not sure. There may be a little situation that's more serious than we first thought."

"Oh damn. You're not talking about your beard rash again are you? Because hearing about that shit once was more than enough, thank you. My ears couldn't take anymore."

"No it's not, dickhead. And you don't even have ears so that's a moot point."

"Oh, but I do have a mouth. Wink, wink. Ha, ha."

"Oh God, kill me now if this is what I have to put up with for the next couple of months."

They all walk down past a few more buildings before both men need to head in another direction. As the two men are finishing up a topic Alexis chances a quick look towards Mr. Stalker and sure enough, he is still there and looking directly at her. This isn't good and we still have a fair way to walk home. I suddenly want to grab hold of Mr. Uptight's junk and make him walk us all the way home.

"Okay kids, this is my stop. Do either of you have plans for tonight? Maybe you two should grab a drink together and enjoy a relaxing moment before all the crazy starts. But as a boss, I should tell you not to stay out too late now. Enjoy whatever you decide. Night."

"Umm, I have somewhere to be so ... sorry."

Well up yours, snob, we wouldn't want to share a drink with you even if you were the last hot, sexy, yummy smelling, fertile male left on this planet, even if the whole of existence was resting on us wanting to mate with you. No, not even then, the human race could go to hell. We don't want in your pants, not now, not ever ... okay. I think that covers it all. Let the anger go.

"I'm not available either. I have work to do."

"I wasn't aware you were still working on another project. I hope it's not going to interfere with our work."

"There's no other project. I'm going home to work on our project."

Yeah! Shove that in your pipe and smoke it buddy! So arrogant. But as my girl takes another quick nervous look in the direction of their building and frowns at the fact that Mr. Stalker is *still* looking her way, when she turns back to look at Mr. Uptight, his face has softened.

"Alexis, is everything okay?"

Brains frozen, gone, short circuited, fallen to the ground. Her name rolling softly from his beautiful lips has tears forming in the back of my girl's eyes and her lip feels as if it's trembling. She has fantasized and dreamed of her name flowing from those exact lips that are now right in front of her. And the concern in his voice is almost our undoing. The power this man has over us is intoxicating, and having to control that while we work together could possibly be what brings us completely undone, in more ways than one.

"It's okay. Umm, I'm okay, I mean. Goodnight Lane."

She's right. We need to move away from him quickly, because for some strange reason, tears are going to fall and we have no way from stopping them. Why do we want him so badly? Why do we want a man that has not treated us with a shred of respect, a man that has pushed us to drink way too much vodka on some very lonely nights? A man that's too cold for us to even warrant thinking about. So why, after hearing our name in his low husky voice do we now feel a single tear roll down our face? Fuck, the female body is a confusing entity sometimes.

"Goodnight, kitty cat."

Oh, he did not go there. I'm so going to cut him off in his sleep if he repeats that name again. But I have a better idea. Hit him where it really hurts.

"Night, Mr. Eight Seconds."

"What? No way! Who told you that? That's a lie! I have stamina baby, I can last ..."

And on the tram we hop. Boys. So easy to tease if you know how.

We were so busy getting away from Mr. Uptight, we forgot about Mr. Stalker for a few minutes, but as we look back towards the other side of the river, we see him moving quickly through the crowd, looking in the direction we were just standing with Lane. This is not good. Not good at all. We need to take this very seriously now.

My girl's smart, she knows we have to start writing Mr. Stalker's habits down and also speak to security for our building. Maybe they can keep an eye on him through the CCTV cameras all over our building. And we need to be careful walking to and from work. In the mornings it's always busy along Southbank, but at night we don't want to lead him straight to our front door. We can't ignore something this serious. For tonight we will just immerse ourselves in work, that will clear the unease of Mr. Stalker, but working on our newest project won't erase the thoughts of Mr. Uptight. Damn this is going to be a difficult project, in more ways than one.

We get home safely and get straight to work while last night's stir-fry heats in the microwave. Yes, she wants to make a large head start on Mr. Uptight, but my girl is also excited about such a large and challenging project. She gets amazing feelings flowing through our body when ideas form that just won't let up until she sits still and draws or writes them all down. I may get ignored quite a bit when her creative juices are on fire, but the feelings of accomplishment when a simple idea grows like rapid fire is freaking amazing. It feels as if all our nerve endings have come alive at once. Actually, it's very similar to how an orgasm slowly smoulders at first and then explodes at climax, causing fireworks in your vision. Even though it has been forever since we had one of those ones. I wonder if it will ever happen again.

After working through dinner she decides it's time to get comfy and slips into her PJs, the best working clothes ever. Seriously, if we could design a pair of work PJs, vaginas all over the world would cry with happiness. No more tight pants in unbreathable fabrics, no more stockings that just about cut off our circulation. We and our owners would be a much happier race.

Just as we sit down in a more comfortable state, she gets an idea. Ahh, I knew this was coming, I knew she would use this as a weapon against Mr. Uptight, I just didn't know she would bring out the big guns so soon. She jumps up and moves quickly to the kitchen, pulling out ingredients from cupboards and the fridge. Deciding she needs to double her efforts, she rushes back to her room and throws on a hoodie over her PJs, slips on her runners, grabs her keys and purse and heads for the door.

No girlfriend, you're not! We're not jogging down to the corner store in our goddamn PJs! Oh damn, yes we are. And I thought you were supposed to be the smart one. What has gotten into you? I have no choice but to go with the flow and just pretend that I'm not embarrassed to be connected to this woman sometimes.

As we enter the grocery store that's two blocks from our apartment, I feel at least four sets of eyes turn our way and then the snickers start.

"Looking for a roof over your head, sweetheart? My guy's got plenty of room to accommodate your sweet sugar."

"Great line, dickhead."

"Hey there my little pussy cat, did someone forget your milk?"

Seriously? Why does my milkshake bring all the boys to the yard?

"Really? I've never heard that one before. Move along gentleman, ladies on a mission."

Seriously, some dicks are more dicks than others. I'm still trying to figure out what head on a man holds the most brain cells. Jury is still out on that one. My girl grabs all the extra ingredients she needs to make her famous, mouth-watering and super healthy blueberry muffins. She makes them all the time for her little office, often by request, but Mr. Uptight's office has a lot more staff, so even doubling her recipe won't cover it. Maybe she is planning on leaving them all on Mr. Uptight's desk, hoping he won't be able to help himself and he will get fat and unattractive after eating the whole two batches. Yep, that's probably it.

Once we're home and the second batch of muffins is in the oven, we get back to some solid work. With Adele crooning in the background, our creative juices are overflowing. After the buzzer chimes to take the last batch of muffins out, we return to work, coming up with some exciting concepts we can't wait to show off to Mr. Uptight. Oh and of course the clients too.

It's almost midnight before my girly starts to finally wind down. This is a late night for us, we normally get more beauty sleep than this, and I need all I can get while I'm still recovering from my tragic injury. I hate to think of what I may look like in the morning. Thank God I won't be parading myself around to anyone, but if I'm all healed by Friday night, I will be more than happy to parade around in front of the right piece of meat. I just pray we get one that knows what he's doing and has *zero* facial hair.

Hey, I would even go for one of those athletic types, maybe even a cyclist for once, just to experience nice, gentle, hair free ... well ... everything.

SIX

He

You're watching her leave, aren't you; you're watching that tram pull off. You really do have feelings for her, not that I think you realise it, but you do. Hold up. Who the fuck is that? No, not the bloke next to her on the tram, that pogo crossing the road towards us. He's been around here a lot lately, although I doubt you really noticed, but you have now though. That's right, keep an eye on him, remember that face, Lane. Now let's head home.

"See you in the morning, Lex, sorry about today."

You really are soft as shit sometimes, Lane, you really are. But why not say it to her face?

•••

Right, don't forget to shut the door this time, dipstick, I forget the number of times we've woke up to find that bloody door ajar.

"Shit, I need a drink. Today has not been a good day."

I swear mate, booze is your go to response for every tense situation. You stood there and peacocked, flaunting yourself, I mean seriously, who calls themselves a freaking tiger? I totally get Andre calling Alexis a tiger, you know, give her a boost and all that, especially after you fucked around with her head all day. But you, calling yourself a tiger, who does that, dickhead? Now because of you and your poxy name, I now have a new nickname. Mr. Eight Seconds, thanks for that.

"Where's my tequila. Come on you bastard, where are you?"

It's not in that cupboard; it's in the one by the freezer. It's always in the one by the freezer, why do you forget that? Hang on, yeah, stupid question. You're always too pissed to remember the day after. Seriously though, you shouldn't jump into that bottle yet, Miss Warm Sunshine and Hot Lips are diving into the work and ploughing ahead, so why don't we? Come on, seriously, folders open on the table, we've got some old shows on the boob tube to create some background noise, so dive on in. Water's lovely as they say, or we could always go through and ditch that bitch once and for all, you know, toss out all her bullshit belongings that still clutter up drawers and other places, especially that bloody bear. Do you know how much of a rod killer that thing is? It just sits there, staring. It creeps me out and I forget the amount of booty that has gotten pissed off at us because that poxy bear has pushed the mood right out of me.

"Ha, found you, ya bastard, time to get drunk."

Oh great, another night spent with your hand stuck on me as you attempt to tug the whisky dick out of me rather than getting work done. There are times when I really do wonder if I was only grafted onto you at the last minute rather than us being attached from your birth. I really do think we are two *very* different people. Well, I'm a penis, you're a person, but still, we are far too separate to have ever truly belonged together to begin with.

Oh God no, the salt shaker and a bunch of lime wedges, did you plan all this in advance or something? I'm so going to make you puke, in fact, I'm going to give your gut a heads up now and make sure you redecorate your toilet seven shades of puke before bed time.

••••

"Oh shit, my head."

That's right, dipshit; it's that bad this time. You necked that bottle within an hour, *then* went down to the corner store and bought yourself another three bottles and necked another one when you got back. Take a look at the kitchen bin, more lime in there than a Cornish quarry, not to mention I literally taste tequila *every* time you take a leak. Do you even realise how much it stings when you drop a load in the bowl? This is getting ridiculous, something has got to give. At the rate you're snorting down the liquor it's going to be you long before me.

"Damn it, this has to change, I can't keep doing this. I'm going to end up drinking myself to death."

No shit, Sherlock! I've been telling you this ever since you hit the sauce after Miss Queen Bitch up and tore you a new one. So are we going to work today, or are you going to be a complete pansy and sit in a dark room all day and fawn over the all-consuming sack of shit that walked out on both of us, with your former best friend no less? Yeah that's right; I actually pay attention to the stuff that happens, to what goes on around us as you walk through the pointless excuse of a life you seem content to live at the moment.

"Shit, I need something to put my head into at least some sort of normal state, otherwise I'm going to puke, or at the very least, end up with a migraine by the time I get home."

Good, we can finally get some bloody work done for once, rather than you fucking around making Alexis's life a living nightmare and ruining my chance with Hot Lips, *if* something ends up happening. Which in all likelihood, it won't, because you're playing the part of Captain Douche Bag in the two month production of the Beauty and the Arsehole.

"Come on, come on, where the fuck did I leave them? They're here somewhere."

Ha, you're looking for the Alka Seltzer ain't you? Well guess what, you used it all, props for not shopping properly, mate. This'll teach you to prepare better, won't it. I swear, this is getting to be a bloody running joke with you. That last box you bought was supposed to last a month, and you blew through it in two weeks. But like every other damned time we go through this, you'll head to work, plough through the job, be a complete arsehole to Alexis, and then drink yourself into a stupor again tonight.

I honestly can't get my head round the way you treat her, but hey, like I have said to you before, not my problem, douche bag, you are going to get stuck with whiskey dick for life until you buck your ideas up and treat that woman with at least some respect.

"Ah, shit, okay, what was it Benji said always perked him up? Right, where's the eggs and tabasco sauce?"

Oh lovely, I'm going to be sieving through that crap again. Why don't you just throw some cold Chinese food into the blender as well? No, oh shit, I was bloody joking, don't actually, ah fuck. This is going to taste bloody awful on the way out. I'm so glad I can't really get the full flavour of anything that I'm pumping out. Damn, can you imagine what it would be like to live with the taste of jizz and piss constantly in your mouth?

••••

"God, why is the world so damned noisy today? It feels like I've got a freaking cement mixer full of marbles in the back of my head."

That's what you get for being a closet alcoholic, mate; you may as well wear a sign around your neck that says "I want to be a brewery," because if it wasn't for your anal retentive cleanliness ritual each and every damned morning, then you would certainly smell like one. Speaking of douche bag things to do in the bathroom, did you bleach your teeth again this morning? I mean, seriously, who does that apart from dumbass American actors or anyone on Jersey Shore?

Hey, ain't that the prick you saw making crazy eyes at Alexis? You know the one who went all Michael Myers crazy stare when he watched you and her talking last night after work. That's gotta be him, he has that same Sheldon Cooper haircut and cheap jacket. Mate, are you blind or what? You've got to be able to see this tosser, come on, take a freaking look for fuck sakes. Seriously Lane, open your eyes and take a damned look at the guy! He's right there glaring at you like he is trying to make your head explode.

For crying out loud, you're more clueless than a blind gay guy in a freaking all female nude review for Blowjob Quarterly.

Okay I'm so over this, you're next to bloody useless. I'm going to give Hot Lips a heads up on this douche bag, maybe she can nudge Lex into paying attention when he's around.

"Morning, Clive."

"Morning Mr. Anderson, busy day ahead?"

"Count on it. I've got my boss chewing on my arse and my new work partner is a bit of a crowd pleaser, never can catch a break."

Oh you arsehole, you know for a fact Lex is doing nothing more than what you used to do and by rights you should still should be doing, being a nice person. So stop spreading bullshit and get on with your job. Besides, you can see Clive doesn't give two shits what you say; he just gets a better report from his shift boss when he clocks out. You don't ever see that from Larry when he's on shift. Oh who am I kidding, you never listen so I'm just going to stop talking and wait for Hot Lips and Lex to get in. At least then I get some intelligent conversation.

••••

"Lex, can you pop up here please, need to chat about some things."

And so it begins; the aimless, pointless, childish teasing of a malcontent. I'm still at a loss as to why you're being like this. I cannot wait to find out what Hot Lips makes of it all. Oh I hear panting, and rushed footsteps. Yup, she ran up here again. You owe that woman some serious compensation. Especially after the container of muffins she left on your desk this morning. You may be trying to show some will power, but we both know by the end of the day you will have eaten at least two. And how sweet was that of her to leave a large basket of them on our front reception desk. Not that you would have noticed.

"Why do I suddenly feel like that public speaker from the Hunger Games?"

"Oh, what, do you mean? 'May the odds forever be in your favour.' Hey, Mr. Eight Seconds."

"Pretty much. I swear, every time these two are in the same room, there is more tension than an Alcoholics Anonymous convention where the coffee just ran out; there is no give or take between them, she's as stubborn as he is and he's just being a right arse of late. I mean hell, you saw that yesterday. How's the pash rash by the way, Hot Lips?"

"It's healing, thanks, and I know exactly what you mean; my girl was straight into her PJs and the funky leftovers as soon as we got home. And then in the middle of it all, decides to make blueberry muffins. Like we don't have more important things to concentrate on. By the way, did you see anything odd on the way home last night?"

"Oh, you mean the Michael Myers wannabe with the Sheldon Cooper hair cut? Yeah, I saw him. The blind Adonis I'm stuck with didn't, but I did. It's astounding the shit he misses that I catch. I mean hell, it was me that first put him in Alexis's direction. This dull git was too wrapped up in his own misery to even see her at first."

"Don't you mean blonde Adonis?"

"I know what I said, but seriously, you need to keep a watch on that guy. I do not like the way he is staring at our girl."

"Our girl?"

"Well, I, uhh, oh fuck, I meant that, well, I uh ..."

Shit, shit, shit and double shit. I cannot believe I let that slip. I swear if I could blush I would be the same colour as Heinz ketchup right now.

I'm just going to be quiet for a while I think.

"What is it, Lane?"

"Look, I know you love your desk, I know you love your office. But this whole running yourself ragged thing, it just isn't going to work in the long run, and I don't want you falling ill or hurting yourself for the sake of this campaign. So; I have an office big enough for multiple desks; I know for a fact we have some of the new pattern ergonomic ones in storage, so I'm going to get one set up in here for you to use."

"Mate, you really need to check that tone. Do you even hear how condescending you sound? Hell, even I know that is the wrong way to phrase things and I'm supposed to be the bad influence, well, that's if you follow the Freudian school of thinking."

"Do I get a say in this?"

Lane, seriously, abort the mission, abort the mission, man. You are setting yourself up for failure here.

"Of course you do."

Oh, so now you're being a gentleman and letting the lady have a say in things. You're such a tool and I swear if I had hands, I would be giving myself the biggest face palm right now. How can I be attached to someone this dense?

"Thank you, but no thank you. I'm comfortable as I am."

"Ha, serves you right, douche nozzle. Did you think my girl was going to go all puppy and roll over for you to tickle her belly? Get real."

"Hot Lips, did you seriously just compare *your* girl to a dog?"

"No I didn't, I used it as an analogy. I realise you only have a small brain in that head of yours but seriously, wise up Mr. Eight Seconds."

"That's rich coming from a talking pin cushion. You know, I'm thinking of changing your nickname. What do you think of Pash Lips?"

"Oh you son of a ..."

"I'm sorry, I didn't catch that, Pash Lips, you're a bit muffled and it's kind of rude of you to leave in the middle of our conversation."

"Fuck you, you limp noodle."

"You wish, Pashy."

Okay, you just called her up and chased her off in one conversation, which has to be the world record of fuck ups, or at least your personal best, bro. I'm really at a loss as to what to do with you anymore; you're really getting to the point of no return. I would say beyond redemption, but I'm an atheist so, redemption is what you make it.

Hang on, you're picking up your phone, who are you calling?

"Viv, can you patch me through to Maintenance please?"

Whoa, hang on, what the hell are you doing, why are you calling Maintenance. Lane, stop and think over what you're doing.

"Yes Mr. Anderson."

Oh no.

"Maintenance."

Lane seriously, what are you doing? If you're doing what I think you're doing, then she is going to be *pissed.*

"Hi, this is Lane Anderson, I'm in office 320 in the south corner. Do you have any of the new ergonomic desks available? You do? Excellent. What is the earliest you can get one up to my office and set up?"

"Well, we have a new cubicle sector going up in the renovated conference area, so probably Wednesday at the earliest, Friday at the latest."

Okay seriously, Lane, you are digging a hole so deep we'll be eating tea in China. Back off now, mate.

"I need it done before Friday, so Thursday is the latest it can go in. Can you also add to it a new posture corrective chair as well and a foot brace?"

"Sure, so, installation before Friday morning. You don't work nights, do you Mr. Anderson?"

"No I don't, well, not often, but I can make sure it is clear this evening if that helps."

"Yeah that'll work; I can get a couple of the guys to do it either Wednesday or Thursday night."

"Okay, thank you very much. Goodbye."
Oh we're so fucked.

SEVEN
She

Mmm, a stretch in the mornings is good for the body and soul. We're relaxed this morning. It could be because the past two days have been uneventful in the war of Alexis vs. Lane, or it could be because it's Friday and we're seeing our girls tonight. Zali was able to organise a table at Vue de Monde on Collins Street through her boss, and after some of the most exquisite food in Melbourne, we will then be hitting the Belgian Beer Café at Riverside Quay. I cannot wait!

I hope after the past two relatively quiet days, my girl and Mr. Uptight have settled into some sort of working routine. But I must say, they're a strange pair when they are together. It is so obvious that there is some mighty chemistry between them and it doesn't take Mr. Eight Seconds and I to point out the obvious. The electricity is floating in the air. But as soon as one of them feel it, if only slightly, they retreat and often retaliate with friendly fire.

I can see it now. The tension will build and build until one of them snaps. And I'm not so certain it won't be my girl. She can be as tough as nails on the outside when she needs be, but on the inside she feels insecure about why Mr. Uptight has given her the freeze from the start. The funny thing is, when they're both completely immersed in their work and she creates an exciting idea, Mr. Uptight lets down his guard for split second and beams at her like a proud boyfriend. He's even squeezed her hand on the table out of excitement before he quickly realised what he'd done and retreated back to his iceberg.

Sometimes I feel a sad vibe coming from him. Like he's desperate to let Alexis's sunshine seep in, but is too afraid of it possibly ending in heartbreak, to let her anywhere near him. But if we live in fear of heartbreak, how will we ever have a chance to experience love? It is a foolish way to live. But that's his loss. My girl deserves the best and he's just not shaping up to be that at all; all the more reason for us to avoid any chemistry where that man is concerned.

Okay, what to wear? We're going out straight from work so let's sex it up a bit while still keeping it professional of course, but it has to make Mr. Uptight's eyes pop out of his pretty little head. No, no slacks. We need to show those long legs of yours, it has to be a skirt. But for the love of God, please do not put on those suck in control stockings. One: because you don't need the bloody things, and two: because I do not want to turn purple due to lack of oxygen. You don't want me dropping off, do you?

"If I wore that smart black dress, with the dark blue panel down the middle, would Mr. Uptight actually take notice? I know it's not a club dress, but it does hug my curves fairly tightly. It has short little sleeves and falls just above my knees so it would still be considered professional enough for the office, but it makes me feel kind of ... sexy. Would he see me as sexy though? Arrrrrr, why am I even bothering to try and impress him? We've been in the same damn building for over a year and his attitude towards me has never changed. Just give up, Lexi."

Maybe if she gives up, she could move on from her obsession over him and then at least she might have a chance at a good professional relationship with him. Because damn, those two brains working together on a project are a force to be reckoned with.

Oh yeah girly, that does show off all your finest assets. Well done and you chose that one all on your own. See, you need to trust your own instincts more often, rather than always relying on Zali or Mel's opinion. You're hot and I know it, because I am. I just have to find a way to make *you* see it. Oo, oo, yes, yes, yes, those shoes are perfect! But you may need to hide some flats in your handbag, because the height of those are not something we can sustain for an *entire* day. But they are pretty.

Okay, let's get to work and make the day our bitch!

••••

We're going to have a great night tonight if you go by all the attention we're getting just on the way to work. We haven't even stepped into our building and we already have the men of Melbourne fawning all over us. A little black dress works every time. It should be a law that everyone with a vagina should have one hanging in their closet.

For the first time in forever we don't see Mr. Stalker waiting across from our building. That's a good sign. Walking across the lobby we get a lot more smiles than usual, and as we enter the elevator we have a few young studs scrambling in after us, all giving my girl some sexy sideway glances. Today is going to be good, I can feel it. Umm ... well ... maybe ... not. As we knock and then enter Mr. Uptight's office, Alexis freezes.

"Good morning Alexis. I have an idea I want to run by you before we contact the client at lunchtime, so take a seat and we'll get started."

Alexis is speechless. Not so much out of shock, but more so out of anger. Anger that is boiling up through her entire body and threatening to explode. Because at the far right of Mr. Uptight's office is a brand new desk! All fitted out with new stationary sitting pretty on it, a foot rest sitting under it, and one of those fancy new chairs sitting behind it. If he hadn't asked and she hadn't already refused, it could be seen as a lovely and thoughtful gesture. But, and this is a big but, he knew she was happy commuting back and forth from her office.

She is breathing deeply, trying to control the reaction she wants to let loose on him, knowing that he is damn well trying to get a heated response from her. For what reason, she doesn't know, but feelings of hurt start to fester inside her mind. She shakes it off, not letting them take hold as she tries to think of a response that will show him she's not willing to be drawn into his petty games.

"*Nice desk, Mr. Anderson. Do you have a twin I wasn't aware of?*" she says in her nicest voice. And much to her delight he squirms slightly.

"*I would much prefer to turn to you when I have a question than have to pick up the phone or email you a hundred times a day.*"

"*I didn't know it was so hard for you to use a phone or computer. I'll keep that in mind for future reference.*"

"*I can use both just fine, thank you. I'm just trying to save us both time. And I don't want you hurting yourself running around on those ... umm ... on ... those ... on those shoes that're so ... very ... ah ... very high. Umm, we should get to work, don't you think?*"

Well, well, well. I thought it would be the dress that would have Mr. Uptight stumbling over his words, but I think we just discovered his weakness. Stiletto shoes! Let's just store that little piece of information away for another day. Oh, maybe he has a foot fetish? Ooo, toe sucking. We've never tried that.

My girl smiles sweetly at him as she goes and makes herself comfortable at her new desk. She makes a big deal of moving things around and repositioning the desk slightly, changing its angle to look out the windows more, at a view she'll never get sick of. She then moves her chair up and down until she has the height just right. She opens her laptop up and begins opening all the documents she needs to work on.

It's silent in the room apart from Alexis tapping on her keyboard. When she looks up she catches Mr. Uptight just staring at her. Was he expecting a fight over the desk? Or is he just mesmerised by her shoes and maybe her dress? Either way my girl is happy with the look on his face.

"*You said you had something to show me, Lane?*"

"*I do. I um ... I have ... I have an idea I want to show you that I think the client would be happy with."*

This is a first, and me and my girl like it.

"What're your thoughts, Mr. Eight Seconds?"

"Umm, what was the question? I'm still stuck on the word stiletto and the images of them up around his ears."

"Focus, Eight. What has your man so stumped? The dress or shoes? I need to know these things. It could be a matter of life or death one day. Are you even listening to the words that are coming out of my mouth?"

"You have lips, but no mouth, so get it right. And yes, my brain hears your words but the big one upstairs is still stuck on the stilettos in all sorts of positions."

"So he does want Alexis is that way? So why the big freeze all the time?"

"Oh yeah, he wants her that way. She is constantly in his dreams in lots of ways, believe me, but he refuses to acknowledge his feelings in the daylight hours. Past heart break and all that crap clogging up his brain. But hey, as long as we can get them to a point where they can work peacefully together, this will be a much happier place to be stuck in."

"Mmm, interesting. Do you think he'll ever stop being hooked on his ex?"

"Well to do that, he'd have to actually rid himself of half the shit in his apartment, which at the moment he is reluctant to do. I don't know why, the bitch really did a number on him and with his best friend no less. So why he would want to constantly think about her is a mystery to me. Sometimes I believe my brain functions better than his."

"Well in my experience that isn't the case. It's usually the little brain causing most of the trouble, but I may have to agree with you on this one. But don't get used to it, Eight."

The remainder of the day runs smoothly. And yes, we have to admit, having a desk in his office is a hell of a lot more convenient than running up and down the stairs all day long. And both Alexis and Lane seem to be getting more work done. The whole day they have both looked up from their desks to ask the other a question. It's turned out to be much more productive, but there's no way she'll let him know that. She is still secretly peeved at his condescending ways.

But there's a distinct downfall to this new arrangement. His sexy as fuck aftershave is messing with us something shocking. She'll be engrossed in typing or researching and I would be off in my own little world and he would move slightly on his desk and then bam! Brain cells on holiday again as a big whoosh of aftershave floats our way. It takes her a good few minutes to pick up where she left off.

Sometimes his scent threatens to cause a flood through my centre. I have to use meditation just to control myself. *Stinky shoes, smelly fish, garbage bin, sushi shop's garbage bin, two week old sandwich left in the office fridge.* Anything to distract myself from the arousal I want to feel, the arousal which is a natural response for me when a potential mating partner is within arms' reach of us. Bloody Mother Nature sometimes makes life more difficult than it needs to be.

They achieve a lot today, and going by Mr. Uptight's sly grin he knows it's because of his desk plan. Stupid smug male with stupid smug grin on his stupid too handsome face, connected to his stupidly too hot body. Mother Nature sucks!

"I'm thrilled with the client's response to all of our initial ideas. If they're that happy now, can you imagine how happy they'll be with our end result? I love it when a client validates all of your hard work."

"I agree. It makes all of the hard work and long hours' worth it."

Whoa! What the hell is happening to my girl's body? It's as if everything just short circuited for a few seconds before it all just went back on line. It takes me another few seconds to realise the problem. A smile. A goddamn, butter wouldn't melt in his mouth, hot as hell and very genuine smile! It is something to behold. All sexy and cheeky with a dimple, with promises of real feelings behind it. It is the first time I think we are seeing the real Lane Anderson. All his walls momentarily down as true joy takes over his face.

Alexis is standing there, mouth open, as she watches him pack up his desk for the day, the residue of the smile still tugging at his very kissable, plump lips. Happiness. I feel happiness start to flow through our body. Happiness is always a good thing, but in this instance, a smile causing this tidal wave of joy may not end well when he reverts back to the coldness we are used to. Mmm, interesting development.

As if sensing her staring at him, he looks up and right before her eyes that smile starts to fade. She can't stand to see what it will be replaced with, so she turns quickly and packs up her own desk, desperate to get away from this confusing man. She swaps her heels for flats, throws her lap top bag over her shoulder and quickly exits his office, offering a *"Have a good weekend"* over her shoulder.

"Hey Hot Lips, what the hell was that all about?"

"That was trouble my friend, trouble with a capital T. See you Monday, Eight."

No Alexis, don't go there. I can feel the gears turning in her head as she rides the elevator down to the lobby. She is so lost in her dangerous thoughts of a nice Mr. Uptight, or Lane as she is thinking of him now, that she doesn't even notice all the interested eyes following her and her little black dress. She doesn't even notice that Mr. Stalker is back. She just keeps walking a few blocks before she hops on a tram and heads up Collins Street to meet the girls.

It was just one rare smile, sweetie, don't let it cloud your head with impossibilities. One smile doesn't change his chill the rest of the time. Let it go and let's enjoy a dinner with our girls.

Vue de Monde is not our usual M.O., but it is a lovely change. Certainly not the type of place for a casual pick up, but we can save that for later. Mel and Zali are already seated so we make our way quietly over to them.

"Quick, tell us how the week working with such a delicious piece of man candy has worked out for you. I've been flat out, well, flat on my back

every moment I'm not working, but that's another story. You first, Lexi."
Zali is practically bouncing in her seat!

"Well ... it's been interesting. You could say it's been much like a rollercoaster ride. Completely up and down. Cold one minute, lukewarm the next, back to cold, then downright heated a minute later. It has my freaking head spinning and I'm worried it's going to affect my work before the project is done."

"Nope, you won't let that happen. You're too good at your job Lex. And Mel and I agree, as soon as you find a way to bang him out of your brain, the better. Then the unknown is known and you can get back to work. No more up, down, back, forth, the tension will go. Easy"

"As I've said before, I wouldn't even have a chance at getting him in that situation in the first place. And after, then what? Adding some awkwardness to the situation is not a good plan. Sorry, you suck tonight."
My girl's right, I don't want awkwardness shadowing us in the office.

"Do you want to fuck him? Don't roll your eyes at me, just answer the question honestly."

"Yes. More so now that I've got to work with him and I know that his brain is as brilliant as the rest of him."

"Now that's trouble. But we can still work with it. Okay, here's the plan. Drive him to the point of no return, where you tempt him so wickedly that he just can't resist you for a minute longer; then grabs you roughly and fucks you right then and there on his desk. Then say thanks and get on with your job. Pretend it didn't happen and it will drive him insane. Then you will always have the upper hand on your attraction to him and be able to control it better because you know it'll be you who holds all the power. You're so distracted at the moment because he has the power over you and your raging hormones. You can do this and we are going to help you. Mel, do you have plans tomorrow afternoon?"

Zali is a fucking genius!

"No, and I know exactly what you're thinking and I know the exact place to take her." Mel, the queen of shopping!

"Wait up, where are you planning on taking me before I have even agreed to your crazy plan?" My girl really needs to lighten up a little.

"Oh darling. We are going to sex you up like never before! We know how to keep it professional but blur the lines in a sexy way. You will have the entire male population of your work place eating out of your hand, but most importantly, Mr. Uptight will be your bitch to do whatever you want with, the poor little puppy. Oh you're so installing a hidden camera in his office. We need a visual of what's about to go down!"

"Well his office is now mine also, after he had a desk installed in there for me even after I protested. But no to the camera. First: it's illegal to film someone without them knowing, and second: I do not want to be working knowing you bitches are staring at us the whole time. That would so put me off my game. But, I wouldn't mind a new wardrobe. This dress made me feel amazing today, so even if the clothes only give me a perk up, that's good enough for me."

"You are sharing offices? Did you hear that Zali?"

"Oh damn! Things just got real. I'm placing the first bet, Mel. One hundred dollars says they won't last two weeks without christening either desk. What's yours?"

"Mmm ... I'll match your one hundred and say three weeks before it happens. But I'll up you fifty to say they will take a turn on both desks. Deal?"

"Deal, girlfriend. This is so much fun!"

"Are you guys serious?"

Zali and Mel just nod, so Alexis knows there is no point in arguing. Even though I personally think it is a pointless bet, I'm happy with the prospect of a new wardrobe and oh, new shoes to match. Shoes are my crack, I think. Especially red ones. Oh yeah, the red ones.

After eating the delicate delights of this place and firming up the shopping plans for tomorrow, the girls head out and down to the Belgian Beer Café. It's really close to our work and it's packed with Friday night drinkers. The smell of testosterone here is almost overwhelming, but mixed with the beer smell, it becomes almost intoxicating, in a good way.

They decide to sit outside in the terrace area as it's a mild night and not quite as loud as inside. Again, my girl's dress gets lots of attention, cementing the idea that a new, sexier, work wardrobe is a good idea. The vibe is good until Mel brings up a touchy subject.

"I've been meaning to ask for a while now. Did you ever hear from Mr. Biggest Arsehole In The World again?"

Okay, queue the plummeting mood. Our head was in a good place after all the dinner conversation, but now, now I know this night is going to end badly.

"Apart from a few pleading texts the week following and then a few more wanting to drop off some of the stuff I left at his place, no. And I like it that way."

Damn straight we do! I wouldn't be surprised if karma has him hit by a tram by the end of the year. But that doesn't stop the feelings of failure that washes over my girly. She wasn't to blame but somehow feels she wasn't enough and that is why he strayed. Some men stray because they are bastards, simple as that. And most don't have a heart, that's a reason too. Okay, I need to help my girly get out of the funk she is in. Think, think.

Just as the girls suggest a spa day together I know will pick up my girl's feelings, she spots him, the cause of all her recent angst; Mr. Uptight himself. His head is buried in his phone as he walks straight past us and towards the entrance of the Eureka Towers penthouse apartments. Yep, we should've known he was a penthouse man. That has Alexis falling deeper into her funk.

No. I won't let that happen. I concentrate on all the yummy male smells in this place and create enough pheromones in her body to have all the male species within a ten kilometre radius come running. Her cheeks redden and her heartbeat picks up. Then the brain chemicals play along too until she is practically panting. Here we go, this is what we need.

"Ladies, find me a hot man stat! And preferably one that's clean shaven. My adventures with a beard are over!"

Woohoo! That's my girl. Zali and Mel just stare at each other, not used to Lexi being so up front, but they soon catch on and start scanning the place for dicks. My girl has so many mixed feelings running through her that I'm thinking maybe tonight isn't the night for a hook up, but when a certain hotty sitting at the bar gives her a slightly shy smile, she makes her decision. Zali invites him and his friends over to join our table.

After an hour of drinking and laughing, the shy smiler whispers something not so shy in Alexis's ear.

"I would love to wake up next to you tomorrow morning."

I didn't say it was original, but with his shy smile still in place, he's pretty damn irresistible and maybe just what my girly needs after all. He suggests his place, which he says is just a ten minute cab ride away, but as always she declines, opting for the safety of her own apartment. He pays for the whole table's drinks, eager to get my girl out of there.

They make it to the corner of the building before he pushes her softly up against the wall, capturing her lips in a soft, eager kiss. He may look shy, but his lips speak another story. His tongue demands entry which she doesn't deny as she lets hers join in a sensual dance of flesh. But as the kiss intensifies, her mind wanders to the man in the tall building above her. What would his kisses be like? Would they be soft, or demanding and hard?

No, girl. We have yummy man candy attached to our lips, we're so not thinking about that iceberg at this moment. She lets her mind get lost in the kiss completely, until both pull away panting. She pulls on his hand and guides him to the tram that will take them to her apartment. He places one arm around her waist as they swing side to side in the busy tram, his thumb rubbing circles on her flesh, setting her alight. It's the little touches my girl loves.

As soon as the door closes to her apartment, they don't waste any time. Shoes are kicked off, clothes are flying everywhere, as they stumble down the hallway to her bedroom. There's no time to turn a light on as they fall to her bed in a jumble of limbs and sweaty flesh. He's tender and attentive, worshiping every part of her body; his words are hot but not crude and has her heart beating against her chest in no time.

It has been a long time since we felt like this, so utterly and absolutely turned on before we even get down to the good staff.

"So, what should I call you, sweet thing?"

"Oh as long as you keep making us feel this way, you can call me anything you like."

"Okay, kitty cat."

"Except that. That will have my claws coming out if you repeat those words again."

"Okay, sweet thing it is. Mmm, I can't wait to sink into you. Damn you smell fine and I can hear how wet you are by the way my man's fingers are teasing your girl. Oh yeah, full mast here we come. Get ready, I've been told I'm quite large."

"Oh God yes, I'm ready stud, I'm ready."

After paying attention to both her nipples he slowly moves down, raining little kisses all over her stomach. So sweet and gentle. I tend to prefer hard and fast and confident, but this is nice, this I could get used to. The first flick of his tongue on my bud has us skyrocketing off the bed. With his fingers and tongue working in tandem, it's not long before the rush of ecstasy hits us and we explode around his moving flesh.

It takes me a moment to come back to earth after that fast climax and another moment after that to realise what is coming for me. Oh no! No, no, no. He said he was huge, but damn, I'm having trouble seeing it.

"Hey dude! Your man needs to google 'manscaping' because I feel like I'm about to get lost in your wilderness."

"Aww don't be like that. Believe me, I'm big enough to find amongst all this, and when you do, I will rock your world, sweet thing, I promise."

Oh damn, here we go. It's like a bloody horror movie, where you can't see what's coming for you. Is that it? Oh God I can feel it but still have no visual. Oh there it is, I think? Oh I can feel it now, it's coming out of the forest, it's … it's … it's bringing the damn forest with it! You have got to be kidding me. No, no, it's too much. Eww I'm choking, I'm choking. Someone perform the Heimlich manoeuvre, I'm choking on pubes. Yuck!!!

EIGHT

He

*"**W**oody, yeah, Lex is a damned workhorse, between me and you she's putting me to shame."*

Too right she is, you suck right now bro; you suck harder than a whore sucking a golf ball up a garden hose. You've let your work slip far too much, it's been beer, vodka, tequila and playtime with floozies, too damned much and not enough knuckling down with the files. Hell, you've got a half dozen project proposals just sitting in your filing cabinets.

"Ha bloody ha Woody. Yeah, you hire her, I doubt her boss would enjoy that much, then again, if you did, hell, I'd just pop down and take her spot with the other team. Right, I gotta go, I'm almost home and I'm dying for a leak. Bye mate."

Oh come on dude, like hell would you do that. For starters, you'd miss the attention you get from those sheilas in the copy department. I'm surprised they haven't pinned you in your office and sucked the marrow from your bones. Okay, let's get into that lift and get home; I need to drain the bank, mate, and to be blunt, it's making my balls ache.

••••

Finally! Close that damned door and get me to the loo. Well, we could wait, but I know for a fact you hate wet jocks and pants. Oh God yes, that feels good, damn that warm feeling in my sack feels awesome. I love that. I know you enjoy that odd feeling you get in the soles of your feet, mate. Why did you wait for so damned long? Oh fuck, phone's ringing, uh, screw it, let it ring off, we've got an answering machine so stuff it, this feels too good and if you cut me off mid flow I'm going to make you piss the bed, count on it.

Yep, that's it, shake twice and dab once, don't want dew drops in your jocks. Oh good, we're just gonna wander round in socks and shirt? Yeah, I love hanging free and easy. Swing, swing, slap, slap, this is the way a penis claps. Just for the love of God, do not do star jumps in the nude again, I head butted my sack last time and it freaking hurt.

Are we going to slip into a pair of silkies or we going full naturist tonight? Because unless you're putting on the heater for a bit, I may uh, shrivel up a little, it's not exactly warm tonight. Well? Oh you're checking the answering machine and stripping down, okay. You closed the blinds this time?

No, no you haven't, you cheeky bastard.

"Lane, you lazy fucker, you coming out tonight? Me and Booker are down at The Dukes, plenty of pussy on the prowl tonight mate, you going to get your arse down here? Give me a call bro."

And delete, good man, naked or not we need to get some work done and this weekend is going to be nothing but work, eat and sleep. I know we need to get a good shag on, but man, you've gotten lazy in the work department. Now, whoa, I'm on the up and up, what's gotten into you tonight? I haven't risen this fast since you were on that eighteen to thirties tour in Spain. That lap dancing club was awesome. Expensive, but awesome.

Hang on, whoa, whoa, whoa, you're ignoring me? Here I am sticking out like a tree trunk and you're ignoring me. You really are intent on work, aren't you? Okay, so I'm just going to hang here and stick out, praying I don't clip the door frame on my back swing. Seriously though, where has this sudden need to work harder come from? I wonder, could it be that little Miss Warm Sunshine, or Alexis as we know she should be called. Has she finally cracked the icy shell that Miss Queen Bitch made crust over your heart? She has, hasn't she. That smile at work, that wasn't from pleasing the clients and positive reviews, it was from working with her and being content with your lot for the first time in years. She really has chipped her way into that shrivelled ball you used to call your heart.

Okay then, coffee pot is brewing; we've got chicken cooking on the stove top and brown rice simmering slowly, so let get down to it, let's show our little ice melter what we can do.

••••

"Righty o, that's file six of eighteen done, now I need to check on the purchase orders for the next half of the project. It seems there is a small error in the finances for that half, might just have been a clerical issue, but I need to have Felix look it over, just to be safe."

Huh. That was something I have never seen you do, actually follow through with clerical errors. You really are pushing for gold this time out, aren't you? Oh, more coffee and back to work. Do you mind if we swing by the loo first, I'm fit to burst here.

••••

Well that was the most productive Friday night in the history of Friday nights. Usually by the time midnight rolls around we're sitting in a booth somewhere with a drunk chick in our lap and our tongue down her throat, but, here we are, sitting in a bathrobe on our sofa watching old reruns of crap TV while sipping at another cup of coffee. So that was what? The Waterman contract, the final parts of the first half of the new package you and Alexis are drawing up, and a new contract from the city confirmed and notated?

What have you done with Lane and why am I now attached to you?

••••

Ugh, I have such an awful taste in my mouth, why do I have an awful taste in my mouth? Oh right, the coffee, always makes everything taste like burnt dust and hot dirt. Are we getting anything close to dressed today mate, or is this a boxers or birthday suit day again? I don't mind the hanging easy modes, just put a towel on that sofa first, my nuts always get stuck to the stitching and it freaking hurts like a bitch when you get up quick. But first, we eat.

I'm really feeling like a full English today, you know, bacon, sausages, eggs, all the good stuff. Washed down with some orange juice and a decent green tea, not coffee and porridge again, it's getting a bit much to be honest. Saturdays are always good for a full English, make a medium late start, sit down and munch on that with some mindless TV before we hit the work stack again.

Oh come on, no, not the porridge and coffee again! Damn you Lane Anderson, I'm going to be pissing dust and dirt for a week at this rate. Just tell me we're hitting the bars Sunday at the very least; just do me that one solid. Hang on, it's nine a.m. on a Saturday and the phone's ringing? Check the caller id first before answering.

Ah, it's only Benji. What the bloody hell does he want this early? Are we answering this or sending it to the answering machine again?

"Laneway you freaky fucker, where the hell have you been the past week? I dropped you a message last night and heard nothing back. Come on man, get back to me asap, we have a massive party lined up for tonight, mate."

Well that answers that, answering machine it is.

"Sorry mate."

Wow, another message from the boys deleted, this is a new horizon for my boy, I'm quite enjoying this new you, the cold air around my balls is a bit of a pain, but the work ethic is a good change.

So are you going to break out your old graphics degree or are you going to wimp out again? You do remember the days when we used to sit there at that old desk of yours and draft out posters and flyers for the packets we were working on; that used to impress a lot of the clients, why did you stop that?

Oh that's right, Miss Queen Bitch thought it wasn't right for a corporate man to sit there and draw silly cartoons and gimmicks. That bitch has a lot of shit to answer for when you think about it. I really wish you had dumped her when you had the chance, rather than going as far as you did.

Talking of going as far as you did, why did you stay with her? She was cold, calculating, lazy as hell and greedy. Shit, she even nicked food off your plate more than once; literally straight off your plate and you just sat there and let her do it. What were you thinking, bro? Okay, now you're standing there and staring at her photo *again,* what is going through your head, seriously bro?

"I was in love."

Hang on, did you just answer me? Did you just reply to something I asked?

"Only answer I've got for everything you did to me you selfish bitch, I spent three years of my life with you."

Goddamn it, you're just talking to yourself again ain't ya? Shit, I honestly thought you could hear me, you really need to work on how you talk when you're alone; or better yet, just don't talk to yourself. It is the first sign of madness you know.

"Fuck you."

Okay, now this really is creepy. I know you're swearing at her and judging by the way you launched that picture across the room, you really are in a bad frame of mind. I think we need to settle you down a bit. How about this, some nice endorphins to get your heart rate down and some warmth going. Hmm, hey big brain! Any chance of you conjuring up some images of Lex, in say, some French panties and a pair of heels?

There we go, that's got your mind going to other places. Okay, now my turn to move this on, get the blood pumping and here we go, now that's got your mind off that bitch and well into other areas. Yeah, I know what I said a while back, but I'm not letting my boy get all stressy over that slag.

Good man, get a nice firm grip, ease up, not that firm, you're making it hard to keep it solid. That's better, my head was starting to hurt with how hard you had me there. Nice long strokes mate, keep it sweet and languid; big brain keep those lovely images coming, our boy is deep into this, throw some kinky dancing into the mix, the sway of her hips and some lace undies.

Okay now, a little faster bro, keep your grip light, maybe a little liquid silk would help the situation. That's my boy, just a little pea sized drop. Now that's a good feeling, oh yeah, rub my head, I can feel my balls crinkling, damn this is good. Big brain kick this up a notch, throw in some tongue work, get her licking anywhere he wants just get him going over the top.

Oh damn, that's it, right there, yeah, here I go.

"Oh Goddamn, Lex, suck me, girl. Yes!"

Oh, damn that was heavy, I almost drowned there. When was the last time you sweated during a long wank, bro? That's right, you can't remember, and why can't you remember, because you've never enjoyed it this much. It has been a heck of a long time since anyone cracked your shell enough to fill your head with kinky fantasies.

Okay, back to work, after we clean up obviously, but back to work.

••••

Now this looks good, this looks very, very good. Some of your best designs, mate, have to say Alexis has brought out your better attributes and she's done it bloody quickly. I have to tell Hot Lips about this when I next see her. Now get the other few done and we can grab something to eat, you have to be hungry after this morning.

••••

Phone's ringing again, what time is it now, six thirty? That has to be Booker or Benji again, you need to answer them or you're going to have one of the wonder twins banging on the door and demanding to know why you're ducking them. Do you really think they're going to like the fact you're avoiding them so you can, as they'll put, score brownie points with your boss and the new piece of arse that has taken residence in your office?

I know they're your best friends, but Jesus Christ are they dull sometimes and I don't mean boring. Both are bright in their own fields obviously, but their mentality are like eight year olds on a constant sugar rush. They only ever want to know one thing when you get to-gether, who you last dipped your wick in and how hot they were on the, as they put it, 'Banging Booty Scale.' I get more intelligent conversation out of their junk than you do the blokes themselves.

So, I want to know one thing: Why do you still hang around with them? They're not the greatest or wisest of company? And all their junk chats on about is pussy and how badly their balls sweat at work and like I said earlier, mate, their conversation is a damned sight more intelligent than Benji's and Booker's.

Ah screw it, they pick some good lays and always buy the next round in, a bit of idiocy can be put up with when it comes to a good shag and a great beer.

Then again, you've got Hot Lips and Alexis worming their way into our hearts and minds, so, are we really going on the hunt tonight? Piss up, yes. One night lay … somehow I don't see that in our immediate future. Well not for us at least anyway. Benji and Booker on the other hand … well … they'd shag a sheep if you put a mini skirt and lipstick on it.

••••

Phone's ringing Lane, sixth time today mind you, and this time, judging by the ID it's Booker not Benji.

"Laneway, you unsociable bastard, what the hell have you been doing the past few days. Benji has called you at least half a dozen times. You ducking us or what?"

See, I told you they weren't going to be happy with you.

"Nah mate, sorry about that. I just had a ton of work to get done and needed the quiet to do it, besides, where's the love? If you fuckers wanted to see if I was okay, you could have always knocked on my front door, Bookend."

Ha, Bookend. I've always loved that nickname for him, why do you call him that anyway? I'll have to ask Henry. I can't believe that idiot named his dick Henry. The poor fucker hates his name. But, then again, what can he do about it, he just hangs there.

"True, but then again, where's the guarantee you would have answered the door, you unsociable fuckhead."

"Yeah, yeah, I get it. You're both pissed at being ignored for two days, I got one thing to say. Suck it up, buttercup, and first round is on me tonight. Meet me at The Duke at eight thirty, I'll be holding the bar up with two waiting for you fuckers, so you better not stand me up in some douche bag form of revenge."

"Nice, see you there. Besides, Benji will forgive you the moment that glass ends up in his hand; me, probably the third."

"Whatever Bookend, see you tonight."

Party time tonight! Just remember, Alexis wouldn't like it if you still smelt of booze on Monday morning. Ha, made you grin.

••••

Well it's time to let it all hang out, to really pull the cork out the bottle and get absolutely wasted. Are we going on a proper crawl or just getting slaughtered at the Dukes? I vote for the Dukes. After spending the last two days in nothing more than a pair of socks, I don't really feel all that up to wandering around trapped inside a pair of jocks for six hours while you pump me to bursting point with cheap lager and round after round of shots and chasers.

You know that's just my opinion, well, more of a request than opinion; but hey, it's your call. But if you have a heart, then for the love of all that is holy, please, please, take that into consideration.

••••

"Laneway, you cheeky fucker, where the bloody hell have you been? Me and Booker were beginning to think you'd started ducking our calls."

Yeah Laneway, you going to tell them the reason you're ignoring their calls so much, or am I going to let their tackle and sack in on the secret?

"I just had a lot of work dumped on me with the new project and have been playing catch up. Sorry fellas."

"Bullshit, you were shacked up with that new bit of fluff from the office, weren't you?"

"No ... I'm ...."

"Yeah, yeah, spin me another one mate, we know you, you were getting your shag on and didn't want to be interrupted."

Ha! If your boys only knew how far they were from the truth this would be beyond hilarious, although mate, I think when they pegged you for bedding Miss Warm Sunshine, they were quite close to the money, weren't they? You'd love a chance to thaw her out; I know Hot Lips wouldn't say no to us if we asked nicely. Hell, I wouldn't say no if *she* asked nicely.

"Whatever."

See, it's answers like that, that make me worried you can actually hear me.

"Hey boy, how's it hanging?"

"Oh hey Henry. Yeah I ain't too bad, been hanging free the past two days, Lane's been on a nude work kick, been nice, but I wish he'd lay a towel down on that sofa of his; the stitching in the cushions get stuck to my sack and it freaking hurts."

"I hear ya, I can't count the amount of sand that gets caught in my eye when Bookend heads to the beach. He always goes for the nude beach and every damned time I end up with mouthfuls of sand. I'd say it's a pain in the arse ... but well ... you get the idea."

"Oh stop whinging you pair of flaccid nancys, this week has been a living nightmare for me. You know what this fuckhead has gone and done?"

"Damn it, Apples, please tell me he didn't!" No, Benji couldn't do that to something so precious.

"No!"

"Yep! I am now the proud owner of a freaking Prince Albert! According to him, it's supposed to make it feel better for both sides, but so far all it's given me is a bloody headache or a freaking runny nose. Well, I'd have a runny nose if I had a nose to run out of, but you know what I mean."

"No mate, I really don't." I run enough sometimes without a bloody nose.

"Oh I forgot, *I'm the only one here with a lump of metal hanging out of his fucking face!*"

"Moving on. What are you guys picking up from Lane?" I need my bros' advice here.

"Well, he's in love, even if the dull git doesn't realise it yet, and I don't think our boys are even noticing the change in him. He's mellowed a lot in the last week. I was going to say something sooner, but I thought better of it, just in case it was something else. We all remember what he was like in college, if it came in a little zip lock bag or he was able to drink it he was in. So ..." Mr. Prince Albert has the best memory, but can't say the same thing about his owner Benji.

"Yeah I remember, he gets the flashbacks every now and then, you know, random bouts of absence or a weird memory, but other than the beer and shots, he's as clean as a baby's arse." Those memories feel like I'm on an LSD trip sometimes. "Henry, you got anything to say here?"

"Well, it comes down to two things. One, are you as invested in the woman as he is, even though he doesn't realise it yet? Are you committed to putting one hundred percent into making him see just how he feels for the woman he is working with?"

"Hang on Henry, I never said it was ..."

"You'd have to be an idiot not to see it, and don't interrupt, it's rude. Now, answer me, are you committed to making your boy happy?"

"Yes I am, I wouldn't be doing the right thing if I wasn't." If Lane's happy, I'm happy.

"Good. And two, is your female counterpart as committed as you are to making her girl as happy as Lane is by just being in her presence?"

"Yes, yes she is. Hot Lips is beyond devoted to her girl. Hell, she makes us look like slugs in comparison."

"Hot Lips huh, nicknames already, that's a good sign. Anyway, you two need to get down to it, settle on a plan to really bring your two together, heavens know that they make one another happy and I can tell that just from how you act when you think about her or say her name, regardless of what Lane is doing pheromone wise. I mean, what kind of man sits in all weekend and works just to make his work partner think better of him? Or have I guessed wrong there?"

"No Henry, you've hit the nail on the head. You know, it really freaks me out sometimes, just how much of a perceptive dick you are."

"My mate may be a drunken moron at times, but me, well, they always say the brains are in us, I guess I'm just proof of the rumour."

"And now I think you're a tosser, Henry. Ha, just kidding, love ya bro." I really do love my bros, in a bro way though, not the other way, ah hell, you get my drift.

"Yeah, you too. Now let's get these morons plastered and see if we can put Baby Apple's new face jewellery to the test."

"Oh God, you just had to drag out my old college nickname, didn't you."

"Well you're the one that came up with Baby Apples, still, it's better than Henry."

NINE
She

This week has flown by and run very smoothly. It seems as if my girl and Mr. Uptight are finally focusing on work, and when they focus, boy do they get a lot of work done. After only two weeks they're ahead of schedule. I knew my girl could do it, but after the first week I seriously doubted Mr. Uptight's abilities. But it seems after a weekend break, he came back firing on all cylinders. I thought he must have got laid, but Mr. Eight Seconds informed me with a dramatic sigh, 'I wish.'

It is Friday again and Alexis and Lane are in the thick of researching. They almost forget to eat lunch and if it wasn't for myself and Mr. Eight Seconds sending their stomachs a message that we all wanted fuel, they probably would have worked through till dark before realising how hungry we all are. Even then, Mr. Uptight had lunch ordered in. I could have done with a nice stretch instead.

They have barely moved from their computers all day except for much needed pee breaks, and even then, me and Eight had to remind them forcefully to take care of us. They were this close to getting wet underwear. That would have been a lesson not to ignore us again. But as the sun starts to lower in the sky, I think the time has gotten away from them again. They are working in companionable silence, which is oh so boring.

"Hey Eight, does your man have plans for tonight?"

"Nope. He's cancelled all Friday night sessions to concentrate on the project; in fact, he has told the guys that weekends are off unless he gives them a heads up that he has time to spare. I think your girl's incredible work ethic the first week kind of scared him straight. At least for now."

"Damn, so no action for you then?"

"Believe me, I still get plenty of action, just not the female kind."

"Well now, I didn't pick him as bi, my radar must be well and truly broken."

"What? No, we're not bi. Well, not yet anyway. But I don't really see that in our future considering he needs me to get it up and there's not been a specimen of the male species to raise me yet, so it's safe to say we only like the ladies. What about you? Any ladies get your motor running?"

"That's a no for us. But, never say never; especially considering the way the male species is acting these days. Don't they realise that playing the field, constantly, is affecting the growth of our population? I mean, if they don't want to settle down, then it's less likely babies will be born; it means our population will one day be almost nothing. Then what happens to the human race, ha?"

"Umm, alien sex?"

"Seriously and I thought you had the big brain. If it wasn't for the likes of you or I controlling some of our owners' actions, there would be no humans left for the aliens to have sex with. But their probing does sound ... stimulating."

"Ha, ha. You're funny, Hot Lips. A guy could really get used to having you around. It's going to be so dull when this project's finished."

"Oh ... umm ... thank you. And I agree, it is going to be dull. But, we can at least make the most of it now. I just wish your man wasn't so cold towards Alexis, because if he wasn't, it could get really interesting for us two, or maybe awkward, umm, yeah."

"Oh Hot Lips. Don't get my brain started on those possibilities. I really need a pee."

"Umm, what does peeing have to do with anything?"

"You're turning me on!"

"Well, that's nice, but, still don't see what the peeing thing has to do with that."

"Do you know how hard it is to pee with a hard on? Even a semi can send that stream sideways."

"Ahh. Now I get it. Nice to know I can affect you in that way."

"Oh you affect me plenty. It's just impossible to get my guy to act on it."

"Maybe we have some hope then. Because I … I … don't worry."

"Because you would maybe like to get to know me a little better?"

"My lips are sealed."

"They wouldn't be if I was banging at your entrance."

"Okay then. Let's leave that conversation for another time. I really need to get my girl up and going home, I'm aching with all the sitting she has done today. I feel as if my flesh is sticking to her thighs. I really need a stretch."

"I could help you with that."

"Eight, behave. It's Friday night and the rest of the office have almost gone. We need to get them out of here and home to begin the weekend."

"Well, I think that may be difficult. My guy has just decided in his head that he's staying until this piece of research is complete. In fact, he's thinking of ordering in dinner."

"Well he can do what he wants. I'm sending sleepy messages to my girl as we speak and giving her tingles like pins and needles, so she knows I will be completely numb in less than ten seconds flat. I'm out!"

"I'm going to continue here for a few more hours, Lex. But if you want to head home that's fine."

Well, where did those manners come from? Maybe these two have come a lot further than I thought. But damn! I can feel exactly what my girl's thinking and I want to cry with exhaustion.

"I'm fine to continue too, if you don't mind the company."

"Hot Lips, wake the hell up and tell me what the fuck is happening here. My guy is fighting the biggest grin he has had in forever! Tonight could be a massive turning point. Come on, do your magic, send out those pheromones."

"Eight, I'm too tired and I have a headache. Not tonight."

"What the fuck! You pull that line on me now, when we aren't even dating? No! Tell me it's not so."

"I'm pulling your chain, dickhead. The minute I knew what she was going to say, I started to send those pheros her way as fast as I could. Can't you smell them?"

"Oh yeah, beautiful, now *that* is my kind of drug. But my boy is resisting like he would a root canal at the dentist. I give him credit, he has a lot of will power right now."

"Damn. So does my girl."

"I don't mind at all, Alexis. What would you like for dinner? I'll order something in."

"I don't mind. You choose."

"Eight, what universe are we in?"

"I'm trying to figure that one out myself."

They sit in silence again, clicking away on their computers, lifting their heads to ask quick questions only. And despite all the happy and horny hormones Mr. Eight Seconds and I are drumming up and shooting through their bodies, neither of them are falling for it. What a pity, because I think I'm really falling for Eight. I can see him as someone I'd like to go to bed with each night and wake up next to every morning. At least a girl can dream.

"Hot Lips, my guy is starting to squirm. Let's double our efforts and see what happens."

"Done deal."

Hormones are flying all over the place, but these two are as stubborn as each other. Alexis starts to squeeze her thighs together to try and alleviate the ache I have created in my centre, as she tries to conceal her hastened breathing. She is squirming in her seat, her cheeks starting to show a distinct flush to them. She swallows hard, keeping her head low as she raises her eyes slightly to check out the cause of our lust induced rush.

She notices him frowning, straightening his spine as he sits up taller in his chair. A low, almost inaudible growl leaves his lips as he reaches a hand down to adjust his package, taking a moment to shift it to a more manageable position. That's it Eight, make him as uncomfortable as you can.

Alexis likes what she sees and uncontrollably licks her lips. I can feel our entire body struggling to control our want for this man. Despite his coldness and sometimes condescending ways, there's no denying that he is hot and definitely a fine male specimen. The images flashing through Alexis's mind are downright dirty, allowing her resistance to begin to waver.

She finally allows herself to think about what it would be like to be swept up into his large muscled arms, with her legs wrapping instantly around his tapered waist, as he raises her from the ground, ravishing her mouth with an urgent hunger to his kiss. She then imagines him turning them around to lie her down upon his desk, too desperate to claim her to bother pushing his paperwork aside.

Her legs, with her stilettos still on, would raise and rest upon his shoulders as he bent down to kiss and suck on her bottom lip, while his fingers are busy unbuttoning her shirt, stumbling with his urgency. He would lift his head to admire her spread beneath him and would then lean forward and lick the tops of her breast, making her breath catch in her throat.

"Hot Lips, are you even listening to me? I said, I think it's working. His thoughts are taking a turn down wicked street, straight for your girl."

"Huh what, oh yeah; my girl has noticed and is trying hard not to show how affected she is by him. He seems really uncomfortable. What're you doing to the poor guy?"

"I'm making him so hard it feels as if I could break at any moment. He is trying to shift me slightly to alleviate the discomfort, but I just keep pumping the blood through my veins, making it impossible to move me. And it's not just me, he has now got on board completely and is imagining all the ways he could fuck her on his desk, so it's not only my fault. I just wish he would get his arse out of the Goddamn chair and do something."

"Oh damn Eight. I'm about to flood my centre, surely one of them has to break soon!"

Alexis tries breathing techniques to try and control her arousal, but I make sure to increase it. There's a knock at the door to announce dinner, which has been brought up by one of the building's security guards. As Lane stands up and walks a little awkwardly to the door to retrieve the bags of food, Alexis take that moment to drool over his tight arse. Damn, those buns are defined. I can only imagine how strong they are when they are helping to pump into a ...

"Damn, I'm in pain, Hot Lips. This security guard needs to leave immediately."

As the guard is handing over the bags to Mr. Uptight, he begins to frown, then looks between Alexis and Lane, obviously smelling the sexual tension that is lingering in the air. He slowly steps back and shuts the door quietly. The guy probably thinks he has something to gossip about with his fellow guards. The problem is there's nothing to gossip about *yet*.

Alexis is too unsure of her body to even chance standing at this moment, so she pretends to be engrossed in her work, leaving Mr. Uptight to sort out dinner. After shuffling around with the plastic bags for a few minutes, he takes a deep breath, turning his head towards Alexis for a moment before he begins to slowly walk towards her desk with two containers of her favourite Chinese food.

He places them on her desk and just stands there, breathing loudly, waiting for her to raise her head. Her heart rate has risen; blood is pumping fast through her veins as she slowly raises her head. The heat she sees when her eyes meet his has her flooding her panties all on her own, as she clenches her thighs together harder.

"Just checking that this is what you wanted, Alexis?"

"Umm, what?"

"Are those the two dishes you ordered?"

"Oh, um, yeah, they look right. Thank you ... Lane."

His low rough voice has her just about jumping out of her seat, but she digs her pointy heels into the carpet, grounding herself in place. Lane bites his lip, taking a deep breath that has his nostrils flaring. He then turns quickly, returning to his desk and sits down on his chair, well, tries to sit down. He sucks in a sharp breath before his hand disappears below the desk, for what I assume is some more adjustments, before he then reaches for his own food.

These two are so worked up they can barely swallow their meals. They steal little glances at each other, both still resisting the chemistry that has this place on fire. Neither wanting to cross that line of professionalism, but both now desperately craving each other. They continue their dinner in silence, pretending not to notice what is happening between them. I can feel it, it's only a matter of time before one or both of them crack. It may not be tonight, but I swear on my most precious jewel, my bud of arousal, that it will happen soon.

"Oh Hot Lips. I don't think I can rev my man up like this again if there is no guarantee of an immediate release. I'm in so much pain I feel sick, physically ill, and it's not just me. My boy is struggling to even swallow each mouthful of his dinner. This level of discomfort is just not worth it."

"Are you saying that my girl and I aren't worth it?"

"Aww sweetheart, don't say it like that. You know exactly what I mean; you're worth everything, but surely you can agree with me, this type of build-up, when it looks like neither of them is going to give in tonight, it's freaking torture."

"Yeah, I have to agree. I'm not looking forward to a round with BOB tonight. That type of release will not cure my appetite. "

"Who the fuck's Bob?"

"Ha, ha. How do you not know BOB? I was sure your guy would be the experimental type."

"I told you before, we are not into guys. Especially if this Bob dude gets around. Haven't your heard of STDs?

"Oh my God! This is so funny. BOB is not a person, he is a ... wait for it, you are going to laugh ... he's a battery operated boyfriend."

"Oh for fuck sakes. You had me going there for a bit. And no, we haven't used one personally and his ex didn't like them, so our experience with BOB is limited."

"You don't know what you're missing out on. They can be pleasurable for both."

"Okay, I'll take your word for it."

After dinner is all tidied up, they continue their game of pretend, as if neither of them wants to acknowledge the feelings that are flowing through their veins. Their questions are short and their answers more so, as if both are afraid to speak. Eight and I try our best for the next hour, but these two just dig their heads deeper into their computers and their heels deeper into the carpet. Both are even too scared to get up and pee.

Tonight doesn't end how I would like, but at least it's a start. I really am feeling numb from us sitting for so long, and thank God my girl finally gets the message. Her head is getting fuzzy and her eyes blurry as she starts to pack up and shut her laptop down.

"Good idea Lex, nothing is sinking in this late at night. I think I'll start to pack up too."

Wow. Someone finally has a voice. By the time my girl is ready to head for the door, Mr. Uptight jumps up and opens the door for her. Okay Mr. Gentleman, nice gesture, but I don't want you to open a door; I want you to open me!

They walk in silence to the elevator and my girl presses the button. Thank God there is only a few seconds wait, because this awkward feeling between them sucks. They both get in and Mr. Uptight presses the button to go down. And the awkward feeling changes to something more serious. As soon as the doors slide close, the smell of hormones becomes suffocating. It is slowly drifting from every pore of their bodies. Alexis's cheeks redden and Lane almost bites his lip off with how hard he chews on it.

The bell dings and the door opens to the lobby. For a few seconds, neither of them move, as if they are both frozen under the spell of horniness. Mr. Uptight grunts before taking the first step and Alexis finally finds her feet and moves after him. They walk across the deserted lobby, her heels echoing through the empty room. Mr. Uptight holds the door open for her and she walks out into the crisp night air. After a few steps they both come to a halt, looking anywhere but at each other.

"Thanks for working late too, Alexis, I really appreciate it."

"It was my pleasure, ah, I mean, it's my job, to um, stay until the work is finished."

"Of course, of course. Um, are you going to be okay getting home on your own this time of night? I could walk you home if you like, or call you a cab?"

"It's okay Lane, I'm used to walking home on my own, even at night. But thank you for your concern. Enjoy the rest of your weekend. See you on Monday. Night."

"Goodnight Lexi."

They have both said a soft goodnight, yet neither of them move. Their eyes are fixed on each other as if they are both mesmerised by what they see. Maybe they finally see the possibilities that they could have together, or maybe it's just the lingering tones of the sexual hormones Eight and I overloaded them with. Either way, they seem reluctant to part. Which gives me hope.

Lane, ever so slowly, starts to lean towards Alexis, and her body follows suit. Their eyes never leave each other as the world around them falls to the background. All they see is each other. Lane starts to lower his head slowly, as if asking in silence if my girl wants what he is about to offer. But then a car horn beeps loudly from the street behind them, breaking their trance.

Alexis slowly starts to step backwards, realising what was about to happen. Uncertainty washes through her as she struggles to recall if it was her or him that was leaning forward. The last thing she wants is to look like a fool if he had no intention of actually leaning in for a kiss. She takes another few steps back before offering him a small smile and turning away from him, heading towards the tram stop, desperate to get home and sort out these vamped up feelings.

"Hot Lips. No! Don't let her leave! He was about to kiss her. Our plan worked. Turn her around and come back here this instant!"

"I think we may have pushed them too fast, Eight. Let it go for tonight and we will make a new plan of attack on Monday. Night. "

"Nooooo! But I wanted to wake up to you in the morning."

"Me too Eight, me too. Sweet dreams."

"You too, baby."

The first step on the tram feels like I'm being ripped away from a loved one, traveling far and wide, never to return. My feelings intensified the minute he said he wanted to wake up with me. Now I know for certain I'm in love. It's times like these, I wish *I* had the big brain.

TEN
He

Damn you Lane Anderson, damn you and your ridiculous sense of professionalism, we were so damned close to sealing the deal with Hot Lips and Lex, but no, you had to go and be the *'consummate'* professional. One of two things are going to happen here; I'm going to nag you to the point you tug one off, or you're going to go chasing after Lex and plough her to oblivion.

It's at points like this where Lane does a runner from his feelings. He's gone before, and no doubt if this thing with Lex boils out to nothing, he may do it again. Last time he spent six weeks telecommuting for work, all the while hiding away in some island shack off the coast of Thailand. I really hate Miss Queen Bitch for what she did to my boy and seriously, I hope he never goes there again. Having Thai ticks plucked off my ball sack from that stupid waterfall is not something I ever want to revisit. But, right now, Laneway here has two choices; I just hope he picks the right one.

Lane bro, seriously, what the fuck happened to the man that would have called over a cab and rocketed off after that foxy lady with the cheeky muff?

I know what's coming, a night of rampant masturbation followed by a round of tequila chasers and a drunken sonnet scrawled into the leather backed notebook hidden in the bottom of the nightstand.

I'm going to be one sore dong in the morning, one very sore and very pissed off dong that will be taking this up with Hot Lips the first moment I get. Oh Hot Lips, how I dearly want to wake up next to you, even if it was only a one night thing.

Well, here we go, one more unto the lube, dear friend. Just remember to shut the front door this time, we don't want the neighbours complaining about the sounds of your jerking off echoing through the stairwell. You're not even going to wait for us to get in before trying to adjust me properly? Get your hand out until you get inside, idiot! Oh shit, hey there, Mrs. Winslow.

"Oh shit, Mrs Winslow, uh hello, sorry um, yeah, good night."

Mate, what have I told you about waiting for a closed door before doing that; I know me and Hot Lips had you pent up and raging, but shit, seriously, how the hell could you be so damned stupid as to do a frontal adjustment in the bloody hallway. I bet Mrs Winslow loved the view though, that old bird is always staring at your arse when you pass in the lobby.

Well there go your shoes, pants, jocks and socks; what's next, your skin? No, just your shirt and jacket, so another nude weekend it seems to be. Seriously, someone is really eager here, already in the bedroom and dragging opening the bedside drawer and yanking out the lube tube.

Damn it, that stuff is cold, but I'll be a dildo if that doesn't feel good on my head. Oh yeah, smooth it in. Yeah that's it, wiggle it a little, oh yeah right there. Shall we start the picture show? I think we shall. Big brain, roll film.

"Oh damn, that's it Lexi, just like that."

Yeah I thought you'd enjoy that; ease up on the grip a bit, big brain, throw in a little tongue action. Oh yeah my boy likes that, I can feel his pulse racing now, yeah, you like it when Lexi licks my head. Mmm, that feels beautiful don't it, her tongue sliding over my head as you curl your fingers into her hair. Yeah, my boy likes that thought.

Okay, a little faster.

Damn it boy, keep that pace right there. Oh shit, big brain, turn it up a bit, half-length swallow with a nice tongue swirl. Mmm that's it, yeah, he's racing now; oh he loves the idea of Lexi sucking me tight between her plump lips. He's been fantasizing about that all damned day. Yeah, oh God, let's keep it right here.

"Yeah Lexi, suck me, suck me hard."

That's my boy, tighten that grip slightly mate and circle that thumb some more. Just like that, that's it, right there, a little faster again, bro. Oh we're drying out a little, get some more lube on me, don't want to start sticking.

"Lexi, baby, Goddamn it, oh yeah, suck me nice and deep, beautiful."

Hell yeah, my boy is really going to town on this. That's it, nice and fast, really get some speed going, mmm just like that. Oh God, here it comes, it's coming. Arrrrrrr! Damn, that was a heavy shot; we ain't cum like that in a while. I swear I'd smoke if I could. So now what, I guess we get up and grab a shower.

Oh you're asleep, well I guess the emotional and physical excitement did wear you out a bit, that and the marathon wank just now, ah well, who am I to go against the tide? See you in the morning, Lane.

••••

Well that was a ... spirited night. I'm still pissed at you, Lane, but that was a good way to end the day. Now are you still going to be a complete wimp and do that whole wait three days bull crap, or are you going to man up, call her up, and take her out on a date; or are you going to do what you always do, hedge in with some daft excuse or implausible reason for calling?

"Hello, Lex? Sorry for calling on the weekend. Is there any chance we

can meet up for a coffee? I'm free from now until around two, if you are? I uh, I need to talk over some points from Friday's research. I was going over it this morning and well, I think we need to iron out a couple of wrinkles we may have overlooked."

Well that is one way of doing it I suppose, still a nancy boy way of doing it, but then again, it can be effective, if used properly. I'm wondering if ten a.m. is a bad hour for her and she doesn't see just how much of a blanket ruse your request is, but what if she does, hey? What are you going to do then?

"If it's a bad morning for a meeting we could always go to lunch or something, I know a few quiet places near the office or say further along the north bank that will allow us to talk in quiet."

Oh come on, just bloody bite the bullet and just ask her out you daft sod, she has to see through this, she has to. I mean Hot Lips is attached to this woman and she saw through me in the first ninety seconds of meeting her in your office.

"Well fantastic, shall I make a reservation for say one thirty?"

Huh, I can always be wrong, wouldn't be the first time.

"Okay then Lex, I will make a reservation and text you the address, or, I could come and pick you up if you like? No, that's fine, I'll text the address and meet you there. See you soon."

Seriously, she actually bought that pile of tripe about the work situation? Seriously mate, you are pushing close to the line on this, you better have a damned good line set for this *'lunch date'* of yours.

• • • •

I haven't found you this nervous since you had to give that speech in grade six. What was it, oh that's right, about the Anzacs and the end of World War One, you were trembling then and you're trembling now. You have spent the last two weeks working with her, what the hell could there be to be nervous about? Ah I get it, to you this is a date, your first date with her and you are thinking back on every girl you've ever dated, trying to discern exactly what you could do to *not* screw this up. Well, considering you're the only one of the two of you that thinks this is actually a date, well, I don't see how you could screw this up. That is, unless you say something completely stupid, or go blurting out those bubbling heartfelt feelings of yours. You always do drop in head first, you daft bastard, and I don't mean my head.

Ah well, your tie is straight and your hair styled properly, professional yet casual, as always. Now go brush your teeth and gargle a pint of mouth wash, otherwise you may end up gassing her to death, you know you get a tinge to your breath when you're overtly nervous.

••••

"Well, this place is nice, a little up market, but nice. A bit more intimate than I was expecting for a work conference."

"Yeah Big Eight, what is your boy playing at?"

"Honestly baby, I ain't got a clue. All I know is that he has planned this to look like a work thing so he can have a stealth date with our girl. He's doing that whole geek in high school thing, where you ask someone out for one reason, but to you, it's something else entirely. To be fair, I would rather he just asked our girl out. I'm dying to wake up with you, but my boy is being a complete ... sorry I have to use this phrase, pussy ... over everything."

"You're forgiven, and yeah I figured it would be that, but my girl is being just as coy and just as dense about it. I saw this coming the moment he phoned, but Alexis, well, I doubt she'd notice a nuke going off, she is so deep into la la land over him and your bloody pheromones. You couldn't drag her out with a freaking herd of wild horses strapped to her ankles."

"Ooo shush for a moment, Lane is trotting out his 'excuse' for calling."

110

"Oh this should be good."

"Shush."

"Sorry."

"I'm glad you like it. It's a small bistro that I take preferred clients to. They have an excellent selection of food; the chef is cordon bleu trained, but they also value their preferred customers' privacy, so there are secluded booths and tables at the back that are perfect for meetings that require a little more finesse than you can apply in the boardrooms back at the office."

"I can see why, but still, can we justify sending this to the corporate account?"

"Let me worry about that. Order what you want and we can get down to discussing the work over some good food. If you like sea food, I recommend the scallops, they use a sweet but dry white over them, gives them a nice edge."

"Cheeky bastard hasn't even hinted at the reason for really being here. He's smoother than I gave him credit for."

"Yeah, that's my boy for you, sweetheart, he's been that way since high school. The chiselled jaw and whiskey brown eyes works in his favour. Hell, he bedded the 'it girl' when he was barely past sixteen. My boy has always had game, but around our girl, he's a freaking mess. He is really working hard to keep his composure, believe me."

"I can tell, your scent has dipped a lot, Eight. I'm going to try something here, let's see if I can get my girl a little … juicy."

"Well, this should be fun."

"Uh Lane, where's the restroom?"

"Through the arch at the back, second door on the right."

"Thanks!"

"Ha, bulls eye! Back in a minute, Eight, my girl is off to … adjust her panties."

"Lucky bitch, I'll just be here, hanging half mast, trying to get my boy to think straight."

"Good boy."

Lane, we need to up our game here, what are you thinking? One slip and this could explode worse than the Hindenburg. You have to be extremely careful here, bro, and I do mean careful.

"Well that was fun, my girl now has one very soggy wad of cotton in her clutch purse."

"You mean that you're ..."

"Yup, I'm catching more breeze than a Bells Beach surfer."

"Oh you're killing me! If it wasn't for my boy's nerves I would be punching the bottom of this table right now. You are one very cruel pussy and it is one of the things I love about you."

"Hang on, what did you say? Did you just say you love me?"

"Uh, huh, uh, no, I just meant that, you have a lot of admirable qualities and I happen to think very highly of them. I'll tell you now, I'm falling heavy and hard, but ... yeah, I'm going to shut up now."

"Well ... okay then ... thanks, I think."

"Okay, I have to ask, and this is hard for a guy to ask, but are we on the same page here? Or do I have to check out and find the right book?"

"No, you're doing okay, maybe a page or two either side of where I am, but you're doing fine."

"Well, okay then, I don't feel like the proverbial idiot lost in a supermarket anymore."

"Good. I would hate to put out the fire before I have a chance to get nice and crispy from the warmth."

"I swear, if I had a face I would be grinning, but we're here for our boy and girl. Let's see what we can do to get these two idiots to actually commit to what they won't yet admit."

"You're full of pseudo poetry at the moment. Have I hit on a soft spot?"

"Huni, when you're around, I'm anything but soft. Well, when my boy isn't as nervous as a kid at the end of year formal at least. Oh shush, Lane's going for it, the whole work excuse, for real this time."

"It better be a good one."

"Should be, my boy doesn't do cheesy, well, not all the time."

"No that's just you."

"Ha bloody ha, now shush, they're getting a little closer, this may actually work."

"So, Lane, you haven't actually told me what this 'meeting' is all about. I was beginning to think you had enough of seeing me all week. A girl could get to thinking this is more than a work thing; but then I know you're not that coy about things. Well, not according to the girls in your office at least."

"Ha, no, well, no, if I did have intentions you'd know it, well, I hope you would. But no, this is purely work. I just like the intimacy and quiet setting, it's more of a change of pace to the office. To be honest, I'd have brought you here sooner if it wasn't for ... well. I had thought at first that you didn't really like the idea of working with me."

"I'll admit, I didn't, what you hear on the grapevine and office gossip that and well ..."

"Go on, tell me."

"Holy shit, that is a smooth move, the leaning in and setting a comforting hand on hers to coax a more revealing conversation. I honestly thought he'd miss that. Hot Lips, are you pushing your girl to open up here? She is being a little more honest than I thought she would be."

"I'm giving her a nudge in the general direction, just make sure you reciprocate, okay. But not too deep, no past love lives crap. We both know the reason behind things, but these two, well, they'd run a mile if it came to a head too soon."

"I honestly thought you hated me. Whenever you see me you always get this cold scowl and it always made me feel a little ... well ... insecure around you."

"Shit, that's a little too open, Hot Lips! Have her do something cute, I just felt his heart drop a bit, damn it. Uh, have her smile and drink while looking at him over the glass, my boy has a big thing for sexy eyes and hers are awesome. Do it now!"

"Shit okay, here we go."

"Whoa nelly, that has sent his heart racing. Tell me, is he holding her hand a little too tightly, his grip just tensed a bit, I'm seeing nothing in his head but the image of her eyes."

"Trust me, it's all good, I'm wetter now than ever. If we're not careful, she's going to leave a patch on the seat."

"Okay, quiet now, we have to be careful here."

"Lex, I'm sorry about that, I know how I can be. It's well, it's complicated. Let's not spoil this nice lunch with talk of old issues, suffice it to say, I have enjoyed these past weeks working with you. Your attitude and enthusiasm is something I had lost a while ago. If anything, I have enjoyed my time in the office more than I ever have since working there."

"Well ... I ... I'm glad."

"Bugger me, is she holding his hand, voluntarily? Or did you prompt that?"

"No, that is all her, even the thumb rubbing the back of his hand is all her. I think we're winning this, Eight."

"Indeed we are, baby, indeed we are."

"So, why did you call me here?"

"Uh, oh yes of course, I have a few design and research ideas that I wanted your opinion on. Before working for the company I was a graphic artist and architect, so I drew out a few ideas that popped into my head last night and well, I wanted your opinion."

"Lane, these ... these are fantastic! Why aren't you head of the design department?"

"Well, Woody prefers me where I am and since ... well suffice it to say I let that side of things slip a bit and well, working with you, it's ... pushed me to pick up the pen again."

"You're going to make me blush, but these are stunning. I love the mixed medium approach. Do you really think the client would like a full

billboard spread like that?"

"Well, it's only my representation of it. With a few simple tweaks we could have it on an animated sign or even set up as a motion graphic for a television ad."

"Oh snap, he's gone for the lower arm. Oh, oh, he's moving round next to her. Hip to hip, shoulder to shoulder, hand on her arm. Eight, we have three point contact, we have three point contact."

"I know, I know, this is awesome. We just have to be careful, we don't want to push them too fast. Even if she feels like she wants to take it deeper, don't let her. A soft peck on the cheek on the way out is enough. My boy already wants to drag her into his arms and ravish her right here."

"Yeah, Alexis is wishing the same thing, but yeah, okay, we'll play it safe."

"Atta girl."

"Oh shush you."

"I'm really pleased you like them, Lex. I was honestly extremely nervous about showing them to you; it's not often I show anyone my other talents, not since ..."

"Not since what?"

"Waiter, can we get a bottle of Chardonnay, a Cherubino Margaret River if you have it."

"Hot Lips, is she genuinely worried over this? I'm picking up some strong tinglings from her. The hand at my boy's elbow while he's ordering the wine is screaming worry."

"Oh big time, but the desire is still there. I think this sliver of vulnerability is playing to our advantage here, Eight, she is drinking it in."

"It's an old and long story, Lexi. I will tell you someday, but for now, let's just enjoy the food and maybe we can work on some other ideas while we're here."

"Okay, if you're sure."

"Oh dayum, that smile just made my boy's heart leap. He has fallen head to toe for our girl. Lane is hooked, all you need to do now is reel him in and mount him on your girl's wall."

"I'd like to mount you on my walls, Eight."

"Oh fuck woman, you are going to make me plant an oyster in Lane's jocks at this rate."

"Hmm nope, I know a place I would much rather you planted things."

"Oh me too, beautiful, me too, but for now our boy and girl's happiness takes priority."

"I'm sure Lexi, I'm sure."

"Ooo, your boy is being a little bold, he's gone for bare thigh contact. Oh the tingles I'm getting. Get him to squeeze a little, my girl is going to leak like a tap when he does. Oh yeah, just like that. Mmm she likes that, she likes that a lot!"

"Madame, Monsieur; bon appetite. With compliments of the chef, Mr. Anderson, I would also like to offer you a complimentary entrée. It is steamed salmon mousse on braised asparagus with a cranberry reduction. A sharing plate, if I'm not mistaken."

"Cheeky bugger's smile has made our girl blush, Eight. Don't let your boy do anything daft, this could play to our advantage."

"Okay, yeah, I'm wheeling him in a little, but for now, this is running on its own steam, let's let them take the wheel for now, see where it leads. If they need it we can give them a ... push ..."

"Mmm, oh I know something you could push and push hard."

"That's my girl."

••••

Well that was an interesting event; I wonder what the boys will make of it tomorrow. I have to admit, you did me proud, me and Hot Lips are actually getting somewhere, and you and Lexi seem to be on a new level with how you two are going, so it should be a good progression all round. Just next time bro, play it on the level. There aren't too many points where we can get away with the stupid 'work-date' combo/ She's a smart girl and if it wasn't for the goofy juice Hot Lips shot her up with, then your plan would have collapsed so fast not even Dwayne Johnson could have saved it, and they've had him save everything!

Anyway, I need a stretch and pee and we need some kip. That wine hit us hard and I always get a funny head in the morning, so please for the love of all that is holy, let me drain out, then drink a couple of pints of water when we get home. I do not want a freaking wino droop when dealing with Heckle and Jeckle tomorrow. I love my bros, but bloody hell are they annoying sometimes.

Okay goof ball, are we stuck with that dopey grin? You look like a kid that just got their first kiss from their playground crush. I have to admit that it worked out pretty well, but hell, what is up with you and that grin, seriously.

All she did was peck your cheek and hold your hand while doing it. Then again, she does always smell freaking divine, so yeah, okay, I can forgive that little grin.

••••

"Hey boys, how's it going?"

"Oh, hey Bookend, look at him. He's grinning more than that gator that ate Mr. Farnam's dog in sixth grade."

"Shit yeah, look at him. I ain't seen someone grin that much in, well, fuck if I know when."

"Oh piss off, I ain't grinning over anything." Oh yeah Lane, you're grinning alright.

"Bullshit, you're either in love or on coke and I know you swore off the hard shit years ago, so fucking spill."

"Seriously, I ain't in love with anyone."

"Benji, hang on a sec. Laneway, bro, we've known you since we were six, hell, we know you better than your freaking parents do. Don't give us the bloody runaround, who is she?"

"Bookend, what do you want to bet it's that tight little thing he's told us he's working with. Well shit on a stick, look at him blush. I was fucking right, you've fallen for that chick in the office. What's her name?"

"Her name is Alexis and yeah, you rotten bastards, I have fallen. She is, shit I don't know, there's just something about her."

"Well good on you mate, she's a good looking sheila by your account, nice to know you've finally gotten over that other rotten bitch." Yep, thank God he has Booker.

"Yeah, to be honest boys, I don't know what took me so damned long to do it. I have had plenty of girls come and go, but I dunno, I guess it took till now to finally break the cycle."

"Shit, she's broke something alright, your balls by the sounds of things."

"Oh shut up Benji."

"Hah, I haven't seen Bookend and my boy take down Benji with an in sync snipe in ages."

"Well, it's been a long, long time since one of the three musketeers had a woman they actually cared about aside from their mum. Laneway is the first of our trio to actually take a step towards that, in what, got to be nearly five years." Henry is right, it's been too long for these idiots to be fucking around.

"But bro, seriously, if you are set on this sheila, you have to make it clean, that witch has got to be gone for good. Every picture, every scrap of crap she ever bought you, everything. It has to go."

"Yeah I know Book, I know, just sometimes, no matter how many times you hit delete, you just can't shift 'em."

"Well fuck, come on then, let's grab two sixers and head back to yours. We're kicking that bitch once and for all."

ELEVEN
She

What a strange weekend. I know that Mr. Eight Seconds and I probably contributed to it by stirring Lane and Alexis up Friday night to the point they were both ready to explode, but damn was my girl and I surprised by My Uptight's phone call Saturday. A work lunch, really? Alexis knows that the examples of the graphic billboards he showed her, despite how brilliant they were, could have waited until Monday. They wouldn't have affected any work either of them was going to do over the weekend.

When Mr. Eight Seconds confirmed that his guy just wanted to see Alexis, hope sprang through my entire centre, making it quite easy to flood hers during that lunch. That and the fact she liked seeing him in a different light.

"I'm so confused. Will the real Lane Anderson please stand up!"

Alexis is leaning on her bathroom counter, staring at herself, trying to decipher the mystery that is Mr. Uptight. Her emotions have been all over the place this weekend and it hasn't been helped by the fact that someone has been prank calling her phone since Saturday night. Just phoning and hanging up. I say, at least have the balls to say something if you are taking so much time calling constantly, be creepy, be obscene, anything is better than silence.

But all jokes aside, Alexis is worried. Could Mr. Stalker have somehow gotten her mobile number? It's usually only clients that may have one of her business cards, so I guess if he asked the right person he could easily have gotten a hold of one of her cards. Damn, I hope it's just some teenagers being stupid. But still, she intends to let the building's security know, just in case.

"He looked so much more relaxed at lunch on Saturday. And damn! That sweet, cute smile of his had me going ga ga. Where has he been hiding it all this time? When I think about it, the truth is, I have seen it before. All over the damn lobby, being thrown at every other female he stops to talk to or that passes him by. But that smile wasn't ever for me. Why? He seems to have walls up most of the time, but why does it seem those walls are only up for me? This man is going to be my undoing if I let him."

I'm not sure he will ever be a man we can figure out, Lexi. I agree with your friends. The sooner you fuck him out of your system, the sooner you can move on to greener, much friendlier, much less Jekyll and Hyde pastures girl. Unless ... you are actually developing serious feelings for this guy? Does she think he could turn out to be our Mr. Long Term Guy? When I think back to lunch, I can see her falling, falling hard for him. And if that happens, there will be no more fun and games to play. Damn, I'm so confused too.

We either stop seeing him as the cold Mr. Uptight and try and discover the real Lane, to see if he is someone who is actually worthy of my girl's affections, or we find a way to just hump and dump him and move on with our lives after their collaborative project is finished. As much as I want to do the nasty with Eight, when it comes to matters of the heart, I will not risk my girl's getting broken again, because last time almost crumbled her. I never want to relive those dark days again. The scar of betrayal never leaves the heart.

"Get a grip Lexi! There are still weeks to go on this project and if you're letting Lane get to you this much already, how the hell are you going to

cope for the remainder of the campaign? Damn stupid men who look too good for their own good!

That's my girl! Okay, but seriously now, we need to stop looking in the bloody mirror for answers, because unless you are an evil queen, it ain't answering you back anytime soon, princess. Let's just get to work and let fate do what fate does best. Umm, well, fate sometimes sucks, so maybe a less sucky fate for a while would be good, thank you.

After a few restless nights over the weekend, Alexis is too tired to walk the entire way to work, so tram it is. Monday morning's tram rides are ... an experience. Usually the busiest ride of our week and one I don't particularly like. Being crammed up against strangers, some of which have scents that just don't appeal to me, is not my idea of a 'fun' ride.

"Hey there, lollipop. I would love to take a lick of you someday. We're having drinks with friends at P.J. O'Brien's tonight at seven. I will guarantee you a happy ending."

"Lollipop? Seriously? Listen up, I'm only going to tell you this in the interest of the dwindling population. Your pick up lines suck! If you want any chance at spreading your wild oats, think sweet, not sickly sweet. Okay? Now move on, knob head."

Sometimes I don't know how the human race isn't extinct already. Thank God for the gentlemen of the old days, or we might not have even made it past the eighties. That was a feat in itself.

"Hey, sweet lips. Move on from that loser and over to my pussy pass. I guarantee you that between you and me, we can have the damn population booming!"

That doesn't even justify a response. Pussy pass? The names men call their junk is just ... juvenile.

"I sense some tension in your core. You really shouldn't hold onto that. You need to find a way to release it. I can help, but after the way you just shot down the last guy, I'm not sure you would be open to my suggestion."

"Well now. As long as you don't use some cheesy pathetic line, I may just be willing to listen."

Okay, he has a lot more control over his guy than I do Lexi, judging by the way his guy just suddenly moved closer to her, almost, but not quite, invading her personal space. Mmm, very stealthy indeed. I like. Maybe he's a spy, about to invite us along for some adventure. Oh, that would surely snap my girl out of her Mr. Uptight funk.

"Tonight, at six, have your girl walk under the Spencer Street Bridge and turn left down the first laneway. You will see a navy blue door, have her knock three times fast, then twice slow. When it opens, walk all the way down the long corridor and I'll make sure my guy is the first person you see. Then we can swing the night away babe. No better way to lose the tension that's wrapped so tightly around that sweet body of your girl."

And … that's our queue to leave. *Hop off at the next stop, Lexi, the next stop!* Seriously, more power to you if you want to swing, but to invite a perfect stranger on a tram to join you at some club hidden down a laneway is not the type of spy adventure I want to be living in, thank you very much. What a wanker. Well maybe not. If he goes to a club like that, he has like-minded people to do that for him. Good luck to him.

As we make our way towards our building, the relief at not seeing Mr. Stalker at the waterfront is short lived as we go to open the door of our building and see him off to the side, looking through the window into the busy lobby area. Alexis refuses to freeze like her body wants to. Instead, she ploughs through the door and marches with anger towards the lift, refusing to look back to see if Mr. Stalker has actually spotted her.

Once we reach our floor, she continues walking with anger towards Mr. Uptight's office, thankful that he's not in yet. She throws her bags on her desk and picks up her phone to call security. After relaying what she just saw out the front and about the mystery phones calls she received all Saturday night and Sunday, to the point she had to turn her phone off, she slams the phone down and finally takes a much needed breath.

Tears threaten in the corner of her eyes as she tries not to think about the possibility that this could get worse. She tells herself he has done nothing wrong except stare at her and maybe the phone calls are not related to him at all. She will be wary but will not let her mind run away with scary scenarios. So far, nothing serious has happened so let's hope it stays that way.

Just then Lane comes through the door with a tray of two coffees and a small white box, along with a huge smile on his face, which falters slightly when he takes in the worry on my girl's face.

"Lex, is everything okay? You look a little pale. Are you feeling alright?"

Damn. Instead of brightening my girl's mood, she struggles to hold back the tears that are desperate to fall. She takes a deep breath and coughs to clear the emotion that has welled up in her throat, not only from the situation, but also from the concern in Lane's voice and the sweet gesture of coffee and sweets first thing on a Monday morning.

'I'm fine, thank you Lane. I just had a rush of too many thoughts in my head at once and was a little stressed. I'm good now; even better by the smell you have just brought into the office and the thought of what's in the little white box you're holding."

I think she would be much better if she had told him the truth, maybe she would feel better getting it off her chest, but his sweet smile and gesture has started to brighten her up some. And I want to know what's in that little white box too.

"Well, I arrived a little early today, so decided to walk down the bank a few blocks to find something delectable to bring back for you. I knew coffee was a no brainer and I was going to buy some still warm banana bread, but when I saw these little gems, I had a feeling they could be your favourite. Am I right?"

He opens the box to reveal, indeed, one of her favourite indulgences. Brightly coloured macaroons! How did he know? It's not something I have ever mentioned to Eight, I'm sure of it.

"Oh Lane, how did you know?"

"So I'm right? Score one for Lane!"

"Eight, who is this man?"

"I don't know, but I like him! The truth is, this is him, well, the him before Miss Queen Bitch came along. Are they really her favourite? Because as soon as his eyes zeroed in on them under the glass counter, he just knew they were what Alexis would like. This is getting interesting, Hot Lips, very interesting."

"I agree, Eight."

"You're very right. I usually just buy one or two, because if I bought a whole box, there probably wouldn't be any left by the end of the day."

"So what if you ate a whole box. You don't have to worry about that. We can both share this box of twelve and finish it off by the end of the day."

"Umm, thank you. But one will do me. A pistachio one please, if it's there."

"Nope. It's six or none. Your body is perfect, Alexis, you can eat as many as you like."

"Eight, I have to ask again, who is this man?"

"May I introduce you to Mr. Falling Hard. Mr. Falling Hard, this is Hot Lips."

"Damn. I kind of like him."

"Me too."

After taking only one macaroon, with promises of eating another one at lunch, Alexis lets everything else just fall away and gets her work groove on. By morning tea, the first draft of the storyboards they had printed arrives. Lane decides they need the boardroom to spread them out and set them up clearly, but when he phones reception to book it in, he is informed that it is being used for the rest of the day.

Alexis suggests they use her office's boardroom and phones through to reception to book it. After the receptionist gives her a time of 1:30 p.m., she also informs her that she has had a man constantly requesting to be put through to Alexis's personal line, and when the receptionist informs him that she can only take a message, he hangs up. My girl's whole body stiffens at this news. Now there are phone calls at her work? She quietly asks the receptionist to call security and let them know, just as a precaution.

"Is everything okay? You look a little worried."

"I'm fine, thanks Lane. The boardroom is booked for 1:30 p.m. I hope that's okay with you?"

"That's fine, Lex. How about we go out to lunch first? We're on top of everything now so we can actually take the time to eat."

"That's true. Okay, lunch out it is. Thank you Lane."

"It's my pleasure, Lex."

"Oooookay. Does this seem to be moving at light speed to you, or is it just me, Eight?"

"I told you. My man is falling. And I really think he's finally ready to move on. And what better girl to move on with than Alexis. She is sweet, caring, beautiful, and in the words of my man, perfect. But not as perfect as you, baby."

"I think I'm in love."

"Then that would make two of us."

"I think I'm going to cry."

"Not yet, your girl has no time to go change her panties, Lane has just come up with a brilliant idea."

"I'll try and hold it in. Until I'm all alone in bed tonight. Well, as alone as I can get connected to another person."

The morning goes fast as both Alexis and Lane are on fire. The ideas are flowing and so are the smiles. Lane really does have an amazing smile when he lets it show, and boy has it been showing today. Alexis has been left staring at him numerous times when he has let his guard down and produced a face splitting grin. These two are going to make beautiful babies.

Babies? Oww!

After lunch, they head back to their office for all of their printing and some supplies before carrying it all down to Alexis's offices. After saying a quick hello to all the staff and introducing Lane around, they head to the boardroom and set up. An hour later there is a knock at the door despite Alexis asking not to be interrupted.

"Come in."

"I'm sorry to disturb you, Alexis and Mr. Anderson. I know you didn't want to be interrupted, but I have a man on the line saying he is a family member and it's an emergency. He said he must speak with you at once. It's a bad line, so I can't tell if it's the same man who has already been calling, but just in case it's not, I thought I better let you know. He's on line three."

"Thank you, Alecia, I better take it. Excuse me, Lane. Hello, this is Alexis Ryan, who is this? I said hello, who is this?"

She holds on for a few more seconds, but no one speaks so she calmly places the phone down. And takes a few deep breaths. Just as Lane is about to ask her what that was all about, there is a large knock on the door before her boss Andre walks in.

"I'm sorry to interrupt, but Alecia just told me about your call just now and all the calls this morning. Security has spoken to me, Lex. Is there anything you need me to do?"

"No thank you, Andre. Security has it under control. But thank you for the offer."

"Okay, but maybe wait until I'm ready to leave before going outside alone tonight, okay kiddo?"

"Okay Andre. Thank you."

After her boss leaves, she tries to avoid Mr. Uptight's eyes, but he just waits patiently in silence for her to look up. When she does, the look in his eyes warms her heart and has her body buzzing with emotion. How did he worm his way into her heart so fast? God, I hope he treats her right. If not, this is going to hurt badly when it ends.

"Care to explain what security has under control? Is there something I

should know, Alexis? Maybe I can help."

Damn! If we weren't already falling fast, it would have happened with that one sentence. She debates about brushing him off, but realises he's too smart for that. So she decides to tell him some of the truth.

"It's just about a pest who has been hanging around the building. And now I suspect he is the nuisance who has been prank calling me on my mobile since Saturday night and now here at the office. Security has all the information and has assured me they are keeping an eye on the situation. There's really nothing more to tell. He's just a pest, he hasn't done anything serious."

"Yet, Alexis. He hasn't done anything serious yet. People that start out as just pests can turn into stalkers or worse. Have you gone to the police about this?"

"He hasn't done anything wrong enough to go to the police. They would have nothing to charge him with. It's really not a big deal, I promise, it's just an inconvenience that he's now annoying my work colleagues."

"Just be careful okay. And let me know if it gets any more serious."

"I will. Thank you, Lane.

"The seriousness of your boy's voice has me looking at this whole Mr. Stalker situation in a new light, Eight. Can you make sure that Lane doesn't let us walk out of here alone at the end of the day, please? I'm suddenly not feeling very comfortable walking home alone at night anymore."

"I promise baby, I promise."

The rest of the day goes by fast, with Lane being extra attentive towards my girl, and we like it. They've been working close all after-noon, even brushing shoulders while checking out the graphic boards, but Eight and I stay in our sullen moods, not feeling as if it's the right time to start playing games with Alexis and Lane in light of the Mr. Stalker drama. Now's the time to just enjoy the simple closeness of the two people who control our lives.

TWELVE

He

"**R**eady to head home, Lexi?"
"Yes, just give me a moment to pack a few bits away and let Alecia know we're done here."

"Okay, meet me out front?"

"Sure, I won't be a more than a minute."

Oh there it is, that smile that you're falling hard on, you know the one that gives her little cherub cheeks and makes her eyes sparkle. The one you've only really seen a dozen times since you've properly known her, but could easily draw from memory. You know that one. Mmm, watching her sashay down the corridor as you head for the lift, nice, there's a good firm backside if ever there was one, just the right side of plump and peachy. Okay, eyes back in your head, bro, or we are going to walk into the lift doors again.

Oh shit, too late.

"Lane, you okay?"

"Yeah, I'm good, just got distracted for a moment."

"By what?"

"Uhh ...."

Better think of something quick, bro, or she is going to catch on you were checking out her arse.

"Oh, just thinking about plans for tomorrow and what we're going to present to the clients and things, nothing real important."

"Oh ... okay."

Does she look a little disappointed to you?

"Damn right my girl is disappointed, I'm disappointed."

"Disappointed by what? By the fact he didn't admit to staring at our girl's arse as we so gallantly walked into six inches of chrome steel?"

"Yes!"

"Well okay then, I'll make a note of that for the next time my boy very nearly busts his nose."

"You do that. I'm going to be watching you, Eight, always watching."

"Okay, are you my girl, Hot Lips, or Roz from Monster Inc.?"

"Ha, ha, I would call you Mike Wazowski for only having one eye, but I get the feeling you're not as short and stumpy."

"Oh sweetheart, you have no idea."

"No, but I really would like to."

"You and me both, baby, you and me both. Right, I'll see you downstairs, lift is here. Be safe."

"Always, Eight, see you soon."

••••

So, long day, hey bro, a very long day, and yet here you are waiting for a woman for whom you are falling head over heels. But somehow you still don't know the state of your own feelings. I sit here, screaming at you, telling you how you feel for her, but do you listen? Do you? All you keep doing is mulling over your schoolboy inadequacy and inability to logically escape your own mind.

You are in love with a woman you barely acknowledged for a year all because she piqued memories of that frozen hearted bitch, yet you still won't let yourself feel it. No wonder you can't pull yourself together enough to simply ask her on a proper date. Oh who am I kidding, there is no point in hashing over this anymore and you can no more hear me than a dog can do calculus, so I guess we're reduced to another pseudo date tomorrow over lunch … or have I just missed the mark slightly with what you were thinking? Ah well, I guess I'm going to find out soon enough. Here she comes.

"Hey baby, did security tell our girl anything?"

"No Eight, they didn't, they're logging all the calls that come in for our girl though and keeping an eye out for the guy with the … what did you say his hair was like?"

"Sheldon Cooper, you know, from the Big Bang Theory."

"Ah yeah, I think our girl actually said that to security, I'm not sure. But anyway, it's still pretty much a waiting game, waiting to see what happens next at least."

"Well one thing I do know, Lane is still pussy footing around with his feelings."

"So is Lexi, they're both as confused as one another, Eight. I'm a little worried at the moment that if we don't play this carefully, we may lose our chance altogether."

"Not gonna happen baby, I won't let it."

"I know, but still, I can't help worrying over it."

"Lexi, do you fancy going out for lunch tomorrow, say, taking an early lunch at around twelve and maybe taking a couple of hours to ourselves? Still in a work frame obviously, but I have a couple of ideas and I wanted to talk you through possible locations that go with them. What do you say?"

"Hmm. I didn't see that coming."

"Neither did I, babe, neither did I."

"Uh, sure, I guess. It's a bit unorthodox, but sure. Do I need to bring anything from the office or prep anything?"

"No, just bring your usual, wonderful self and that awesome smile of yours. I dare say you could charm birds from the trees with that."

"Okay Lane, peel the cheese off and stop, you don't want to choke her to death with it."

"I thought you said he didn't do cheese, Eight?"

"Yeah well, this dumbass hasn't exactly been himself the past couple of days."

"That's a bit obvious, Eight."

"Lane, are you feeling okay?"

"Yeah, why?"

"Because that is the corniest thing I have ever heard anyone come out with."

"Yeah well, it's the truth, you do have a gorgeous smile."

"Well, uh, thanks. I'll, um, see you in the morning, okay."

"Oh, she's getting all squirrely, I'm literally drowning here. I bet she bites her lip in a second and tucks her hair back a little, she always does that when she is really into the moment and feeling a strong pull to someone. *Yes!* Right on cue, this is a really good sign, Eight. Just ease your boy back a bit, don't let him lean in or anything, she may be firing off an okay signal, but her professional side is still leaning hard on her heart at the second. We really need to be gentle. Just have him take her hand and 'help' her onto the tram. That will be enough for the moment."

"Yeah, I'll see you in the morning Lexi, sleep tight. Remember, just bring yourself and that smile. That's all I need."

Did you seriously just wink at her? Holy shit, she's blushing, how the fuck did that work? You lay out some of the cheesiest lines since the eighties and then wink at her and it freaking works.

"Eight, remember, no calls or messages, let her simmer with this. We will be there, I can guarantee it. But let her simmer."

"I'll do my best, baby, I'll do my best. See you tomorrow."

"Bye Eight."

••••

Office is quiet today, a little too quiet. Everyone is on site as far as security goes, Oh there's Clive, why don't you see if he has any information.

"Clive, what's going on, where is everyone?"

"Seems we had an attempted break in, got the department heads for most of the companies in a meeting with the security chief. Doesn't look like they made it into the building, but the camera on the east corner that overlooks the storage entrance was smashed to pieces so there's no guarantee. It might just be a bunch of teens on a stupid dare, but better safe than sorry; especially with the whole thing going on with Miss Ryan. Chief wanted to be double sure it wasn't related so we are scanning all internal footage and carding anyone we don't recognise, as well as scanning everyone who enters. Which reminds me, card please, sir."

"Yeah sure, here. Has Lex been through yet?"

"Yeah, she went up a few minutes ago, want me to phone through?"

"No that's okay, just checking. Catch you later."

"See ya later, Mr. Anderson."

••••

"So do you have anywhere you would prefer to go for lunch, Lex? I hadn't picked a specific restaurant or anything, I can work my ideas in around wherever you pick."

"Hmmm, well ... I've had my eye on Rosetta for a long time, but that is a bit of a stretch just for lunch ... so ... I guess we could try Rockpool? It's another that has always caught my attention, and if we're pimping out the corporate cards, well, might as well get our monies' worth."

"I like how you think. Rockpool it is."

••••

"Well, that was something different."

"Was it what you thought it would be? Rockpool is a pretty high end joint."

"The food was wonderful, but quite pricey for what you actually get, although I suppose most high end places are like that. Still, the views from the place are stunning and I love the idea you had. A barge banner would certainly capture a lot of attention from the riverside restaurants and offices."

"Well, from what the client has said, it would be a viable avenue to put forward, but we can discuss all this at the office. I'd much rather just enjoy the time and company on the way back. If that's okay with you?"

"Certainly is."

"There's hope yet, baby."

"There certainly is, Eight."

•••

"Morning, Clive."

"Morning, Mr. Anderson."

"Did anything come from that incident yesterday?"

"Not really, although we do now have Larry running night patrols every forty-five when he's on shift. Same applies to the other staff when they're here."

"Small mercy being a static day shifter then I'm guessing, hey Clive."

"Ah, I dunno, I quite like the nights, I like the quiet, but I get the roster the boss dishes out so ... it is what it is."

"I hear ya. Have a good one."

"You too, sir."

Well another day, another dollar. I can feel you're eager to get up there, but there's something off in you today. You were all happy chappy yesterday, but now, not so much; are you pining from not sending me swimming in her pink lagoon? You know my girl wouldn't like me calling her that, but you only deal in crass rubbish with your boys so I guess it's a good way to get my point across. Oh for the days when you could actually be swayed by my suggestions, although I suppose you still can to an extent, but nothing like you used to be. The days gone by when all I had to do was twitch a certain way and off you would go, like a whippet out of the starting gate. Now I'm lucky if I can convince you to fart to order, let alone do anything else. Getting you this far with Alexis is proof enough of just how blind to my influence you've become.

I really do think some days it would have been better if I had packed up my balls and left with Miss Queen Bitch. She tried hard enough to take them when you two broke up. Oh, umm, sorry, I didn't mean that, yeah I felt that pang, sorry Lane. Ahh fuck, I've gone and woke up those old memories. I better warn Hot Lips when I see her. Today is not going to be a good day.

••••

"Morning, Lane."
"Yeah. Hi."
"Is something wrong?"
"Nothing, I'm fine, let's just get to work."
"Uh, oh okay. You just look a little upset, that's all."
"I said I'm fine. Now can we please get some work done?"
"Yeah sure."
"Uh, Eight, what is up with our boy?"

"I sort of woke up some bad memories, by accident and on the way in he kinda got a bit moody."

"A bit. He's acting like King Twat again. My girl is fluxing all over the place; her heart is going very cold at the moment, fear and worry cold. She used to be like a freaking super nova around our boy, now it's like Antarctica in there. What the fuck did you do?"

"He was being a bit of a nob and trying to squash his feelings down, you know after Tuesday's lunch date and all going so well. He kinda scared himself and I didn't want to have to redo all of our work on him, so I gave him a bit of a nudge, but I must have gone a bit too far."

"What did you do?"

"I mentioned Miss Queen Bitch to him, and pulled on the strings linking to her leaving."

"Oh Jesus, you fucking idiot."

"Yeah."

"I'm going to have to really pump in the empathy today, try and get my girl to empathise with him rather than take it to heart. This ain't good, you could have fucked this right up you know."

"You think I don't know that!"

"Don't you shout at me Mister, I ain't the one who just butt shagged Pandora's Box into opening."

••••

"So Lane, what's on the agenda for lunch today? Got any plans, another idea trail or maybe lunch in?"

"Nothing actually, I have some conference calls to make."

"Uh okay … have I done something to upset you? If I have I am sorry."

"No, I'm just busy. I'll see you back here after lunch."

"Fuck, Fuck, Fuck, Hot Lips I'm sorry, I will fix this. Shit."

"You bloody well better, my girl is close to tears here."

"Fuck!"

••••

"Morning, Mr. Anderson."

Are you going to answer him? No … ah shit … I have messed up big time, you have a deeper cloud over you than the ash clouds that buried Pompeii. Damn it, there has to be a way to fix this.

"Mr. Anderson?"

"Sorry, he's well, ah, shit I fucked up mate; tell your boy I said sorry."

"Yeah, no shit."

"Hold the elevator, please."

Oh now that was just cruel, that kid was just delivering the mail. Did you have to stand there and watch him drop it all as he tried to stop the doors closing? It wasn't *that* bad … was it? Let's have a look. Oh … oh no. Damn it.

"Morning, Lane"

"Hi."

"Is everything okay? You look a little pent up and your eyes are a bit dark. You're not falling ill from over working are you?"

"I'm fine."

"You really don't look it."

"I said I'm fine, let's just get to work already."

"Okay, sheesh. Sorry for caring."

Yeah now you felt that one, that's a good sign, you're not too far gone. I may be able to pull this back from the edge after all. Right, let's see.

"Eight, you need to get to work on this. My girl is really going through a spin because of how Lane is acting towards her. I don't know how much more she can take before she snaps at him."

"I'm working on it, just a little while longer I promise, sweetheart. I promise."

"Okay, I trust you."

"I know."

Come on bro, we can do this, find that happy point, where is it, ah how's this, Lexi's giggle, you always like that. Yeah that'll take the edge off of this. Oh yep, that's a twitch in me, we're hitting a nerve with this alright and it feels like a good one. Okay, now just sit down at your desk and close your eyes a moment. Holy fuck you just did that, are you really back to that point. Let's test it, okay, um, adjust me to the left. Christ on a bike, you just did it. Okay then, sit back, recline your chair and breathe deeply. Atta boy, okay now. Focus on her smile, that soft dimply one where she cocks her head to the left a little, you know the one where her hair falls just past her ear and a few strands catch on the edge of her eye making her brush it away behind her ear. That's it, you like that a lot, don't you bro, yeah focus on that, focus on how it makes you feel. Focus on how she makes you feel.

"Eight?"

"Not now babe, we're getting there."

"No I know, the pheromones are strong off you, but Lexi is about to say something and I cannot stop her, she is determined to ask."

"Oh crap, what is it?"

"She's going to bite the bullet and ask him about it."

"It?"

"It, as in what he wouldn't tell her, she thinks that it is what has made him switch like he has."

"Oh crap, well, she's right, but, fuck! Okay, uh."

Bro, I need you to call Woody, now. Make it about the security issues, say that Andre mentioned something about Lexi and you want to follow up on it.

"Lane, have you got a minute?"

"Uh, one sec Woody. Not really Lex, can it wait?"

"Yeah I guess so, I was …"

"What?"

"Well, after yesterday and that, I was just a little worried about you, that's all. Just wanted to see if you wanted to talk about anything."

"No I'm fine …. Thanks."

"Okay. I'll maybe talk to you later then. I'm going to go and get some more of the designs printed out."

"Yeah okay. Sorry about that, Woody."

"Too close, too bloody close."

"Yeah, but it still doesn't help my girl feel any better."

"Sorry baby, but Lane is getting there. I've taken the edges off it, he's still a little dark, but it should be an easier fix now."

"It better be. My girl isn't going to take much more of the sudden chill down."

••••

"*Well, I'm heading home Lane, see you tomorrow?*"

"*Yeah, I'm packing up myself now.*"

"*You know, I know we've not been working together all that long in the scheme of things, but if you need to talk about anything, I'm here, it's what a colleague and friend does.*"

"*Thanks, but as I said, I'm fine.*"

"*Well, okay, but still I stand by what I said.*"

"*Yeah, thanks Lex, see you in the morning.*"

••••

"*Hey boys! Fuck this has been a fucking awful week.*"

"*You're telling us, what happened to the 'no mid-week sessions until the job is done rule' that was a pretty stringent point of yours? And by the looks of things, it is one you're about to shoot in the back of the head.*"

"*Yeah well, despite the whole Lexi thing, I have had a pretty shitty couple of days. Memories of Miss Queen Bitch came rolling back into town and has plagued my every damned thought. I just need someone or something to blow it all away. Just completely glass her clean.*"

"*Well shit, me and Bookend will take care of you, what you looking for, tall, short, blonde, brunette; Asian, Caucasian? What?*"

"*I don't give two shits mate, as long as I can wipe this shit from my head and forget about that bitch, Lexi, and the whole damned scenario.*"

Hey! Hang on one motherfucking minute, you are not fucking around on Lexi, fuck no, that girl deserves better, Lane, and you bloody well know it. I'm not letting this happen, no way no how. Now, let's get some sabotage going. Tequila shots. *Now!*

"*Boys, line 'em up, I'm one thirsty dude and if we are going hunting I need to get my war face on.*"

"*That's my boy. Benji, line them the fuck up.*"

Here we go, yeah, I can feel my walls softening, no way in hell you're getting a steeler out of me. I hope your date likes soft sausage, because at this rate I'm going to be softer than a boiled hotdog.

••••

"*Whoops, ha, shush, you'll wake Mrs. Genaro and she is a whiney old bitch at the best of times.*"

"*Ha, like I care, I don't live here and all I want is what's in here.*"

Lovely, I have drunk slut's hands on me. Ugh I feel dirty already.

"*Well good, because you are going to get it and get it hard.*"

"*Mmm, I hope so, I've been wanting this all evening.*"

"*Then brace yourself sexy, here it comes.*"

Oh fuck no, I'm not hitting that! There is no way in hell I'm slipping into that velvet pocket. Do you know what Hot Lips would do to me if she found out?

"I've got some Hot Lips right here for you, big boy."

"You can shut it as well, I'm going nowhere near you. Hell, I can smell from here that you've taken more poundings than Frank Bruno. Besides, I'm spoken for."

Lane, don't do this. Seriously, stop! You're going to regret this; I'm not going to rise to the event no matter what you do. Nothing and I mean nothing is going to make me harder than an overcooked noodle no matter what.

"So, what she doesn't know won't hurt her, so why not pull on out and slip on in. Hmm?"

"I said no, and I mean it, you drunk scrag."

"Well fuck you."

"No! That's my point."

"Come on then stud, slip him out and slide him in, I am more than ready."

You're going to regret this, Lane, I mean it, do not pull me out of your jocks; seriously mate, last warning. Oh you idiot, you really are going to regret this.

"Well, it's uh, longer than I thought, but, well ...."

"Yeah I uh, I don't know what's up."

"Well it certainly ain't him."

"Hang on. Come on, don't do this to me."

Rub me all you want Lane, I ain't getting up, nope, not even rubbing on my eye is going to get me up tonight. Lexi and Hot Lips deserve more than this, they deserve the real you. Not the drunken idiot that is trying to get between this bar skank's thighs.

"Uh, so are you going to lift his head anytime soon, or am I going to just be staring at a lump of limp steak now?"

"Fuck, hang on, give me a minute. He is going to be harder than iron any moment now."

"He better, because watching you stroke that lump of limp skin is boring as fuck."

"Hold on, ahh for fuck sakes come on ...."

"Look, if we're not going to fuck, I'm going to go."

"No hold on, I seriously don't know what is going on here."

"I do, whiskey dick, you're too pissed to get it up and I can see from here he ain't going anywhere, so I'm outta here. Have fun with that piece of wet sausage, I sure as shit didn't."

"Ha, bye, bye bitch, go find some drunken trucker to suck and fuck, because my boy is off limits."

"Shit, thanks mate, thanks for making me look like a limp dink. Ah who am I kidding, this is my fault. What was I thinking when I came up with the idea of shafting some one-nighter to try and get Alexis outta my head.

Damn it, that girl is in my every waking thought, what the hell am I going to do?"

Well mate, you could start with admitting that you love her.

"I guess it's time to face facts. I'm well and truly in love with this woman, damn it! What the hell do I do now?"

THIRTEEN
She

*"**W**hat the fuck is wrong with him? He is worse than yesterday and I have just about had enough of his Jekyll and Hyde routine. I was stupid to even think Mr. Uptight would disappear completely. But I did get my hopes up with all his cute smiles and sweet gestures. I'm such a fool."*

No, no Lexi, you are not a fool, he is. He is a fucked up, cold, emotionally stunted piece of male stupidness. Even Eight is having trouble understanding his boy. I mean, he got rid of his ex's stuff, decluttered his life of all the emotional attachment to her memories, but didn't have a clue on how to move forward. Fear, fear of love can bring down even the toughest of men. But that doesn't mean we have to sit by and take his crap.

Alexis stays in the break room, taking a little longer than normal to make her morning coffee after being subjected to Lane's foul mood the minute she walked in this morning. The first feeling *I* got from him was sadness, a deep-seated sadness. I was hoping it was because he realised what an arse he had been to my girl the past two days, after being so damn sweet the two days before that. But no, his sadness was soon superseded by his grumpiness and his need to push Alexis further and further away.

My girl may be frustrated by his grumpiness, but more than that, she is hurt. Within a few short days, she had started to invest her heart in her attraction to Lane, only to have him practically throw it back in her face. The sting of rejection can cause more harm internally than would ever show on one's face; and the deeper cuts, well, they don't always heal so well.

I do the best I can to pump her with happy hormones after giving the brain a heads up to boost all her creative juices. She needs to re-focus solely on this project and do what she does best. Kick some corporate butt! But it's going to be a challenge with the cause of her discontent sitting barely five feet from her all day long for weeks to come.

"Hey Hot Lips, sorry about my boy, I'm trying my best to reign in his crazy emotions, but I must admit, it's a struggle. He's literally all over the place. But rest assured, his feelings for our girl are still strong, stronger than ever in fact. It's just that the idiot is still trying to fight them and he's fighting them hard."

"I don't care what his feelings are for my girl at this moment, Eight. She's hurting and I don't like it! I really think this rollercoaster he has her on will have whatever chance they had at making a go of their attraction crashing and burning before it even has a real chance to take off."

"What're you saying?"

"I'm saying that it'd take a miracle for him to repair the damage he's done by acting the grumpy sod, after only days ago giving her a taste of what you tell me is the real Lane. His mood swings aren't worth the risk to my girl's sanity."

"Are you giving up on ... us?"

"I'd never do that, I'm just trying to face the harsh reality of the situation. The only chance you and I may ever get to be intimate is when the project finishes, and we somehow get them to go out and celebrate, then they both get shitfaced together and accidentally fall into bed. The regret the day after would be worth it, if I got to spend only one night joined to your heat."

"Oh damn, beautiful, one night will never be enough. Let's just hope my boy gets his head out of his arse sooner rather than later."

"Fingers crossed."

Alexis sits at her desk and tries her hardest to concentrate on the work in front of her, but when she lifts her head slightly to glance at Mr. Uptight and sees the deep frown masking his features, her heart plummets to the bottom of her stomach. Old insecurities come rushing back with a vengeance as she once again feels that somehow she isn't good enough in this man's eyes.

Between big brain and I, we pump up her creative juices so high that she produces some of her best work yet. Instead of running her ideas by Mr. Uptight, she just forwards them straight to the client for pre-approval. She continues working in silence while at least feeling good about the work she is creating. When lunchtime comes around, she doesn't even bother checking what Mr. Uptight wants to do, she just throws her phone in her bag, places the strap over her shoulder and walks out of the office, needing a break from his angry grunts and the swearing under his breath.

"Hot Lips, where's your girl going?"

She's moving so fast, I don't even get a chance to respond.

She walks out of her building and strolls down Southbank, not noticing that Mr. Stalker was back at his usual lookout point and did indeed see her leave the safety of her building. She has no appetite so continues to walk off the tension that has taken up residence in her chest. Her mind is everywhere as she begins to doubt herself again due to the mixed treatment she has received from Mr. Uptight. She now begins to think that maybe he was only happy with the work they were producing together, not actually happy with *her*. My poor girl's heart is breaking and there isn't a damn thing I can do about it. She feels like a fool for even believing for a few brief moments that he could have been our Mr. Long Term Guy.

"Hey there, pussy cat. Maybe I can help cheer up your lunch break with a little Friday fling? My guy works in this restaurant, so if you go around back, I can get him to open the kitchen door and we could have some afternoon delight in the storeroom. What do you say?"

"I say you're a dickhead and fuck off."

"Damn. What's up your arse? Or is it that time of the month, hun?"

"Oh don't you dare go there! If I had my period, I would being going all roid rage on you, I would be that pissed at your comment. Now go back to the sleazy hole you crawled out of before I really bite your head off."

"Oww."

After walking for almost a half hour, we turn and head back towards our building, still no clearer on her feelings for this confusing man. We knew he would be trouble the minute we found out we had to work with him. So why didn't we just keep our distance and put up our professional walls? Mmm, I think Eight and I have to accept some blame here, maybe even accept it all. Damn I feel so bad.

Alexis walks back into their shared office and Mr. Uptight Bi-Polar doesn't even look up and acknowledge her presence. She takes a deep breath, gets comfortable at her desk, and begins to work on the files she knows she can do on her own, not wanting an excuse to have to interrupt his cocoon of shitiness.

"Hot Lips. I can't stand the thought of losing you before I even get a chance of making you mine. Damn this hurts."

"I agree Eight, it hurts bad."

"I bet this hurts worse than what it would if Lane decided to get my knob pierced. I think that would have me passing out."

"That pain would be over and done with within a few days, never to return. Try having period cramps for a few days *every* few weeks and that's not the worst of it. Clotting fucking sucks! Oh and the mood swings, those would give you whiplash they swing so fast *and* being extra horny due to hormones racing around and not being able to do a thing about it, that's the worst. Unless of course you're in a committed relationship. I imagine then there would be lots of shower sex at that time of the month."

"Umm … I would prefer not to have the words period, shower, and sex in the same sentence thank you. But I must admit, it wouldn't stop me from wanting you, moods and all."

"Aww."

The day is coming to an end and there's been nothing but tension-filled silence *all* day. Mr. Uptight has only grunted out quick questions to Alexis, who has not lowered herself to his level and has answered him as sweetly as she normally would. It did nothing to improve the frostiness that's settled in the air of this office. I think tonight might see the return of the vodka lows.

Great, I'll be peeing acid all weekend.

Alexis gets a text from Mel, asking if drinks are on for tonight, or is she too busy being banged by Mr. Uptight on his desk. It sends my girl's mood even lower. She sends off a quick reply of no, she's too busy, not in the mood to discuss the past few sucky days with the girls and goes back to finishing up the last of her work. She was so preoccupied in trying to drown out Mr. Uptight that it's now an hour and a half after finishing time already.

She looks up to see that Lane is frowning at her and finally gives in and sends him a frown back, then proceeds to loudly pack up her desk and switch her laptop off before packing it in her bag. She tidies a few more things before finally standing and making her way towards the door. She is stopped by the chill in Mr. Uptight's voice.

"Alexis, what's this email?"

She makes her way behind his desk and leans down towards his laptop, locating which email he seems to be pissed at.

"Those are the ideas I emailed the client earlier today. I didn't realise they'd got back to us."

"And you sent them ideas without going over them with me first?"

Whoa, back off man, my girl's not in the mood for your shit right now.

"Yes I did. You didn't seem to want to be interrupted today so I sent them for the client to get an advance look at before we sent them the final concepts."

"This is too important to mess around with, Alexis. You need to show me the ideas first before you even think of sending them to the bloody client!"

"Don't you dare yell at me! I know what I'm doing!"

"Obviously you don't if you're sending half-arsed crap like this!"

And *that's* my girl's breaking point! As Mr. Uptight is fuming at her, she grabs the glass of water that was sitting on his desk and throws it right in his pretty face! The look of shock on his face is nothing compared to the shock my girl feels at his next actions.

Before either of us knows what's happening, Lane rises quickly from his chair and grabs both of Alexis's arms, pulling her roughly to him as he smashes his lips against hers. Her breath's caught in her throat as sensations begin to run riot through her body. She's angry and wants to scream at him for grabbing her roughly and assuming she was up for a kiss from his rude arse, but on the other hand she can't help but lean into his body as her mouth automatically opens to his demanding tongue.

He's giving all he has and demanding everything in return. His grip softens slightly on her arms as she feels his arousal harden against her stomach. Her mind's a swirl of emotions as she allows her tongue to dance with his, the sensation making her nipples harden against his chest, causing a delicious friction. My core is flooding without any prompt from me; I feel as though time's suspended as we struggle to comprehend this sudden change in Lane's behaviour.

But only another second passes before Alexis realises exactly what's happening, and to my dismay, she pushes hard against his chest taking a step back, making him release his grip on her upper arms as she whispers angrily, *"How dare you!"*

What? Wait! But before I can grasp a complete thought, she is storming out of his office.

"Hot Lips! Make her come back!"

"Oh God, Eight, I can hardly think let alone try and send a message to my girl."

"No! You can't go! I need you so much it hurts. You're mine, Hot Lips, only mine!"

Before I have a chance to respond to the one I love, my girl is storming down the stairwell, taking two steps at a time in her stiletto heels, which has me holding my breath. When she gets to the bottom she slams the door to the lobby open, not realising that it's completely deserted apart from the two security guards watching the monitors quietly at the main desk.

She doesn't hear them ask if she would like to be escorted to the tram stop, she is just intent on running, and that's what she almost does. Her heart is hurting and her head is confused, as she tries to piece together what just happened. That man has gone from the cold Mr. Uptight, to the sweet and caring Lane, back to the arsehole we always assumed he was, to the filled with immense passion man who just gave us the best kiss of our lives, we think. It finished as fast as it started and we're still confused as to why he kissed us in the first place.

Talk about women's mood swings causing whiplash. Lane's are making us feel as if we are in a bloody car accident every Goddamn day! The tears start and I welcome them as I'm unable to cry my own. I was so caught up in the kiss I didn't even think to talk to Eight about it. Did he know that Lane was about to kiss Alexis? Or was it just as much a shock for him? Going by his silence, he was just as stunned. And then I didn't even get a chance to say goodbye and that I loved him. What if this is the end of their working relationship? What if I never get a chance to say goodbye?

Suddenly all thoughts of Eight and Lane are thrown out the window as a large male hand grabs my girl over her mouth and another comes around the top of her shoulders and forcefully drags her backwards. Alexis is dragged a few feet down an empty laneway before she finally snaps out of the shock of being grabbed in such a way and starts to fight away this attacker. She screams behind his hand while trying to dig her feet into the ground to stop his movements.

She manages to turn slightly, loosening his grip across her jaw, allowing her to take a large breath and scream with everything she has. He tries and holds her mouth again but she turns her head sharply, slipping out of his hold. She turns to get a look at her attacker's face, but it is covered with a black balaclava. It is so dark that she is unable to see his eyes.

He reaches a hand out to grab her shoulder again as his other grabs ahold of her shirt. She screams again as she tries to kick in the direction of his groin, but misses. But it's then she hears Lane calling her name from a distance.

"Lane!"

"I'm coming Lexi, I'm coming!"

As she hears Lane's response, she turns her head and sees him running into the entrance of the laneway. Her attacker's grip disappears instantly and then she hear his footsteps running away, but she doesn't turn his way. She focuses on Lane's form running towards her, not realising just how far down the laneway her attacker had dragged her. Lane grabs and hugs her painfully before pulling back, looking over her frantically.

"Did he hurt you?"

She's lost her voice and can only manage a shake of her head to tell him no, before he suddenly lets her go and sprints in the direction her attacker ran. She stands there, silently, her body trembling with adrenaline as the realisation of what could have happened invades her thoughts. She always assumed she would be able to instantly fight off an attacker. She has done many women's self-defence courses over the years with Mel and Zali and keeps her body strong with Pilates, but when you add shock to the equation, everything you have learnt can sometimes go out the window and it feels like that just happened to my girl.

What if she didn't snap out of the initial shock soon enough, what if she was struck over the head and knocked out? The what ifs are making her tremble more as shock takes over her body completely, weakening her knees, causing her to collapse to the concrete ground beneath her. It's harder to breathe now; her heart is pumping blood faster through her veins, causing a loud roar inside her ears as she stares down at the dirt beside her knees.

Lane comes running back towards Alexis, but she doesn't hear his footsteps. He kneels down in front of her and gently lifts her chin, asking again if she is hurt, but she doesn't hear the words. He tells her to take a deep breath, but it doesn't register. He gently grabs her under her arms and helps her to stand, scanning her body for any injuries before gently folding her into his arms and against his chest, his hand softly gliding over her hair. Holding her tightly, rocking her slightly as he tries to sooth her with his words, words that are not penetrating her shocked brain.

"Lexi baby, we need to call the police or drive you straight to the local station to report the assault. Security have enough information on the creep that's been stalking you out the front for the police to at least question him about this. Lexi, can you hear me? Do you understand what I'm saying?"

I think she does hear him, but she is still unresponsive to his questions. My girl is having trouble accepting what could have happened if Lane hadn't heard her scream and come looking for her.

"Oh my Hot Lips, my sweet, sweet Hot Lips. I feel sick, sick at the thought of that fucker trying to touch my girls. Thank God, a minute after Alexis stormed out, my boy *finally* got his head out of his arse and realised what an epic mistake he had been making with her and then panicked that she was now walking out in the dark alone. If he hadn't run after her ..."

"Oh I know my love, I know. My poor girl, oh dear God, the thought of what could have happened ..."

"Shh baby, shh. You're safe now. I've got you."

I'm waiting for the flood of tears to start, but Alexis is still too numb to feel more than shock. I'm so worried, it's not like my girl to stay this silent. I'm not sure what to do.

"Lexi baby, look at me. We have to go to the police. Are you able to walk?"

"No police."

What? She finally talks and she is refusing to go to the police? Oh Alexis, you are not thinking straight, my girl.

"Lexi, we have to report it to the police in case it's connected to the stalker or the phone calls."

"No, no, no. No Lane, please."

"I will be right there holding you the whole time. They will just ask a few question and then I will put them in contact with our security. That's all, I promise."

"No. They will keep me there for hours asking the same questions over and over again. I can't do that. I won't. I can't identify the attacker so I can't connect him to the stalker, who security hasn't even been able to do anything about because he has done nothing but stare. Nothing can be done! No police! No! No!"

"Hey sweetheart, come here. It's okay, it's okay. I won't force you. Maybe when you have had more time to think about it. It's okay, I've got you now, you're safe in my arms, always."

"Please take me out of here Lane, please."

"Okay baby. I'll take you to my place. Now's not the time to be alone, okay?"

"Oh God, Lane. Take me out of here, out of this city, these buildings feel like they are closing in on me. It's suffocating! I can't breathe here. I need

to breathe."

Her knees go weak again as her shaking increases and finally the tears start to fall. Lane catches her against him and then bends and picks her up in his arms, cradling her close to his chest while raining sweet kisses all over her head. He leans down awkwardly to grab her bag and then swings it over his shoulder and walks back out towards the waterfront.

He walks only another block then turns left down a quiet street, walking only minutes before stopping at the side of a tall building, where he punches numbers into a keyboard. There's an electronic click before a door opens to reveal stairs that lead to an underground carpark full of luxury cars.

He walks past a few bays before stopping beside a black sleek car. He slowly places Alexis's feet on the ground, still keeping a supporting arm around her as he uses his free hand to reach in his pocket, finding his keys and pressing the button to open his car. He opens the passenger side and carefully, tenderly, helps my girl into the car, grabbing the seatbelt and strapping her in safely. He brushes tears from her cheek before placing a feather light kiss to her nose. He then walks around and slides into the driver's seat.

The engine roaring to life has Alexis jumping out of her skin. Lane reaches over and gives her hand a reassuring squeeze before returning both hands to the wheel and proceeding to drive out of the carpark and down the street. All of us are silent, as the weight of the night's event starts to lay heavily on our hearts.

The tears have stopped but I can still feel their wetness on her cheeks. Her thoughts are muddled as she watches the lights of the city go by. Soon it darkens as we drive onto a freeway and further and further away from the city. Lane reaches over and places his hand on her knee, his thumb rubbing soothing circles over her skin.

My girl is confused. She was so frightened tonight and fears she may never feel free again to walk the streets of her city. She feels as if she just wants to curl up into a ball and cry for days, but not alone. As much as she is conflicted about her feelings for Lane and his towards her, there isn't a single other person she wants to be sitting next to right now. His tender ways have her heart aching, but it's worth it, in this moment, when she needs the caring Lane she only got to see for a matter of days. She would take anything he would offer right now than not have him at all.

She just wishes there was a guarantee that this is the Lane she will see when the sun rises tomorrow, because this is the Lane she could see falling hopelessly in love with, which, if she was honest with herself, was what her heart has already started to do.

We feel as if we have been in the car all night. I feel squished, sweaty and exhausted when Lane slows and winds his car down a small dark road. When Alexis turns her head towards him, what she thinks she sees outside of his window has her heart racing.

He then turns slowly to his right and pulls up to a small gate before hopping out and quickly pushing the gate open enough for his car to pass by. The smell from outside has tears forming in my girl's eyes and the breath catching in her throat as Lane quickly hops back in and drives down the long dark driveway before stopping in front of a large two story beach house.

As he hops out of the car and walks around to open Alexis's door, he is treated to a sobbing mess. The realisation that Lane has brought us to a beach house, obviously his beach house and something she has been dreaming about for a lifetime, has her completely and utterly falling apart. Damn, I hope this Lane is the real Lane, because if it's not, it's going to hurt my girl more than any attack down a laneway could.

FOURTEEN

He

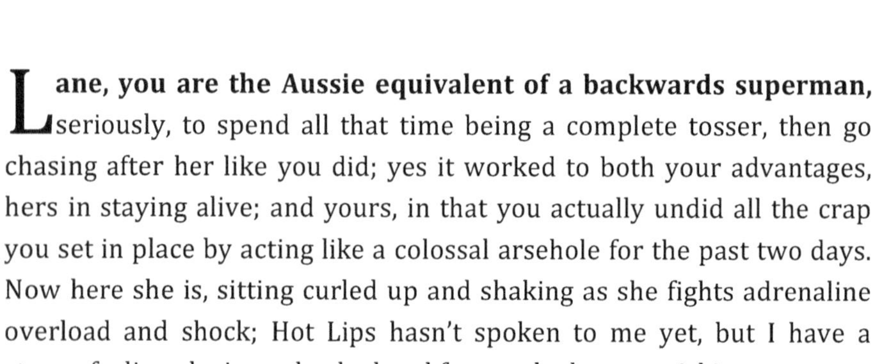

Lane, you are the Aussie equivalent of a backwards superman, seriously, to spend all that time being a complete tosser, then go chasing after her like you did; yes it worked to both your advantages, hers in staying alive; and yours, in that you actually undid all the crap you set in place by acting like a colossal arsehole for the past two days. Now here she is, sitting curled up and shaking as she fights adrenaline overload and shock; Hot Lips hasn't spoken to me yet, but I have a strong feeling she is as shocked and fear soaked as our girl is.

I'm just thankful beyond belief that in the closing seconds of your work day you actually felt something akin to shame for the way you'd been acting and charged out of that building faster than a coke-fuelled Batman. The feeling in your chest and the pounding of your heart when you heard our girl scream was something that I honestly have two feelings on. One, that it is proof, solid and quantifiable proof, that you are head over heels in love with our girl and two, that you hold far more value in not only hers but also many other people's feelings, especially when it comes to how you feel about them. I truly pray though, that nothing ever causes our girl to scream like that again, or you to feel like you were. I think this could be a true turning point for the both of you.

Sitting here, staring at her as she slips into a fitful sleep curled into our chair, sure is making my balls ache. Why don't we put her to bed and take a walk, just leave the door open a bit. Feeling as she does, I don't think she should be left alone for too long.

"Lexi is sleeping deep, Eight, you two can go out for a while if you really think he wants to, if ... you want to."

"Baby, I never want to leave you again, never, for as long as I'm alive and pulsing with the rampant energy of life will I ever leave you."

Well Lane, what are we doing, are you heading out for a walk or are we going to move Lexi to the bedroom and make sure she isn't alone when she wakes up?

"Lexi, it's me, I'm just going to carry you to the bedroom okay, come on, put your arms around my neck and hold on."

She smells like sunshine and warm summer mornings. How could you have ever been angry enough to ignore anyone who smells and looks like she does? Besides, she is filled with a love and kindness so boundless that no one in this lifetime could ever be assured of finding another person such as her. To drive her away like you did, well, you're either so darkly masochistic that you enjoy the pain and torture that comes with it, or you really are that damaged that you find your own self-loathing and fear preferable to actually embracing the love that was being offered by the slumbering woman in your arms.

"I'm sorry Lexi, I was a fool to act the way I did. I never meant to hurt you or to be so negligent with your feelings and your heart. I've just, well, I've had a hard time opening up to everything that's happened in my life."

I think she is still too out of it to even hear those words and the meaning behind them. Set her down in the bed; if you truly want some kudos from her, slip her shoes off and leave it at that, do not, for the love of God unbutton her shirt or undo her bra. Booker did that once with a girl who passed out at a house party he threw and she went ballistic at him when she came too. Bad memories that night is.

"Eight?"

"Yeah baby?"

"Don't leave me alone, stay here with me."

"I promise baby, I promise."

Lane, pull in one of the light rattan chairs from the deck, I don't think Lexi or Hot Lips should wake up alone. I would throw in some macho phrase like, "I want to be here to protect my woman from anything that threatens her," but we failed that task in epic fashion when you went all moody bastard and sent her running out the door of our office in an anger-filled huff.

You have a lot to answer for, Lane and I pray you're going to be the man our girls deserve. I would step up but, well, I'm attached to you and kind of just a penis. Right, so grab a damned chair and get comfortable. With God as my witness you are going to prove to our girls that you deserve them, and if you are asleep when she wakes up, mate, you are not going to get a fucking boner for a damned year.

••••

"Lane! Lane, where are you?"

"Hey, hey, shush now, I'm here, you're safe. As long as I'm here, nothing and I mean nothing will ever hurt you."

Careful mate, she's still half-asleep and still shaken from what happened only a few hours ago. I doubt she'll say no to a comforting cuddle though, just be careful with the hands, after that fucker grabbing her like he did, well, you never can be too careful.

Damn that scent of hers, how does one person smell that good? She is so soft and warm, fits us both like she was made to be in our arms and she's melted that ice right out of you. I cannot believe you let yourself doubt that and acted out against her. Oh damn, she's crying again. That's it, pull her closer, let her snuggle in tight. She needs your arms tonight.

"Baby, you okay?"

"No Eight, I was so damned scared; scared we'd never get to be together, scared I'd never get to say … get to say …"

"Get to say what?"

"That … I love you."

"I know you do, I love you too baby, I love you with everything I am."

"But you're just a penis."

"And being this guy's penis ain't easy, but that doesn't mean I don't love you more than life."

"I know babes, just trying to lighten the mood."

"I know, beautiful, I know. How's our girl?"

"She's still shaken, very shaken; but she'll be okay, it's mostly shock. As long as we stand tough and Lane stands with her and *us,* our girl will pull through it all."

"Lexi, baby, why don't you try and get some more sleep, I'll be right here when you wake up."

Damn it, I feel she's too scared and in too deep of shock to even reply properly. Best to just make her comfortable, bro, and see how she feels in the morning.

"Baby, I'm going to leave you some of my sweats and a tee to change into in the morning okay? I'll be right here all night. Sleep, beautiful."

Okay, careful now bro, you don't want to wake her up completely, it would be better if you could nap in the chair next to her. Just be bloody careful when you're, um, 'extricating' yourself from our girl's grip. Damn it she's stirring; be careful you freaking klutz or you'll wake up sleeping beauty and damn … is she a beauty.

"No, no, Lane no, don't leave me."

"Hey, hush now, I told you, I'm not going anywhere; I'm just fetching you some of my clothes for the morning, then I will be right back, okay."

"Okay."

God, seeing her like that is making my heart clench, well actually it's your heart but you get the idea. Curled up in the foetal position right in the middle of the bed, she just, well, she looks lost. Like a kid lost on the beach, just so small and fragile; scared beyond recognition of any form of comfort, except of course, for you. For some reason, you great oaf, she feels safe when you're holding her, so I don't think that you sitting in a chair all night is going to cut it.

Just do yourself and me a favour, change while you're picking some gear for our girl. Sleeping in a shirt and trousers is um, well, just get changed, or you'll find out quickly why sleeping in suit trousers is not the way to go. Yep, that's more comfortable.

"Hey Lexi, I'm back."

That's it mate, slow and tender, show her you're a positive presence. A person in her state doesn't need sudden surprises. Oh, uh, okay, that's not a move I personally would have done, but yeah, brushing the hair out of her face and kissing her forehead seems to have made her a little more settled. Nice one. Well I guess now it's just time to get comfortable again and see if she responds in a positive way to you settling in next to her on the bed.

Ooh ouch, shit, careful how you move around here, I just head butted my own ball bag. Okay, now shuffle around and see if she wants to be held the same way as earlier, which, yup thought she might. Okay, slouch down, let her use you as a pillow, just make sure you can sleep like this bro, don't want you suffocating on me, I don't think a dick can be reincarnated.

••••

Ugh, I hate waking up in these, I always feel like I'm coated in extra thick lube and not in a good, I'm going to a nice tight warm place way, but the, ugh you should shower more, it's going to cause a fungus. There is a reason they call these 'sweat pants.' I'm so damned sticky I'm stuck to my own balls and Lane's thigh. Speaking of which, are you awake yet, bro? Nope, you're still in the land of nod. What about our girl? Nope, she's still deep in dreamland. How about my girl?

"Hot Lips, you awake yet, baby?"

"Mmm, morning handsome. Sleep well?"

"Somewhat. How's our girl feeling?"

"Let me check those brain waves. Oh she's a lot better, still not right, but the panic is gone and she's dreaming of, well, if I told you, you'd pitch a tent faster than the circus in holiday season, and if I stay watching these for too much longer, Lane will have a very big wet patch on his mattress."

"Well, uh, yeah, okay, wet patch not so good, but the thought of you all sexy and wet, damn I'm fighting a woody here."

"Naughty boy. Play your cards right and I might just get Lexi to show you just how warm and wet I can be. But ... maybe not so soon after ... well, yeah."

"Oh come on! That is just cruel. How am I supposed to get Lane to deal with me when he is curled up against our girl? It's not exactly going to benefit our cause if she wakes up to find his morning wood."

"Yeah, yeah, I'm sorry, but after having spent so long cooped up in that office and being within a couple of feet of the man I love and now to be only inches apart and separated by a few millimetres of cloth and an arsehole of a circumstance, well, I just had to be cheeky. Sorry baby."

"Don't worry about it, babe, I'm used to dealing with bits like this. Lane has, uh, a very active libido. My skills at falling limp at a moment's notice for work reasons should be worth logging with the Guinness Book of World Records. Well, if there was a case for world's fastest boner loss. Oh, looks like the children are waking up, that means dreams of morning sex are out of the equation."

"Oh God, if only we could."

"Oh we will, we will. One day."

Careful bro, you don't want to startle her by moving too quickly. But by the look on her face and the little smile she has I think it should be okay to make the first move in. You know, hello and maybe a kiss on the forehead that you like so much, nothing more.

"Morning beautiful."

"Uh, hi. Did I sleep like this all night?"

"Well, apart from the occasional twitchy nightmare and dream-induced whimpering, yeah you were here all night, safe, with me, just as I promised."

"I've no doubt you did promise, but, well, I don't remember much after getting into your car."

"I actually hoped that would be the case. You weren't exactly in the best frame of mind last night."

Too right she wasn't. Damn, I've never known someone to twitch and move as much as she does in her sleep. Shit, I have known puppies that whimper and move less.

"I brought you some of my older clothes, well, not older, they're just smaller than what I wear now, nothing wrong with them at all. I just thought you might like a shower and something fresh to wear."

"Umm, thank you."

"No need Lexi, no need. Now you go and shower and get changed, en suite's through there. I'll get some food on the go."

Well that was smooth as silk, bro. Leaning in like that and kissing her softly on the forehead, judging by the soft blush to her cheeks there, she actually liked it. Well shit, why wouldn't she like it? It was tender and oozing more love than a Shakespearean sonnet, only I'm here wondering if we should have pressed our advantage while we had the chance. Oh well. Hey, now someone is being very proactive. Careful Lane, soft and tender remember, damn her lips feel wonderful, soft and a little powdery, like marshmallows dusted with icing sugar. Try toying gently with the hair at the top of her neck quickly. Yeah, she's pushing into you, she likes that, ease up a bit. Okay lover boy, break off now and go do some breakfast, she is starting to get a little overwhelmed again.

"Just wanted to show you not everything about me is cold and fierce. Now go change, I'll get some breakfast on."

"Uh, okay."

Damn, dude, look at her. She doesn't know which way is up now. Hot

Lips, baby, can you pull our girl's brain back into her head? She seems a bit lost.

"Shit babe, *I'm* a bit lost by that kiss. It felt freaking awesome from this end, so God knows how my girl is taking it. Why can't he kiss *my* lips like that first thing in the morning?"

"Grrr. Damn babe! Give it a day, he may just do that or I might just force him to."

"Mmm a girl can hope. Just be careful, remember, nothing too soon, she's still not out of the woods yet."

••••

You know I'm really impressed right now, Lane. You've gone from zero to hero in no time flat. Here we are, listening to the sounds of a running shower and rather than go creeping in there and ploughing her in the shower like you would have any other bit of fluff that happened to be in our bathroom back home, you're here, cooking bacon and scrambled eggs, and I have to say, you make some mean scrambled eggs. Oh, going all out with this, pulling out the herbs, better be careful though, you don't know if she is allergic to any of them. Hey, here she comes all drippy and sexy in your clothes.

"Feel better? You look refreshed, and I have to say that Tee and those sweats look good on you."

Damn, she is one stone cold fox; bro, if you blow this, you are never and I mean, *never,* going to find anyone like her. No matter how hard you look.

"Mmm I needed that; you have one hell of a power shower in that bathroom."

"Yeah, when I had this built, I figured I may as well go big or go home. This place is my home away from home, a place for me to decompress and unwind. Just know, if you ever need to get away, just give me a shout and it'll be here."

"You really mean that don't you?"

"Wouldn't say it if I didn't mean it, Lexi."

"I know, I just have a hard time believing people, with everything that has happened in the past few years, it's become more and more obvious that honesty is a hard thing to expect or even find."

"I know, but enough of that. Eat up; we're going for a walk."

"Where?"

"Fucked if I know, we'll find out when we get there."

"You're a very hard man to read, Lane Anderson."

"Not really, you just haven't had a chance to see the real me."

"True, but what I have seen, those little glimpses when you let your guard down in the office, I liked."

"Well eat up then and I will let you see as much as you want."

"Hmmm, that's a very open invitation."

"And not one I make to just anyone. Before we head off for a walk though, I have to take a small spin into town. Need a few things for dinner. You okay to wait here or do you want to come with?"

"No I think I'll be okay, but umm, you do have an alarm system or something here right?"

"Yup, alarm code is two zero eight six. I'll set it before I leave, I shouldn't be more than an hour."

••••

Well this is nice; warm sand, fresh clean ocean, and yet, we both know she is still as tense as a cat on a hot tin roof, no matter how flirty and relaxed she seemed back in the beach house. We need to find a way to make her more comfortable, Lane, to let her really know we aren't just in this for a quick fumble. You love her, and her, well, she's head over heels for you. No, don't blurt it out you dumbass, that's just going to make shit awkward, I know what you were thinking, thank fuck you kept your trap shut.

Take her hand gently and lead her to that cove you found when this place used to have a campsite. Weird how things go, really. Anyway, get moving, the path is over there, unless something has messed up the place. The views from up there were stunning when we were little, so now, well, that should get her head calm enough to have the fog fading fast.

"So what did you get that was so desperate when you took off and left me to fend for myself?"

"None of your business, cheeky, besides, I can't give away all my secrets can I? Otherwise what would I have to surprise you with later? Anyway, come with me, I've got something I want to show you."

"Lane, what ... where are we going?"

"It's a surprise and if I tell you now, then what's coming next won't be nearly as worth it."

You've gotta love this place, mate, the views around here are freaking phenomenal; I just hope Lexi loves them as much as we do. Just for the love of God, do not do what you used to as a kid. You know, taking a running leap from the top into the pool below and be careful with the footing mate, remember the pathways here are crumbling. Keep a tight hold on our girl, bro, we don't want her taking a tumble.

The air is a little colder up here. I'm so glad you wore your sweats and not those daft cargo shorts. The wind would have had me shrivelling fast. Just hope that if I do end up going tortoise you can get something warm on me sooner rather than later. I don't fancy having you tease me back into life like the last time we were up here.

"So, what do you think?"

"Oh Lane, this is beautiful, you ... it's like you can see forever up here."

"I know, I used to come here a lot as a kid, it's one of the reasons I bought the extra land around the house to try and keep developers off of it. Come on, let's sit, you've got to be a little worn out after I dragged you up here."

Nice move, bro, nice move. Uh hang on, did you bring a blanket or something? The bench that was up here rotted out years ago. So it's either get grass in your arse crack, well more accurately a grass stain on the seat of your pants, or stay standing the entire time you're up here.

"I wonder."

What are you doing now? You look like some scrambling hermit looking for a hole to crawl in. Hell, I can feel the disturbed curiosity coming off of Lexi and Hot Lips. Mate, you really aren't doing yourself any favours … hang on, what the fuck is that.

"Uh Lane?"

"A friend of mine stashed this here back when we were teens, we used to come up here and go base jumping into the pools or climb down and into a couple of the small caves in the cliff face. It got to a point where we were risking chest infections and flu a lot of the time, the wind can get pretty cold up here closer to winter, so he stashed this bag here. I'd forgotten all about it until he called recently to catch up."

How do I forget these things? You could have at least given me a heads up. Ha heads … up … I crack me up. But seriously mate, that was a dick move, and I should know.

"Oh handsome, stop pouting. I can feel the indignant cringe from here. If you're a very good boy I may just kiss it and make it better for you later tonight."

"Oh come on girl that is just mean, you know Lane has no jocks on under those sweats, having me rise and tent them now would be …. Oh …. Damn that is genius."

"I know."

"Damn it, I fucking love you."

"I know that too, now hop to it and see if we get the reaction we want."

Okay here it goes, one involuntary woody coming up, right okay, think kinky. Lexi lying on the beach, naked, legs open, fingers toying with her wet lips. Yeah … that's good … can feel the blood pumping. Okay, another push should do it. Lexi, leaning forwards, her pert butt pushed high in the air as she looks back at us, slowly and I do mean slowly teasing her panties down over her cheeks.

"Uh Lane."

"Yeah babe?"

"I think ... um ..."

"Huh? Oh shit, sorry."

Hey bro, why are you acting so embarrassed about this? You know she wants you and me just as much as you want her.

"Well that wasn't exactly what I was hoping would happen, but it was worth a try, hey Eight."

"No, wasn't exactly the best response but, oh hang on baby, I think things are going to get a little serious, can you feel the energy off our girl?"

"Yeah, this is a bit, um, let's just see what happens, but no matter what babe, I love you."

"I know baby, I know. I love you too; let's just hope my boy doesn't fuck things up again."

Okay Lane, let's see what's up with our girl. Ready and ... go.

"Lane, I ... I think ... that guy, the one that attacked me, I think he might be my stalker. It has been driving me insane, I see him every morning, just standing there across from work. He's there when I leave. I keep getting all these phone calls, none of them have a message, just this sweaty, stale, breathing. I get the calls day and night, I have trouble sleeping I get so paranoid that the phone is going to ring, so I sit there staring at it half the night."

Mate, she is starting to cry, what are you waiting for, put your arms around her and hold her close to you, she needs it, you need it, and it sure as hell will be one step closer to you two finally making it abundantly clear how you both feel. So don't be a fucking idiot, hug the girl.

"Hey, come here, come on. I know we can stop this from continuing. I won't have you trapped like this by some psycho with an obsession.

Security have enough on him, calls logged with dates, times and numbers when the fucker called the office, they have him on CCTV standing out front. And you've got me to corroborate the attack, even if we didn't see his face; we have all we need to put this to bed once and for all. So Lexi, as soon as we get back, we're taking this to the police, okay, I won't take no for an answer this time."

Nicely put bro, even if all you got for an answer was a soft slightly sullen nod, but nicely done. Okay my balls are starting to freeze being stuck against the cold earth here, any chance of us heading back and getting dinner sorted?

••••

"Baby, is our girl allergic to anything?"

"No, just cheesy pick-up lines."

"Funny. But seriously, is she allergic to anything, or can't eat anything?"

"No, you're all good."

Well okay then, Laney boy, let's get cooking.

••••

"Oh my, uh, what is all this?"

"Well, I wanted to do something to cheer you up, so we have some dishes that I, while simple, know you would probably not have tried before."

"Well okay, still doesn't answer my question."

"Okay then, we have, Sope, it's essentially a very thick tortilla, made with maze and limes, baked and then topped with refried black beans, aged cheese and a smooth tomato based sauce mixed with fresh tequila cured pork. Following on from that is one meal that takes a while to prepare so I always keep some curing in the fridge. Cochinita Pibil, it's a

slow roasted pork dish, served with steamed rice and diced tomato and cilantro, simple really."

Okay enough showing off, you know you got that recipe from a DVD, so stop bloody gloating.

"He got it off a DVD?"

"Yeah, one of his favourite films, I can't remember the bloody name, but credit to him, he's made it his own. I wonder if it would ever pass muster with ... hmm."

"What?"

"Never mind, baby, just enjoy the time with me, I think this might pay off in the end."

••••

"Damn Lane, this is delicious. Where the hell did you learn to cook like this; wait no, don't tell me, I don't want to know. I like a mystery."

"So I guess you like it then?"

"Like it, I freaking love it. It tastes fantastic and you can hardly sense the tequila in it, it smooths out so well with all the other flavours."

Okay that's all well and good; she loves your cooking, but what now? Where do we go from here, it'd still be too bloody weird if you dragged her into bed and, like swimming, you should really wait an hour. Plus, I'd let her make the first move anyway, just to be on the safe side. So, um, I guess, you could always get the hearth going and curl up with a film or something, or just some soft mood music and the fire. You know, enjoy each other's company a bit more intimately. Hint, hint.

"Seriously baby, if he doesn't get the lead on from that, I have serious doubts about my boy's intelligence."

"Give it time Eight, give it time, we've got the whole weekend ahead of us and I for one have no doubt we will end up together before Monday rolls around."

"I know baby, but we still have to be careful with our girl, we don't want to damage things more than they already are."

"Yeah, I know, she's getting hard to read now, so just give it time, she'll be ready soon enough."

FIFTEEN
She

Feeling the heat from the flickering flames of the open fireplace, while lounging on the softest sofa I have ever laid my bits on, I'm still amazed that we are here, in a real beach house, Lane's beach house to be exact. If this was ours, I'm sure we would find a way to work from home and move in here permanently, ditching the city apartment lifestyle we currently live. My girl could afford it if she wanted to, but feels as if it would be too isolated living in a house like this all alone.

Despite the reason we are here, today has been wonderful, in a quiet, understated way, but still wonderful. The gentle caring and subtle affection that Lane has been showing Alexis is mesmerising and has had my girl's heart rate rising more than a handful of times today. He has been a perfect gentleman, which to be honest, has been frustrating at times for both my girl and I.

His light kisses and gentle touches have flooded my centre more than once today and has my girl's brain overflowing with naughty thoughts, which then have her feeling guilty, thinking that she is here recovering from an attack and was not invited here for a dirty weekend away. But damn it if we don't want a naughty weekend desperately with this man, right here, right now.

Even Eight has been restrained, to a point. The respect they are showing us is heart-warming. The quiet walks along the beach were so very sweet, the silence saying more than mere words could have expressed. Then Lane understanding Alexis's need to focus some of her restlessness on work, their laptops opposite each other on the dining table, was a vision that had my girl craving that kind of companionship every weekend here.

And then dinner! Holy fucking meat on a stick was that a beautiful and yummy surprise. The old saying, 'the way to a man's heart is through his stomach,' could so easily be translated to, 'the way to a woman's heart and soul and panties and everything in between, is through her stomach,' when it comes to a man who can cook more than just a BBQ. The meal was delicious, but even more than that, the time spent looking into Lane's eyes and his looking right back, was … heaven. We can't help but think what a good Mr. Long Term Guy Lane Anderson would make.

But now, sitting here, in front of the fire, with Lane sitting beside us, his arm casually hanging over Alexis's shoulder while she is snuggled comfortably into his side, is pure torture! I'm trying so very hard to not let our arousal become too obvious, because if he was to reject my girl in this moment, I honestly don't think she would survive too well at all. And the restraint that Eight is showing would be admirable, if it wasn't so hilariously painful to hear.

"Arr Hot Lips, make your girl get up and go to the toilet, or grab a drink, or say she needs some fresh air, anything, just pleaseeeeeeee move her from our side. I'm in pain and I don't know how much longer I can hold onto these freaking hormones without letting then smash into my boy's already barely there restraint. Move her, *now!*"

"I hear you babe, I do. My girl is barely hanging on herself. If it wasn't for a recent serious event which has her believing it's an inappropriate time to have these feelings flowing through her entire body, she would be all over your boy in a flash. It would be so fast that you wouldn't even see it coming. You're not the only one in pain here."

"Remind me again, why are we both restraining ourselves? Aren't these feelings what we have been striving for these past few weeks?"

"We don't want to risk our girl thinking that Lane is taking advantage of her while she is in a vulnerable state. She may get caught up in the moment or the night, but what if she wakes up pissed or upset tomorrow? We don't want to risk ruining what beautiful progress they have made in the last twenty-four hours."

"True. It hurts to say, in more ways than one, but I agree with you."

"Good boy."

Alexis continues to snuggle tightly into Lane, believing that, if this is just a one night, emergency type of comfort thing, then she will make the most of it. She takes a large inhale of his scent then snuggles tighter into his side, her heartbeat kicking up a notch when he squeezes her tighter to him and places a feather light kiss on her head.

Then something changes.

Alexis starts to change her thought process, so fast in fact, I'm having trouble keeping up. She is thinking of throwing caution to the wind and making a move on Lane, damn the consequences.

"Lane?" she says in a deep, lustful tone, as she lifts her head from under his shoulder, staring longingly into his eyes. When she sees the same hunger and barely there restraint shining back at her, she decides to take a chance on her feelings for Lane and rises slowly towards his lips, giving him time to back away if that is his intent, but he starts to lean in as well.

"Oh my God! Eight, this is it! All our restraint was for nothing, they are going to make this happen on their own."

"I'm not sure, Hot Lips. He's holding back, he still feels as if she is too vulnerable to take this further than a quick peck."

Their lips meet gently, brushing slightly over each other. It is Lane's low growl that has Alexis leaning in with more force, deepening the kiss, begging for more. When Lane's tongue traces her lips, our body comes alive. I can no longer hold back the arousal I have been fighting near this man. Her tongue meets his, which has his grip on her shoulder tightening as he pushes his tongue all the way in, desperate to dance with hers.

Eight is right, I can feel his restraint. The want is there, I can smell the testosterone his body is releasing, but he's trying not to hurt our girl, which shows what he truly does feel for her no matter how much he has been trying to hide it behind his coldness.

All of a sudden our restraint breaks as our body is engulfed in flames. Alexis reaches a hand up, grabbing the back of Lane's neck, pulling him closer, demanding more. He still tries to refrain from letting go, but when Alexis moves up higher, not breaking their heated kiss, while moving her leg over his lap, straddling him and pressing her body flush against his, he completely and utterly loses it. Both of his large hands grab hold of her arse and he forcefully brings her closer, smashing hard against his solid erection while he growls loudly into her mouth.

"Fuck, Hot Lips, I can feel your lips part over me through the cotton fabric. Your heat is scorching and … oh Goddamn it, your wetness is soaking through our clothes. Need you, need you now!"

"Holy fuck, Eight. You feel so hard, so good. I want you, I want you inside me. I'm going to die if it doesn't happen this second."

Alexis rubs her centre against Lane's hard cock as one of his hands travels up her spine, reaching into her hair as he smashes their lips together harder, bruising the delicate pink flesh as he then sinks his teeth into our bottom lip before soothing it with his tongue.

Weeks of pent up frustration releases, causing a heat to rival hell as they both consume each other, feasting on the hormones that are seeping from their bodies. I'm flooding like never before as Eight hardens to the point of breaking. Lane and Alexis are almost clawing at each other with a passion neither has experienced before, trying to get closer, trying to feel more.

Lane reaches both hands to the back of her tee shirt, pulling it over her head and throwing it to the side. His hands reach up and cup her breasts over the top of her silky black bra, still not breaking their kiss. His hands move up to her shoulders, dragging her straps down her arms softly, freeing her as he breaks the kiss long enough to bend down and take one of her hardened nipples into his mouth. She throws her head back, her moan echoing around the room as Lane once again reaches a hand around to her arse, pushing it hard against his arousal.

"Need you Lane, need you so bad."

"Oh Lexi baby, I fucking need you too. But ... I don't want to take advantage of you."

"It's not taking advantage if it's offered up freely to you. I want you Lane, I want you right now. Please don't make me wait."

Without hesitation, Lane throws her down onto the sofa beside him and starts tugging at the baggy sweatpants along with her panties, roughly pulling them down her hips as she lifts slightly to help him. He then sits back and stares at her bare body spread out before him.

"I'm sorry Lexi, I'm sorry I resisted this for so long."

Before she can answer, his hands grab her knees and open her to him, displaying me and our arousal that has spread down her thighs. He starts to slowly lean forward, not breaking eye contact as his tongue lashes out to make a single swipe between my lips. Alexis bucks her hips into his face, increasing the pressure, almost causing us to climax.

Lane enjoys her reaction going by his husky laugh as he repeats his actions, but this time holds her thighs down. He then sucks our entire clit into his mouth, his warmth encasing my bundle of nerves. Then he's thrusting two fingers into our soaking core, causing a delicious friction on my internal walls and that's all it takes for the explosions to begin. The wave takes over as Alexis screams his name, our climax shooting electricity through every nerve in her body.

"Oh my, oh my, oh my Eight! It has never felt like this before, we have never exploded like that from oral *ever!*"

"Damn, damn, damn, baby. That was beyond my expectations. And that was just the beginning, Hot Lips. You just wait until *I* rub your internal muscles, the neighbours will know Lane's name I guarantee. Hold on tight, baby. I'm going to take you for the ride of your life."

Lane pulls his fingers free of her body and begins to crawl slowly up, biting her sensitive skin as he goes, at her hip bone, her stomach, her ribs, one breast, collarbone, neck, jaw and then sucks her bottom lip into his mouth before giving it a quick bite also. She can taste our arousal on his lips and moans as the taste seeps into her mouth.

Just when she thinks he is going to settle against her, he suddenly stands and pulls her up with him, reaching behind her, grabbing both arse cheeks and pulling up. Alexis wraps her long legs around his waist as he pulls her tightly to him, our wet centre soaking the front of his sweatpants.

With one hand holding her arse he attacks her lips again, sending his other hand up into her hair, grabbing roughly, anchoring her to him, moulding them into one, as he then starts to walk towards the stairs.

"Dear God don't let us fall Eight, unless I fall straight onto you, but then I don't want any injuries stopping this arousal. I want more, much more. Take me Eight, take me."

'Fuck, Hot Lips. This is really happening, I'm going to make you mine. I hope this is just the beginning."

Lane's strength is amazing as he rushes up the stairs heading towards his bedroom, while holding Alexis tightly in his arms, still kissing the fuck out of her, stealing every breath she tries to take. Lightheadedness isn't even the start of it. She feels as if she is floating on clouds above a raging volcano.

When he reaches the edge of his bed, he places one knee on the mattress and slowly lowers Alexis down, still holding her tightly in his arms as he moves her higher up the bed. He wastes no time in breaking their kiss and lowering his head to capture a nipple roughly between his lips. His other hand moves slowly over her stomach, sending delicious shivers through her entire body.

His hand teasingly moves over to her thigh instead of where we need it most, his fingers rubbing in the groove between thigh and pelvis, as he then moves over, ever so lightly, barely brushing our centre. He strokes down her other thigh, kneading her flesh roughly, before finally moving to where we so desperately want to feel him.

He pushes all his fingers through our wet folds, the slick noise filling the room as he spreads our juices, growling at the evidence of arousal due to his heated touch. He shoves three fingers in at once as he bites down on the nipple he was sucking, causing Alexis to slam up into his body with a loud, drawn out moan. He continues to cause havoc on my centre as his movements become faster, more frantic, his breathing becoming laboured.

"Eight, Eight, I will fall apart if he makes me come like this again."

"We need you wet, baby, we don't want to hurt you and by the way my boy's heart is beating against his chest, there is no way we will be holding back when we finally enter your slice of Eden."

"If I was any wetter, you could bottle it up and sell it! Just make him hurry, baby, I need to feel you."

Lane curls his fingers forward and hits my front wall, causing sparks to fly through my entire centre, making my bud of nerves throb and enlarge, begging for attention and that's exactly what he gives it. He presses his thumb down with such force, we climax so hard it feels as if Alexis is going to passing out.

"Yes Lexi, yes! Give it to me baby, come for me, only for me. Fuck I need this, I need you."

"Lane!"

"I need you now Lexi, I can't wait."

The minute he moves, she misses his heat. He reaches over to his bedside table, opens the draw and pulls out a condom, opening it with one hand and his teeth while the other hand rubs over a very hard Eight. He rolls it on quickly before moving over her, placing a soft kiss to her lips while he positions himself at my entrance, anticipation rolling from them both in waves as the heaviness of the situation finally hits them.

This is happening, there is no going back. After weeks of mixed emotions they are both throwing caution to the wind and giving in to the chemistry between them, risking their hearts, risking their souls, risking their professional relationship for this moment, a moment to be free, a moment to be themselves, a moment to show the true Lane and Alexis.

"I need you Lexi, more than you'll ever know."

"I need you too Lane. I need the real you."

And as she says that last word, he pushes into her hard all the way.

"Eight!"

"Oh baby. I feel you, I finally feel you. This is, this is … I'm lost for words, baby."

"You are so *big*. I could sense that you were large, but damn baby, you are hung!"

"Oh baby. You are perfect, absolute perfection magnified by a thousand. Ah, oh, no, no, no, don't squeeze me that hard. I won't last!"

"I can't stop it, my muscles have wanted you for so long they're afraid to let go. Move baby, I need you to move, I want to feel your entire length."

Lane is panting, his head buried in her neck, lost in the moment, as Alexis holds on tightly, digging her nails into his back as she struggles to breathe. He slowly pulls out until he almost slips free, before slamming back in, reaching her resistance, growling with satisfaction at hitting her deepest muscles.

"Oh fuck, Hot Lips, I can feel all of you. I can feel where you begin and where you end. I can feel every ripple your muscles are making as they try and milk me, begging me to move. I can feel your heat, I can feel your juices sliding all down my shaft. My head can feel your pulse as it's crushed up into your deepest crevices. In this moment, I own you. I own every inch of you. You … are … mine!"

"Eight, I don't want this moment to ever end."

Lane moves out again, but slows down when he pushes in this time, finding a rhythm that's most pleasurable for them both. He kisses her lips, then her jaw, over both her closed eyelids, then over to her ear, before biting it softly, still moving, still dragging heavily through my tightened muscles.

The friction builds, his pace quickens, as he reaches between them to rub over our clit. The flood of arousal is everywhere, slick and hot; the smell is intoxicating as hearts beat erratically, the heat scorching as their bodies slide against each other.

Alexis has never been this turned on in her life. Even when she started to let her hair down with her ex Mr. Confidence Smasher and finally embrace her sexy side, it was still nothing compared to the way Lane is making her feel. He's reaching places that have never been touched before; nerves that have lain dormant are finally feeling alive for the first time. Sparks are flying between every piece of connected flesh.

He continues to push slowly, but once inside pushes up hard into her deepest point, causing a new sensation we've never experienced before. He has found a new g-spot I'm sure of it. I didn't even know it was there. Now I feel as if I'm losing my mind and that goes for both brains.

"Oh Eight, how did he know where to find that spot? Oh, ah, ah, ah, yeah, that one."

"He didn't baby, I did. I just knew if I bent the right way I would find a way to set you on fire like no one ever has, like no one ever will. This space is mine, Hot Lips, only mine!"

One more hard push, up high into this new spot, has Alexis screaming Lane's name so loud, the neighbours will indeed know his name. He continues to thrust, harder and harder, growling with each strain, Alexis gasping with each push, struggling to catch her breath.

The climax eclipses anything our body has ever experienced. There is a blinding light as everything explodes in colours, a delicious burn along my internal walls as the heavy, fast pull of Eight continues to slide in and out in a desperate chase to their own explosion. Every part of me becomes sensitive as the wave continues to move throughout my core, shuddering, gripping, muscles jumping in spasm as the feeling of euphoria takes over all of our senses.

"Hot Lips! Fuck! I can't hold back, I'm coming, I'm coming. You're mine, do you hear me? You're mine!"

"I love you Eight, I fucking love you."

Lane pushes harder, faster, chasing that last piece of resistance and smashing it to pieces as the tingle in his spine spreads and causes a fast rush of an explosion. He roars Alexis' name so loud it rings in her ears as his grip tightens on her skin, sure to leave the evidence of his climax on her body for days to come.

Fast heartbeats, gasping for air, fevered heat, slick skin, wetness running down thighs, the smell of ecstasy saturating the air. A climax that has left them spent and sated, unable to move from their joined bodies, not wanting to break the connection they just created, all thoughts of reality crushed beneath their sweaty bodies. Fuck reality, it can wait until the sun rises in the morning.

SIXTEEN

He

Oh damn, what a night. That was freaking amazing, knackering, but amazing, I don't think me and my boy have had such a wild, passion filled time in … well … ever. Waking with my boy in the night, finding our girls there soft and supple, it's what dreams are made of and yeah, Laney boy, you're right, the last couple of times it wasn't just sex, it was something else entirely. It was slow, sensual, filled with love and passion. Truly, before we all finally fell to sleep we gave a true home to the words love making.

"Mmm, good morning baby, how is my girl this morning?"

"I'm very, good, a little worn out and sore in certain places, but still very good."

Mate, if I weren't still spent from the boiling torrent of love, sex and rampant fucking of last night, her smile would have lit my boiler once more. I think you owe that girl a very tender, cuddle laced kiss, don't you. Oh good man, ahead of me as you should be. I have to say though, she was brilliant with those soft lips of hers, in more ways than just one, haven't felt anything that good in a *long* time.

"I'm not surprised, baby, not surprised at all. If I wasn't still worn out from last night, just being here would have me rising again."

"Mmm, yeah, Lane careful, I'm a little sore after having you and big boy so many times ... but ... we ... maybe we ..."

I do not like the look in her eyes, Lane, shit, you've got the same damned look, no, no, no, fuck no. You can get rid of those thoughts right now, you are not putting the brakes on this now, it's only just started.

"I know, it's okay Lexi. I can see it, it's running clean as day in your eyes and I think I feel the same. Despite us, the night we've had together and all that's just started; it could be ... disaster for us if it spilt over and affected our work, we both know our careers are riding on such an important campaign. Both our lives revolve around our work, that's who we are and why we ... are so Goddamned good at what we do; I don't ever want to let this, us, or anything we have together go, but I guess in the light of day, we can see what's at stake."

No, no, no, no, fucking no. Stop right fucking now Lane, I mean it!

"I know, I was thinking exactly the same thing and if it did ... spill over ...or somehow got out, it could ruin everything. Everything that is just starting between us, everything we have at work, all the time we have put into building our careers, could just vanish, even if this is everything I want, all I have ever wanted. All that I've ever needed, we've got to ..."

Don't even think about it Lane, don't bloody do it, we've only just got our girls; me and Hot Lips have worked too hard and too fucking long to get you two together. You do this Lane, to me, to us, to Hot Lips and Lexi; and I swear, I will *never,* and I mean *never,* forgive you, I will never rise again, do you hear me Lane, *never!*

"Yeah, so ... what do you want to do? We could ... plan ahead; from this moment on, our sole focus is our project, nothing else even ventures into the frame. We work our arses off, grind ourselves to the bloody bone and then, once everything is done, once we've given it all we have, we can be us and finally see just where we are and then, well ..."

"Okay, but Lane, there's ... there's something I want to tell you, something I need to tell you."

"I already know what it is Lexi, I already know."

Okay, after all that, all that crap about keeping it social and business-like, which by the way is fucking awkward as fuck when you're sitting naked in bed together after a night of fucking each other senseless, you don't even have the decency to let her say what she needs to say to you? You should be beyond bottling everything up, you should have let her finish, oh hang on okay, this isn't something I saw coming. You and her, lips locked and hands roaming.

"Baby, did you hear what Lane just said?

"Yeah I heard it all, but, you do know what this means, means for us and our relationship."

"Yes baby I do, but did you just hear what our boy told our girl … baby … baby?"

What the fuck is going on here, I'm losing my fucking mind. First you two spend a night humping like bloody rabbits on Viagra, then, in the morning, when you should be relaxing in each other's arms and basking in the afterglow of the night before, you scrap everything and make plans to live like workaholic monks for the foreseeable future. Then not only do you do that, but you do a full one eighty and silently admit your feelings for each other and to top it all off, I talk to my baby and see if she has heard all that has gone down and she says she has, then clams up on me. So … *what the fuck is going on!*

"Well, um, I uh, I need a shower, so … yeah … I'm just going to, uh, grab one before we head back to work."

See, that's just what I'm on about, what the hell is going on. Damn it I'm so freaking confused. Lane, what's happening bro? Oh come on, talk to me mate, and don't just sit here with your head in your hands, bloody talk to me, my girl's not talking, Lexi has buggered off into the shower and you're sitting here looking like some depressed skinny Buddha. Nothing, alright then; I guess I'll just hang here and block the flood waters from getting in your butt crack, because it seems like that's as much use as I'm going to be for the next couple of months at least.

"No, I'm not letting our weekend end like this … no way no how."

Okay what the fuck, you just said … but … hold the fuck on, what are you doing? Grabbing another condom? What? Wait damn it.

"Lane … what the …"

Okay then, damn she feels good when she is all wet and slick.

"Oh damn yeah, here I come baby, I'm going to give it to you good."

"Oh hell yeah, I was so hoping your boy would do this, baby I need you, I need you in me, I need one more goodbye. Get him to slip that rubber on now!"

"Here I come baby, oh damn you're so tight, I can feel you clenching me, oh baby you're pulling me in. That's it baby hold me tight, never let me go, I love you so damned much baby, so, so, much."

"I love you too, Eight, I love you more than anything, stay with me baby, please stay with me. But harder would be better if you don't mind."

Lane cups her breasts, twisting her nipples between his fingers. I slide deeper into my girl, the water crashing down over our bodies, my girl clenching around me, her soft walls rippling as Lane drives me deeper with each thrust. The sound of his hips hitting Lexi's slick backside fills the air as she gasps and moans.

"Oh yes! Lane, yes, yes, harder, I need you harder, I need more of you. One more time."

She leans back against him, her head resting against his shoulder as she drags his lips to hers, their tongues dancing as her fingers slip down and she draws her nails slowly over my tightened sack. That one stroke, with her sharp, almost razor edged nails is all it takes before my limit bursts and I explode with want and need.

"I'm coming Lexi baby, I'm coming, oh fuck!"

I feel Hot Lips clench as Lexi screams, her nails digging deep into Lane's thighs as I empty everything I have, my girl draining every ounce for me in one, long, explosive, burst.

"You feel it baby, yeah, milk me dry, do you feel me baby, do you feel me deep inside you?"

"Oh fuck yes, give it to me Eight, fill me up, make me yours again. I want it, I want it all."

We all slump to the floor, our lust and need finally drained, sated and yet tinged with pain at the thought of this being the last time the we'll be together, until we can finally bid goodbye to the project that is standing like a wall between our lives together.

"Baby?"

"Yeah Eight?"

"I love you."

"I know baby, I know, this sucks …"

"Big time, but at least we had one last big one together, I just … well … it's going to be hard baby, very hard and not in the way we like it to be but, if it's what our boy and girl need to do … well … ah fuck, no, I don't want this, I don't want you to leave, please baby make her stay, stay with me."

"Oh Eight, I want nothing more, I really don't want to go, but, shit, I know if I had eyes I'd be crying right now. Fuck, I want to cry so badly my girl is welling up, I want to stay so much, I really do. I love you Eight, with all I am, I love you."

"Lexi … I …"

"Don't Lane, this is hard enough as it is, you know how I feel, and I know how you feel, just leave it at that. Please don't make this any worse than it already is. Just hold me … a little while longer."

••••

This place feels different, it feels, well, empty. Even though she's there in the bedroom, just slowly packing up and sorting herself out before we leave, this house already feels like a tomb. You built this to be your home away from home and now, yeah, I know you'd rather sell it than come back again.

There are some dishes in the dining area, mate; you left them there last night, don't forget them. There's no telling when we will be back here again, *if* we will ever be back here again. I know I couldn't stand to be anywhere that you and Lexi have been, when she isn't there. Why is this so damned hard, bro? Why is it so damned hard to let go of it all, I know we've only just had her after the epic chase that, if it had been a movie would probably have spanned six years and seven continents, but why can't we just switch off? It's not forever, I know it, and you know it. So even if it is only a matter of a few weeks, why can't you or I just shut it all off and then turn it back on when we can finally be how we want to be, huh, come on, tell me why?

Fuck this hurts. Can we go out onto the decking or something, I need some air. I need to at least get out of the building for a few minutes, so come on bro, let's, I dunno, go stare at the waves or some shit? Great, that did a whole lot of fuck all, Lane, I know you're hurting and trying to tough it out for Lexi's sake, but mate, you're driving me *insane.* The morose thoughts that are floating through your head are worse than when Miss Queen Bitch was there in front of you fucking Dave in your own bed. Sorry, that was a bit too far, but it's true, this girl, no, sorry, this woman, has come into our lives, burrowed and carved through the ice that had surrounded us both and awoken desires and feelings that we thought had long since shrivelled to nothing.

Just look at us, we're standing here staring at a damned beach that only a week ago held such vivacious joy and memories so dear to our hearts that it would have worn a hole through to our soul if we lost them. And now, neither of us can bear the sight of it, the mere thought of it tearing us apart as all the memories, that even now are only days old, shift around inside that confused noggin of yours. The one of you and Lexi and the long walk along the shoreline, hand in hand, a companionable, if stressed silence between you both. The slow, slightly taut conversation that you both had atop the cliff. All of it, and I know right now you want nothing more than to claw your own eyes out, all in the name of keeping the vow you made to the woman you are hopelessly in love with. It's only for a small amount of time, but I can feel your fear that it may never be again. That's where all these depressive thoughts are coming from.

Fuck, what are we going to do Lane? We need to figure it out and soon, otherwise we're going to either go crazy, or ruin the one chance we've had at being truly happy in over half a decade. Lane, I don't think I can go through that again and I know you can't. So, what mate, are we going to do?

"Lane? I'm um, ready when you are."

"What, okay, yeah, let me just grab my car keys, I'll meet you out front."

••••

Silence, I hate silence, it never bodes well for anything; from family to work and anything beyond that, nothing good ever comes from silence and this car is thick with it, the tension in Lane's body making me shift and shiver as I fight to silence my words.

"Hot Lips … baby?"

"Yeah Eight?"

"Are we okay, nothing has felt right since this morning and I truly can't lose you, I'd rather cease to exist than know I lost you over something we could fix."

"Baby, *we* will always be fine, there is nothing wrong between us, between the pair we're attached too, well, that remains to be seen; but we, my sexy phallus, are always going to be fine, this isn't forever and I love you too."

"But I didn't say I love you."

"You didn't have to."

The thrum of the engine shivers through my sack as I feel the heat radiating off Lexi as Hot Lips soaks the car in a comforting blanket of happy pheromones. I feel my boy sink into his seat, the tension in him pooling and flowing free as he struggles to keep the grin from his face.

Lexi squirms slightly as she sighs softly, her smile teasing at the edges of her mouth as she turns her head and stares out the window. I know Hot Lips is trying in desperation to quell the tension but I still feel the horrid layer of depressive anxiety lingering just under the surface.

I find myself flinching as my boy grinds his teeth silently as he watches Lexi out the corner of his eye, all the while still trying to keep us on the road as he moves through the coastal roads towards Melbourne. His thoughts are a jumbled mess, I mean seriously, one moment it's complete acceptance of the task he and Lexi have set themselves, then the next in rolls a wave of doubt at whether they can pick up where they just left off. On top of that come sprinklings of deep loss, loss at the thought of what lies before them, the weeks and months of utter inhospitable loneliness as they try to drown their desire for each other and the carnal feelings of love and lust that even now is gnawing its way through both of them.

Several times I have had to force his mind back onto the task at hand, even if it is the basic one of merely driving in daylight, with his mind so unfocused, so torn between every little thought, or snatching scent memory as he catches a teasing whiff of Alexis's perfume. My boy is completely incapable of keeping his mind on track and it is driving me to insanity.

I'm just glad that this is only a short car journey, anything longer and we would all end up dead.

••••

"Well babe, here we are, home sweet home. I know what we've decided, but I have to ask, are you still sure you want to move ahead with it. I'm willing to try and work with us staying behind closed doors."

"Lane, you know we can't do that, it'd be too dangerous and we've both got too much to lose if it comes out at the wrong time. I'm sorry, but we have to stick with the plan."

"Okay, I know that is what the best course of action should be. Still, it doesn't mean I have to like it."

"I know, neither do I, but it is what it is. I'll see you Monday, Lane."

"Hang on, at least let me walk you to your apartment."

"Lane, it's a hundred feet from the car door, I'm a big girl, I'll be fine."

"I know that, I guess, I'm just looking for an excuse to stay with you, even if it is only for a few seconds more."

Yeah, way to look needy Laneway, shit, at least do something debonair to smooth over the childish whining. Ah fuck, who am I kidding here, I don't want her and Hot Lips to leave any more than you bro.

"Baby, please, do something here, I can't bear the thought of you being away from me, please, drown her arse in happy juice, anything, just make her stay, baby please."

"Eight, you know I can't do that, I love you, I love you more than anything, but her mind is made up, and so is Lane's even if he can't see it yet. Nothing is going to stop this, not me, not you. Only thing that would make her stay would be a tranquiliser and a net and you and I both know Lane isn't that kind of person."

"No I know, I just can't bear it, the thoughts of us only having that one night together, it's going to be hell and I don't know if I'm strong enough to live through it. Nor is my boy if I'm reading him right."

"We're stronger than we realise, baby, we'll live through this, now make Lane let go of Lexi's hand. We have to go baby, I love you."

"I love you too, I'll make him let go. Night, baby girl."

"Night handsome."

The apartment is cold, flat, lonely. We're not even inside the door more than a minute and I'm already getting pangs of hurt and loneliness. My girl, my soul mate, the one person in this entire blue marble we call a planet that actually understands and completes me, is now beyond my reach. Hell, she may as well be on the other side of the solar system for what I can do about it right now, and going by the feelings I'm getting off my boy, well, he is feeling it deep inside his shuddering heart.

"Fuck I need a drink."

You and me both Lane, crack that bottle and run a bath, I can't be bothered with a shower bro.

••••

God that feels better, but now bro, can we really stand to walk away from everything? From Lexi, from Hot Lips, you're seriously considering keeping to the deal between you two? It's going to drive you insane, Lane, hell, it's already sending me mad.

"Am I really making the right move here?"

No, no you're not, fuck I have been telling you that all you're going to succeed in doing is making our life completely and utterly miserable. Which, as I know you all too well, will turn you into a moody prick again and that will drive a wedge between you and Alexis, which will put even more distance between me and the woman I love. That's right, you heard me Lane, I'm in love with Hot Lips, head over freaking heels, up to my freaking pubic follicles in love with her. All this pact between you and Lexi is doing is ruining any chance I truly have at happiness right now, so I hope you're proud of yourself, because, dickhead, *you're ruining my life!*

I want you to know one thing though Lane, one thing, it's not only my happiness you're ruining here, it's yours as well. Just think about that.

"Fuck I don't know, on the one hand, it makes sense for me and Lexi to put it all on hold until the project is finished. On the other, it is going to drive me absolutely insane being unable to even hold her close when I get the chance. Shit, why do I always do the debonair thing and agree to other people's plans without even thinking them through before opening my mouth, am I that much of an idiot?"

Yes! Yes you are! You are a grade one prat, and one I truly wish I could freaking leave. Why in the name of all that is holy was I attached to you? Am I being punished? Was I Hitler in a past life or something?

"Working with her, in that office, I don't know if I can do it, I really don't. I mean, shit I'm sitting here in the bath talking to myself, so I guess I'm already crazy, but, ah fuck it, I can't turn round and just say 'deals off babe, let's fuck on my desk.' Well I could but, shit I don't know, I wish someone could just tell me what to do."

I have been, I have been all the way along, it's just you, you cloth eared dickhead, that doesn't want to fucking listen to a word I have to say and now we stand to lose it all because you don't know how to listen to other people, or more to the point the one person here who actually knows how to use that lump of flesh between your ears. *Me!*

Damn it, all this is doing is making me feel all the worse, being stuck between your legs like a rotten sausage while you refuse to listen to reason. It's damned depressing, sometimes I really wish there was a company that made anti-depressants for dicks. I sure as hell could use some right now.

SEVENTEEN
She

As soon as Alexis shut the car door, she went numb and her mind went straight into survival mode, running on auto pilot. She walked into her apartment and started cleaning everything! Every room, every surface, even cupboards we barely open were pulled apart and re-stacked. Laundry was done, fridge cleaned and sheets changed. Her apartment was sparkly by the time she realised it was now nine p.m. at night and our tummy was rumbling in protest.

When she allowed herself to think, all that crept into her thoughts was doubt, doubt over whether they really could pick things back up when this project was over. Yes, it was only a matter of weeks, but depending on the client's needs, it could take longer and a man like Lane Anderson didn't seem the type to go without, even if he had almost admitted to the depth of his feelings for her.

She has to admit, he was wonderful over this weekend. He was caring and attentive to her needs and trauma of her recent attack. He was gentle and loving and genuinely seemed to like taking care of her. His guard was down and she liked what she saw. And the *sex!* Holy fuck! Hands down the best sex she has ever had, if I may say so myself and I *am* more of an expert in that field than her I think.

Everything just seemed to fall into place this weekend, but I could feel her holding back slightly, trying to resist the urge to let her heart completely fall for this man. But she couldn't control it, like she hasn't been able to control the pull she has had to Lane from the very first moment she saw him across the lobby of her work. Her heart fell long before she even allowed it to. And now, now it was breaking slightly due to her past insecurities.

She wants to believe they can put things on hold for the sake of their project and pick right up from where they left things today, but history tells her not to believe everything that is being said to her. Her ex made all sorts of promises for the future and to the outside world, and to Alexis it appeared he kept those promises, until one moment in time where all his words suddenly meant nothing but lies. To a moment that would forever be etched into her brain, playing on repeat at her weakest moments. Like now.

The pain hits so suddenly that she falls to her knees, wrapping her arms around herself and cries. She cries for all the past pain of a broken relationship, the betrayal of his actions right before her eyes, and the months it took to recover from it. She cries for her issues that are making her judge Lane's words in the same way, when she knows it's not justified. She cries at the possibility that for some reason she may never get to experience that kind of passion and love she felt from Lane's every touch and the sincerity in his every word.

She hates that she is doubting the wonderful weekend they just shared, when she should be happily counting down the days until this project is finished and she can see where these feelings for Lane will take her. I need to snap her out of this funk, but to be honest, I'm a little destroyed at having to say goodbye to Eight, so I'm not much help at the moment either. God we make a sorry pair.

The only plan I can think of is to get her creative juices going with some help from the big brain, get her finishing up some documents and projections for work ahead of time and hopefully make her so exhausted she will find some sleep for us tonight.

Well, my plan didn't exactly work how I was hoping it would. It's almost one in the morning and yes she is exhausted, but not exhausted enough to go to sleep without first falling into bed in a sobbing mess. The pain of her self-esteem issues is crippling as she finally lets everything out, and hopefully in doing so, lets everything go after the tears wash away all the past and present pain.

I really wish Eight was here. He would know exactly what comforting words to say to make this all bearable. I miss him so badly and it hasn't even been an entire day away from him. What will it feel like if, after the project finishes, they can't work things out and go their separate ways? Oh dear God, I wouldn't survive that. I'd become a dark lonely place covered in cobwebs because there is no way I would ever let myself get aroused again.

●●●●

The next morning is the beginning of an entire week of 'Awkward with a capital A.' After waking up with not much sleep behind her, Alexis surprised me with her positive attitude. She told herself in the bathroom mirror, *'Don't expect the worst, this could turn into something lasting, just focus on work and think positive.* I'm so proud of my girl. But so much for that little speech, the minute she walks into the office, things become strained.

Monday:

Lane is just about to walk out of his office when Alexis goes to walk in and they almost collide. He takes a step back as his lips stretch into a face spitting grin; he begins to lean towards her before his smile falters and slips from his lips, as he seems to remember at the last second that they are only work colleagues for now. He straightens and only offers a small smile the second time around.

"Good morning, Alexis."

What happened to Lexi? Damn this is not good. But my girl plasters a smile on her face and soldiers on.

"Good morning, Lane. I did a little work last night and came up with an idea I would like to run by you."

"Sounds good. I'll just grab a coffee and be back in a minute."

And with that he practically runs out of the office and down to the breakroom, with Eight yelling out to me as they go.

"He just needs a moment, baby. It's so fucking good to smell you again, Hot Lips. Fuck have I missed you. Talk soon, my love."

At least when Lane comes back he has made a coffee for my girl too, which she takes with a shaky smile, not sure on how to navigate this new vibe that is settling over them both.

"Eight, are we going to get through this? Well, more to the point, do you think Alexis and Lane are going to make it?"

"Hell yes, baby. Despite them agreeing to place their relationship on hold for the welfare of this project, it has made Lane more determined to make it work. We just have to be patient and let them do it their way for a while. These next few weeks will go by fast, I promise."

The rest of the day doesn't fair well. They say very few words to each other and keep their distance when looking over storyboards side by side. Lane asks her if she intends to go to the police today to lodge a report, to which she quietly answers yes. He seems to want to say more, but decides against it and just lets a silence drift over them instead.

"He wants to go with her to the police station, Hot Lips, but feels that he can't now considering their agreed situation. But he's hurting baby, just wanted you to know that."

"I understand, babe. She wants him to offer to go with her, but feels that it's overstepping on what they have agreed on, so she won't ask. This sucks Eight, and not in a good way."

"I agree baby, I agree."

We head to the police station during our lunchbreak, after Lane and Alexis look at each other for far too many seconds before she left, neither wanting to be apart at this moment, but we go alone, because that's for the best? This hurts.

We are at the police station for almost three hours, with them contacting our building's security while we're there and requesting all of their documented evidence of Mr. Stalker and any CCTV footage of the outside of the building, as well as the lobby area. They already have the information on what they are referring to as 'an attempted break in' a few weeks ago at the building and said they will now attempt to retrieve any security footage that may have been taken down the laneway of her attack.

But all in all, because the suspect works in the building next door and has every right to enjoy the waterfront at the entrance of both their buildings before and after work, there isn't much they can do unless they find CCTV footage of him doing anything more than just staring at my girl. She knew this would probably be the result, but feels better making a statement and giving the police all of the information she has just in case something changes in the future.

Back at the office, after relaying what the police said to Lane, they get back to work, in silence, in an awkward as fuck silence with Lane's sexy as fuck aftershave floating in the air. This is going to be a long, very long few weeks.

Tuesday:

And if we thought it would get better the next day, we were wrong. Neither Lane nor Alexis know how to find a middle ground. When they feel as though they are speaking too friendly, they stop mid-sentence and put on a flimsy professional tone instead, which just sounds strained. When they are looking over printouts or storyboards and accidentally lean too close, they straighten up so quickly it's leaving Eight and I dizzy.

"This is *not* freaking working, Eight. My girl can't concentrate for shit and all these near touches are causing her heart to beat erratically all over the damn place. She may just have a heart attack by the end of today and then where will it leave us all."

"Hang in there, baby. It's only the second day, it's going to take them a bit of time to find a comfortable middle ground to work in, but they'll get there, I promise. We just have to ensure they concentrate on work only and withhold all steamy hormones when they do get too close to each other. They can do this. But me ... damn Hot Lips, you smell better with each new day. It is a major undertaking to not rise the minute you walk into the damn office every morning. I just have to hold it all in until we get home and then let it all go to my head and ... well ... let's just say Lane will develop a few more callouses on his hands over the next few weeks."

"Fuck Eight, that is just torture to my ears."

The rest of the day is such a wash, Alexis decides to take a lot of work home to catch up on, since today hasn't been very productive at all, for both of them. Eight tells me Lane will be burning the midnight candle also to try and stay ahead on this project. Damn I wish we had a time machine to jump ahead to the good stuff again.

Mmm, yeah, the good stuff. Eight, filling me, stretching me, making me ... Oops, didn't even know we had left work and now on a tram heading home. I will have to finish that little daydream tonight when Lexi crawls into bed. Shit! I have to make her stop by the grocery store, BOB's batteries are flat and we have none left and there is *no* way I'm going to let these visions go in my head without a little bit of release tonight.

Wednesday:

Thank God today is super busy. They are getting ready to send their client some more ideas and both want to get it right before they forward them on. The morning goes by fast and when lunchtime arrives, Lane suggest ordering in so they can continue on the creative run they are both feeling, even suggesting ordering from Alexis' favourite Thai restaurant, which makes her smile and has us all believing that they can indeed find a comfortable medium to work in.

After lunch they decide to spread everything out in the boardroom to get a better look at the campaign as a whole. It begins by both of them respecting each other's personal space and being cautious not to lean too close to the other. But an hour later, that all goes to shit! Lane seems to be leaning in closer each time, leaving Alexis to wonder if it's deliberate or if he is just so engrossed in work he doesn't notice he is doing it, but either way, it's making her on edge as our body starts to react to his nearness without any persuasion from me.

A few minutes later Lane brushes her arm in a very deliberate way while praising her idea. She pretends she didn't feel it, but when he does it again less than two minutes later she can't help the obvious shiver that takes over her body. Lane stares into her eyes for a little too long, waiting for something, but Alexis diverts her eyes back to the work in front of them, ignoring his stare that seems to be drilling heat into her core.

"Okay Eight. The first time I thought it must have been an accident, but that second, tender brush over her arm was *so* obviously deliberate. What is your boy playing at?"

"I'm still trying to figure that out, baby. He knows they have to wait, but sometimes the need to touch her is so great, he just has to, but he is trying to hold back and I promise I'm not encouraging this at all. As much as I want to get near you, I know it's best that they wait. Let's just hope all this restraint doesn't screw up their project after all."

The little bumps and little touches continue until Alexis's nerves are wound so tightly she feels as if she will scream. She starts packing things up, mumbling that she needs to get back to her computer to complete some research she was working on this morning, and practically sprints from the room, leaving Lane trailing silently behind her.

Looks like it will be another long night catching up on work again. As long as she's not too tired for ice cream and a roll in the hay with BOB, I'm okay with it. After being around Eight every day and not being able to get as close as I would like, BOB has been my only sanity. If he breaks,

I may just die.

Thursday:

They spend the morning ignoring each other, which is a good thing, because the tension in this office is laying thick in the air today. Quick questions are the only thing that's breaking the silence, apart from Eight and I talking up a storm.

"It's too quiet in here. I'm bored. Entertain me Eight, tell me stories of conquests from the past."

"Umm, bringing up the past doesn't always have a happy ending, baby."

"Just tell me some of the funny moments you've had. Something to lighten the mood a little. Please."

"Well, I won't get into my past, but I do have some hilarious stories from Benji and Booker's crazy antics. I don't know how those two haven't been arrested by now, by how brazen they both are. At one stage, it was a competition to see who could have the most public sex! Thank God Lane opted out of that one, because I'm too pretty for a jail cell.

"But there was this one time Booker talked this chick into getting it on in one of those cabins on the Melbourne Star. He had only been seeing her for two weeks when he paid a fortune and booked a cabin, just for the two of them, saying it was for their anniversary. The entire cabin is bloody glass except for the floor, so God knows how they were discreet enough to move clothes out the way, while standing, looking like they were just a couple cuddling, when the truth was they were fucking slowly up against the glass. He won the competition with that one."

"That sounds quite romantic actually. In one of those glass cabins, late at night, watching the sparkling lights of the city slowly go by. The public fucking thing sounds a little too risky, but it might be something to try in the future, who knows."

"Damn girl, stop talking like that. We're at work, remember."

After lunch the silence somehow turns to snappiness. Both being short tempered with the other's ideas and suggestions. There are grunts and growls and banging items on the desk harder than what's deemed polite. Frustration at themselves and at the situation seems to be coming to a fast head, and Eight and I work frantically behind the scenes to tone down their agitation. But after Lane gives a straight no to one of Alexis's ideas without letting her explain, my girl breaks. She packs up her laptop and storms out of the office, mumbling she has an appointment to get to. Eight and I are just speechless.

Friday:

Alexis knows she can't let Lane get to her like she did yesterday. This is already becoming increasingly hard, but snapping at each other will only make things worse. So she decides to be her normal sweet self regardless of what he says and does. She will not snap back.

"Hot Lips, my guy feels so bad for snapping at Lexi. I know he will be on his best behaviour today."

"Well that will make things easier. But my girl had already decided to be the grown up here and not let his snappiness bother her."

"He's not trying to be childish, it's just frustration and believe me, I know how he feels. His frustration is leaving burn marks on my delicate skin. I think I'm close to getting a blister for Christ's sake. I'm all for a release and as often as I can get it, because I'm a dick after all, but damn, three to four times a night is a bit much, even for my head."

"Aww poor baby. I would kiss it better if I could."

"Just promise to get your girl to kiss me better when these two are finally back together and all will be good in my world."

"Deal, big boy."

The morning runs smoothly and so does their quiet lunch in, but something changes in the afternoon. The vibe in the air heats as both Lane and Alexis steal little glances at each other for a few hours. Lane clears his voice. Alexis crosses her legs, then uncrosses them and crosses them the other way, which has Lane growling softly under his breath. Something is changing and anticipation is flowing through Alexis's body.

"Eight. Do you feel that?"

"Yep and it's making me nervous. I think my boy is about to break and I'm not sure if I can stop it or what *it* will even be when he does. Big brain and I are trying to pump him with creative juices to try and get his focus back on work. I'll let you know how it's going."

The tension in the air feels as if it will strangle my girl, who is clearly feeling as though something is about to happen. Her release of pheromones are only just holding on, waiting to respond to whatever Lane is going to throw her way.

For the next hour things start to settle down and Alexis actually loses herself in work for a while. Lane getting up from his chair and mumbling that he needs a coffee doesn't even have her looking up, but the sound she hears next has her full attention. The door closing and the click of the lock has her head lifting so fast she feels dizzy.

Her eyes lock onto Lane's. He's still standing at the door, his hand gripping the handle so tightly his knuckles are turning white, the look in his eyes pure hunger as he slowly lets go and starts stalking towards her. He looks aroused and angry at the same time, and the testosterone flowing from his body is off the charts as he walks around her desk.

"Eight? What the fuck is going on?"

"This is the other side of his breaking point, Hot Lips. Hold on tight."

Lane's large hands wrap around both of Alexis's cheeks, gripping tightly and pulling up, guiding her to stand, and before she can even take a breath, his lips are on hers, taking, demanding, desperately wanting to claim them as his. Her brain is in shock but her body catches on quickly and melts into his hold, wanting to claim him just as desperately.

Lane mumbles something about *'Can't resist you any longer'* and *'We will work it out,'* before pushing her back against her desk and smashing their bodies together. She can feel his heart beat against her ribs as his arousal has her full attention near her stomach. She moans into his mouth which fuels him on even further.

He reaches behind her to the zip at the back of her skirt and practically rips it down, and before the skirt is even off, his hand comes around to her front and slides down her stomach, under the elastic of her stockings and panties and slides straight through a very wet centre. The minute she heard the lock click on the door, she flooded with arousal and I wasn't to blame this time. But now, now I ensure to flood her even more as he slides two fingers in and growls at our wet heat.

"Arrr, I needed to feel this heat so bad, Lexi baby. I need you, I need you in every way and I can't fight it anymore."

The only response Alexis has is a long, drawn out moan as he attacks her mouth again, while continuing to cause a delicious friction between her thighs. She can't help but push against him, wanting more, seeking his own heat to mate with hers. She fumbles with his button and zip before getting her own hand down the front of his slacks and grabbing a firm grip of his scorching flesh.

The growl that rumbles in Lane's chest is almost primal as he pulls his hand free of her panties and yanks her skirt, stockings and underwear down to the ground before reaching up to grab a handful of her hair and smashing his lips to hers again. He bites the plump flesh of her bottom lip before pulling back and slowly guiding her to turn around so her back is to him, as she kicks off her clothing.

He runs both hands slowly up the outside of her thighs, moving to her arse cheeks, before up and over her back, slowly adding pressure, guiding her to stretch over her desk. He reaches his hands up to hers and places them up at the edge of her desk, spreading her over the top of contracts and spreadsheets. His hands then slowly brush down her arms, over her spine, slowly down and over to her hips, before pushing around to her stomach and sensually down, over her silky waxed skin.

When his fingers rub over our clit she arches her back with a moan, which sends him wild. He reaches in his pocket for a condom before he shuffles his pants down to fall at his ankles and spreads her thighs with his knees. He rips the square packet open with both hands and eagerly rolls it down before placing Eight's head at my entrance and oh so slowly pushes all the way in.

"Ah Eight. That feels so good. I need more, I need all of you."

"Let me relish the feel of you baby, before you start bossing me around, beautiful."

"No! Now Eight, I need all of you now!"

Lane controls himself and pulls back slowly before he rams back in fast, making the desk move a few good inches across the floor. Our entire body is alive at this surprise attack and is on the verge of exploding already. And by Lane's desperate moves, so is he.

He reaches a hand under Alexis to pinch a nipple, making her scream in ecstasy, forgetting that other offices are nearby. Lane uses his other hand to cover her mouth as he continues to torture her hardened nipple, panting out his own arousal. He lets go of her nipple and smooths his hand down towards her centre, feeling where they are joined, rubbing his fingers around their combined wetness before pushing firmly against her clit, making our climax shoot hard through our body.

His hand muffles her scream as he buries his head into the back of her neck, muffling his own growl at his powerful explosion. They both become acutely aware of voices down the hallway, making them stumble apart, fixing their discarded clothes back into place quickly, my girl still in disbelief at the powerful sensations Lane brought to her body in record time.

He reaches out and grabs her, cradling her to his chest, holding her lovingly as they both struggle to maintain a normal breath. Tears form at the back of my girl's eyes as emotions start to rise to the surface, but she fights them back, not wanting to dampen the great desk sex we just had.

"Eight, how the hell did that just happen and before you answer that, please promise me that will *not* be the last time we have desk sex. That was freaking hot!"

"Holy fuck, baby. I knew he was about to lose it but I didn't know he would take it that far. But damn I'm glad he did. I've always wanted desk sex and I'm so glad it was with you, Hot Lips. And if this is the beginning of regular sex with you, I guarantee I will do all that's within my power to make it happen on the desk at least once a week. Hell, once a day if that's what my girl wants."

"Damn I love you, Eight."

"I love you too, baby."

While *we* are thrilled at the result of Lane's restraint being broken, the two with the big brains are struggling a bit.

"Lane ..."

"I know Lexi baby. I'm so sorry I broke our plan. I just couldn't continue another minute without feeling you close to me and ... well ... I kind of lost it when I got you in my arms."

"This week's been hard and we've been completely distracted by each other, but Lane, this intimacy is just going to make it worse. It will become too hard to maintain the professionalism we need to finish this project. And what if your colleagues in the hallway just heard us, how is that going to look for the both of us? They might applaud you, but the woman in these situations don't always fare so well."

"Fuck Lexi. I'm so sorry, I didn't think of that, I would be gutted if this got out and your work ethic was criticised because of it. Damn, just the thought of it affecting you that way ... I'm sorry, I really am. I will try my hardest to keep it out of the office."

"Lane, not just out of the office but ... it has to stop all together for now. We both live in the city, our current client's main building is only a matter of blocks away, and we need to be seen as the professionals our reputation precedes. We have to stick to our plan, if ... that's still something you want."

Lane pulls her into his arms in a tender embrace, both sighing with the simple contact. Heartbeats settle and breathing returns to normal, but the reality is that even this simple pleasure has to be placed on hold if they are to stick to the plan they originally agreed upon. Lane places a soft kiss to her forehead before pulling back, dropping his embrace of my girl.

"I'm sorry again, Lexi, I didn't think through all the consequences and I promise I'll try to be on my best behaviour from now on."

"Then why are you grinning, Mr. Anderson?"

"Because … I said I'll try. Now let me walk you out to your tram stop before you disappear into the night."

Lane's gentleman act lasts until we reach our stop. As the tram pulls into place, he cups Alexis's cheek and plants a hard kiss to her lips, a kiss with promises of things to come, before pulling back with a panty dropping smile and turning to head back towards our building. My girl's head is spinning as she stands in the middle of the tram carriage, swaying as it moves slowly, smiling despite trying not to. Yeah, Mr. Uptight has turned our world upside down in more ways than one.

The tram ride is short as we head to a quiet little bar to have a quick drink with our girls. We have so much to catch up on I'm not sure where to start. It's not until we walk into the urban modern entrance and take two steps down, walking towards the laughter of Zali, that I come up with the first words I need to tell my fellow intimates.

"I just had DESK SEX!"

"Oh my God! Welcome to the club, babe." Yes, Mel was the first to join that club.

"Congratulations on having your desk cherry popped! It is so freaking hot isn't it? Did everyone look at Lane and Lexi different when they walked out of the office? I remember Zali blushing up a storm after her first desk romp. She is a screamer, so no wonder the entire floor heard her. Thank God she had the confidence to carry it off with just a smile before going back to work." And Zali certainly didn't stop there. Lucky girl.

"Well, that's the problem right there. No one heard them I think but, if it did get out, Alexis was in a bit of a panic of how it would make her look."

"She would look hotter than she already does in people's eyes. Your girly overthinks things a lot. But enough of her thoughts, tell us yours. Was it scorching, was it fast, was it hard? Men seem to think because there is a solid surface underneath, they can go as hard as a bloody bull. Which feels fucking awesome, but my girl has received plenty of bruises due to frantic desk sex. But it's a good kind of pain, a sensual kind of pain, a steamy kind of pain. Oh damn, my lace agent provocateurs are getting wet! I better sniff out a hotty in here to blame it on." Zali does wear her sexy bruises like medals at times.

"There's two sitting at three o'clock. One's a suit, I can smell his silk shirt that he probably paid way too much for and the other is a tradie, he has that raw wood kind of smell. Mmm, raw wood. Oh yeah, I'd like to get up close and personal with his raw wood alright." Sounds like Mel's in for a woody night.

"Well you two can have one each, because Alexis is so wrapped up in the former Mr. Uptight that she is silently counting down the days until this project of theirs is over. But I need details next time. Especially about the tradie's wood."

Alexis spills the beans on everything Lane, while the girls sit there silently, which is odd, because they are never silent. My girl tells them all of Lane's sweet words and the situation at work and everything she is currently feeling. I feel the relief washing over her body, it feels good to get it all off her chest. But the girls still sit there in silence.

"Say something, anything."

"You might not like what I have to say. But we have all vowed to be honest with each other, always, even if we know it may hurt, so here goes. You are not falling for the man, Lexi, you have already completely fallen. You, my sweet friend, are utterly and completely in love with him."

You can't hide a single thing from our girl Mel.

"I'm falling, I agree with that, but I'm not there yet. It's too soon."

"You're not being honest with yourself, if that's what you think. Because it's written as plain as day across your face and in between the words you're speaking. You ... are ... in ... love. You are just scared to admit it because of Mr. Confidence Smasher and I can't blame you there, but if you don't love again, you will never truly feel again. So honey, let go and enjoy that fine man who rammed you over your desk. If he can do that, he's a keeper."

Oh Zali, I love your brain.

"And if it is love and we screw it up because our work situation gets difficult, then what?"

"You need to find a balance of both. You can do it. But right now, I need to talk Hot Tradie into doing it with me tonight before Miss Bleach Barbie at the end of the bar walks over to him and sinks her claws in."

EIGHTEEN

He

You know, I think we can do this; we can get everything back to what it needs to be. I can feel the confidence flowing out of you like a hole in a keg, bro. *Please* don't let it just be hot air and foolishness, I don't think either of us could take that fall.

You know what we need? We need to go see the boys, get a few down our neck and have a decent night of it. Maybe you can see what they would do. Well, we both know what Bookend would do, and we don't want that, but when paired with Benji, well, they can be, *insightful*, and I'll see if the guys, mainly Henry, have any ideas. Okay, so that's what we're doing. Just toss your jacket and briefcase in the car and head on down, don't sod about getting changed. Come on, let's get going.

••••

"Sup bitches, how's it hanging?"

"Hey, not bad bro, not bad. Henry's been waxing philosophical all evening, I think Bookend has a new squeeze. Not seen him like this since that Russian chick got her Cyrillic muff on Henry."

"Yeah I remember her, couldn't understand a single word she said, but shit, her girl could drink with the best of us."

"So what's new with you and B.E?"

"Well, uh, you know what, fuck it."

"Come on bro, spill, we can both see something is up with you, spill."

"Uh, well, you know what, I'm in deep and I mean deep. Lexi, shit, she's perfect, she's everything. I just don't know how to tell her exactly how I feel, I've fallen hard for her, boys. I really have, but, I just, ah fuck. You know what I mean."

"Yeah bro, I do, I was this way with Natasha, you'll know the time when it comes. Just for now, try the little things, you know, keep it subtle and soft."

"Well you boys heard that, and know my boy is head over heels and well, so am I. Hot Lips is fucking amazing, she makes my world complete and well, I love her, I absolutely and unequivocally love her. No two ways about it boys, I'm in love."

"Well, I for one am thrilled for you. You deserve a chance at happiness. I know Lane's last girl wasn't one to sniff at, but we all know you never felt like you have here, when it came to her camel toe. That girl was septic, yeesh, bad hoodoo."

"Thanks Henry, and yeah it was, bad everything when it came to that bitch, but Hot Lips and Lexi, they've washed everything away; nothing is left behind to tarnish anything when it comes to our love for her."

"You really are head over heels for her ain't you, bro. Kudos, it's rare to find that kind of love, I hope it pans out, bro, you deserve it."

"So Benji, Booker, I know you're holding something back, so come on, lay it on me."

"Mate, we've both been there, the ache in your gut and the thump in your chest when you're near her. Yeah we've been there, best thing either of us can tell you is, don't wait, don't be a pussy and hide what you're feeling, just tell her. No if's, and's, or but's; just straight up honesty. Look her square in the face, take her hands in yours and tell her."

"Benji is right, Lane, you have to tell her, sooner rather than later, bro.

You don't want to fuck it up before you get started or let her slip through your fingers."

"Thing is boys, I just don't want to scare her off, with all that has happened with both of us … well … there is a lot of professional crap we have to deal with and I'm worried that if I do something that brings it all crashing back, it will … well … just turn us both on our heads."

"What the hell are you on about, Lane?"

"I don't want to fuck up and scare her off by saying something wrong."

"Then why the hell didn't you just say that, you dickhead!"

"I did! You two fuckers are just too dull to see it!"

"Oh fuck off! We're here, trying to help you and you go and insult us, well fuck you very much Mr. Anderson, next time we'll just tell you to get piss off, shall we?"

"Sorry Booker, seriously, sorry, you too, Benji."

"So you fucking should be, but seriously mate, you need to tell her how you feel before it's too late to salvage the situation. You guys can find a way to work it around your work, ya know."

"I know Benji, I know, I'm just terrified of what could happen."

"Aren't we all when we love someone?"

••••

Well Lane, are we going to tell Lexi how you feel? It's blatantly obvious she knows already, so what are you waiting for? The rapture, the end of days, your mum to swoop in and do it for you? Man up and freaking do it already. I'm open enough to tell Hot Lips I love her and just how much she means to me and as you well know, *I'm a freaking penis!* You're a grown man, so fucking act like one. Go out there and tell that woman just what she means to you, or both you and I are going to lose the women we love.

"They're right, I know they're right and I know exactly what I need to do … so … what is stopping me? Why am I hesitating so much? I love her, I

love her unlike anyone else, hell, I think she is the one. But, why am I so scared, is it just because I'm afraid of the vulnerability that comes with it? Shit, I don't know. Lexi is my one and only, but here I am acting like a child wanting some comforting arm to take me in and do this all for me, which is, well, simply not me. Fuck, no, I can't carry on like this, Lexi is my beginning and my end, she is it for me, she deserves to know. I need her to know exactly what she means to me. Monday, Monday is the start of it all, no more avoiding it, I am telling her. Project be damned, she deserves the real me and I need her to see me for who I am. I just hope I can be the patient man she needs me to be. Come what may, I'm going to try, for her, I'm going to try, even if it breaks my heart in the process. She's worth the risk."

Yes! That's my boy, about Goddamned time, where's the champagne? We need to pop a cork to celebrate this, this is one moment that needs to be celebrated. Atta boy, Lane, fucking hell yes. Let's do this! Oh, yeah, you want to celebrate by popping *that* type of cork. Okay, I'm up for it.

I'm coming, Hot Lips, your man is coming home.

••••

Monday:

That's it, new week, new progress and a chance to actually change Lexi's mind and get our girls back. I really hope you can pull this off, Lane, I don't know how much more I can take of this; the awkwardness, the need to feel her, the sudden snatches of her perfume as she moves through the office or past us to get something from the printer or the filing cabinets. Those soft little glances she casts at us when she thinks we're not watching her. I really don't know how close you can force me before my limit kills me.

Friday was fantastic, we needed it, but it's like putting a plaster over a hole in a dam. I don't know if it's going to be enough to sate all that we're keeping inside. Fuck, I need my woman, Lane, and I know you need yours. Miss Queen Bitch is gone, bro; she is dead, buried and locked so far in the past that not even Jacques Cousteau could find her arse.

So there is now nothing and I mean nothing that can stop us. So, get your warrior face on bro and go, go tell our girl exactly what she means to you and get our women back.

"Lexi, can I ..."

"Not right now Lane, we've hit a solid vein here, come on take a look, tell me what you think of this!"

Damn she smells great today, and so does my girly. Mmm damn bro, hang on what are you doing. Oh nice, little stealthy touches. Yeah okay, soft and slow, run that little finger of yours along the outside of her hand, get her distracted, just play it off as nothing, don't even acknowledge what you're doing, just slow and easy, back and forth along the top of her hand. Just like that.

"These designs are fantastic Lexi, freaking fantastic, you've got a great skill with Photoshop and an eye for spacing. Great work, I think the client will be impressed with these."

Okay now, while she is struggling to separate from the physical and mental affection, cover her hand with yours and squeeze gently for a few seconds and then at the last moment make deep eye contact. That's it, just like that. God, her eyes are like falling into lagoons of cool tropical water. Damn it, if I were you I'd never look away. But we have to, it's been six seconds too long already.

The rest of the morning carries on with more of the same, Lexi and Lane dancing around each other with my boy casting sly and overt passes at our girl, soft little strokes here, the back of his hand over her hip as he passes her on the way to the in-office photocopier and a quick brush across her back as he leans in past her to stare at what she has worked on in the intervening hours. Lunch comes all too quickly, but the scent coming off both my Hot Lips and Lexi, well, Lane would be a fool to miss his mark and Lane's mama didn't raise a fool.

Lane is following a few feet behind Lexi as they head towards the stairwell, the rest of the offices a hive of after lunch activity, as they catch up and follow on with calls and work. A sly grin falls over my boy's face as he speeds up, catching hold of Lexi's elbow and drags her into the emergency exit access, the rarely used off shoot of the main stairwell, standing cool and dark as the door starts to swing shut.

"Lane, what on earth are you ..."

"Shh."

My boy rips his tie from his neck, jamming it into the hasp on the doorframe before the door swings shut. The bunched up silk stops it from trapping them inside as he pins Lexi to the wall, his lips snaring hers as I hear my girl moan.

"Mmm Eight, our girl needs this and she needs it bad even if she has been trying to fight it! Come on, get your big self in me and fill me up, my walls are aching for your touch, baby."

"Damn it girl, here I come, open wide baby."

The condom in Lane's grip slips over me as he spins Lexi to face the wall, her hands coming up as she spreads them flat against the cold surface of the stairwell. He flips her skirt up onto her back; the sound of tearing nylon fills the air as he rips the crotch out of Lexi's tights. The sodden cotton of her panties is pushed aside as she gasps at the sudden and all too welcome assault on her and her clothing.

"Damn baby, my girl is loving this, now get your sexy self inside me. I need my man and I need him now."

"Oh here I come, baby, here I come."

With an echoing slap across Lexi's backside Lane spears me in, the feel of her soaked panties scraping along my shaft making both of us shiver as his hips slap against her warm skin.

"Fuck baby, I just couldn't hold back, I needed you and I needed you bad."

"I don't care Lane, I need it too!"

He curls his hand in our girl's hair as he drags her blouse upwards, his hand slipping inside her bra, thumb and finger twisting and teasing at her nipple as he drives me deeper into her wet core.

"Oh baby, you feel so good, oh yeah Eight, fill me deep, that's it, oh fuck yes, fill me till you break me!"

"Keep talking like that and I will do more than break you, baby."

Lexi yelps slightly as Lane sends another stinging crack across her backside as I sink deeper into Hot Lips' scorching heat. The sound of my boy's hips slapping against Lexi's taut butt fills the air as he grunts and groans, the sound of her panting breath driving us both crazy as I feel myself swell inside her, Hot Lips clutching at me as I feel my head catch at her quivering entrance before I drive deep into her shivering wetness again.

"Fuck Lane, oh God, yes, yes!"

"Damn it baby, I just couldn't help it, I was dying trying to stop from taking you in the office again."

The smell of sex fills the air as Lane ravishes Lexi's neck, her skin turning a soft pink as he continues to drive me into her to the hilt.

"God, I'm coming baby, I'm coming."

"Oh yes I can feel it, yes, oh God Lane, I'm coming, I'm coming."

His lips snare Lexi's again as she struggles to stop herself screaming; my head explodes as I feel Hot Lips ripple around me, her walls dragging me deep as she drains everything from me. They stand, leaning against the wall, panting as sweat rolls down Lane's neck, Lexi's supple form moulding against us as I slowly begin to shrink.

"Fuck, baby, that was intense."

"God, was it ever, I haven't felt my girl go so fast in years and you and your boy are magic. Mmm damn, I love you."

"I love you too baby, I love you too."

The rest of the day passes in a blur of quiet flirting, sly petting and subconscious need as they both bask in their secret stairway tryst.

Tuesday:

Well today is a hot one, and I don't mean hot as in sexy. Clients are in and they're looking for something impressive or blood. Either way they're going to be leaving with something and my boy and girl, well, they're more nervous than a Jew in the Vatican.

So I guess there's nothing for us to do but wait and see what the rest of the day brings. Which, if I'm getting the feel of things from my boy correct, a lot of tension, a lot of 'business' and finally, a hell of a lot of squeaky bed springs if he has his way. But he doesn't, neither of them do and it looks like, as they're standing here waiting for their clients, that nothing is going to stop the hammering of my boy's heart.

Lane turns and smiles at Lexi, her eyes wide as she clutches at her hands. My boy reaches out, his hand finding hers, offering a soft comforting squeeze as she turns her gaze upon his. Her blue eyes are brimming with a mix of fear and excitement as my boy's heart skips a beat. Both of them snap back to reality, the moment shattering as the door to the boardroom opens and the clients walk in.

••••

The meeting drags on, the clients resisting slightly as both my boy and Lexi fight to lay out their combined ideas. Eventually, after what feels like a century of smashing their heads into concrete, the clients begin to see sense and listen to what my boy and girl are saying.

"So, that's basically the entire proposed design, from the campaign's initial run right through to the multi-media distribution. I think the only thing we haven't worked in here is a mass leaflet drop from a C130."

Oh Lane, dude, really bad call, bro.

"What Mr. Anderson means is that we both feel we have covered every conceivable angle. If, in the next few days before we wrap up designs and send it through to the distribution teams, you come up with anything else you feel is needed or should be included, do not hesitate to call or email either of us."

"Thank you, Miss Ryan, we may just do that. Mr. Anderson, thank you

as well, although the jokes ... well ..."

"Yeah, sorry about that, I get my sense of humour from my father ..."

"Don't we all. Anyway, congratulations to you. I feel we certainly made the right choice hiring the both of you. I shall forward my findings to the board and be in touch soon. Good day to you both."

Come on dude, that was pretty lousy, but, oh okay you're not even paying attention here, well, screw you then.

"So Lexi, what would you say to dinner?"

"No Lane, we need to keep this professional."

"Professional, you didn't say anything like that yesterday, or Friday. So if you don't want dinner ... how about we ... toast this some other way."

His lips slip along her neck, leaving a soft shimmering trail of flushed, pink skin in their wake. My boy's fingers dance along the buttons of Lexi's blouse as she tries in vain to fight the growing arousal that Hot Lips is goading into a raging inferno.

"Mmm Lane, not here, oh, oh God that feels good."

A deep growl leaves my boy as Lexi's backside grinds against me and Lane's lust builds. I need to be free, free to sink deep into the moist centre of Hot Lips, but damn it if her arse rubbing over me doesn't feel delicious.

Her fingers reach around to snatch at the zip to Lane's pants as he slips his fingers through the layers of Lexi's skirt and panties, her wetness soaking them as he rubs slow circles over her clit.

"Damn baby, your boy's fingers feel gorgeous, oh please have him sink them deeper, we both want it bad."

"Oh he will be baby, just you wait."

Hot Lips swallows my boy's fingers whole as he slips one after another in Lexi's dripping heat. Lexi claws at her panties, forcing them down her legs as Lane drags me free, a condom already lying partially open on the table as Lexi reaches round and begins to stroke her hand along my thickening shaft.

Without another word, the skin of latex slips over me and I'm sinking deep into the rippling warmth that is Hot Lips.

"Fuck baby, I have wanted this badly, I cannot keep you out of my head. The amount of time I spend at night coaxing everything I can from me, I don't know how I'm standing."

"Stop talking Lane, and go harder."

The table rocks and shudders as Lane drives me deep, the sound of skin meeting skin filling the air as Lexi fights to keep her moans soft. Lane reaches around, her bobbing breasts teasing his fingers as he snatches at her nipple. She whimpers, biting hard on her hand as he teases the soft bud between his thumb and forefinger.

"Oh God, keep doing that, I'm going to come."

I throb and flex at her words, Lane's lust and desire rising as I swell another inch inside Lexi, Hot Lips cooing as I sink as deep as I can into her soaked silk, feeling her walls slide against me. Lane grins as my sack tightens, their growled words lost amidst the sounds of their animal lust.

"Oh damn, I'm coming, I'm coming."

"Damn girl me too. Fuck!"

"Eight, baby, that has to be the quickest orgasm my girl has ever had. What is up with these two?"

"I don't know baby, I just don't know. Lane just can't turn it off. Hell, I probably have blisters with all the midnight strokings I'm getting. Wouldn't surprise me if we give Kleenex this year's sales quota single handed!"

"Well, whatever it is, he can keep doing it. Mmmm, he can keep doing it all night long."

Wednesday:

Today, well, it's an odd one. Lexi seems a bit peeved, yet yesterday, she was all for it. I swear the boardroom still smells of sex and sweat. Hell, client satisfaction has tripled overnight after Lane and Lexi's after party, but still, today's odd.

No matter what my boy does, he is rebuffed at every turn, it's like she's suddenly become a nun. No matter what he does, be it a cute little kiss on her cheek when no one is looking or a sly touch here and there, she just glares daggers at him and swats his hand away. I'm confused as hell and so is Hot Lips. She is getting so many mixed readings from her girl, one side is as wet as the ocean and the other is drier than the Sahara desert in summer time. I mean seriously, you could sand a wall with how dry one side of my girl is right now.

Still, the day rolls on, with my boy being rebuffed at every turn, those frowns never straying far from Lexi's forehead as she aims it at us again. Hot Lips tells her to stop, the noise tearing at me as I struggle to comprehend the change in our girl; it's not as if it's *that* time of the month. My girl would have given me a warning if that was coming; being on the receiving end of a red bashing is never a good thing. People think oh yeah, safe day, messy, but safe. *Fuck off;* do you have any idea what it does to a chap's moral to be sent into that on those days? Regardless of the fact that she is weeping *and* screaming at you while you're doing it, it's like the first night of the Somme, no one comes out of that situation without some kind of scar.

"Baby, what the hell is going on? I haven't seen someone this frustrated since I watch Benji's mum kick his third girlfriend out because they'd had sex in the bath after she'd just cleaned it."

"I wish I knew, Eight, I wish I knew. She is totally confused; hell, there is less sense coming out of her than a Chinese VCR manual."

"Did you just make a culture pun?"

"Yep."

"And you wonder why I fell in love with you."

"I never said that."

"You didn't have to."

"Lexi, hold on for a moment."

"What, Lane?"

"You've been pushing me back all day, have I pissed you off?"

"No."

"Then what did I do?"

"Nothing, it's fine."

"Oh come on."

"Seriously, it's fine."

"Lexi, that is bullshit, there's something wrong, and I get the feeling it's my fault."

"I said, it's fine, so it's fine, okay?"

My boy steps forwards, his arms slipping around her waist as he pulls her close to him, his lips finding their way to her neck as she pushes back slightly.

"Are you sure now?"

"Mmm, uh, what? What was the question?"

"Nothing important."

Well, that was quick. Lane turns Lexi to face us as I stir against his briefs and zip, the scent of my girl making me throb as I ache for the feel of her. Lane nips and sucks at her neck as he sinks his fingers in Lexi's backside, lifting her from the floor and carrying her to his desk.

"I want you so badly, I just don't know how I stop myself from taking you in the lobby each day. You've woken something in me, Lexi, and I just can't stop it from taking over."

"Lane ... umm ... ahh ..."

The condom is out and unwrapped before I can even think, Lexi staring at us as I push past the rapidly descending zip, slapping against her bare thigh as she sinks her heels into Lane's lower back.

"Just how many of those do you have, anyway?"

"Enough."

"You knew this was going to happen again, huh?"

I drive deep into Hot Lips' waiting silk as Lexi pulls us tight to her, Lane's sudden grunt making us both jump as the desk shakes under the sudden pressure. Lexi groans deep in her throat as I bottom out and fill her completely.

The smell of sex soaks the air as Hot Lips floods us with desire,

Lane's thrusting hips slapping against the back of Lexi's legs, the desk jumping under each rampant spearing.

"Yes, oh yes, Lane, fuck."

"Oh fuck Lexi, take it baby. Take it all."

Time blurs as Lexi and Lane's coupling sends work scattering to the floor, his desk shuddering as he drives me deep into our girls' soaked depths.

"Here it comes baby, open wide, I know you want it."

"Oh yeah, Eight, give it to me, let me suck you dry."

"Oh fuck baby, take it, take it all."

Thursday:

Well another day, another dollar. Are we going to get some actual work done today, bro, or are you … oh, okay then.

"Lane, we haven't even started work yet!"

"I've locked the door and work be damned. I want you, and I want you now!"

"Lane, seriously, I … I …"

"I need you Lexi, so damned badly."

"What the fuck, baby! Does your boy ever stop? I'm still sore from yesterday's romp."

"You and I both, baby, but Lane is pumping so much blood into me I couldn't stay limp if I wanted to."

"Well, I guess we better just go with the flow then."

"Yeah baby, I guess we better, open wide babe."

"Come on in then, big boy."

••••

"Baby, please tell me your boy is out of juice for the rest of the day, I don't think I can take much more. I love you, but I'm exhausted and need a rest."

"You and I both, baby, but I honestly don't know. I don't know where he is getting it from, it's insane, he's never been like this with anyone before. I think my head is developing an RSI from all the thrusting."

"You think that's bad, I think I have friction burn on my bloody internal walls. You do realise that is supposed to be impossible!"

"I'll do what I can, babe, but I can't promise anything; you've seen how he can get."

"Thank you, baby."

"Anything for you."

The rest of the day is thankfully sex free, Lane and Lexi both diligently working to catch up on all the work they had 'fucked away' the past week. Day folds into afternoon before either of them rises from their desk, Lane's only contribution to the day's 'conversation' coming in the form of asking if Lexi wanted a coffee. A soft muttered no thank you was his only reply.

I can't help but notice that as the day has worn on, the energy that usually fills the air has begun to darken, Lexi's shoulders dropping a little with each passing hour as she buries herself further and further into her work. I need to ask, but I'm afraid of the answer I might get if I do question Hot Lips on whether or not our girl is feeling okay. I bite my tongue, or I would if I had one, and press on with keeping Lane on task and try to ignore my mounting concern for the wilting flower in the corner.

I can feel Lane begin to come around to what I have already noticed, his brow furrowing as he casts his eyes over towards our girl. I can feel concern flowing off him, his gaze lingering a lot longer than it ever has before, as Lexi sits hunched at her desk.

••••

Time clocks out well before anyone in the office, Lexi ignoring the shuffling growl that is now audible as the rest of the floor filters past the door. In silence they move, packing up their bags and cases, neither uttering a word to the other. Lane too unsure of what is going on, and me, well, I'm terrified to even ask my girl what has so suddenly switched between our two.

The walk to the elevator reeks of silence, the clicking of Lane's shoes and the dulled tapping of Lexi's heels the only noise in the now tomb like floor. The ring of the elevator bell is deafening as they both step through the open door, not a word passing between them as they are ferried down to the bustling foyer.

My boy keeps casting furtive glances at Lexi, her stoic, almost stonewalled face making him more than nervous as he watches the doors in front of them open, tracking her face in the polished chrome.

Even now, with the fervour of the foyer, the silence that cocoons them both shatters everything, not one word uttered between them as they move through the hustle and bustle of departing office workers and rapidly moving night cleaners. The torrent of the outside world slams down around us, the noise crushing everything and still they remain silent. I'm beyond terrified and into a world of fear so pronounced that I don't think I can ever fully pull myself from it at the moment, let alone Lane.

The walk to the tram stop is slow, measured by each step, the tap of Lane's shoes echoing the click of Lexi's heels as they make their way towards her ride home.

Standing in front of the tram, I finally find my voice, calling to my girl at the last moment, all the while Lane and Lexi stand staring at each other in silence.

"Baby, I don't like this, it's worrying me. A lot."

"I know Eight, it's come out of nowhere, but I'll try and fix this. I love you."

"I love you too, baby, please always remember that, no matter what happens, I'm yours."

"And I'm yours too, baby, nothing will ever change that."

"Well, goodnight Lexi."

"Yeah, night Lane."

Fuck, do something Lane, lean in, kiss her, do something. Okay better than nothing, a quick peck on the cheek, shit, something is wrong, big time. Fuck!

••••

Okay, okay, okay. Oh, crap. What are we going to do, bro? Something has changed and I don't know how to fix it. Damn it, why can't you just duct tape emotions like you can everything else? Damn it all to hell, Lane Anderson, what have you done?

"Fuck. That was frosty, so damned frosty, what the hell happened? I don't know, whatever it is, it needs to be gone. No matter what, I'm going to try and fix this. I need her to know now, she deserves to know, to know that I love her and I'm not leaving work tomorrow until she knows it. I'm not going to risk her slipping through my fingers. We'll work it out. We've got to work it out."

Yep, we *have* to work it out, because I can't live without my girls. That is a reality I refuse to think about.

NINETEEN
She

My girl is in a strange place. We came home; she turned the TV on and just sat. We never just sit and watch mindless TV or news. We usually come in, maybe chuck on a load of washing so we don't have to do it over the weekend, organise some dinner, answer personal emails or Facebook messages, then we may sit with dinner and our laptop open at our small dining table. We usually clear all thoughts of work by the last mouthful so we can either settle in to watch our favourite reality show or shove on a movie. If we really want to chill we would have the bath running during dinner, then slide in with a good book waiting beside us. We don't just sit and stare at the boring news.

I can't quite tell where her mind is at and that's probably because she can't either. She is torn between loving all the sneaky office sex this week and the way Lane brought her body to climax faster than she knew was possible and feeling insecure, wondering if Lane is just attracted to the thrill of an office affair.

She is not that type of girl. She has always held her work with the highest of respect and if one of her friends had ever asked if she would be involved in an office fling, she would be the first to say 'hell no.' She loves her job too much to ever risk it on a casual desk fuck. Was that what it was for Lane? Damn, now she has me doubting the poor man.

Eight has told me the depths of Lane's feelings for Alexis so I doubt her thoughts are correct. I believe that past insecurities could be at play here, insecurities that never seem to be too far from the surface.

Do we ever truly lose them? Our past pains, our past heartbreaks, our past issues with ourselves? Even when we have found our happy place, it only takes one song, one scent, one taste to have us crashing back to a place of considerable pain and doubts. But that's what makes us who we are. Our past. The good and the bad, the happy and the sad, the pleasurable and the painful. All of our past makes us who we are today. And because of that, we will always be wiser today than yesterday. We learn how to be better people with each passing day.

But some scars are deeper than others and finding your boyfriend, the man you love, in bed with another woman is a scar that cuts so deep it can never truly be erased despite all the happiness in the world coming your way. Despite knowing deep within her heart she is indeed head over heels in love with Lane, the past will always have her doubting his motives and that is something I'm not sure I can ever truly help with.

She is thinking that if she does throw all of her trust into this thing with Lane and he turns out to only be attracted to the thrill inside the office walls, what happens then? They work in the same building, they enter the same door, they walk through the same lobby, they may end up in the same elevator more than once a week. How in the hell will she ever recover with him constantly within reach?

I try and flood her with happy juice and give the brain a heads up to fill her full of memories of their weekend at Lane's beach house. The way he swooped in and rescued her, the way he was so attentive to her needs and vulnerability, his quiet caring and loving side. The way he kissed her lips, both sets. His soft words, his gentle touches, the way he fucked her and the way he gently made love to her, revealing the depths of his feelings without using words.

That weekend certainly wasn't about a thrill behind office doors or in cold stairwells. It was about a woman and a man no longer able to fight the chemistry between them. That weekend was real, that's where we met the real Lane Anderson. She needs to remember that, she needs to see that his feelings are as real in the office as they were that weekend. Yes, I admit, his way of showing them now is a little more risqué, but the truth behind his actions is still the same. He wants her in his life.

As much as I pump her with the good stuff, it doesn't work. The visons of her ex in bed with that barely legal piece of candy keeps playing on repeat in her memories. She was too boring and nice for him, so she thinks there is every chance that Lane may come to that conclusion one day also. And by then, she may not be able to salvage her poor heart.

With that thought, before I even have a chance to come up with a plan, she decides she needs to stop what's going on between her and Lane completely. Nothing here, there, or in between. It is causing her to not work at her full potential. And if it's truly meant to be, then after the project is finished and their campaign is a success, they will still have their feelings for each other and the time to pursue them outside of the office. If he really does feel as deeply for her as she hopes, as he has displayed in his own way, he will understand and he will wait. Won't he?

Oh dear God. I feel this is a big risk. It's like that saying, *'If you love someone, set them free, if they come back, be sure to have them tested for STDs.'* Oh fuck, not that one, that's Mel's favourite. The other one. *'If you love someone, set them free, if they come back, it's meant to be.'* But will she be able to cope if he doesn't come back? Surely that will hurt more than the possibility of their current situation damaging their careers.

This is all just fucked and not in a good way. I hate this, I hate the thought of her walking away now and Lane deciding not to follow. Big brain and I flood her with memories and feelings of the beach weekend, but it does nothing to change her resolve. She wants to protect her heart and truly feels that her plan is the only way. I really hate that word plan at the moment, that word is fucking everything up for me. I finally found the one and she is sending him away.

BOB is so not getting a rise out of me anytime soon.

••••

Alexis gave herself a talk in the mirror this morning but I tuned her out. I don't care what she has to say. To save her own heart she is breaking mine in the process and I just don't know how to deal with it. I feel more out of control at this moment than I have ever felt in my life. Who am I kidding, *my life*, I don't have a life apparently. I'm only here to remove a person's waste, give them pleasure and push out something the size of a watermelon when the population needs a boost. My feelings are never taken into consideration. Why were we made with lips if they don't come with a voice? It sucks lemons, I tell you, not that I have actually sucked a lemon, but the rumour is, some women in the Philippines have, along with ping pong balls apparently. Why? Who the hell knows that answer!

I don't feel up to walking today so I send out tired hormones to make her ride a tram instead. I don't even care about the squishy crowd or odour coming from the hippy dude next to me. My caring has left me temporarily.

"What's up, kat?"

"Nothing much. How about you, um, dude?"

"Nothing, until I got a whiff of your girl's natural smell. She is sweet. Do you taste as sweet as she smells?"

"Well Mr. Dreadlocks, why don't you shimmy up a little closer and see if you can find out."

"What the fuck? Seriously? I've never had a chick respond to my words as fast as that before. Maybe that weed Jake got for me last night really does have super powers like he said. Hey, maybe I can even stay hard longer than thirty seconds now. Watch out kat, my doggy is coming to play."

Oh shit! He really is coming for us. His guy pretends to bump into Alexis, mumbling a sorry, but not moving away from her personal space. As much as I was pissed at my girl, I don't really want to invite strangers to get up in our junk, especially one that smells like a lawnmower that hasn't been cleaned since last century. This trip is not the holiday I dream about.

"Hey kat. Your girl's not responding. What are we doing wrong? Fuck, maybe I need to re-boost my superpowers. Hang on, I'll get my guy to light up another doobie."

And *that's* our sign to get of this ride, man.

After feeling uncomfortable with Mr. Dreadlocks pressing up against her and hopping off two stops early, our uncomfortable feeling doesn't stop because as we reach our building we can clearly see Mr. Stalker at his usual lookout point at the waterfront. Lexi raises her head and continues to walk confidently towards her building. She will not show her fear or panic at the thoughts that this man may have been her attacker down the laneway.

As she turns towards the door of our building, she notices he doesn't turn her way, but can still see his creepy stare as he watches out of the corner of his eyes. A feeling of nausea washes over us. My girl struggles to maintain her composure as she makes her way through the crowded lobby. She is about to step onto the elevator when someone grabs her elbow. She screams in fright as her mind imagines Mr. Stalker slithering through the crowd, waiting to catch her with her guard down.

"I didn't mean to scare you Lex, I just wanted to tell you we haven't received any phone calls lately. "

Holy fuck! It's just Alecia, the receptionist from our own offices. Damn, my poor girl's heart is taking a pounding with that fright. She has tears at the back of her eyes she is desperately trying to keep from falling.

"Thank you Alecia, I really appreciate you letting me know."

I'm thankful the ride is packed as we all cram in and Alecia starts to talk to someone else she knows. My poor girly needs a moment to compose herself before heading into Lane's office.

I don't want to walk in there. How is my Eight going to take the news that the waiting game is back on? Will Lane agree or will he get sick of the complications? Work romances aren't always romantic, they can be complicated and dangerous in more ways than one, but with their workload only going to increase with each coming week, distracting each other will only cause unwanted stress. Well, that's what Alexis is thinking when she walks into Lane's office ready to tell him her thoughts.

"Oh Hot Lips, today is going to be a good day, baby."

"Umm, I'm not so sure about that, Eight."

"What? Why baby?"

"Maybe you should just wait for Alexis to start talking. Just remember, it's not forever."

"What the fuck?"

Lane is just finishing up a phone call when Alexis walks in and places her laptop and bag down at her desk. She is trembling with fear and doubt, yet I can still feel that she is adamant that what she's about to say is for the best.

"Good morning, Lexi. I have something important I need to discuss with you."

"Morning, Lane. There is something I also need to tell you. Do you mind if I go first?"

"Of course Lexi. Go for it."

He is awfully chirpy today. I'm not looking forward to the aftermath of this next conversation.

"Lane ... I've been thinking. With the pressures of this campaign only going to increase, along with the workload, I can ... I can no longer continue what's going on between us right now. It's becoming difficult to

separate life and work and that's resulting in my productivity decreasing. I'm having to do more work from home when it's late and I'm tired and I feel as if I'm not giving our client my best. I just … I just never saw myself in this type of situation. An office affair is not something I ever considered being a part of my life. Maybe when the project's finished we will both see things differently, but for now, work has to be my main focus. I hope you understand."

"Whoa, Hot Lips. This is bad, this is real bad. My boy's blood pressure just went through the freaking roof. He planned to confess his feelings for her and she comes out with that!"

"Hang on, what did you say?"

"He had this whole speech prepared and was going to tell her exactly how he feels, I mean *exactly* how he feels. He wanted to make her officially his and then was going to promise that he wouldn't let it affect their work. He had it all worked out in his head and now … fuck! This is bad."

"I understand, Alexis. This has been affecting our work and I can see the quality in what I produce is not up to my usual best. I agree it's for the best that we stop."

"Eight, he sounds so cold. This is breaking my girl's heart. She was hoping they could go back to their friendly selves and at the end, start something really meaningful together. Now she feels as if her worst fears are coming true and he really didn't have strong feelings for her."

"This is beyond fucked up, babe. My boy is pissed and hurt at the same time. These two are in exactly the same spot but neither realise it because they hold their feelings close to their chest for too fucking long. This is such a clusterfuck!"

"Oh Eight. What's going to happen now?"

"We pray, baby, we pray."

Alexis swallows hard as Lane stares at her with no emotion on his face, like she is a stranger who is interrupting his work day. She shifts from one foot to the other, not sure how to deal with this awkward moment and the feeling of her heart breaking in her chest.

"Lane ... I hope we can go back to our friendly selves. We still have a few more weeks left of this project with the stress only mounting. I hope this situation doesn't add to that."

"It won't. We will just focus entirely on work. So let's get started, shall we? We need to go over the change in colours for the digital campaign's main title; the last one looked too bland."

Okay, that right there was a direct hit to our girl. She had chosen that original colour, and at the time, Lane loved her choice. So this is how it's going to be now? He is going to revert straight back to Mr. Uptight? No in between, no real Lane, no compromise at all? To Alexis's credit, she holds her head high and moves over next to Lane to choose another colour while trying her hardest to hold her heart in place.

"Baby, I'm sorry. This is just ... self-preservation. He is hurting and his only way of coping is to completely shut himself off from her. Give him time, he will realise it soon enough."

"I just hope it's not too late when he does."

The rest of the morning is suffocating. You could cut the tension with a knife it's lying that thick in the cooped up air of this office. After choosing a new colour for the main title of their digital campaign, a colour Alexis believes will not work so well, but didn't want to cause an argument with Lane by speaking up, they spent the rest of the morning at their own desks in silence. The click of their keyboards is the only sound in the room. That and the loud beating of my girl's shattering heart.

She decides to be herself despite the ache in her chest and reach an olive branch out to Lane.

"I'm on a roll here, Lane, and it looks like you're also on a streak. Would you like me to order some lunch in so we can continue working?"

"No thank you, Alexis. I have a meeting to get to. In fact, I better get going. If anything work related comes up just text me."

Lane shuts down his laptop then pushes it into his briefcase before taking his suit jacket from the back of his chair and sliding it on. He grabs a set of keys from his top desk drawer and walks out of this office so fast I don't even have a chance to say a goodbye to Eight.

Alexis sits stunned for a few more minutes before she quietly gets up, walks over to the door and closes it. Flipping the latch to lock it, she slowly walks back to her desk and sits down on her chair. Then there is silence. Her breathing is slight and her heart is slow. It's not a reaction I was expecting and quite frankly, it's more alarming than if she was to burst into tears and drop her head onto the desk.

She breaths in slowly, lets it out just as slow, and then turns her attention back to her computer, continuing with the research she started an hour ago. I'm not sure what to do. If I knew exactly where her head was at, I would know what hormones to pump her with to get through the sting that Lane has left by his cold demeanour.

Seeing as it's work she is currently focusing on, big brain and I pump up her creative juices to hopefully keep her distracted, but the nothingness she is displaying is still alarming. She continues to hold her emotions back as the day slowly turns into night. When it's time to finish and Lane still hasn't returned, or messaged that he has been held up, well, that's her breaking point.

A single tear slips down her cheek, gripping the edge of her jaw for a few seconds before dropping to the document below. Her head quietly falls forward, and she stares at the water stain on the white paper slowly spreading out before it comes to a stop. Time is frozen in this single moment of silent pain. Soon another stain appears and another and then another. Tears silently fall as she tries to hold onto the heartbreak that is threatening to suffocate her.

As she sits there quietly sobbing, I feel a loss I have never felt before. Even the ex didn't cause this type of devastation. Is it because she truly saw Lane as being different despite her fears? Or is it because she was hoping he would understand and respect her need to quell things between them until the project was over? He agreed the first time they decided to put their attraction on hold. She didn't even get a chance to tell him she wanted to see where things went when the campaign was all over. His cold response left her feeling unable to ask him if he would … well … wait. His quick agreement to her words was not the response she was dreaming of.

So what now? How do you move on when you were doing everything you could to protect your heart and it ended up being broken anyway? You call your friends. We need our girls, stat!

••••

Even though the girls know Lexi isn't in the mood for some male company, they believe a little man candy wouldn't hurt, so that is why we are sitting in the garden of Largerfield Bar and Beer Garden, up against the glass, watching the lights of the city sparkle away.

"So what happened exactly? You told him that you both need to concentrate on work and he basically blew you off?"

"Something like that. I just … I really thought he would understand and say at least he would be willing to wait before we really started something, well, something more than office fucking. I feel like such a fool."

"No honey, you are not a fool, you did what you thought was right. We know you, we know your ironclad work ethic, so we understand and you were right to hope, no, expect him to respect that and in turn respect you. He's the fool, not you.

"I agree, Lexi. You did the right thing for both of you. You were thinking with your big head, and he wasn't, obviously. You deserve better. Like that tall glass of yumminess checking you out at the doorway. Now he looks like the respecting type. Enough respect to make a woman come first."

"Umm, thanks, but not tonight, Mel."

"Hey, a little harmless flirting will perk you up faster than that Cosmo

in your hand. Just saying."

Zali and Mel give Mr. Yumminess at the doorway and his three mates a couple of sly smiles, which of course have them walking over within a minute flat and joining our little group for more cocktails and beer.

"Hey sweetie. Your girl is giving off some pretty sad vibes. Is everything okay in your world?" Aww how sweet. Some dicks are nice.

"Just had a bad day, handsome, that's all."

"Well if we play our cards right, I could get my guy to make things better by morning. Unless she just needs a good cry and sleep to get her out of her funk. I don't want to cross a line or anything here."

"Thanks for the offer, but tonight's not a good one for us. But thanks for being sweet." My girl is in no shape for a one nighter at the moment and I have to agree, neither am I.

"Oh come on, Lexi is so in need of a good shag, something to fuck away her funk is definitely called for. Nothing better than the endorphins of an amazing O to wash away the sads. That's why so many single people hook up at a wedding. All those lonely people wishing it was them that had found true love, mixed with free booze, creates a wonderful shagfest." Mel can have all those type of hook-ups thanks, we'll pass.

"The way my guy just moved closer to your Lexi chick indicates he is about to try and pick her up. If you want me to back him off, please just say so, sweetie." As I said, some dicks are sweet, and some can be sour, but now's not the time to pay any attention to my tastebuds' memories.

"Aww, see, all dicks are not dicks all the time. You are so sweet. If Lexi is up for at least some harmless flirting, send your man my way." Yep, Mel is not fussy at all.

Lexi smiles at Mr. Yumminess but it's not her true flirty one. But I feel her wondering if this man is any better than Lane or will he also turn out to only be attracted to the thrill of something new and then move on. He places an arm around Alexis's shoulder and she doesn't shrug it off. She just sits quietly listening to the chatter around her.

"Hun, are you and your girl okay? I can feel Zali worried about her. She was hoping the man candy might at least distract her, but it's obviously not working."

"She's not doing so well. I think we should call it a night actually. She needs time to think and let today sink in. Then we need to find a way to move forward. I just ... I just wish my Eight was here."

"Oh babe, I'm so sorry. If it's meant to be it will all work out. Don't lose hope just yet."

Alexis announces she is going to hop on a tram and head home. After saying our goodbyes, we are surprised that Mr. Yumminess says he will walk us to the tram stop to keep us safe. We are even more surprised when he grabs Alexis's hand as they stroll down towards her stop. When she turns to say thanks and goodbye, we are stunned silent when he leans in and places a soft sweet kiss to the corner of her lips.

"I know that just cheered my night up, I hope it cheers yours up also, if even just a little bit. Night, Lexi, it was lovely to meet you."

Aww, what a nice man. Maybe we should have got his number, just for future references of course. The ride home is a blur as my girl's emotions start to catch up with her. Once inside the door of our apartment, she heads straight to our bedroom, strips off, gets under the covers and lets go. All of her insecurities come crashing down at once. Her worst fear was realised today as Lane did nothing but turn his back on her.

If only she knew that he was about to tell her he loved her. Bad timing fucking sucks!

TWENTY

He

Lane, where the hell are we going? Lane, Lane! For the love of God Lane, slow down, where the hell are you going? We need to go back, we've been gone an hour, Lane, we have work to do. Lexi is going to worry. You're taking me away from my girl, Lane, now fucking stop and go back to the office this instant!

"I spend all this time, showing her the real me, letting her in, we spend a weekend at the one place in the world that no one but me has been to in years; and now, she just tosses it all back in my face. Did none of it mean anything to her?"

Lane, get your arse back to that office *now*, stop being a complete punk and moping over the situation. I think you have it wrong, get back there and fix this. In that office are the women we love, the woman who, for the first time since Miss Queen Bitch, managed to chip her way through that iced block and deep into your heart. So get back there and talk to her, Goddamn it.

"Fuck it, I'm over it! I'm done, finished; file this under 'O' for over. I only agreed to that insane idea to save face, not just for me, but for her, and what do I get a face full of? Rejection and nothing more. Damn it, I could cry right now, this is so fucked up."

Lane, are you going to listen to me? Lane. Lane!

••••

Bro, you've got to slow down, you're going to crash and burn if you keep up this pace. Oh for crying out loud, at least use a glass for pity's sake. Oh Hot Lips, I wish you were here baby, this is too much for me to deal with on my own. Lexi has shattered him with a single sentence! Damn it, baby, I need you so badly right now.

Lane, lie down, stop, cease and desist. Put the bottle down and go to bed, please for the love of God just stop. Damn it Lane, I love you, man, but you are seriously testing the limit here, there are only so many times I can wake up to the daily sting of the night before, before it becomes too much. Or causes internal damage down my shaft.

Oh why do I even bother now? You stopped listening ages ago and now, well, Lexi and you weren't even officially in a relationship and here you are, falling apart at the first damned hurdle. I'd hate to see what'd happen if you two had had kids.

Can you at least call the boys and drunkenly pour out everything before you get to the third bottle?

"I ... I uh, I call need to Bookend phone."

Okay, so you're pissed already, not good, but you're thinking ... I think. At least you can have someone here that isn't so far into the wind that they're passing Mary Poppins on the inside lane. Just call Benji and Booker and get them over here, now Lane.

"Benji, Benji. Fucked Benji. Everything, nothing right all gone fucked."

"Lane, what's wrong, do you need me there, mate?"

"Fucked Benji, all fucked."

"I'll be there in ten bro, and I'm bringing Booker."

Lane, I would say it will all be okay, but that is only going to happen if you actually turn round and fight for the women we love. *Yes we.* I know you love Lexi, you fell almost the moment you saw her, all that bullshit coldness was fear, childish, fear. All pushed forwards by that witch that broke your heart, only yours, not mine. I never liked her, she smelled *wrong, very wrong*. And her muff, well, she was caustic; every time I was with her I was surprised I came back whole.

But now, now we need to get the boys in and you, you need to get your head out your arse and make a move to get our girls back. Ah shit, you've passed out. Well, I ain't going to piss your pants, no matter how relaxed you're getting. Don't need to make you any worse emotionally than you already are.

••••

"Damn Bookend, take a look at this drunk bugger."

"Good thing the dull git left us both spare keys to this place. Guess it's his old man's prepper nature, most squaddies are like that. But still, shit, Laneway, look at you, your folks would be mortified. Fuck, I'm mortified. Get your arse up."

"Fucked, all fucked, tried to say. I tried to say."

"Balls, he's on a bloody loop. Benji, put the coffee machine on, we need this dickhead sober enough to talk us through what the hell has happened. I don't think he can be without adult supervision at the moment."

"Yeah, no shit. Ain't seen him this bad since … well …"

"Yup."

"Let's get some coffee down his neck and then see where we are."

"Hey boys."

"Hey, man."

"Hey bro, everything okay?"

"No, everything ain't okay, it's all on its head at the moment, Lane is fading fast. I don't think he's going to be 'okay' for a very long time."

"Well what the hell has happened? Last we knew, you and your boy were doing the horizontal tango all over your boy's office."

"Everything was going perfect, me and Hot Lips, together virtually every day, Lane and Lexi, falling head over heels for each other. All was looking rosy, then, well, I don't know. Lexi just dropped right out of the race. She's putting up more walls than an Irish brickie. Hot Lips hasn't had a single clue as to what is going on. It's just silent. Lane went in yesterday with the intention of making it clear to Lexi how he felt, what she means to him and where his heart is in all of that, but well, it just went to shit so quick that none of us could find the floor let alone the door."

"So what did Lexi tell Lane then? Did she say she didn't feel the same or something?"

"No, she didn't even give Lane the chance; she just ripped the carpet out from under us and then, well, here we are with my boy so many sheets into the wind that we could open our own bedding store."

"Yeah I get the idea, well our boys should be able to pick him up. Here's to hoping that Lane can piece this together, or that Lexi can get her act together and see Lane for who he is, but I guess he has muddied the issue with the constant office sex so she could have gotten the wrong idea. But, yeah, this ain't good for anyone."

"No, it certainly ain't."

••••

"Damn, hang on. Oh fuck."

Lovely, nice start to the morning bro, when was the last time you spouted some stomach chutney after a heavy night? It's got to be at least a few years. Yeah, a few years at least, and I know your boys ain't going to clean that up for you; at least there was a bag in the bin by your bed.

"Morning Laneway, feel any better than last night? I'm going to say no, but then you really weren't making much sense other than the fact you were crying over everything being 'fucked' and you said that a lot. So what the hell happened?"

"Do we have to do this as soon as I wake up?"

"Mate, when you ring me in the middle of the bloody night, drunk as a skunk and babbling about everything being messed up by saying and I quote, 'fucked, all fucked, tried to say. I tried to say,' it kinda gets your mates' attention and has both me and Bookend bouncing over here faster than a Roo on coke."

"Fair point, I guess I did hit most of the alarm bells pretty hard. Sorry."

"Don't be, it's what your bros are for. Besides, you'd do the same for us."

"True, but still, can I at least get some water in me or something before you go all Gestapo and start in with the third degree interrogation?"

"I suppose that's a fair request."

I hope the boys can get Lane back on his feet. He's fallen hard and fast and not in the good way when he fell for Lexi. No, this, this was like he fell from a plane strapped to an anvil, nothing but the grace of God could stop him from hitting the floor and nothing did. Damn it Lexi, why couldn't you have waited, we only needed a few minutes, a few bloody minutes longer and all this would be totally different. I'd be here waking up next to my girl instead of my boy's disappointed best friends and waste paper bin full of puke.

There really are points where I wish I had the power to go back in time, and others, well, those points I just wished I could cease to exist. Although lately I just want to stop this world and get off. Nothing has made a lot of sense in a long time, my boy included.

Lane shifts lazily, his movements lacking any cohesive motivation as Benji stands there, a wry smirk on his features as Lane tosses the covers aside.

"Why am I still dressed?"

"Because I ain't your fucking butler that's why. Do you think me and Booker are going to strip your drunk arse down and then put you to bed? Fuck off."

"Fair enough, I didn't realise I was that bad last night."

"Mate, you necked three bottles of tequila in the space of three hours,

I'm surprised you're not dead and I ain't talking the mini personal bottles you get off the planes or in gift sets; I'm talking those big buggers you pick up from Cellarbrations. I'm seriously surprised you are standing right now."

"Well I wasn't until you pulled my bloody curtains open."

"Yeah well, I owed you one for scaring the shit out of me. I love you bro, but never fucking do this to yourself again. I saw what happened when that bitch fucked you over, and now here you are drinking yourself to oblivion over what? Another chick who is by all accounts just trying to get her head straight after you fucked, literally, fucked her senseless."

"What?"

"I dragged some of the details out of you last night, all of this, all of it, is basically your bloody fault. I told you to be straight with her, I told you not to fuck about and just tell her. And yet, what do you do? You go and spend the next week shagging her everywhere you can think of. I'm surprised you didn't have a photocopy of you sliding in and out her muff. You missed your chance, not by an inch but by a fucking mile. You have got some serious ground to make up Lane, and you ain't going to do it by sitting about getting shit faced."

"Yeah, I know."

"Too bloody right you know. Now me and Bookend are going to bounce. You get the three S's done and meet up at mine; we're going out for some decent tucker and a laugh, you need it."

"Yes Dad."

"Ha bloody ha, don't be a prick."

"Hang on, what time is it?"

"A little after three p.m."

"Fuck, I slept that long."

"Yeah you did. I was toying with the idea of getting Booker to tell you it was December third or something, but that just seemed a bit too cruel, all things considered."

So you're being hauled off for a meal with the boys. A couple of bevvies and a good blabber should set you straight, although I don't think the drinks will do you any favours, hey, captain puke bucket. There's a fine line between a good, relaxing drink and a chill down, and the raging piss up you are continually set on. I'm really beginning to doubt your mental integrity, Lane.

••••

Well we may just have a decent night of it, decent grub here and a nice scent from the eye candy floating around. So, we'll see. Oh for fuck sakes, *no, no, no,* put the fucking tequila down Lane, put it the fuck down. Do you hear me? I'm already fucking scorched from spouting out battery acid this morning.

"Oh no, no way boyo, you are not going down on that worm again. Tequila is not your friend bro, beer or nothing tonight; you are cut off from spirits."

"Well shit, why not just cut off my cock and balls while you're at it. I seem to be the only one around here that isn't in on the plan to control and fuck over my life, so go on, have at it."

"Lane, sit down you dickhead. We're not controlling or fucking up anything and I sure as shit ain't fondling your rod and sack; we just don't want to see a repeat of what happened with Miss Queen Bitch, her and Dave. You went through the floor and kept on going. Are you surprised by how cautious we're being?"

"No, it's just fucking stupid, I'm a grown man, I don't need a nursemaid."

"None of us are saying you do, now, shut up about it, have a drink, and let's gets some grub going. We're here to have a chill out not a barny."

"Yeah, you're right, sorry."

"No worries. Now shall I call her over?"

"Yeah go on."

Here we go.

"Hey saucy, how's your girl doing?"

"Knackered but horny, why, your boy looking?"

"Nah, I'm just being friendly. My boy's not in the best place at the moment. Any chance you could get your girl to perk him up with a bit of flirting or something?"

"I don't see why not, sexy, would rather get more acquainted with you, but hey, if your boy ain't 'up' for it then I guess I can at least be nice."

"Thanks, babes."

"No problem, handsome. What about your friends here, they up for a bit of pickle tickle?"

"Henry, the nice lady has a question for you."

"Sorry love, what, I wasn't paying attention."

"I said do you fancy a quick one with me and my girl later? I'm sure I can get her to slip her number with the bill, she's not fussy."

"Sure why not, you smell a little spicy, just how I like it."

"Well then, that's good to know. I've been told I have a bit of a sharp bite at times. See ya later, fellas."

"Later sweetie, oh and thanks."

"No worries huni, just remember to slip my girl a big tip, and I'll be back for your friends later."

If her girl can perk him up, the tip will be worth it.

"Well Henry, that was a turn out for the books, nice one. Show that sheila a good time, okay, and don't let Bookend get freaky. She seems like a chatty one, especially her slick spot."

"Yeah I picked that up from her. She's a bit 'too' friendly, gave me a weird vibe."

"Sorry mate, what was that? It's kinda hard to hear you with a mouth full of metal."

"Oh shut up."

"Come again?"

"Fuck you."

"Okay, now that I heard."

"Man, stop winding him up. Ain't his fault that Benji decided to jam a lump of tin in his japs eye, is it?"

"No it ain't, but hey, it's the most fun I've had in a few days. It's been frantic and fun but … well … lacking bite for a lack of a better word." I love having fun with my dudes.

"That piercing sure as shit didn't lack bite."

"I bet not bro, so … uh … can I ask …"

"What did it feel like?"

"Yeah."

"Remember when our boys were tots and teething, and we could feel the bloody things pushing through their gums?"

"Yeah."

"Well, take that sensation and transfer that to your head, then you're pretty much on the money."

"Ouch."

"Yup, that ain't the worst of it though. The worst part is the salt baths and disinfectant, those sting like a yeast infection bathed in hot sauce."

"So … just wondering, why did Benji get that done in the first place?"

"Well, according to some crackpot message board and blog site he reads, it aids in sensation and enjoyment during sex, but take it from me, this thing is just distracting. It tugs at my face, aches like fuck when I'm slipping through the pink, and just generally gets in the damned way. I haven't had a decent shag in ages thanks to this bloody thing."

Why go through all that pain then? Men, so stupid sometimes.

"I'm seriously loving my new piercing, boys. Damn the sex has been great since I got it; it makes everything sharper. I feel every movement she makes, every time she even quivers. It's fantastic."

"Bro, I'm trying to eat here, I don't want to hear about your pierced prick, although judging by the way our waitress is looking at us, she wouldn't say no to you slipping your pierced dong into her velvet handbag." Velvet handbag? Ha ha, good one, Lane.

"Nah Lane, she's giving you the goo goo eyes. I think she's after you."

"Well she's out of luck there lads, although Booker, by all means go in and take her off my hands."

"I might just do that, bro, she's pretty cute, but then again, she does look a little feral; although I don't think that's a bad thing in a one-time shag partner; a little freaky deaky always makes things more ... interesting."

"You really are an odd dude Bookend, but I love you bro."

"Not going to propose to me now are you?"

"The burger maybe, but no Bookend, not you."

As the evening wears on I can feel my boy starting to loosen up, the alcohol in his system brushing aside the brooding pain that is slowly eating away at his heart and soul. The pain of possibly loosing Lexi and my pain that still spears through me at the thought of losing Hot Lips, all of which boils back on Lane just making him feel all the worse. I just hope his boys can pull his head out his arse and push him onwards into everything he needs to do.

"So dude, you going to dip your head? It seems as if that bit from earlier was more interested in you than any of us."

"No bro I ain't. My heart belongs to Hot Lips and only Hot Lips; no other velvet handbag is slipping around me while there is still a chance we can be together."

"You really do love her, don't you, man."

"Yeah, I really do, she is the most wonderful person I have ever met."

"Okay, who are you and what have you done with my bro?"

"I'm sorry, what was that?"

"Oh fuck off."

"Love you too."

"Well boys, you ready to make a move, although by the looks of Laneway I think a cab would be a better bet than walking anywhere."

Oh damn bro, I take my eyes off you for a few minutes to have a conversation with my boys and look at you, so drunk you can barely speak let alone do anything else. Oh shit no, don't try and pick up that waitress, bro, no, just stop.

"Hey there ... uh, you ... uh you ..."

"Me what, sweetie?"

"You, me, bed uh ... bed ... sexy fun ..."

"Well as entertaining as that sounds sweetie, I don't think you would be up to the task."

Lane, chill bro, you're drunk. We ain't got the coordination now to even raise a semi let alone slip into her love glove, which I wouldn't let you do anyway.

"You bed, me call cab. You boys okay to look after your fella here?"

"Yeah we've got him hun, although I wouldn't say no to your number, if it's on offer."

"Well, it may just be."

"Well good, and I may just give you a call if you make it so."

"Call, you, I'll ... uh ... sexy ... fun ... sex."

"Whatever you say darling, whatever you say."

"Come on Lane, let's get you home."

"Ruined, I'm ruined ... sex fun, waitress sex ... all ruined."

"Taxi."

"No, no taxi, sexy fun, with ... uh ..."

"Louise, her name was Louise and the last thing you're having is sexy fun with anyone, so come on Romeo, I'm putting you to bed and tomorrow we're getting Lexi back for you."

Well this is confusing. Who's doing what and where are we doing it?

"From the looks of things, Booker is going to be shagging the waitress, Lane is going to be put to bed by Benji, and we, well, we're just hanging here trying to maintain some semblance of sanity as you watch your boy nurse a hangover in the morning."

"Well okay then. I guess I'll see you all in the morning. Later ladies."

"Night, dude."

"Night bro."

••••

Well last night sucked donkey balls; Lane, I'm officially declaring you T-total, you are banned from drinking again, ever, do you hear me? Not another drop from henceforth. The choices you decide on, paths you take and moves you try to make, are beyond ridiculous; fuck, you are one awkward drunk.

Look at you now, you've gone from sitting in a cab propped up by your two mates on the verge of puking your lungs up to sober, for what? A few blurred memories and lost moments of pain all drowned in a wave of inadequacy, but hey, at least you got blitzed out of your skull.

Come on dude, hold it in, at least get out of bed before chucking your lungs out the window. Oh Lane, bro, damn it, in the same bin as well. Shit, that thing is going to smell worse than a McDonalds dumpster if you keep doing that.

You know what, no; this is the end of it. Starting now you are changed, see this face, see the one you're aiming at the damned toilet bowl, yeah, this is my serious face. Oi, let me talk first, damn it, are you trying to drown me? Ah fuck it all, fine. Done? Good! Don't forget to shake the dew from my tip, now where was I? Ah yeah, *enough is enough*! The drink, the partying, the nights with the boys so lost in a tidal wave of booze that you barely remember your pin code for the door, all of it stops, even your bros are not impressed with your shit any more.

Lexi deserves better, bro. You know it.

"God Lexi, I'm so damned sorry. You deserve better than this, you deserve everything and I know that with me like this there is nothing I could do or say to make my actions right. But with God as my witness Lexi, for you I'm damned well going to try."

Okay, I don't get this. I swear you're hearing me, but then you go on these long peals of raucous confusion and I just sit here in your jocks along for the damned ride. Even now, you're standing in the bathroom staring at yourself in the damned mirror and apologising to a woman on the other side of the damned city. If you're so set on making these changes, bloody well show her.

"Come Monday, baby, you are getting the real me, no matter what happens. I just hope I don't fuck this up like I did last time."

TWENTY-ONE
She

Alexis spent the weekend completely engrossed in work and work only. Because that's what she wanted, wasn't it? That's what caused all this heartache in the first place. Her work ethic and her need to separate it from her personal wants and needs. But to be fair, she was also trying not to feel the pain of rejection, which is exactly what she felt on Friday when Lane left the office and never returned.

All she hopes for now is that they can continue to work together in a friendly manner until this project has finished. Then ... pray Lane doesn't walk away from her. Because even though she is trying to be strong now, I know that if Lane doesn't suggest that they pick up where they left off, it will be impossible for Alexis to continue working in the same building as him, especially if she has to witness his Mr. Uptight persona flirt with every female in the lobby. That, she couldn't handle.

We will walk into the office and be nothing but ourselves. That's all anybody should be. After walking to work, which did us the world of good, we stop two buildings from ours, sitting on a bench to slip off our runners and replace them with our heels. Yes, the red, sky high ones that make my panties wet that has nothing to do with sexual arousal at all. Then we continue to our building.

Mr. Stalker is at his usual waterfront post, but when he notices my girl, he looks the other way. Could we have wrongly accused this man of being a stalker? I have a feeling we haven't, but Alexis is hoping an innocent man wasn't questioned without merit. I'm just happy he's not giving us his slimy stare anymore. Creepy was not the word.

My girl smiles at people she knows across the lobby, being the chirpy girl they all expect, while on the inside she is terrified that Lane may not turn up to work, or walk out again without telling her when he will be back. She hates to think that she may have been the sole reason for him not returning to work Friday. Is she really that bad? I make quick work of getting rid of those thoughts with the help of big brain, instead filling her with all the ideas she came up with over the weekend and the good feelings that came with them.

As we walk down the hall towards Lane's office, I feel my girl struggle to maintain her composure. Even the daggers being thrown at the back of her head again by Vivian the receptionist, who seems to be blaming Alexis for Lane's lack of attention towards her, don't have her grinning as usual. When she opens the door and finds that he hasn't arrived yet, instead of feeling relieved that she has a few more minutes to gather herself together, like I thought she would, she begins to believe that maybe he won't be in today also. At this thought, her mood plummets deeply.

Taking deep breaths, she goes to her desk and sets up for the day, fighting off the tears that want to fall. Brain! Happy thoughts, happy thoughts, stat! We will not let this get to her; she will concentrate on work and forget to check the clock every five minutes that Lane doesn't arrive. Work, work, work, is the mantra we will be pushing through her brain.

She opens a document that needs some changing and is engrossed with its finer details when Lane does indeed arrive at work, with two coffee cups in hand from the break room. Oooookay. This day should be interesting.

"Good morning Alexis. I was hoping this coffee wouldn't get cold

waiting for you. I've a great idea for our client's brochures I need your opinion on, so let me know when you're ready to take a look. Oh, and sorry about Friday, my phone went flat and my charger wasn't in my briefcase to let you know my meeting went a hell of a lot longer than I was expecting."

Umm, okay. He is a *lot* happier than Friday. It's as if he got laid over the weekend. Fuck! No! Please don't let that be it. NO, no, no. Please just let it be a Jekyll and Hyde persona.

"Baby, how could you even believe that I would let something like that happen? Just because these two idiots can't get their shit together, doesn't mean I would go and throw away what we have. Is that what you think I would do?"

"Oh Eight. I'm so sorry. The thought just entered my brain before I really thought it through. And no, I don't believe you would ever do that to me intentionally. But Lane is the one in control, I wouldn't hold you to blame if that was to happen, just know that, my love."

"He can't make me go up on his own, that's all up to me, so at this point in this screwed up situation he won't be getting a chance to even try. Besides, he has had a very long, hard look at himself over this weekend and will be treating Alexis with the professional and personal respect she deserves, I guarantee you that, baby."

"Thank God, because I think my girl may just break if he walks out on her again like he did Friday. Fingers crossed we can all make this work, Eight, because I don't want to lose you."

"Me either baby, me either."

The morning runs smoothly, with Lane being friendly without being flirty, which I hate, but my girl needs. They work on some great ideas together and the atmosphere is comfortable. This is how it should be, how it should stay, until the end of their project at least. They email their client their revised ideas, who then phones back immediately to tell them they are delighted with what they've come up with. The feeling in the office is easy, happy, which is just what they both need after the last few tumultuous weeks.

"Let's hope this day is how it will be until this project finishes, hey, Hot Lips."

"Oh my, Eight, I freaking hope so. My girl has been up and down like whore's drawers since they started working together, well, in more ways than one. I think I've aged ten years in the last few weeks alone. In fact, I know I have. I can feel grey hairs starting to prick through my skin and just because they're waxed away doesn't mean they're not there."

"Oh hush, you crazy thing. There's not one grey hair around you, I promise. But yeah, we need this peace to continue too, for the sake of my boy's sanity. He agrees within himself that work is what they should be concentrating on, but he's finding it hard to stow his feelings away when they are so strong. After Alexis dismissing him on Friday, he's struggling to contain them at all."

"She wasn't trying to dismiss him at all, she just felt like her work was slipping because of their 'involvement.' She doesn't want to lose her job over it, as much as she also doesn't want to lose Lane. It's one big catch twenty-two. But she does want him, Eight, badly. It's just bad timing right now."

"I know baby, the timing sucks. But know my boy still wants her too and feels like shit for walking out on her Friday."

"So he should, that was an arsehole move. It shattered my girl, badly."

"Sorry baby. You know that his feelings for her are still strong. And I think that if they're both still feeling so into each other, we've a fighting chance at being together when this is all over and done with. That's an exciting thought."

"Oh hell yeah it is, babe."

••••

The next few days are much the same. It's as though a cease fire has been called and they are indeed focusing entirely on work. Well, Lane and Alexis are. Me and Eight, that's another story.

"Can you stop that please?"

"Stop what, my Hot Lips?"

"Stop sniffing the air like that. It's distracting."

"Why is it distracting, baby?"

"Because I know exactly what you're doing, Eight!"

"And please do tell, what am I supposedly doing my love?"

"You are trying to get a whiff of me! And if I know you are trying to get a whiff of me, then I will automatically try and get a whiff of you, and if I do succeed in getting a whiff of you, I won't be able to control my reactions to your glorious smell and will have Alexis's panties so wet it will be as if she just peed herself!"

"But babe, I can't help *but* get a whiff of you, your scent is floating around this entire office."

"What? Do I smell? Alexis washes me more often when it's that time of the month, so you shouldn't be able to smell it!"

"Well, I don't smell *that*, but I do know you're riding the red sea at the moment."

"What? How? I haven't had a chance to tell you it started over the weekend and it's nearly over anyway, but how the fuck do you know?"

"Okay kitty kat, calm down. That's one reason right there, Miss Snappy Tom."

"How dare you! Are you trying to tell me I have been going all PMS on you this week? Because listen here buddy, if I was going all crazy PMS on your arse you would know it!"

"Chill baby, I'm just messing with you. I can tell because the pheromones you and your girl have been releasing have a different feel to them, so I just guessed it was that time of the month and ... you have been a little bit short with me a few times this week for no reason at all."

"Oh Eight, I'm sorry. I've just been a little under the weather, I think. All the stress of last week and then getting our period in the middle of it hasn't been pleasant. Thank God we only have two heavy days and then spot for two more after that, because if we had a heavy flow like Zali does, for almost five days straight, I think I would drown in sorrow … or blood, either way, not a great way to die."

"Okay, I do not need to hear the phrase *heavy flow* from you ever again, thank you. I have a fear of drowning and will have nightmares all night if I can't get that vision out of my head."

"What? But you have baths and not just showers, am I correct? And with Lane having a beach house I'm sure he has gone for a swim in the ocean more than a few times, so how can you have a fear of drowning?"

"It's not clear water I have a fear of drowning in babe, if you get my meaning."

"Seriously? So if Alexis was really horny and begged Lane to take her in the shower, while she had her period, you would stop Lane's attempts?"

"Well, I have never come across that situation before. Miss Queen Bitch was even more evil when it was that time of the month, so we stayed clear, thank God, until it was all over with."

"Can I ask you a personal question, Eight?"

"Of course you can baby. Ask me anything."

"Did you … umm … love Miss Queen Bitch's other … umm … brain?"

"No baby, I never loved her and to be honest, she never loved me. We just co-existed in a friendly manner, but that was it. I mean, we would talk, but it wasn't anything deep like you and I. We would just guide each other on how best to get our owners off and then would sit in comfortable silence. She wasn't *as* big a bitch like her owner was, but she wasn't exactly the most friendly muff on the planet either."

"Thank you, Eight."

"For what, baby?"

"For being honest with me."

"That's all you'll ever get from me, baby, I promise."

Work becomes such a focus between Lane and Alexis, especially since their client hinted that they may have more requests for their services after this project is done, that it has really become a bore to live with.

"Eight?"

"Yeah babe?"

"I'm bored. Entertain me please."

"Ah babe. At the moment, I'm trying to get Lane to go for a walk so we can pee, you know, just something to move me from this uncomfortable position he has me in. My head is sticking to my balls and they feel as if they have gone numb. If things weren't going so good at the moment, I would pump him with horny hormones just to get him to move me. I need a stretch."

"My poor baby. Want me to try and get Lexi to lean over his desk again? I could tell he loved that she had an extra button undone on her shirt, which is completely *not* on purpose by the way, but the way his breath hitched, I thought he was about to begin office sex round two. Bugger."

"Oh don't remind me about that. Round one is still etched at the forefront of my mind and the mind of the big one too. That's our spank bank fuel every night."

"Yep, ours too. Especially that whole stairwell scenario. Oh yeah, the fast, desperate way Lane took us, ahh, that's a highlight when we're taking a tumble with BOB."

"Okay, I know BOB is not another man, but I still don't like hearing *its* name please. It just gives me a chill."

"Oh no baby, it doesn't give chills, it gives nice vibrating sensations that you can feel from your head to your toes. It is nice, real nice."

"Is it better than the real thing?"

"Well, my girl doesn't use it so much for penetration, mainly just for clit friction, but when BOB 1.5 was still operating, and she had the two going at once, it was thrilling. But still never as good as a real hot blooded rod like yourself, baby, especially if you combine you with

Lane's hot lips and talented fingers. Oh damn, that's a nice feeling. Oh yeah, I like those memories."

"Oh baby, don't get me started. You sigh like that again and I'll be tenting so fast, I may just break my head against the underside of the damn desk."

"I would kiss you better, Eight."

"Ahh, you're killing me!"

My erotic thoughts are interrupted by Lane's cough and Alexis getting up and mumbling that she is going to powder her nose. Shit! I think Eight and I both got a little carried away with our memories of that wild week of office sex. Mmm, desk sex. I hope that's in my future again. If I know Eight, he will make it happen, just for me. Damn I love that dick.

As Alexis washes her hands after cleaning up my wet mess (oops), she looks at herself in the mirror and smiles. She is happy with how this week has gone. The past four days have been perfect and their creative brains have been on fire. She is more optimistic about the future than she ever has been, especially with the whispers that the client is so happy they're considering requesting Lane and herself to work with their company again.

But what will that mean for her and Lane's relationship? Will they survive another project together? If this does turn into more work, my girl is determined to figure out a way to make it all fit. She will not give up on her feelings for Lane and I will not give up my love for Eight. This just has to work out. I need that dick in my life more than the air I breathe.

TWENTY-TWO

He

I **can feel it burning deep in my boy's gut, the aching indecision** coupled with the shattering frustration of having to stem all that he feels in the name of keeping his woman, *our women,* within arms' reach. I can honestly say this would crush a smaller man, but my boy, Lexi's man, well; we've fought through tougher things, this one just happens to have a sharper hold on Lane than either of us first thought.

His thoughts are a whirlwind of random chaotic noise. Fear at losing Lexi wars with his need to finally lay it all on the line and tell her just how he feels. It's so crazed in here that nothings gone down on the screen in the last hour. He just sits at his desk staring at the woman that owns his heart. With all the relationships that have come and gone over the years, nothing has made my boy feel the way Lexi does.

Hell, I'm stuck here, coiled against my own sack as I begin to throb and grow against Lane's leg and yet, even with the testosterone that roars through our veins making me harder than steel, he still can't shake the aching worry over whether or not he should finally fess up and tell Lexi just how he feels about her.

I'm just thankful the day is nearly over.

••••

Bro, I have one thing to say: Thank you. Thank you for phoning Booker to come over and not sinking into another bottle of tequila as soon as we got home, I really don't want to taste that again in a *very* long time.

"Lane, bro, you need to calm down. You're going to give yourself a bloody heart attack seriously."

"I know, but what do I do? Do I tell her how I feel, now that we're just getting back on track and making a soft go of still being work partners? I mean, I can see in her eyes that she wants more. Wants us to be more than we are at the moment, but her damned professionalism is pushing her to keep it on that one level. I just don't know what to do."

"Mate, if Benji were here he would say the exact same thing that I am. You need to tell her, you can't move on with anything in your life until you do, your work is suffering. That desk behind me in the corner there has sat as empty as a blonde's brain for the past week. All we've seen of you is either a drunken puddle of man shaped vomit or a passed out skin suit that would be better suited as a freaking scarecrow. So like we've been telling you for the past month, just tell her, you need to tell her, bro."

"I know Booker, I know ... but when ... how? I'm so fucking confused right now."

"Bro, sit and calm down. We will get this sorted, I promised I would help you through this didn't I? So come on, chill for a minute and we'll figure this out."

••••

Okay new day, new start; but hang on, something ain't right, something really ain't right. What the hell is wrong? Desks are okay ... cabinets aren't moved ...what the hell is wrong?

"Hot Lips, baby, is everything okay?"

I'm there waiting for any kind of answers, my mind whirling over everything that has happened in the last few days before I begin to question the situation as an entirety.

"Hot Lips, baby?"

Nothing. Silence. What the hell is going on, where is my girl and Lexi?

"Morning Lex ... Lexi, odd, okay, she's usually here by now."

I know Lane, she usually is, but, oh right you can't hear me, um, I guess it's nothing to worry over. She should be here anytime now.

"Okay Lane, nothing to worry over, she's probably just taking her time getting in, just get started with work and she'll be here before you know it."

Yeah Lane, great idea, just get stuck into work; before we know it our girls will be here, saying hi and how eager they are to get started with the day. Oh Lane ... phone's ringing.

"Lane Anderson speaking ... oh hey Woody ... yeah everything is going great, just waiting on a few bits to come in but ... what? No I haven't seen Lexi yet. Yeah, her ideas are fantastic. I'll get her to check in with you as soon as she strolls in. Yeah, have a good one, Woody."

This is getting worrying, mate.

••••

Well the day has dragged by; it's weird trying to work without Lexi's soft scent filling the room as we stare at the screen, I miss my woman, Lane, where is she?

Okay, so morning tea has come and gone and she still ain't here, bro. I can feel the worry eating its way from the soles of your feet through to the hair on your head. You have checked for a message on your emails and checked for a text or message on your phone, but nothing. You're going nuts trying to figure out where our girls are, so ... where the hell is she, bro, where the fuck is my woman?

"Okay, don't panic, there could be a perfectly reasonable explanation,

no need to start worrying needlessly. I'll ... just call, yeah, call and see if she is coming in. She could just be running very late or ... maybe she had an appointment, I'll just call her and check, it's what any concerned colleague would do."

Well it's ringing bro, it's ringing. Anything yet, no, okay ... how about now ... no ... damn it Lane, why isn't she answering. I'm going crazy here, she should have answered by now for fuck's sake.

"Lexi, it's Lane, sorry to ring you on your personal number but, well, just a little worried about you, you're never this late and well, I guess, just give me a call when you get this message, let me know you're okay."

Damn it, bro, I have a really bad feeling here, this ain't right, can we check with security or something? I'm really freaking worried.

"Hey Clive."

"Hey Mr. Anderson, everything okay?"

"Sort of; you seen Miss Ryan today? She's usually in by now but, well, she's running extremely late, can you do me a solid and check if she's either signed in or well ... you know what else."

"Sure thing, sir."

"No, it's Mr. Anderson or Lane to you Clive, we've known each other almost five years now."

"Sorry Mr. Anderson, but no, nothing on either the watch list or the entry log, sorry again Mr. Anderson."

"Okay thanks."

Uh Lane, check with her receptionist, what was her name, Alecia wasn't it?

"Damn it okay, okay, come on fucking elevator, where the fuck are you? Screw it."

Damn bro, you're sprinting down these stairs faster than Usain Bolt. Come on, calm down a little at least, it won't do anyone any favours if you kark it on the bloody stairs. Damn you can still smell the sex in the air in here I think, fuck, run you bastard, run.

"Alecia, have you seen Lexi?"

"No Mr. Anderson, she's not been in all day, why?"

"Well she hasn't shown up yet and I can't reach her on her private line. Do you have her address? I'm getting worried and I just want to check in, see if she's okay."

"Okay yeah, that is odd, um, I can't really hand out her personal details."

"Damn it girl, just give me the address."

"Okay, okay, here. Please let me know how she is."

••••

Okay, here's her apartment complex, um, she's number 316, so go on, what are you waiting for? Go see if our girls are okay. Thank God she gave her security code to her receptionist for such an emergency so we can at least get to her front door. Slow down, ow, fuck, will you watch those corners? You just cracked my head against the banister end. Fuck that hurts, right, 312, 314, bingo! Now come on, knock on the door, hurry up, damn it.

"Lexi, you here, come on babe, answer me."

Try knocking harder.

"Lexi?"

"She left about eight thirty this morning mate; she ain't been back yet. She works over near those posh apartments on the waterfront. You her boyfriend or something?"

"Something like that, thanks, mate."

"Want to leave your number or something so I can ring if she comes back or what?"

Lane, you going to answer him … no … okay then. Where are we going now?

"Lexi, where are you baby, damn it."

••••

This office is dark without her in it. I'm beyond worried here, Lane, maybe we should call the cops or something, you know, see if there's any reports or anything.

"Fuck Lexi, where are you?"

"Lane, everything okay? Alecia said you'd been tearing your hair out looking for me; Clive downstairs made the same comment."

"Lexi, where the hell have you been? I was so freaking worried! God, I'm glad you're okay. Fuck, I was so worried something had happened to you; don't scare me like that, baby."

"Hot Lips, baby, where the hell have you been, we've both been going crazy."

"Baby, calm down, it's okay, we had a doctor's appointment, just a routine check-up and we took Alexis's mum to her appointment too. I thought Lexi told you both, I made sure she emailed Lane."

"Lane, hey, it's okay. Come on, don't squeeze so tightly, I'm fine, thank you for worrying, but I did tell you. Didn't you check your email?"

"Baby, I have been checking those every ten minutes all damned morning! Hell, I checked there, the security desk, your offices and even got your home address and checked there."

"You checked my home?"

"I was worried you'd been hurt or were too ill to call in; I just wanted to make sure you were okay."

"I swear I emailed and told you."

"Honestly baby, I haven't had anything from you since yesterday."

"She really did email, Eight."

"No doubt, but I think I know what might have happened."

"Shit, fucking internet, it's in my damned drafts folder, Lane, I'm so sorry."

Whoa, hold your horses, bro, the door's open. Oh damn, she feels good. Mmm I've missed this, baby I've missed you and Lexi so damned much.

"Missed you too baby, oh your boy's tongue is driving my girl wild."

Lane's teeth nip at Lexi's lips as he reaches past her and pushes the door closed. Her body moulds against him as he deepens the kiss, pushing her against the door, hunger and passion burning through them both as his hands reach her backside and pull her tight to him.

He pulls back for a moment, Lexi and Hot Lips both mumbling as they struggle to think of a response to the sudden, passion soaked attack.

"Lexi, I have wanted to say this to you for so damned long, I wanted to tell you from the moment I saw you, I ... I love you Lexi, I love you with everything I am and ever will be. These past weeks have been a trial on my heart and soul. I've wanted to tell you so many times how I feel but, well, you wanted professional, to see how the project goes, but I can't wait, I need you in my life, Lexi, and us being in the same office with how I feel and how badly I want you each and every day, professional is something I just cannot keep to. I want us to be more than work mates and I want so much more than a simple office fling, if you're willing, willing to try and make this work then so am I, and I promise, nothing sexual will ever happen again in this office unless you want it to. You deserve so much more than that. I love you Lexi, and I want this to work."

"Lane, I ... well ... I ... uh ... Okay, we can try, we can try and make this work. I've wanted this just as long as you have, I just didn't want to ruin our careers over it, but as long as we can keep this out of the office, especially while this project is still on, then, yes, I think we can make us work."

"Good, I love you Lexi, I'm so damned sorry for the way I have acted. I was just terrified after how things played out last week, I know that sounds stupid but I was. It was like my world collapsed and I just couldn't keep up the image that you wanted. Hearing you say that you wanted to keep things 'professional' it just killed all that I had wanted to say right then, it felt like I'd been rejected before anything had started and in that moment I just couldn't face you or us. Before you'd said anything I had everything, everything I've said now, all of that was waiting, waiting for

you to hear, but well, you know what happened and I just, well, I'm sorry, sorry for acting how I did and not being strong enough to tell you then just what you mean to me.

"Oh and one more thing, you're staying at my place tonight, and that's not a request."

"Mmm, now that's fine with me."

"Eight, pinch me."

"What the fuck?"

"Eight, I said pinch me."

"Um, why baby? I really want to kiss the fuck out of you right now, or at least get Lane to do it, so why do you want me to pinch you?"

"Because I'm sure I dreaming."

"Oh baby, this is no dream, this is happening, this is really fucking happening."

"You're right it is, and I cannot wait to have you in me tonight. Oh by the way we were freshly waxed last night, nice and smooth."

"Fuck baby, you're killing me."

TWENTY-THREE
She

The worry that was radiating off of Lane when Alexis walked into his office just after lunch yesterday was heart-warming, and the kiss, ahh, that kiss said everything. Well I thought it did, but apparently he had more to say. The words *'I love you'* slipping from his lips were an absolute shock to my girl and almost had her legs buckling from under her.

It was the truth, so clear to see in his eyes, that had her falling even harder for this man. A man she thought might never feel for her as she was beginning to feel for him; a man that in a single moment revealed his true self and the love he has for her. After the way he walked out last week and didn't come back, she can't believe it came to this, Lane declaring his love for her.

The honesty behind his words when he explained his struggles with his feelings, then feeling rejected by her calling everything off and then him admitting he handled that rather badly, was all Alexis needed to hear to give this relationship a real go, with some conditions of course. No more office sex? Are you fucking kidding me! How could she deny me that? It's just cruel, I tell you, and secretly I felt a slight pang in her feelings when she said that was a no go if they were to be serious about making this work.

As much as she insisted that it can't happen again, I think there still may be a chance of it in the future. Maybe after the stress of this campaign is over and they are back to their own offices, Eight and I will have a good go at initiating something that's a bit naughty during office hours.

But after heading to her place to grab a few things to stay the night at Lane's and then realising he does indeed live in a penthouse apartment on the top floors of the Eureka Towers, things start to feel a little off. Especially after he opens the door and says welcome, to a very cold and stark penthouse, because this is certainly no home.

Alexis starts to feel a little uncomfortable, but it has nothing to do with the loving man beside her who still has a firm grip of her hand. No, it has to do with this place not fitting the true Lane she now knows. The beach house, that was all Lane, or who we saw as the real Lane that weekend. A man who was gentle and caring when we needed it the most. It was warm and homely, but this, this just seems to fit the Mr. Uptight persona we gave him before we got to know him.

Lane seems to sense Alexis's change in mood, grabbing her face gently while kissing the corner of her mouth.

"So, what do you think?" he asks while walking her further into the apartment, towards the view that is seen through an entire wall of glass.

"Wow. That view is to die for, Lane."

"To be honest, that's the only reason I'm still here. The company owned this first and then it was offered to me as a sweetener when it looked like I was going to take an offer from another company instead of taking 100 Design's offer. They threw this in, fully furnished at a heavily discounted price. So I thought, why not. I'll always have the beach house to escape to. I just haven't had the time to really make it mine, I guess, too busy working or hanging with the mates or weekends down at the beach to be bothered picking furniture I would actually like."

'Thank God' my girl is thinking, because apart from this view, the place feels very corporate, almost as if they are in a business, not a home. Maybe one day, she could add her own touches. That thought makes her smile grow bigger.

"Oh baby, I have been dreaming of this day since I first laid scent on you. And to now have you here, in our home, well, I'm struggling to maintain my excitement, if you know what I mean."

"Damn Eight, I know exactly how you feel and so does Alexis if the grin she is wearing is any indication. Do you really think you can stand at half-mast and not have her notice?"

"We weren't trying to hide it, baby. I'm not the only one struggling to compose myself, but Lane is trying to behave better than he has in the past, because he knows Alexis deserves better, that she deserves the best, so that's what he intends to give her."

"I love that we're here, Eight. It feels right, despite this cold display home atmosphere that is going on in this place."

"I love that you're here more than words could ever explain, but I'd be happy to show you after dinner, baby."

"Cheeky."

"You know it."

Lane does indeed behave despite tenting in his slacks; my girl pretends not to notice, sensing he is struggling to behave, but she loves it. The doorbell rings, making her jump. Oh no! I hope it's not one of his mates. Even though she thinks it would be lovely to meet some of his friends, she kind of has her heart set on spending some quality time getting to know Lane better.

"That would be dinner from the Thai restaurant you like. I hope you don't mind eating in tonight? I don't want to share you with anyone at the moment."

"Staying in sounds perfect, Lane. When did you organise dinner?"

"While you were packing a bag at your apartment, I placed an order. I wanted to feed you dinner as soon as possible, so then I can eat you for desert, for the rest of the night, if that's okay with you?"

"Damn, Lane. That's more than okay, as long as there is desert for me

too?"

"Oh fuck. I hope you eat fast, Lexi baby."

Alexis giggles to herself as Lane goes to the door to greet the delivery boy. When he comes back he grabs one of her hands. She thinks he is going to lead her to the grand, black glassed, dining table next to the kitchen, but instead he leads her over to the only comfortable looking piece of furniture in this apartment; a grey coloured sofa with about ten large cushions leaning against its back.

He walks a few steps further and places the bags of food in front of the wall of glass before coming back and walking behind the black coffee table. Alexis has no idea what he's up to until he bends down and pushes the coffee table until it's almost up against the glass, then walks to behind the sofa and pushes it until it almost meets the coffee table. He then bends down and picks up the food, pulling out the containers and spreading them out over the table.

"I've always wanted to do that."

The boyish grin that spreads across his face as he says those words has Alexis's heartbeat racing and not a single bite has been eaten yet. Yes, I hope she eats fast too. Lane goes to the kitchen and returns with plates and cutlery and tells my girl to sit as he dishes up a combination of all her favourite Thai meals. He remembers, which has her heart melting this time. Poor heart is getting a bigger work out than I so far. The race is on. Two to heart, zero to V. Let's see who the winner is by tomorrow morning, shall we.

"This is so right, Hot Lips. You and Lexi, here, in our home. Home, hah, it's never really felt like a home until right now. It was just a place to crash, even when Miss Queen Bitch was practically living here for a while and it wasn't so quiet, it still didn't feel right. Don't leave baby, ever."

"Oh babe, I won't intentionally leave, I promise. And I agree, this feels right, I can feel Alexis's every emotion and though she is trying not to get ahead of herself, she's feeling it too, like this could finally be it and she can't believe she fought it and nearly lost Lane. I feel this is the start of something beautiful."

"Damn baby, this could actually be forever."

"Aww, my man is such a romantic."

"A romantic that can't wait to stick his dick in you. Just saying."

"There's my man!"

Lane is as relaxed as Alexis has ever seen him. He's laughing and opening up and is an absolute delight to share company with. But as much as they are both enjoying this simple time together, one amount of pressure is building, starting out as a slow burn and simmering up to almost boiling point. The sexual tension between them is about to fly off the charts.

Lane clears the coffee table of their leftovers and plates and returns with a glass of wine for Alexis and a beer for himself, snuggling up close to her on the sofa, looking out to the spectacular view of the city skyline. He stretches his free arm up and lays it over her shoulder, bringing her closer to his side. She rests her head on his chest and listens to his heart beat ... and then things change.

"Is it getting hot in here, Eight?"

"Fuck, I hope so. I want you Hot Lips, I want you now."

Lane's fingers slowly rub circles on the top of Alexis's arm, causing shivers, which turn into butterflies, which take over her stomach with anticipation of what's to come next from the man who earlier today declared his love for her. She's still in disbelief over his words and how true they sounded. And now that she is confident in his feelings for her, she is finally allowing herself to feel her own true feelings.

She knew she was falling and here, right in this moment, with all of her walls completely down in this man's warm arms, she can finally admit to herself that she loves him also. But, and it's a big but, fear is holding those words hostage, fear that the past may one day repeat itself, so for now she will hold her emotions close to her heart where they remain safe.

Lane places a soft kiss to her head and she sighs. He then places another at the corner of her eye, then down her cheek and one at the corner of her mouth, before leaning forward and placing his beer on the coffee table, doing the same with her wine glass, as she lifts her head from his solid chest. When he settles back against the sofa he places a hand gently against her cheek.

He stares into her eyes for what seems like eternity, showing her that the love he has declared for her is true, before leaning in and softly placing a kiss to the centre of her lips. He stays there, frozen in time, lingering against her lips, making her feel the passion he has for her lying just under the surface.

Alexis reaches a hand up and behind Lane's neck, adding the pressure she so desperately craves and that's all it takes for him to stop behaving. His lips start to move sensually over hers, teasing, taking what he wants, his tongue darting out to lick between her seam. His other hand brushes against her hip as he reaches around to her back, placing it low and pulling her closer to him.

It's my girl's brave move of pushing her tongue through his lips that has him breaking the tender moment he has created and turning it into something else, something burning hot. He tugs at her waist, moving her until she straddles him. He pushes firmly at her back until she feels his arousal bulging, rubbing against her centre.

"Oh fuck, Eight, we won't last! I can feel your heat through the layers of their clothing."

"Damn, baby. You're soaked already, I can feel it while I'm rubbing through your centre. Lane's trying to slow down, but I'm not helping him, not one bit."

Lane's hands both run up Alexis's sides, taking her shirt with her, throwing it to the side, then making fast work of the clasp on her bra, placing his hands on her shoulders and slowly lowering the straps until it falls to her waist. With her breasts bare to his eyes, he takes a moment to enjoy the view.

"Fuck baby, you are even more beautiful than the first time I saw you bare. I need to taste you, I need my desert, Lexi."

He takes a nipple in his mouth, his growl vibrating against the sensitive nub causing her head to fall back in a moan. He continues this sweet torture as she pushes down hard against his throbbing cock. He gives the other nipple equal attention as one hand comes around to unbutton her slacks.

"Fuck this. I need you in my bed, I need to spread you out so I can take my time. I won't last much longer if we stay here. Hold on, baby."

Lane grabs on to Alexis's arse and then he stands as her long legs wrap around his waist, holding her tightly as he moves towards the far side of this vast apartment to a hallway which must lead to his bedroom. The whole way their lips are locked in a fevered kiss, breathes stolen, heart beats skipping, as they stumble through a door and towards Lane's bed.

There is no time wasted as he throws Alexis onto his large bed, her laughter stopping as he follows her down, spreads her legs and begins to rain kisses and bites all the way up until he meets the apex of her thighs. I can feel the heat of his breath as he leans in and places a hard kiss over her now damp slacks.

He slides the zip down, reaches under her arse to the waist band of her slacks and panties, and peels them down and off her legs. The cool air does nothing to dampen the heat radiating from my wet centre. He looks directly in her eyes as he leans forward, placing a forceful kiss directly on my core that has Lexi raising her hips against his lips, releasing a long moan.

"Eight, Eight, I won't last long if he keeps this teasing up. Make him stop, ahhhhh."

"Oh baby. There is no way in hell I'm going to make him stop. As much as I want in you, right now, the teasing is the best part. Believe me, I will make this torture worth it."

When Lane's hot tongue darts straight for my clit, my girl screams as she grips handfuls of Lane's hair, making him growl, which vibrates against my already soaking centre. He adds two fingers, the friction causing Alexis to lose her breath as her panting increases. So much for taking his time to enjoy; he is jumping in head first, literally.

He then sucks my entire bud into his mouth and that's all it takes for the wave to begin. Lexi calls his name loudly as her stomach muscles clench and her thighs begin to tremble. All of my muscles contract tightly as the pivotal moment of our climax is reached; the after-shocks begin and ripple around Lane's still moving fingers as I flood all over his weapons of mass destruction.

My mind is scattered as we come down from the high that is Lane Anderson. He crawls up Alexis's body with a sly grin, proud of himself for bringing her apart beneath his lips. My girl's legs fall open, welcoming him in close to her, wanting more of his magic touch. He kisses her hard, claiming her, demanding everything she has and she gives her all. She finally decides not to hold any part of herself back. I feel those three little words will slip out soon.

"Hot Lips, be warned, I'm as hard as a fucking rock, baby, I hope you're wet enough for me, because as much as Lane wanted to take his time, he can't hold back; he's too emotional and turned on to show any restraint."

"Oh, I'm wet alright, Eight, there is a massive patch on the bed because of how much I flooded, but there's more where that came from. Come and get it, babe."

"Fuck! I'm going to explode before I even get in you. Stop with the kissing, Lane, and commence with the fucking, pleaseeeeeeee."

While still kissing my girl, Lane reaches down and removes his pants and briefs, kicking them off his feet as Lexi reaches for the button of his shirt. Too impatient to wait, she pulls hard and the buttons take flight across the bed as she rushes to push the sleeves down his muscled arms. Thank God he had already undone the buttons at his wrists and rolled his sleeves up, because he slides out of his shirt with ease.

When he lays his naked body against Alexis's and I feel Eight rest against my folds, I feel as if I can come again with just the heat radiating from his solid form. Lane bites her bottom lip before sucking it into his mouth to soothe the sting and then begins to kiss her slowly, teasing his tongue over hers, making her moan.

"Lane, I need you now, please."

"I just need a moment, Lexi baby. I will not last if I sink into your beautiful body right now."

Lane's tongue continues to dance with Alexis's as one hand roams up to cup her breast, kneading it, then pinching the aroused nipple, making her rise from the bed, bringing their bodies closer together. Eight's solid form slips against me, causing sparks, flaring my desire even further, making Alexis moan in ecstasy. She is barely aware that he has reached over to his drawer to grab a condom and is rolling it on.

Lane's control breaks as he grips Eight to guide him slowly inside our scorching centre. The heavy push along my walls has Alexis gasping at the delicious intrusion. Once he reaches our resistance, he slowly, oh so slowly pulls out, almost all the way, just about slipping from my core, before he's suddenly slamming back in with such a force we slide up the bed.

"Oh, oh, oh, Eight, Eight! You feel so good, I want more, I want all of you, I want this all the time, day and night, make it happen Eight, make it happen!"

"Damn baby, can we just get through this night first?"

"Oh baby! Just like that, yeah, bend that way a bit, find it, find it, oh hell yeah! That's the spot, baby, that's the spot. Keep hitting that. Fuck!"

We are close, so freaking close. Heart beats quicken, breathing turns to pants, sweat drips down every bit of flesh and Lane picks up the pace, pounding into Alexis with fevered abandonment. Oh yeah, even in the throes of passion, I'm still a fucking romantic.

"Almost there, Eight, almost there."

"Oh I feel it baby, I feel it. Grip me, grip me harder. Oh yeah, that's it, that's what I like."

Lane reaches down and pinches my centre of nerves hard and the explosions begin. Alexis screams out his name, over and over as our entire body feels as if it's shattering to a million pieces. Lane is close; he grunts her name while still pounding, pushing through my muscles desperately trying to milk him, trying to squeeze him, chasing the reward of him falling apart.

He pushes twice more, almost lifting Alexis from the bed before he growls her name in a long, drawn out moan.

"Oh baby, I feel you rippling around me, grabbing me, wanting me. It has never felt this good in our life and that's the truth, my Hot Lips. You are mine!"

"Oh Eight, I'm so happy I could cry."

"Well you are so wet no one would notice your tears, if you could cry, that is."

"I love you, my cheeky man."

"I love you too, baby, I love you both."

As my girl and Lane float back to earth, he moves to the side and drags her back up against his chest and spoons her while raining little kisses all over her neck.

"Thank you, Lexi baby, thank you for taking a chance on me, on us. I promise to never let you down or chase you away again. I love you."

"Oh Lane. Thank you for wanting me, for loving me. I ... I ... I love you too, Lane."

"Oh fuck Lexi baby, that's music to my ears. I ... fuck ... I think I'm going to freaking cry. I love you, I love you, I love you. I'm thankful every day that you came to work in my office. Now, I'm never going to let you go. Thank you for loving me back, baby, you have no idea how badly I needed that."

"I do now, babe."

"Oh Eight. I'm so happy I can hardly breathe. It happened, it finally happened. They are in love and they both know it. This is the happiest day of my life!"

"No baby, the happiest day of your life will be when I make you my wife."

"Oh baby. Yes, it will be. Let's not jinx anything by getting ahead of ourselves, shall we."

"Okay baby. But it *will* happen, I can feel it. But for now I'm happy to live in sin, if it feels this fucking good."

••••

The rest of the weekend is a blissful blur of love and, of course, sex. Oh, plenty of sex. Waking up in each other's arms was the sweetest feeling and one Lane wanted to continue. He held Alexis hostage the entire weekend, driving quickly to her place to grab more clothes so she could spend the entire weekend at his place. Most of Saturday they just laze around and enjoy being relaxed in each other's presence after the last few tumultuous weeks. Saturday night Lane takes my girl out for a romantic dinner, their first official date, and afterwards they barely make it through the front door before clothes are flying off and landing all over Lane's apartment.

Sunday morning is a lazy day in bed, making slow sweet love and talking. They talk about everything. Their childhoods and family, both making plans to introduce the other to their parents soon. They talk about past relationships and the painful breakups they both endured, understanding each other a little more with each passing word. They make plans for after their current project is finished, promising to have lunch together as often as their work allows.

The future looks brighter than it has in a long time, for both of them.

TWENTY-FOUR

He

Oh damn, what a night. God, I'm shattered, but I'm buggered if that is going to stop me. I love waking up with my girls next to me. Life is so damned good right now.

"Morning, baby."

"Morning, handsome, how's my man today, mmm? You made me feel sooooo damned good last night, baby."

"I aim to please and I'm good, still worn out but boy is it in a good way."

"Morning baby, how's my girl today."

"Oh I don't know, I'm a little sore in places that I never was before you got into my bed."

Well okay then, wasn't expecting that answer, but after the way we've been going at it these past few days, I'm in no way surprised that Lexi or my boy are sore, I know I'm amazed I don't have blisters on my head. Shit, they're at it more than a colony of Viagra drunk rabbits. But I guess that's not a bad thing.

"Mmm no, baby, it's definitely not a bad thing. I haven't been this wet since Lexi discovered her first sex toy."

"Well baby, I guess we have to get dressed and go to work."

"Yeah, I guess so."

"Well, we could do that, or …"

"Lane, stop that, you know I don't like to be tickled, no, stop it mister or no more sex for you."

"Yes ma'am, work it is."

"Good boy, now let me get dressed, damn it."

"Hmm, now that is something I do enjoy watching. I think you're the only woman in the world that can make putting clothes on as sexy as taking them off."

"Oh shut up, but thank you."

••••

Well, all is right in the world; Hot Lips and I are together at last, our boy and girl are now so deeply in love that it's leaking from them like sap from a tree and well, life is freaking awesome right now. Work is going so damned well that with each new email more and more is being asked from them by the clients, they are *that* impressed, and I have to say I'm not surprised, because these two when they're together, they're just awesomeness incarnate.

"Baby, have you seen these latest emails from the client? They're going insane of the latest ideas you sent them. Great point by the way, I completely missed the possibility of using the taxis' internal signboards."

"Hang on Lane, I'm reading it now; give me a few minutes to get my head around it. I'm still kind of, well, a bit distracted by last night."

"You're not the only one, but hey, weren't you the one who said to 'keep it professional' in the office?"

"Ha bloody ha, mister, I did say that, but well, that's a bit redundant now."

"I guess so. I'm going to grab a coffee. Want one?"

"Yes please, but aren't you forgetting something?"

"I don't think so …"

"Kiss me, damn it."

"I love you too, baby."

"Ditto. Now go get my coffee."

"Yes, ma'am."

Well, this day has gone epically. Possible pay rises, new requests from the same client, and everything has been on the rise so damned quickly I'm surprised my boy and girl are able to stand upright. Like I said, life is damned good right now.

"Baby, I was thinking, how about we go out for dinner with the boys and you can bring your girls along. I know Booker has been wanting to meet them, I can probably guess why but still, it seems like a fun idea. What do you think, babe?"

"Sure, when did you have in mind?"

"How about Friday? That way we can avoid any possible 'hangovers' at work?"

"No, you just don't want to miss morning after sex. I know you, Lane Anderson."

"Guilty as charged, but what do you think?"

"Sure, go for it."

"Thank God you said that, I'd kind of already sent a text."

"Then why bloody ask me?"

"Because I knew you'd be pissed if I didn't."

"But ... you ... oh whatever. Friday, yes?"

"Yup, Friday. Where do you want to go?"

"Honestly I don't know. How about that place you first took me to, that little Italian place on South Bank?"

"Sure, if you want I can get us a back booth. They have larger ones that should fit us all in. It'll be quiet but that shouldn't really matter. I think it'd be a good starting point for our two ... uh ... groups to meet at."

"My thoughts exactly. Zali and Mel aren't exactly quiet when they get drunk."

"Nor are my boys. Okay, give me twenty and I'll make the booking. See

you in a minute, baby."

••••

Well this week is shaping up to be a week to remember. I have never felt two people so right for each other. Everything about my boy is just, well, happy; it's as if my boy has finally lifted all the crap and junk from his shoulders and for a few days found what it's like to be truly worry and pressure free. When Lexi is with my boy, which, since he confessed his love, has been just about every second of every day, he is a completely new man. Nothing has fazed him, well, I say nothing, nothing except that damned Michael Myers, Sheldon Cooper mash up that is constantly watching our girl.

That dude is always out the front of our building. I mean, what the hell is his problem? Yes, Lexi is gorgeous, sweet, kind, caring, and everything a man wants in a woman, but … um … where was I going with this? Oh right, yeah, that dude has got to back off, although I must admit, since Lane has been at Lexi's side like they've been surgically grafted together, he's not been … so … obvious. He's been looking away each time he sees them together so I'm a little less concerned, but shit, I so wish I could make Lane walk over there and toss him into the river. That creep deserves a good dunking and possibly holding his head under till the bubbles stop, but I know my girl would probably shout at me if we did that.

Anyway, it's now Friday, so time to get our groove on. It's going to be interesting with the boys and girls together in one place, especially since Lexi and Lane are officially an item now. Well, we'll just have to see how this goes. Fun times ahead.

••••

"Can you believe I'm a little nervous about our two groups meeting up

for the first time? I just hope that Benji hasn't nailed one of them before in a freaking club or something; he does tend to roll in those circles."

"He sounds like a charming person, babe."

"Ah, he's a solid bloke, I've known him since I was six and would trust him with your life as well as mine. Hell, he's had my back through many a twisted situation. He's actually one of the reasons I fessed up, well, him and Booker. I owe them a lot. Without them ... well ... I might not be standing here right now."

"Are you telling me, Mr. Anderson, that if it wasn't for your boys kicking you up the backside, you would probably still be umming and ahhing over whether or not tell me how you feel?"

"Mmm, probably."

"Well, I owe them a beer. I would have said something else, but those, I only do for you."

"What?"

"Never mind, baby."

"Did she just say what I think she said?"

"Yeah baby she did. My girl has been a lot cheekier since our two got together. It's great to see my girl finally burst all the way from her shell. I swear, if I wasn't just a vagina, I'd be all over Lane like a rash on a baby's bum. He is sex on a stick."

"Okay, not too sure how to take that statement, baby; it's words like those that make a guy a bit paranoid."

"Well, considering you're the stick I want, there's really nothing my man has to worry about, is there."

"You are such a bloody tease at times, you know that?"

"Yeah I do, but, it's one of the reasons you love me."

"True baby, all too true."

"Lane, you ready to go, babe?"

"Yeah, be right there, just grabbing my wallet and keys."

I hear Lexi gasp slightly as she takes in my boy's outfit. The custom cut suit accentuates every line and facet of my boy's trim and highly toned figure.

"What's with the deer in headlights look? You've seen me in a suit before, hell, you've seen me in one every damned day for the last few years."

"Yeah, but that ... damn, does my man look fine."

"Don't look so bad yourself, gorgeous. Mmm, if we weren't going out to eat I'd spread you over the table and eat you right now."

"Easy there tiger, you may just get to do that tonight if you're a good boy."

"Well, I'd better behave myself then, hadn't I?"

"Oh I never said that."

••••

The restaurant is quiet, warm and cosy, the scents in the air rolling over everything as Lane guides Lexi towards the back of the room. The maître d' grins at them both as they walk hand in hand through the tactfully lit room.

"I'm glad to see my thought was correct when I saw you last time, Mr. Anderson."

"And what thought was that, Leon?"

"That you and the fine lady with you would be more than just companions before the year saw its end. I just didn't think it would be this soon."

"Well, Leon, you know me, when I see a good thing I go for it without care for the consequences, and I struck gold this time."

"I'm glad, sir. Now, there are several people in your party already here. If you'll follow me I afforded you one of the best spots in my restaurant."

"As always, Leon, your service is impeccable. Would you be kind enough to send over two bottles of red and white wine? I'll leave your distinguished palette to decide the vintage; you've never steered me *wrong before."*

"Very good sir, enjoy your evening."

"Thanks Leon."

I feel my boy's heart hammering in his chest as he approaches the table, Lexi squeezing his hand lightly as she feels the trepidation in him as much as I do. Zali and Mel both turn to watch us all approach, their eyes widening as they catch sight of Lane and Lexi together.

"Wow girl, you look stunning and I'm guessing this tall drink of water here is the mysterious Lane Anderson. I'm not sure whether to shake his hand or jam it down my panties. You, girl, you scored big time."

"Uh, nice to meet you too, miss."

"Oh, polite too, well okay then."

"Zali, behave and back up. He's mine; I saw him first."

"Girl, if I didn't love you, I'd steal him right out from under you. Damn you're one lucky bitch."

"I know one thing, Lexi, Booker and Benji are going to love these two."

"Okay ladies, so here he is. Zali, shush for a sec. Mel huni, meet Lane. Lane, this is Mel. Zali already made herself quite known."

"Pleasure, Mel."

"Likewise Lane, I hope you're treating my girl right. If not, I'll rip your heart out through your backside."

"Okay, her I like."

"And what about me?"

"Zali, well, give me a minute, let me think on that and I'll get back to you. Kidding babe, after what Lexi has told me about both of you, I know you're good people, crazy as an outhouse rat, but good people."

"Okay then, Lexi, what the hell did you tell him?"

"The truth."

"Ah crap, you know I hate that."

This is so much fun!

"Okay, baby, I'm feeling rather outnumbered here."

"Eight, you'll be fine. My girls are awesome, just be your gorgeous

self and you'll do great."

"That's not exactly comforting, baby, being myself in these situations usually ends up with me in trouble."

"Eight, my girls will play nice so relax. Trust me, you've nothing to worry your sexy head over."

"Right, if you say so, baby."

They are so going to eat him alive. Ha ha!

"So this is the impressive Eight. Hmm, well, impressive Eight, impress me."

"Hey behave, chick, just because Zali got you inked last week doesn't mean you can have a dig at my man. As for you, Tibby, don't you dare try and one up her, I know how bad you can be."

"Fine, I'll play nice. I remember the nights when you used to be worse than us."

"Oh come off it, I was never worse than you. Half the time we'd stagger out the clubs and find you wrapped around the bouncer's stiff one."

"True, but still, I hate playing nice, it's no fun."

"Who's playing nice, what did I miss?"

"Oh thank God, I was praying you boys would get here soon."

"We're here bro, sorry for taking so long but traffic was a bastard."

"Any excuse, Henry. Any excuse."

"Ha I'm serious, that and Benji kept stopping for every kitten he caught a whiff of. Speaking of which, hello gorgeous, my name is Henry, and who can I say I'm having such a delectable pleasure in meeting on this formerly dreary evening?"

"You're meeting someone who is tired of the gentleman act and just wants a man big enough to fill me up till I all but split at the seams, and who can last more one round."

"Well that is brutally honest, still doesn't tell me your name though."

"You can call me Tibet."

"Why Tibet?"

"Because the only way you're getting in me is if you've got the stamina of a Sherpa or you're hung like a donkey."

"Okay, Eight, this one is freaking hilarious. I love her, not in the way you love Hot Lips obviously, but damn is she fun."

"Henry, Eight, what the hell is all this? Lane told my boy we were meeting a few friends here and I turn up and find an enclave of the sexes. This is like a damned scene from Jabba's palace."

"Well, why don't you play Jedi so I can show you my dark side."

"Well hello gorgeous, I'd rather show you my piercing to be honest."

"Hmmm, sounds like a plan, big boy. You show me yours and I'll show you my new tattoo."

"Oh now that sounds fun. Let's see if we can get our two to agree on something more intimate and get to know one another better, shall we?"

"I like how you think. Tibby, Hot Lips, I'll see you two later. Boys, it's been fun."

"Well, uh, yeah, that was Benji and well, um, okay; this has progressed a lot quicker than I thought it would."

"Told you my girls were fun."

"A little too much fun by the looks of things. Please tell me you were never that easy."

"Nope, I made them work for it. I prefer substance over everything else. I picked you, didn't I?"

"Yeah baby, and I'm glad you did. I love you darling."

"Love you too."

TWENTY-FIVE
She

"**I'm going to pee, I'm going to pee, quick, quick, it's coming out.** For the love of God, Lexi, listen the fuck up and get me to the toilet again!"

"Relax baby, it's just nerves. You have already been twice, surely there's nothing left in there."

"You are not in my vagina at the moment so you don't get to comment, so shut up please."

"Seriously, you are getting yourself in too much of a tizz. Please calm down, baby, for me?"

"This is so fucking nerve racking. I feel sick, I'm serious when I say I'm about to pee and throw up discharge at the same time. Arr, I need some air or something!"

"Oh my poor love. Calm yourself please. There is nothing to worry about. The clients have loved Alexis and Lane's work when they have been presented with glimpses of the project, so there is no reason to panic that they won't like the finished product. You know our two are going to freaking rock the clients' minds with what they came up with."

"I know, I know. But why are they taking so long to call Lane and Alexis back into the boardroom? They spent all morning presenting this campaign and it's been a half hour since they completed their presentation, so what's taking so long?"

"I have no idea, babe. But you felt the vibe in that room, it was freaking electric with what our two were showing the clients. They are going to kill it. This is probably just protocol or something. Please, please just relax a little, baby. I don't like seeing you this wound up … well … unless it's with me inside of you that is."

"Shut it, Eight. Now's not the time."

"Yes, dear."

Most of the morning was spent in the boardroom with digital slide shows and mini movies presenting all of Lane and Alexis's ideas on how to make this company number one in their field. My girl and Lane held up great all the way through, but now my girl's nerves are starting to get the better of her and it's affecting me big time.

"I'm so proud of you baby, so proud of us. I just know they're going to say yes to our entire campaign, I can feel it."

"Oh Lane, I hope so. I know they were all so impressed throughout our entire presentation, but I can't help but feel nervous. For Christ's sake, I feel like I need to pee again, but I know it's just nerves."

"Aww baby, come here. I truly believe we have nothing to be nervous about."

As Lane is rocking Alexis in his embrace, the phone rings from the boardroom signalling that the clients are ready for them to return.

"No matter what they say in there, I'm proud to have worked alongside you, to have worked alongside one of the best in the business."

"Oh Lane. You're going to make me cry."

"No. No tears until they are happy tears after these next few minutes."

They make their way down the short hallway, knock and then enter the room they spent the morning pouring out their blood, sweat and tears into. They both take a seat at the head of the table, next to their handouts and notes, as Alexis takes a slow deep breath to calm her erratic heart. Lane grabs her hand under the table and gives it a reassuring squeeze just as the client begins to speak.

"Miss Ryan and Mr. Anderson. Let me start by saying what a pleasure it's been working with the two of you over these last couple of months. Your professionalism has outshone your reputations."

Ha, if only they knew how professional they *were not* sometimes, in fact, right on this very boardroom table at one time.

"What you have presented us with is beyond our expectations. So much so, that not only do we want to implement all of this campaign into our business immediately, we would also like to hire you both exclusively to re-brand our entire company and the other two sister companies we own. We believe with the ideas that you have presented us with today, that you could help our overall company become number one."

"Eight! Did you hear that?"

"I knew it! I knew our two could conquer the world together. Damn baby, I'm so happy that you and our girl became a part of our life."

"Thank God your boy pulled his head out of his arse."

"Thank God your girl helped him love again."

"Aww. My romantic dick."

The next few hours fly by like a blur. The company wanted Lane and Alexis so badly, they already had their entire offer written up by their legal team and ready to hand over for consideration at the end of the presentation. They'd even consulted with Lane's boss yesterday about what they were going to offer Alexis and Lane today and he, in turn, had arranged a meeting with my girl's boss Andre to discuss it. Both of whom have been in this boardroom all afternoon going over the finer details with the power duo.

It has been decided that Alexis will officially be employed by Lane's company, something Woody and Andre had been working at when they put these two together for the initial project. Andre will still get a percentage of the campaign that was presented today, but will let go of my girl completely, with the promise that she will come by for a coffee at least once a week. It is late in the day by the time our two slip away for a few minutes to discuss whether to sign on the dotted line or not.

"I told you, I freaking told you they would love it all. Oh baby, we hit the jackpot!"

"Oh Lane. I'm speechless."

"Tell me honestly, do you have any reservations about signing the contract they presented? Our legal expert said it's the best contract he has ever seen, but if you think this job is too big, or it's not something you would be happy taking on, please tell me. I want you to be happy, baby, so if you want to pass on it for whatever reason, please just say so and I will knock it back also."

"How did I ever stand a chance of not falling for you, Lane Anderson? I love you and if you are prepared to take a chance on this crazy, freaking awesome and profitable offer, then so am I. Let's jump together, baby."

"I love you, baby. We can do this. As long as your hand stays in mine, I would be happy to jump into anything."

The cheers when Lane and Alexis give a very big yes to the clients' offer are deafening. After a few little details are changed and the documents are signed, the client offers to take everyone out to dinner. Apparently they were so hopeful that they had already booked Mo Vida, which stands ready for this large gathering.

At the restaurant, once all the excitement dies down and the congratulations have been said, boring corporate talk takes over all of the big heads.

"So, how do you handle the long hours these crazy people work, sweet cheeks?"

"I'm not that sweet when you get to know me and my girl is smart; she stretches often during a work day."

"Yes she is sweet, but if you call her sweet cheeks again, I will find a way to head-butt your arse."

"Eight, calm down boy. He was just making conversation."

"She's right, chill dude. I was just being nice. I have had a long day stuck in these crappy jocks and the tight cotton edges are cutting off my blood supply. I just wanted to know how the rest of you coped."

"Sorry mate. Just love my girl a little too much I guess. And as for your uncomfortable situation, you need to guide him to the new Calvin Klein's, those boxer briefs are like wearing nothing at all and the fabric, ah man, so freaking breathable, it's like going commando every day. Your circulation problems will disappear."

"Thanks mate, I'll make sure he stops by them this weekend."

"Since you're handing out advice, care to give us a hint as to how your team came up with that social media ad? My guy could use a bit of help in that area."

"Hold on there, we are not giving away any trade secrets. I know for a fact my girl was as proud as punch for initiating that idea, so your guy will have to learn how to come up with his own ideas, or get another day job."

"But how did they predict the exact market trends for our industry? That is something I have never seen before."

"Again, I ain't spilling any trade secrets. It's enough that we have to listen to the big ones jabber on about business, can't we talk about something else for a while? Like why is your male-female ratio so off balance? You have too many dicks. Where are all the chicks?"

"Well, gossip is not my specialty, but five years ago the head of finance, Tom, was caught having an affair with his receptionist. Not such a big deal, if they were single that is, but Tom was married and so was the receptionist *and* she was also the CEO's sister. If that scandal didn't rock the boat enough, someone had taken photos of them in the boardroom one night and posted them on social media. So a no fraternization policy was implemented and since then, if they need a receptionist or PA, all the men in power mostly hire male secretaries. Strange but true."

"Well, that's a bit sexist. How do they get away with it?"

"Sexist, slightly. Safer, hell yeah."

"I see your point."

After dinner and some supposably more important business talk,

Lane and Alexis excuse themselves, claiming they have some work they need to attend to early tomorrow. But work is the furthest thing from their mind. They want to celebrate, in private. Lane suggest taking a late night drive out to the beach house and Alexis is quick to agree. They go back to Lane's and pack a bag, easy, considering that half of my girl's stuff has ended up here. Mmm, I hope it all ends up here. I love our apartment, but there is sooooo much more closet space here.

On the long drive down the coast, Lane and Alexis steal little glances at each other, with happy smiles on their face. After all those stressful weeks trying to figure out their feelings for each other and then trying to navigate a new relationship with the balance of working together, all worked out in the end and neither of them could be happier.

"Oh Eight. I fucking love you, do you know that?"

"Damn babe, I sure do. I love you just as much. And to think, I get to spend every day with you now. I was worried that when Alexis returned to her own company I would only get to see you on an occasional lunch break, but now, oh baby, I will get to see you all the time. I'm so excited I'm just about busting the zip on Lane's slacks."

"No sexy thoughts while driving, babe. You know the rule. Safety first."

"Fuck baby, I know, but I can't help but get excited about all the opportunities that will present itself by working closely again. Mmm, I'm rock hard just imaging the positions I can get you in."

"Eight! Don't distract Lane from the road! Or I will suddenly develop a headache as soon as we get to the beach house."

"Now that's just cruel, woman."

It's late when they finally reach their home away from home and both are utterly exhausted now after all of the adrenaline from today's events has seeped from their bodies during the long drive to Sorrento. Salt hangs heavy in the air as they slowly get out of the car and make their way up the steps of the weatherboard house. My girl leans on Lane's shoulder as he places the key in the front door and clicks it opened.

"What a day, hey baby? I can see you are done for. Why don't you grab some wine while I head upstairs and run us a bath? Sound good?"

"Yes baby, that sounds perfect."

She places a soft kiss to the corner of his mouth and then watches his fine arse walk up those stairs before turning towards the kitchen. She grabs two glasses, a bottle of wine and an opener, before following the steps that fine arse just took. My poor girl is dragging her feet as she makes it up the stairs and into the master suite, exhaustion settling into her body very fast.

Lane has already started the bath and is stripping down. Alexis places everything on the bathroom counter before slowly stripping herself free from clothes. Lane pours the wine and sits the glasses on the far edge of the bath before hopping in and sliding against one end and reaching a hand up for his love, knowing she is tired and wanting to make sure she hops in safely.

She sinks down into the water and leans her back against Lane's chest. He offers her a wine, but she shakes her head no, already feeling the effects from the few glasses she had at dinner and the exhaustion that is taking over her body quickly. Lane places both glasses back down and wraps his arms around her tightly, resting his head against the top of hers and they just enjoy this quiet moment alone, in the warm water, feeling each other's hearts beat in tandem.

"Eight, I love you."

"Aww baby, I love you too."

"Eight?

"Yeah baby?"

"I don't have a headache."

"Is that so?"

"Yep, but my girl and I are so freaking knackered that we are almost asleep. Will you take a raincheck until morning, babe?"

"My poor baby. Of course, anything for you. Come on, let's get you dried and in bed. Let us take care of the two of you, okay Miss Independent?"

"Yes please, my Eight."

Lane notices pretty quickly too that Lexi is on the verge of sleep and carefully stands up and helps her out of the bath. He dries her quickly then guides her to bed, pulling the covers back and laying her down before going back to empty the bath and tidy up. Then he joins her and pulls her sleepy form in tight to connect with his. As much as I want to celebrate in a sexy kind of way, my girl and I have nothing left after all the weeks of ups and downs and sometimes stress to think of anything but sleep.

"I'm tired, baby."

"I can tell, my beautiful girl. Close your eyes and sleep. I got you."

"I know you do, that's why I love you so much."

"Love you too, Lexi baby."

••••

After waking up with Lane's tongue between our legs and spending all Saturday in bed, only hopping out to cook dinner, then going back to the twelfth round of love making, they spend Sunday morning walking along the beach before taking the ferry over to Queenscliff and slowly wandering around the shops and shoreline there. Finally, they head back and clean up, ready to return to the city.

With their workload ready to increase, they vow to spend almost every weekend at the beach house, bringing whatever work needs to be done with them, ensuring they have some down time so they don't burn out.

••••

When Monday morning comes around, both Lane and Eight are

bouncing around like little boys hyped up on red cordial.

"Eight. What's going on?"

"Just excited about working side by side with you again, that's all, I promise, I really do."

"Umm, okay. Then why are you twitching like Lane just stuck you in the top of a toaster?"

"What? Ha, ha. You are so funny, baby."

"Eight Anderson, what the hell is going on? You are acting stranger than when Booker suggested Lane get your head pierced as a surprise for Lexi. And Lane is overly attentive this morning and it's making my girl nervous. So what are the two of you up to?"

"Baby, please don't make me tell you. It's a surprise and I don't want to ruin it. Can't you just pretend all is okay until we get to work?"

"Fine. Just know that Lane's behaviour has my girl on edge. She doesn't need that the first day back into a new project, Eight. This better be bloody good."

"Oh it is, babe, it is."

Alexis gets more worried during breakfast when she notices Lane's knee bobbing up and down with nerves under the dining table while they eat their breakfast in silence. She gets even more worried as his hand starts to twitch as they walk hand in hand to work. She is so worried about what's wrong with Lane, she doesn't see Mr. Stalker openly gawking at her as they arrive to their building and make their way inside and across the busy lobby.

The nervous energy radiating off Lane has Alexis almost in tears, as her imagination runs wild with the possible reasons. She is so distracted that when they walk into Lane's office it takes her a few seconds to realise what she is looking at.

"Oh Lane," she says on a struggled sob as her hands go to her mouth and she takes in the changes that were obviously made over the past weekend. His entire office has been redesigned. New sleek black desks sit side by side, slightly angled towards each other, sitting in the middle

of the room. A long, dove grey, four seater sofa sits in front of them, with aqua blue cushions scattered on it. There are aqua blue picture frames on the dark grey walls framing famous inspirational quotes.

There are black bookshelves on both the far walls, as the view still remains the highlight of the room. A large bouquet of colourful gerberas sit in a crystal vase with a glass name plate in front of it, with the cursive words *'Alexis Ryan'* sparkling brightly. As Alexis throws herself into Lane's arms, crying at his thoughtfulness, I also begin to feel something amazing.

"Well baby, do you like it? What are your thoughts, my love?"

I tell him the honest truth, the first thought that comes to my small mind.

"DESK SEX!"

TWENTY-SIX

He

These last few months have been one hell of a jumbled mass of hectic awesomeness. Lane and Lexi, the dynamic duo, working flat out for one of the biggest clients they have ever had and now, probably one of the most permanent. No sooner are my boy and girl finished with one aspect that the company wants, they then turn round and scream 'it's freaking awesome, here, we want more, do this.' Neither of them could have anticipated the amount of work one client would entrust them with. Hell, I don't think any PR firm ever could.

Hot Lips and I have gone from strength to strength. There isn't a woman on this planet I would ever want more, in my heart or in my life. Lane really did strike gold when he found Lexi, but me, I became the richest dick in the universe when I was granted the honour of being with Hot Lips. Sounds cheesy as hell I know, but no one and I do mean no one could ever make me feel how she does.

Take a look at our situation. Our boy and girl are working their fingers to the bone, but neither could be happier, because, despite the hours, the work and their hectic tours of their clients' other companies, they still make time for each other, they still go home to one another and no matter what time of night it is, they are always awake to greet each other with a comforting, if sometimes, sleepy smile and a warm cuddle, Lane especially. Lexi, bless her, has shot up the promotional ladder with the company since landing in Lane's office. She is now on par with my boy in terms of leverage and responsibility, with Woody finally getting his wish of poaching her to his company.

And I know that my boy, bless his heart, was so damned proud when she told him, well, he already knew Woody's intentions and that he and Andre have been working on this before their current client had even approached Lane's company, but it doesn't make his pride in her any less.

On the other side of this we can find our duos of craziness, Zali and Mel and Booker and Benji. All four of them get along like lifelong friends and a little more on occasion if Henry and Tibby are to be believed; or Chick and Kong. Bloody Kong. Benji never could pick a decent nickname. Henry is bad enough, but Kong? Seriously, that name has got to change at some point. I really do have to ask Kong about Chick's ink. I still haven't found out what it is and Hot Lips just won't bloody tell me.

But now, well, they may be 'seeing' each other, but that lot are like bloody wolves when they're out together. It's scary. They pick a target for each other and move in like the SASR, taking them down with deadly precision. Makes me shiver just thinking about, especially Chick; she can be brutally predatory. I have even seen her chase off other competition just so Henry or Kong can get a good chance with the one she has cornered. I know they say a wounded tiger is the deadliest animal in creation, but I don't think Discovery Animal Planet has ever seen Chick on the hunt. Yikes!

But, back to our favourite boy and girl. If I'm reading my boy right, sometime soon Lexi will be in for one very big and very happy shock, something that, well, has been a long time in planning for my boy, and not a decision anyone would ever make lightly. I just pray that Lexi feels the same way he does. That girl is my boy's universe; the world doesn't even come close to describing her worth to Lane.

••••

"Boys, can I talk to you for a bit in private?"

"Sure bro. Zali, Mel, we'll be right back."

"Lexi baby, I won't be a minute okay, just need to uh, run some bits by the boys, back soon baby."

"Okay, this is a bit odd, babe, but sure. Is everything okay though?"

"Yeah, never better baby, just got a couple of things that only the fellas can help me with, just guy stuff."

"Right ... okay."

Guy stuff ... really Lane, I thought I'd taught you better than that. For shame bro, for shame.

"Lane bro, what's with the Mickey Mouse cloak and dagger crap, what do you want to talk to us about?"

"I'm going to ask Lexi to marry me."

"What the!"

"Yeah, I'm sorting the ring out this afternoon. I want your help in making it as special as possible. Now, I know you both still have connections with our old high school's band, so I was wondering ..."

"You were wondering if we could arrange for them to do a flash mob song when you pop the question."

"Something like that, maybe, yeah."

"Done deal, bro! Fuck, I'm so freaking happy for you. Lexi is a diamond girl. If you'd waited any longer I was going to ask her for you."

"Honestly boys, I just cannot imagine any future without her in it and, well, apart from asking her to move in, which I plan on doing tonight, there is nothing I want more than to make her my wife; so you two dopey buggers, there are no other people I could ever dream of having help me make this a reality. You two really are family to me, and well, I love ya, both of you. Thank you."

Damn it Lane, you're going to make me cry, fucking emotional twit, shit. Just man hug and get your arses back to the women, I can feel them getting a little curious already.

"*Lane, is everything okay?*"

Told you so.

"*Yeah baby, everything is fine.*"

"*But your eyes are a little glassy. Have you been crying?*"

"*No babe, just got some bloody moron's cigarette smoke in them when we were outside. I'm okay.*"

"*Right. I love you, Lane.*"

Okay, now she is getting a little worried; this sudden secret streak has her dredging up old memories. I can smell them. Careful, bro.

"*I love you too Lexi, but seriously, that's all it was.*"

"*Okay, okay.*"

Well, she's still wary but she trusts you, Lane, so don't play on it too much. I know you won't, but there is a dark and very painful history to it, bro, and hell, it would shatter her in an instant to think that you were repeating the cycle.

Lunch with the crew rolls past as smoothly as Lane's first morning coffee, nothing phasing any of them as they drink, laugh, and joke long into the evening, the orange rays of the fading day streaking the sky as Lane curls his hand into Lexi's.

"*I'll be heading off fairly early tomorrow; I have some paper work to sort out with the council and a couple of bits to pick up from a retailer I know. I'll be into the office at around eleven at the latest if you're going in, okay, baby?*"

"*I can wait if you want and we can sort it out together, I don't mind.*"

"*No baby it's fine, it's nothing drastic, just time consuming. I'll be okay, you head into the office tomorrow and I will be right behind you as soon as I'm done. I promise.*"

The apartment door swings open, my boy and girl stumbling in, a fit of giggles and passionate kissing flowing off them as they toss their clothes aside a piece at a time. The hall and front room are littered with discarded shirts, socks and pants as they fall in a tangle of limbs and lust into the king sized bed that fills the centre of the master bedroom.

Despite the agitation and curiosity laced fear, my girl is really in the mood tonight; my boy must be doing something right this time.

••••

Light slants in, making Lane wince as he shifts in bed, Lexi curled in his arms. He plants a soft kiss on our girl's forehead, whispering a soft good morning to her before slowly and carefully slipping out of her grip.

The sound of running water fills our ears as Lane hops into the shower, the glass door pulled tightly closed as Lexi sleeps, my boy conscious of the noise and wanting to let her sleep as long as he can.

He winces as his mobile chirps and buzzes as he steps from the shower, his feet slipping over the marble tiles as he dives towards the sink, reaching for his phone.

"Booker, that you?"

"Yeah, good morning to you too by the way, what the fuck do you need so badly that you have me calling you at five in the bloody morning?"

"I need you to get into contact with Julio. I can't get an engagement ring without Lexi's ring size, and the only way I'm going to get that is if Julio can work his magic for me with a pampering session. I don't give a shit what he wants, just tell him yes and that it's for three people. I can't really get away with just sending Lexi yet, so all three girls are going. Just do this for me, bro, you know he has a thing for you. I will make it worth it, trust me."

"Fuck, fine, but you really do owe me for this, Lane. Bloody Hispanic fairy always tries to cop a feel somehow."

"Like I said, I will owe you big time. Just do it, Booker, and I need it done a.s.a.p."

"Fine, fine, give me two hours."

"Thanks bro."

"This will cost you more than a bottle of Scotch this time, you do realise

that."

"Whatever you want, it's yours, just do it."

My boy hangs up and finishes his shower. His heart is hammering as he carefully pulls the door open and slips into a pair of slacks and a lightweight cotton shirt before padding through to the lounge room and open plan kitchen.

He pours his heart into the breakfast he is slowly concocting for the sleeping woman in our bed, and I have to say, out of all of them that I have seen him make over the years, this one blows them all away. He knows her tastes like the back of his hand and caters to her every need, all of it fit for any member of any Royal household.

Damn bro, you have really gone all out here. I'm proud of you! You really thought of everything; just don't forget to wake her and let her eat it while it's warm and not leave it to go cold.

"Balls, almost forgot the O.J. Now, to wake my girl slowly and then go see the body corporate."

Damn, my boy is on over drive; his heart is racing here. We are going to have to play this bloody close to our chest, otherwise he is either going to get a stress boner or kark it from a heart attack, or, as with Clive at Booker's thirtieth, both.

"Baby, breakfast is ready. Come on, Lexi, eat up. I know it's a Saturday but I have to go see the body corporate early about some paperwork, but before I go I wanted to make you breakfast."

"Mmm, whaa... Lane, what the ... God, that smells delicious. Baby, you are one in a million, fuck, I love you."

"I love you too, baby, now enjoy this and I will be back in a bit. See you in a little while, baby. If you're intending on popping into the office quickly before I get back, just leave a note and I can meet you there. Love you."

"Love you too."

"Morning, Hot Lips, love you, got freaking epic news, I will tell you as soon as I can, bye baby."

"Huh, morning, handsome, what news ... what ... oh okay ... uh, love you too."

••••

"Okay Mr. Anderson, that is the registration for dual occupancy done and the body corporate papers adjusted for the increase in insurance. Uh, I think that is the worst of it out the way. Now, when will the co-owner be in to countersign these?"

"Uh well, as soon as she says yes to a question I want to ask, then I will bring her by, I guess."

"Well Mr. Anderson, I must say, congratulations at the wonderful change in situation. I always thought a man such as you deserved more than the bachelor life."

"Well, thank you, Mr. Wells, so, I just want to ask one thing. Can you keep this between us? You know how quickly gossip rolls through this building."

"That I do, Mr. Anderson, that I do, and again, congratulations."

••••

Okay, gotta give it to Lane, he is one clever fucker at times. Setting up the whole package with Julio on a moment's notice and renting out at least half his spa just for the three of them really is beyond the call of duty. I just hope Booker plays nice, but then again, Julio can give as good as he gets. He's one tough little guy.

"Okay Booker, you set everything up and texted the other girls?"

"Bro, you know me, it was done within thirty minutes of that call. The girls are excited and the bloody little dancing queen here was more than eager to help me help you."

"Who you call a dancing queen, darling? I pamper and polish and make you look like Beyoncé on her wedding day. Dancing gets you all sweaty and I don't do sweaty, it gets all sticky and you know I hate that.

Lane darling, sweetie Booker told me all about it. I'm so happy for you. I promise not to say a thing, darling. Okay babe, get going, let this froo froo queen get her groove on. I can't work with all this distracting manliness around, you know how it makes me all gooey."

"Okay and that is my cue to leave. Booker, Julio, you are both freaking awesome."

"Oi, where the hell do you think you're going?"

"Oh, I thought you'd gone and booked yourself in, bro, I know how you and Julio get along so well. Besides, you're sagging around the edges a little."

"Oh yeah Booker, darling, just slip out of those grubby old things and come with me, I'll take care of you."

"Uh, thanks but, uh, no, I'm good, cheers though."

"Oh well, a girl can try. Bye boys, and Booker, tell that cheeky sister of yours she still has my copy of The Notebook."

••••

Well, I guess it's time to see the lights in Lexi's eyes when Lane sets this all in her lap, although I know I'd rather be there than anywhere else right now.

"Lexi, uh, you got much planned for today?"

"No, why?"

"Well, I kinda booked you and the girls a day at 'Euphoria and Beyond.'"

"You what? That place is impossible to get into! Julio and Zane are booked months in advance; you're lucky to even get a five minute phone call let alone a day with them. Oh Lane, how?"

"I have my methods. Just enjoy it, baby, you deserve it. You better move it though, Zali and Mel will be there in twenty minutes."

"Oh my God, Lane Anderson, you are the best! Twenty minutes, ha, then that gives me a few minutes to say thank you."

TWENTY-SEVEN

She

Life is freaking awesome. The new project is kicking Alexis and Lane's butt and despite working on side by side desks, they still work hard to find some quiet time for each other, whether it's at lunchtime or when they get home late at night. Their friends have been missing them, because most weekends they have been taking work down to the beach house to relax away from the city's stresses.

Lane has been hinting that my girl should just move in because they spend so much time at his apartment anyway, but she hasn't wanted to put any extra strain on their relationship just yet. This weekend, I have a feeling she may just say yes. They spend every night in each other's arms anyway, regardless of whose bed it is, but it would stop the stress of not having the right shoes we need, at the right apartment, for a particular outfit, when we're rushing for work in the mornings.

"Thank fuck it's Friday, Eight. I need a rest!"

"Poor baby. But I get it, this project is tiring and with having to visit all the branches of all the businesses that belong to this client, it has been putting our boy and girl behind slightly. But thank God they have agreed to no work this weekend at the beach house. I think it's exactly what they both need. Not just them, but us too; I haven't seen you much this week, babe, and I'm missing you badly."

"Aww, I miss you too, babe, but you need to get Lane to shave first, above and below. He has really neglected his manscaping the past few weeks. Lucky his sexy as fuck aftershave smells so good, or he wouldn't even be getting my girl's yummy kisses."

"What? Are you serious? I haven't been in you in over three days. Who cares about a few spiky bits?"

"I care! I still have nightmares about my encounter with the porcupine. Alexis might not mind pash rash, but that's not happening to my lips again. Do you hear me, Eight?"

"Yes, dear."

The morning's a busy rush as Lane and Alexis try to cram in as much as they can so they can enjoy a work free weekend. There are emails, phone calls, knocks on the door by their newly appointed assistants, much to the dismay of Vivian, whose nose is now out of joint because she's not the number one go to anymore, and packages delivered from the printing company. It's like Flinders Street Station in this office today.

They eat lunch on the run as they both head over to one of the client's offices, then head back so Lane can get ready for his conference call with an overseas supplier they're thinking of using. This call is long and still isn't finished by the time they had planned to leave. Lane writes a quick note before gesturing for Lexi to come and take a look. It says *"This call may still take another hour."* She writes then slips a note back to Lane while his call continues, letting him know she is going to ride a tram back to her place to pack a few extra things and will meet him back at his apartment.

She places a soft kiss to his hair, which needs a haircut soon, yep, manscaping is slipping, before she grabs her bag and laptop and heads out the door. She's stopped looking for Mr. Stalker now, but every so often catches his stares out of the corner of her eye, like now, but she refuses to react. Instead she simply keeps walking past and along the banks of the Yarra River to her stop where a tram is waiting.

"Hey kitten. Got much planned for the weekend? My boy is going to a bucks' party tonight at the Woolshed Pub. We could do with some entertainment like your sexy girl. They all have big bucks, so the tips should be worth your time."

I think back to the outfit Alexis is wearing before answering this moron.

"Do I *look* like a hooker to you?"

"Umm, no, but that doesn't mean you're not a good time kind of girl."

"Oh, I'm a good time kind of girl alright, but only for my boyfriend, dickhead."

Some dicks are just delusional, seriously. We hop off at our stop and head over to our apartment. Once inside, my girl starts going through her room, making two piles on her bed. One, to take to the beach house, with a few extra things she's planning on leaving there. And the other is things she plans on leaving at Lane's. She should just pack it all with how bare her wardrobe looks right now.

As she's going through the fridge, tossing any out of date products in the bin, there's a loud knock on the door. She's only been here about half an hour; Lane's call must have finished up earlier than expected. She goes to the door with a goofy smile on her face, one she's been wearing a lot lately, and without looking through the peephole she opens the door wide, ready to throw herself in her man's arms.

What she wasn't expecting was this stranger standing before her, a stranger she has been seeing for a few months at the front of her building, a stranger we refer to as Mr. Stalker. It takes my girl a few seconds to truly register who it is standing at her door, and she wonders how the hell he got into secured apartments without a personalized pin code. As soon as the initial shock starts to wear off she uses all her force to try and slam the door shut.

But it's too late.

He shoves his entire body against the door, shoving it and my girl out of the way as he then reaches for Alexis's shirt. He misses and she moves quickly, darting towards the kitchen where her mobile is ringing, dancing with vibrations on the marble surface. As she throws herself at the edge of the bench, reaching for her now silent phone, she feels Mr. Stalker grab a handful of her hair and yank back hard.

She screams as loud as she can, twisting in his grip to face him, trying to bring her knee up towards his groin. But he anticipates it, twisting out of her aim, still clutching tightly to a chunk of her hair, almost toppling them both over. Alexis tries to punch him, but he dodges her swing. She screams out for help while digging her nails into his arm, hopping to force his grip from her hair. He brings another hand up, trying to grab her shoulder, but this brings him closer, allowing her to bring her knee up hard and connect with his groin.

He doubles over, groaning in pain, and lets go of her hair as she screams again for help, seeing that her door is wide open. She reaches for her phone, grabs it tightly and runs around the other side of the kitchen island, making a dash towards the front door. Lexi doesn't see him coming at her as he shoves a leg out and trips her up, sending her crashing to the floor with a hard thump, her left arm protesting in pain.

She pushes her hands under her and tries desperately to rise onto her hands and knees, trying quickly to gain her footing as he grabs the back of her slacks, trying to pull her back to him. Through it all he's said nothing, no cursing, no hate filled words; he just grunts and growls like an animal. It makes this attack all the more frightening. She manages to rise despite his grip on her slacks. She turns again and this time her fist connects with his jaw.

His hand lets go of her slacks as he stands, momentarily stunned by my girl's punch. She goes for the open doorway again, screaming for help as she lunges forwards. He reaches out, quickly grabbing her long trailing hair behind her, stopping her escape. But she is close enough to the small table to the left of the door. She reaches out to grab the large crystal vase she has sitting there and, after a prayer to God for help, she uses her whole body to swing around fast, aiming the solid piece of glass at his head.

It connects with a dull crunch.

They both stumble to the floor, and he's shaking his head, trying to get back on his feet as Lane suddenly comes through the doorway like a freight train and rams straight into Mr. Stalker, sending them both sliding across the floor. When they come to a stop Lane is on top of this creep and starts pummelling his face with his fists.

Lexi grabs her phone and dials for help, quickly explaining the situation before dropping the phone and rushing over to Lane.

"Lane, please! Stop! He's not moving, baby, he's not moving. You've stopped him, he can't hurt me now!"

Lane looks up at my girl before staggering to his feet and grabbing Lexi, hugging her tight to him.

"Oh baby, are you okay? I was so freaking scared when I saw the smashed pin pad out front and came running up, but when I heard you scream, I don't know, I just saw red! What did I do, I don't remember anything after I saw you on the floor. Fuck baby, I'm so freaking sorry I wasn't here, please tell me you're okay."

"Oh Lane. I thought it was you at the door and that your call must have finished early or something, so I didn't check the peep hole like every other damned time and when I opened the door ... I ... I ..." She sobs.

"It's okay, baby, you're safe now, I've got you and you are never leaving my sight again."

As Alexis falls apart in Lane's arms, sirens can be heard in the distance.

"Fuck baby! Fuck, fuck, fuck! I'm so sorry we weren't here, so very fucking sorry. Are you okay baby? Did that fucker hurt you or my girl?"

*"No Eight, he didn't hurt us, just scared the living hell out of us. We still don't know what he was after. He never spoke, he never uttered one single word. It was the creepiest feeling ever. But she fought back, babe, oh she fought so fucking hard. I'm so freaking proud of her right now. But she's in shock and her body is staring to shake. She'll not get over

this easily, baby, and ... neither will I."

As both Alexis and I fall apart in our men's embrace, the police come charging through the door and the next few hours are a horrible, stressful, long ordeal.

After hours of questioning the attacker, Alexis and Lane and even the head of security that takes care of their office building, the police finally have a few answers. They're calling it a case of deep obsession. Mr. Stalker had been watching Alexis for a lot longer than she'd even realised. When she didn't seem to notice him, he started waiting outside the front of her building, morning and night, watching her come and go. When she first smiled politely at him, he thought it was true love, but shortly after that she started to ignore him and that's when his thoughts turned dark and violent.

Apparently he confessed to what looked like an attempted break in at their office and admitted it was to get her attention. He also later admitted to the attack down the laneway, saying he only wanted to talk to her. But it was when Lane and Alexis started walking hand in hand every day that he really stared to lose it. He admitted a few times to sneaking past security in their lobby and making his way up the stairwell in hopes of bumping into her, but he could never find her office.

When he did discover which company she worked for he started leaving messages, but by then, security got tougher and he couldn't get into the building. One day he overheard Alexis's boss giving her mobile number to an associate outside of the building and decided to unsettle her by constantly calling and not talking. When asked by the police why he was so obsessed with Alexis, he stated because she looked too good for him and he wanted to prove to her that she wasn't. He was taken away for psychological testing and a date for a court case would be made soon.

Alexis is not handling the situation very well at the moment; her shaking is getting worse and Lane has been pleading with the officer in charge to please let him take her home. Finally at around midnight they are told they can leave, but the officer says he will need to speak with them sometime the next day. Lane arranges a time for him to stop by his apartment and quickly walks Lexi out of there and into a waiting cab to head back to his place.

On the way he sends off a quick joint text to their friends, letting them know what happened, but pleading with them to give Alexis until tomorrow afternoon before coming over to check on her. They arrive at Eureka Towers and Lane helps Alexis out of the cab. They walk through the lobby and past the night security officer before getting into the lift. Once in, my girl's legs buckle and she falls into a wracking fit of sobbing.

Lane scoops her up into his arms and holds her tightly, rocking her, soothing her with words of love. When they reach their floor and head into their apartment, Lane heads straight for his bedroom, crawls onto the bed with Lexi still in his arms, and lies them both down, Alexis clawing to get closer to him as he drags her in and tucks her head under his chin. Both of them are in tears at the possibilities of what the night could have brought.

"Hot Lips, baby, are you doing okay?"

"I'm not sure, baby. I feel scared and saddened that something like that happened to my girl, happened to us, but I just knew that Alexis would be able to fight him off. I was confident that the arsehole wasn't going to hurt her as badly as he may have intended to. I'm so freaking proud of her that it's making it all not so bad. Is that confusing?"

"No my love, it's not. Yes, it was a horrible thing to have happened, but you are right to be proud of our girl. She is a strong woman, a woman that will never be without Lane's love, ever."

"Oh baby. Don't let go of us tonight, please."

"I won't baby. Not tonight, not tomorrow night, and not a single night after that. I'll hold onto you forever."

"I love you, Eight."

"Love you too, baby."

TWENTY-EIGHT

He

My boy can't sleep. The thought of anything that resembles sleep makes his heart and stomach clench harder than a dying man's hand. All he sees anytime he closes his eyes is that bastard, that bastard and his hands on our girl. I honestly cannot fathom how Lane didn't crush the bloke's skull; the shimmering madness that was in his eyes just crushed anything that even whispered mercy, yet, when Lexi called out, her voice sliced through everything as he heard his name slip across her lips, and he stopped near instantly. My boy's hands still ache, the dull throb in his knuckles makes his arms shiver as they continue to swell.

The police did warn us that the fucker may try and press charges claiming assault, although the officers, even the station chief said they'd do everything they could to uh ... politely dissuade him from trying. Although reading between the lines, the officer that took their statements, who was luckily a friend of Benji's, hinted at the possibility of the complaint files going for a walk about.

Yet despite it all, Lane still can't sleep. Our girl squirms in his arms, fearful whimpering and frantic twitching jerks rolling through her as he tries to softly soothe the nightmares away.

"Shh, I'm here baby, nothing is going to hurt you anymore, I promise, sleep baby, sleep."

"Eight ..."

"Yeah baby?"

"Lexi isn't doing well. These nightmares are terrifying, he keeps grabbing her, over and over. It's the silence, there's no noise in them, even when she smashes the vase against his head, there's just silence. I don't like it, Eight, please baby, make it stop."

"Damn it baby, fuck, I'm not letting you go, you know that. Just please, baby, try and relax, they're only nightmares. That freak is behind bars now; with all that Lane and the others had on him and what he admitted to, he won't be seeing the outside of a six by eight square for quite a while. You need to help Lexi relax, baby."

"I've tried, but all it's done is make the dreams worse. I tried relaxing hormones and all it did was make that fucker seem stronger. She is so scared right now."

"Damn it baby, I love you, I just wish there was something I could do."

"Try sending out a scent to her, see if that helps, please baby."

"Okay, hold on."

"No, no, don't, no, get away, leave me alone, no."

"Lexi, baby, it's just me, it's Lane, come on baby, wake up."

"Huh, no, no, Lane, help."

"Lexi baby, I'm here, no one else, only me."

"Lane, God, I'm sorry."

"Don't be. Tomorrow's a new day and the nightmares will be gone before you know it, and that is all it was, just a nightmare."

"I'm sorry, baby."

"Hey, come on, enough of that, just snuggle in tight, baby. I'm never leaving you, no matter what happens, you're safe with me."

"I love you."

"I love you too Lexi, now relax, you're safe with me."

"Mmm, I know."

••••

On Monday, Lane is there, hovering and overly attentive, his mind racing as he second guesses everything he does. It would drive me nuts, but then again, I already have two of those so I guess this comes with the territory. Through it all, Lexi seems her bright bubbly self, but Hot Lips and I know the truth all too well, as does Lane. Just below the surface sits everything that psycho pried loose.

Lane's phone buzzes in his pocket, my head vibrating. Any other time I would find it arousing but now, well, I don't think a boner would help Lane's situation, let alone Lexi's.

"Baby, you sure you want to head back into work? Woody would be more than happy to let you have the time off for as long as you want or need it."

"No Lane, no. I'm not letting that obsessed arsehole mess with my head or my life. I'm going into work no matter how hard it is."

"Baby, I fucking love the no guts no glory attitude, but seriously, I have been in this sort of mindset and I just want you to be sure you're ready. I'll be by your side no matter what happens."

"I know Lane, I know, I love you too and thank you, baby. I cannot tell you what it means to have you with me right now; I don't think I would trust anyone else to be near me at the moment."

"I know. Right, if we are going to do this baby, well, we need to go now. But, before we do this, I want you to know one thing, Lexi ... you are the love of my life, and everything to me, so, no matter what happens today or any other, I'm going nowhere without you."

"I love you too Lane, so, so, much. Thank you, thank you for everything."

"No need baby, no need, just doing my job as your boyfriend and partner."

That's my boy, that's my fucking boy. I knew there was a solid bloke beneath all that flirty bullshit. Now, let's see if you have what it takes to really be the husband Lexi deserves, provided she says yes of course. Speaking of which, you better talk to Benji and Booker to make sure everything is in place at the beach house for this weekend. The earlier it's set up, the less can go wrong.

So you better get some time soon to make that call, otherwise, well, you're going to be dropped head first into a half cooked idea that could have been sorted in plenty of time.

"Right babe, I have a couple of calls to make, so you take your time and do what you need to do. I'll be in the kitchen if you need me. Love you baby."

"Okay babe, love you too."

Yeah, way to go Lane, that's not suspicious at all. For fuck's sakes, you really are an idiot at times.

"Booker, you with Benji?"

"Yeah, why?"

"Just checking in."

"Well, you know, we've been here, sorting out your uh, special party."

"Yeah, thanks guys, I appreciate it, you know that. Anyway, how's it all going, any problems?"

"Nothing major. The fireworks guy is mapping out where he is going to be running all the cable work out to the barges, and the old crew is getting some practice in back at their studio. You wanted James Blunt's Bonfire Heart right? Because that's what Benji told them."

"Yeah, that's one of Lexi's favourite songs, it'll be perfect. Tell them all that if they can get it all sorted and in place early I will throw in some beer and a forty percent bonus."

"Shit, you really are dead set on this ain't you?"

"Bro, I'm asking the woman of my dreams one of the most important questions a man ever can, so you bet your life I'm making sure this is perfect."

"Okay lover boy, get your lady sorted and get your arse to work. You do know it's now eight thirty in the morning? It's a good thing me and Benji fluked sickies for this."

"Yeah I know, thanks again guys."

"Anytime."

"I hope not, it's Lexi or no one. Oh, and one last thing, don't forget to send out the invites to Lexi's girls and the rest of the crew."

"Yeah, yeah, go on, fuck off and get your arse to work."

"Catch you later, boys."

Well, seems like it's full steam ahead for you, broheim. Let's see how the rest of the week plays out, but first, we have to attend to one of the most important things that needs attention this week: manscaping! Because I don't want my girl refusing you or me on what could be one of the most sexually charged nights of our life, *if* they say yes.

••••

The office ... is tense. Very tense. It's like they're all waiting for something, anything to happen. Like a bomb tech making the long walk, it's just one huge tension filled lag in time, and Lexi, well, she's like a cat on a hot tin roof. Nothing that my boy says or does makes a lick of difference to her or the way she feels and it is killing my boy to see it.

Security is there, stern faced and wary, eyes scanning for anything on the other side of the front doors. With the events of Lexi's attack and everything before it still rippling through the workplace, Woody and Andre both poured money into the building's security as did the other companies that hold offices in the glass fronted tower block. So now, well, for anyone coming in, it's like walking into an embassy: a bank of three metal detectors as well as dozens of cameras ring the foyer and the exterior. There is not a single inch of ground in or around the entrances to the offices that cannot be seen on one of the dozens of monitors that now fill the wall of the security office.

"Morning, Mr. Anderson."

"Morning Clive. How's it going?"

"Not bad, not bad. The new set up makes me feel like a guard at Guantanamo Bay, but yeah, all in all, it's not a bad day really. If you don't mind me asking, how is Miss Ryan?"

"I'm fine, Clive, thank you for asking."

"Oh damn, didn't see you, ma'am, I hope I didn't cause you offence."

"Don't be silly, Clive, it was kind of you to ask, but I really am fine, thank you though."

"No problem, have a great day."

"You too Clive."

They move away from the wide eyed, coffee driven security guard and towards the elevator, my boy's hand itching to take Lexi's, but he knows that until she is ready, the work place is one spot where their relationship will always be behind closed doors ... well ... that is unless they can't get it to stay closed.

"You still sure about this, Lexi?"

"Yes Lane, I am. I'm not going to let him win no matter how bad my nightmares are, or how bad the bruises show. I'm not letting that mother fucker win."

"Atta girl. I would say something else but, well ... crowded foyer and semi crowded elevator."

Okay, Lane keep your hands in neutral zones, even if you want to pull her close as she whispers in your ear.

"I love you too."

"I know."

Yup, semi hitting the front zip. Damn it, sorry bro, you're going to be popping a chubby for a while today. Nothing I can do about it.

••••

"Eight?"

"Yeah baby?"

"My girl isn't doing good."

"What do you mean?"

"She keeps flinching at every random noise. Hell, the phone rang earlier and she all but screamed in fright. I'm surprised you and Lane didn't notice. Every knock on the office door, every smile in the corridor, hell, every bloody shadow on the blinds over the windows at the front of the office causes her heart to leap into her throat. Our girl is not okay, baby, and I just don't know what to do. She doesn't want Lane to know, but, well, I had to say something. It's really worrying me and I need help, baby, I need help to make my girl feel better."

"I hear you baby, I hear you. I'm going to get Lane on this, trust me, he knows exactly what to do."

The rest of the day passes in a blur of tension and anxiousness, a foreboding cloud that lines up the rest of the week for them both. Despite it all, Lane slowly chips away at the doom and gloom. My boy swings into action, his credit cards screaming in fear as he lavishes Lexi with dinners out and trips to every place he can conceivably think of. Slow hand in hand walks along the Quay and Southbank, making each small break seem like the first days of summer, the tenderness not lost on even the most casual observer. He caps it all off with lunch three times that week in their favourite restaurant. Lexi sits grinning at him as Leon fawns over them both like a clucky mother hen, the stout French man only too aware of what had befallen his favourite customers. His determination to see Lexi happy rivals Lane's, with the paunched and moustachioed man going so far as to offer them free meals for the remainder of the week. A surprise which even had my boy lost for words.

By the time Friday peers round the corner, the cloud that had so plagued Lexi seems to be lifting. Even the front page of the paper that day does little to darken the slowly brightening world of our girl.

"Well, that settles that."

"What does?"

"The paper here, it says that your Mr. Stalker and head case could end up getting a ten year stretch without possibility of parole. Apparently he had warrants out on him in Denmark and Hungary for similar offenses, but they weren't flagged, so it took a while for them to filter down the chain. Seems that is the last anyone this side of Engoordina will see of him."

"Well good. I hope no one else ever has to suffer through his sick adoration."

"You and me both, darling. Tell you what, why don't we head down to the beach house this weekend? I'll invite the gang and we can have a blowout, see if we actually remember it on Monday. You never know what will happen when we're all together. What do you say?"

"Yeah, sounds like fun, just please don't do anything too stupid. I know how you can be when Benji is around. I love him, but you turn into a seventeen year old pot head when the two of you are together sometimes."

"I'll try and behave, I promise, baby."

"Good, okay, you ready to head home?"

"Damn I love the way you say that!"

"Say what?"

"Home, it just makes my world seem all the more complete to know that you truly do see that apartment as ours and not just mine."

"Babe, anywhere with you is home to me, you're all I need to make it so."

"I love you, Alexis Ryan."

"I love you too, Lane Anderson, with all my heart and soul."

••••

Lane slowly pulls along the gravelled drive to the beach house, his heart softly beating in time to the soft snoring of Lexi. She leans against the passenger door, her lips curled in a small smile as she shifts, mumbling his name as she moves into a more comfortable position.

Shadows move across the lights in the living room as he fishes his phone from the cup holder in the armrest, then steps from the car.

"Booker, can you get everyone to slow things down? Lexi has nodded right off and I'm going to put her to bed before we make the final preparations for tomorrow. She knows you're all here, but I just want to let her sleep. This is the first time she hasn't woken in a cold sweat from nightmares and I don't want to chance ruining it."

"Sure thing."

"Thanks bro."

"No problem. Oi you lot, shut it."

My boy grins as he watches Booker's unmistakable form march across the curtained windows, his arms gesticulating wildly as he ushers everyone into the back rooms and away from the front entrance.

Lane softly shuts the driver's side door before moving to Lexi's side and carefully opening it. He watches her jump slightly in her sleep as the door clunks with the lock opening. Easing the door open, he lets the seatbelt take her weight before he sets a hand to her shoulder and reaches to release her from the strap.

"Lexi, it's me, we're here. I'm going to put you to bed, okay? Come on baby, put your arms round my neck. Atta girl, Goddamn it I love you, babe."

"Mmm, love you too."

Her sleep addled words ring with serene honesty as Lane effortlessly lifts her from the passenger seat, lifting her in his arms and pushing the door shut with his hip. Benji grins from the porch as he moves towards them, his hand finding my boy's shoulder as he leans in and softly whispers, *"Everything's set. I even turned down the bed for you so no need to faff around with covers or anything; just set our girl down and close the door, bro, you're good to go."*

"Thanks mate."

Lane moves quietly through the entry and up the stairs, closing the door to the master suite as softly as he can before placing Lexi's sleepy form on the bed. He tucks her in, placing a kiss softly on her head before turning to leave. He casts his eye back into the room and sees Lexi curled up, sleeping quietly in their bed. My boy smiles, simply content as he watches our girl sleep for a moment before turning and moving along the hallway.

Zali and Mel stop talking the moment Lane enters the lounge, both women turning to watch my boy, the look in their eyes making him pause.

"What?"

"Thank you."

"For what?"

"For giving our girl what she wanted most."

"What are you on about? I just did what any guy would and stood by my woman."

"No Lane, you did a lot more than that. We won't go into details, that's for Lexi to say, but we just want to say thank you for giving her someone to believe in again. So ... thank you."

My boy nods, not really knowing what to say to the two women as they smile at him. He subconsciously scratches the back of his head and moves towards the kitchen, Benji chuckling softly as he watches my boy stop in front of the fridge.

"So you ready for the next chapter, bro?"

"As I'll ever be."

"Well mate, I'm pleased for you. She's a fantastic girl and I have never in my life seen you happier than you are right now. So ... don't fuck this up. As much as I love you, if you hurt her, I will kick your fucking arse."

••••

The air stands warm and soft and Lexi's face is bathed in dancing mists of blue and red, eyes glittering as the sky lights up with the shimmering bursts of fireworks. My boy's stomach is a knotted mess as he nervously fidgets with the box in his pocket. He takes a deep, steadying breath before closing his eyes and stepping away from Lexi, then casts a glance at Booker and Benji, who nod to the people around them. One by one they lift from hiding their instruments and begin to play a song they spent the last three weeks rehearsing relentlessly.

"Lane, what the hell is happening? Why is there a band playing music? What are you doing?"

"Alexis Ryan … there is something I want to ask you … but first … I want you to know, from the first moment I saw you, this wide eyed woman with a constant smile on her face, you have filled my every thought. To be honest, I actually tracked you down through my boss the same day. I just had to know your name, and since that day, it has never left me. You are truly the centre of my universe. I've been through so many ups and downs that I never thought I could ever find someone to make me feel the way you do. There isn't a single moment in my existence that rivals waking up next to you each and every day. You make every moment, be it at work or at home, so phenomenally special that I never want to be anywhere else.

"Each day is like the start of some grand adventure and I never want that to end. I never want to wake up next to or be with anyone other than you for as long as I live, and even then, when I do find out what is after all of this, I want to find it with you. So Alexis Ryan, will you do me the honour of becoming my wife?"

My boy kneels, sand tricking through his curled toes as he opens the box in his hands, the ring glittering as the band plays. The echoing crack of the fireworks punctuates everything as he watches the light play over her face.

Time seems to drop to a crawl as my boy's heart hammers in his chest, his throat running dry as he waits for her answer.

"Lexi?"

"Yes, oh dear God, Lane, yes."

Lane leaps to his feet, the box tumbling into the sand as he scoops her up into his arms and kisses her. I can hear Hot Lips screaming with joy as our boy and girl stand wrapped in each other's arms. Benji and Booker hoot and holler as the girls try and hide their tears.

"Oh my God, Eight, baby, was this ... did you know ... oh my God."

"Yeah baby I did! I wanted to tell you so badly, but it would have tipped off our girl and, well ... yeah ... fuck, I love you baby! I promised you I would never leave you and now you know I never will."

"I love you so damned much, Eight. God, I'm going to cry."

"I love you too, my darling wife."

DO YOU WANT MORE?

Would you like to read the continuation of
Hot Lips and Eight's story?
This will only happen if you wonderful readers ask for it.

Visit and like our Facebook pages at

Tania Cooper Books and **Ricky Cooper Books**

and post a message saying 'More Naughty Bits'.
Or send us an email at **cooperbooks100@gmail.com**
with the same message.
If we hear back from enough readers, we will make it happen.

If you loved this book, please take the time to leave a review on

Amazon and **Goodreads.**

To find out the results of this question
and to keep up to date with all of our writing adventures,
please sign up for our newsletter:
http://eepurl.com/bi8xgr

We love to hear from our readers,

so stop by for a chat about what your favourite naughty bits were:

Find Tania on her

Website: www.taniacooperauthor.com.au
Facebook page: www.facebook.com/taniacooperbooks
Amazon: www.amazon.com/Tania-Cooper/e/B00IOBWNDO
or follow her on Twitter: https://twitter.com/TaniaTmcoops

Find Ricky on his

Website: www.ricky-cooper.co.uk
Facebook page: www.facebook.com/R.C.books
Amazon: www.amazon.com/Ricky-Cooper/e/B00BRZZ9V2
or follow him on Twitter: https://twitter.com/RJwC20

You can email them both at

cooperbooks100@gmail.com

ACKNOWLEDGMENTS

First and foremost, a BIG, HUGE, BULGING thank you to you, our reader. Thank you for reading this quirky tale and wanting to know the intimate details of everyone's naughty bits.

Thank you to our friends and family. Without your support and belief in us, these writing adventures wouldn't turn into a book. Thanks especially to Nic Nic, Ann, and Casey for making me (Tania) believe in myself.

To all the bloggers and reviewers who have taken the time to read our book and then spread the word around all of your beautiful pages, thank you. Our book would be lonely and collecting dust in a corner if it wasn't for you guys.

Thank you to our hard working publicist, the lovely Neda Amini of Ardent Prose PR. Where have you been all our lives? Now you are here, we are never letting you go.

And a big cuddly thanks to our amazing editor extraordinaire, Monique. You are a talented lady in so many ways and we are truly blessed to have you in our corner and in our hearts.

Our naughty and fun playlist:

We cannot work without a little mood music.

Dirty Talk – Wynter Gordon

Shut Up and Dance – Walk The Moon

Awake My Soul – Mumford & Sons

Poison – Rita Ora

Run the World – Beyoncé

This Summer's Gonna Hurt – Maroon 5

Let It Go – James Bay

Good for You – Selena Gomez

Milkshake – Kelis

No Scrubs – TLC

Boombastic – Shaggy

Peanut Butter Jelly – Galantis

Crazy in Love – Snow Patrol's version

U Can't Touch This – MC Hammer

Hey Mama – David Guetta feat. Nicky Minaj

Time of Our Lives – Pitbull & Ne-Yo